Melanie —
It's choice — not
Chance
determ...
destiny. Enjoy!

Once Upon a Choice

By

Linda Lee Smigel

∞INFINITY
PUBLISHING

ISBN 0-7414-6809-3

Printed in the United States of America

Published October 2011

INFINITY PUBLISHING
1094 New DeHaven Street, Suite 100
West Conshohocken, PA 19428-2713
Toll-free (877) BUY BOOK
Local Phone (610) 941-9999
Fax (610) 941-9959
Info@buybooksontheweb.com
www.buybooksontheweb.com

DEDICATION

Once Upon a Choice is dedicated in loving memory to my parents. To my father, who taught me my love of books. I love to read---thanks, Dad. To my mother, who encouraged me to live my dreams. I choose to write---thanks, Mom.

To my loving, patient family, thanks for the unconditional support and constant nagging- Bob, Kaylie, Kyle, Dave, and Joanie. I couldn't have finished the book without you.

To Robbie, my deceased stepson, my very own angel in Heaven. Your advice is always welcomed, anytime, anyplace, and I'm always open. Just give me a holler. God Bless.

To my close, steadfast friends, thanks for the continuous encouragement, the pushing, the pulling, the bitching. You all made it possible and kept me on track---Jud, Mitch, Gai, Loren, Vicky, Kath, Athena, Karen, Judy, Pat, Diana, Linda Lu, Erin, Cheri, Moira, Sue, Gary, Mary, Al, and Stacey.

To my spiritual psychic friends---my very own personal ESP hot-line. May Light and Love shine upon you always---Lois, Sharon, Sandra, Victoria, Stephanie, John, Eleanor, Anne, Renee, and Chuck. Thanks for the guidance and the exceptional counsel.

And then there's TK, my editor, who took a diamond in the rough, carefully trimmed it down, and buffed it up, ultimately creating this polished gem of a story. You have my gratitude.

And of course, I thank God, and all my higher spiritual guides, who showed me the way, reminding me that we are all Divine and that life is but a journey, full of choices.

An imprisoned person, with no other book than the Tarot, if he knew how to use it, could in a few years acquire universal knowledge, and would be able to speak on all subjects with unequalled learning and inexhaustible eloquence.

Eliphas Levi (1855)

PROLOGUE

The visions stunned her, froze her in place like that awful moment in a nightmare when the monster is coming, coming, but the legs won't move.

She felt them, lived them, became part of them like never before in all the visions, all the dreams, all the cards turned to life.

Her shoulders heaved as she groped for breath. She tried to let go, to cut the cosmic ties that bind, but the bonds were too strong. The psychic shock waves seared her mind with scorching images of violence and death.

Atlanta

There was a woman, a lovely woman with auburn hair and emerald eyes flashing with anger. She was dressed casually in a pale green jogging outfit.

"Don't open the door," Gem felt the warning flash and tried to send it on, channel it to the familiar young woman, her body tensing with the effort. "Don't..."

She opened the door. A man was there. A big man in a black suit, his face a blank slate with the lifeless eyes of a shark.

Undeterred, she spoke to him sharply. "What are you doing here?"

"Evening, Miss McAlister. I was told to pick up some papers."

She looked him up and down.

"I thought he was coming himself."

"He is in a meeting. Two more hours. He said he will call you later, when it is over. He said he was sorry."

"I'll bet." She turned and walked away, leaving the door open. He took it as a cold invitation to enter and stepped inside.

His hooded eyes scanned like searchlights. Spotless white walls and creamy white floors, with splashes of her colors in the furniture and paintings, muted ambers and greens. Across the wide living room, sliding glass doors to a balcony were opened slightly, a breeze rippling the curtains. He glanced down the hall, listening for any sound. Nothing.

She was alone.

She crossed the room and plucked a sealed manila envelope from the desk.

"Here," she said, holding it at arms length. "And tell him to call me tonight or forget it. Tomorrow is too late. I'm not going to wait any longer."

An obedient nod. "Yes. I will tell him."

She crossed her arms, eager for him to go. He turned, stopped to cough, lightly at first, then harder, a spasm of coughing. He braced one hand on the desk, patting his chest with the other.

She softened at his distress.

"Are you---Can I get you some water?"

He waved her off, still coughing.

"No, no...allergies. I only need air."

She gestured at the glass doors and he staggered toward them, stepping out to the balcony, coughing and wheezing. He leaned on the railing, trying to catch his breath.

She followed him.

"Are you sure you're all right?"

She took a step closer and the coughing stopped. "I am fine."

His hand flashed out and quickly grabbed her wrist so suddenly that she could not react. He seized the waistband of her jogging suit with his other hand and flipped her up and over in one motion. Three seconds. She was there, and she was gone.

Gem shared the terror of the hot air shrieking past, the final blur of light, and then the darkness, sudden and complete.

Three hundred feet above, the man paused to listen. She didn't scream, made no sound going down. He stepped back instead of peering over. No need to look.

He left the balcony doors open, walked back through the room and out, closing the door with a soft click. He was more than a block away, a businessman walking at a measured pace down Peachtree Boulevard when he heard the first distant wail of a siren.

Gem groaned with the mournful cry.

Cleveland

A running man in shorts and a t-shirt striding across a wide downtown street, soaked by his own sweat and a steady drizzle.

Up ahead, the hulking black SUV turned the corner too fast, tires squealing, headlights flashing across his eyes. Stupid drivers. He was a veteran street runner. He knew there was always a careless kid at the wheel or some old codger riding the curb. He'd had his share of close encounters, but he was cautious and alert, always ready to quick step out of harm's way. He picked up his pace, sprinting to the curb.

3

But the SUV veered at him, picking up speed. He stared over his shoulder in disbelief as it jumped the curb, framing him in the headlights. He made one last move, a desperate headlong leap, but the car was too close, too fast. It caught him in mid-air, flush against the grill, flipping him into the windshield, bones and glass cracking. The momentum carried him up and over, landing like a rag doll in the crosswalk. The SUV careened down the sidewalk, swerved back to the street, clipped a mailbox and roared off into the night. The brake lights never flashed.

He lay there, alone in the night, face against the dampened pavement, feeling nothing. The raindrops fell, glistening in the street light, exploding like tiny fireworks before his unblinking eyes. He thought of Eleanor. Sweet Eleanor. In the last moment, he thought he heard her voice calling out to him.

"Nicky! Nicky!"

He tried to answer but no sound would come.

He longed to see her face, touch her one more time. But he could not stay. He closed his eyes and entered the dark.

"Steady on, gentihomme, the light ahead is yours," she whispered.

And still there was more to come. The onslaught was not over. She waited for the worst.

Kanduhar, Afghanistan

"Cobra One, Cobra One. Double-R... do you copy?"

The message squawked in his earpiece, loud and clear. The ensign sitting at the console six hundred miles away and three decks down on the USS Ronald Reagan was right on time.

Major Cameron Chambers responded. "Cobra One. Read you, Double-R."

Sacre dieu. Her own son, strong and fearsome in battle gear, trudging a barren path in a faraway place, a man on a mission. She ached for him.

"We have you on the mark on GPS, Cobra One. Cobra Two is in place at Charley-Zebra-Five-Five, looking good."

"Roger that."

"We have bogeys on wheels at six k's coming your way at one o'clock, Cobra One."

Military talk. She had heard it before, but it was still like a foreign language, all clipped and quick, codes and numbers. She strained to understand.

"Roger. Is that the target?"

"Cannot confirm, Cobra One. Three vehicles, high speed. But say again---cannot confirm. You will have to eyeball and make the call."

"I'll send the welcome wagon."

"Roger. We will lose the bird in oh-thirty. Blind as a bat until two-one-seven. You are on your own 'til then, Cobra One."

"Roger, Double-R. We are moving to position. Out."

The major nodded to the man on his left to move ahead, then watched him spin and fall at the first step.

Major Chambers heard the shots that pinged off the outcrop of rocks to his right and recognized them immediately. AK-47. He could feel the adrenalin rush as he started to turn and return fire, finger already squeezing the trigger. He did not hear the shot that hit him in the back.

So many thoughts filled his mind in that last second as he pitched forward. He thought of his friend, Captain Les Higgins, Cobra Two, 300 yards to the west, perched at the rocky outcrop overlooking the narrow trail, the only passage to the Pakistan border. Higgy was watching his back, and he was as good as you get. Cool, calm, invisible and deadly. Where was Higgy? He must be dead.

Shot in the back. What a strange sensation. He knew the bullet was less than 8mm in diameter, but it felt like a cannonball smashing between his shoulder blades.

He thought of his brother, Chase. He was supposed to call Chase that night. He had promised. It would be the first time he had ever broken a promise to his brother.

He thought of Diane. He hoped Chase would break the news to her. She was so vulnerable, so fragile. Only Chase would know how to---

The last thought stopped short as Major Cameron Chambers landed hard on his face in the dirt.

She shut her eyes, hoping to blot the visions. They blurred instead, melding into one.

- 1 -

GET THE DEVIL OUT OF TULANE!

There weren't that many protesters in front of Carlisle Auditorium---just enough to catch the attention of the *Times-Picayune* and TV station---but the signs were brutal.

BEGONE SATAN!

NO OCCULT ON CAMPUS

JUST SAY NO TO TAROT!

About fifty determined souls had braved the sweltering heat, all members of the fundamentalist Church of the Lamb of God on Beale Street. The pastor had seen a mention of the new summer class at Tulane in the paper and rallied the parishioners to march against the latest encroachment of the wicked.

Inside, the lecture hall was filled to capacity, overflowing into the aisles. Twenty years ago, such a class would have been unthinkable and probably illegal. But times and tides had changed. The Department of Metaphysics was one of the largest in the School of the Arts and the advanced classes in occult phenomena and spiritualism were not only permitted, but embraced, among the most popular in school. The new course, Metaphysics 440: The Tarot, had almost 1,000 students vying for the 258 seats in the largest lecture hall on the premier campus in the heart of New Orleans.

In the anteroom, off stage, the new visiting professor straightened her flowing skirt and checked to make sure her hoop earrings matched, touching with both hands like a girl playing Simon Says. There was a full-length mirror right next to her, but she didn't use it. She had little interest in her own reflection. She knew that there were times when seeing an image of herself had a disruptive effect, fraying the ethereal bonds that linked her to the mysterious cognitive stream.

Her earrings matched, but looking down, her shoes didn't. Oh, well. No time to change and she wasn't about to explain how she was trying on shoes with outfits when her left foot started aching from the---never mind. Let them call her the absent-minded professor.

Best get on with it.

She looked up and whispered, "Here I go, Cheri'. Wish me luck."

In her mind, the reply came quickly.

My sweet Gemini, don't you know by now? You make your own luck. You just go out there and knock 'em dead.

It was her deceased husband Mitchell's voice, loud and clear.

"Love the play on words, my love," she answered aloud.

Professor Gemini D'Orlow Chambers walked out into the light. The cacophony of young chatter dissipated into murmurs of awe. They expected an old woman, wrinkled and worn, with gray hair pulled back into a bun, wearing granny glasses and a faded hippie dress. What they got was a striking woman of indiscriminate age, silver-blonde hair swept in a French twist, clad in airy layers of diaphanous silk, sheer enough to hint at a sleek figure. The shoes anchored her ethereal presence with two bright dots, one yellow, one blue.

Five hundred eyes widened in anticipation.

She stepped to the podium and embraced her audience with a look. The crowd settled, then hushed. She waited for total silence, then a full minute after, and finally spoke.

"Good morning."

"Good morning," they answered in a motley chorus.

"I don't know anything about Tarot cards."

A few gasps, then a wave of laughter rolled through the crowd.

"I'm serious.

"Oh, I have some familiarity, and a little knowledge---but that is a dangerous thing, no?---but very little in the way of hard facts. What is the Tarot? What are these cards? How do they work? Where does the power come from? Is it real?

"I cannot tell you. No one can tell you. Let me tell you what little is known.

"The cards of the Tarot are infused with images of sun and moon, fire and water, earth and sky. Encoded

with icons of man----cup and coin, club and sword---
they are cast with the players of the human drama:
king and queen, knight and maiden, page and fool.
Abundant with color, layered with the symbols of this
world and the next, the cards are the heirs apparent of
the petroglpyhs of the cave men, the Runes of the
ancient Goths, the Egyptian hieroglyphs and the I
Ching of Confucian China.

"In wise hands, the cards are said to be transcendent, beyond conscious limits of space and time,
revealing arcane messages in a montage of meaningful
image."

She leaned forward, intent, "Is it magic? Mystic?
Divine or demonic? True psychic or a grand hoax? In
the sixteenth century, the Renaissance artist, Benevenu-
to Cellini, posed the question in a letter to a friend,
'Who is master of the Tarot?'

"The reply came quickly: 'The Tarot has no masters, only servants.' And that from Leonardo da Vinci,
one of the great minds the world has ever known.

"Tomorrow, bring your set of Tarot cards and an
open mind. Your assignment for the rest of the day?
Carry your cards around with you. Hold them in your
hands and let them absorb your energy. Look at them,
feel them, get to know them. Sleep with them if you
like. Think of them as a little tools, little maps, little
friends.

"The cards can help. They want to help, to in-
struct, elucidate, suggest, point out things you may
have missed. The Tarot are candles; they can shine
light. Open your hearts to the light.

"Now go; lift your spirits. That is all for today."

The students gathered their books and bags,
spirits already lifted by the surprise free pass from a

three-hour class. The professor watched them hurry for the exits.

Ah, youth. To have the whole world before you, full of choices.

◻

The middle-aged man in the last row stayed in his seat, eyes glued on the professor. He wasn't a student or a teacher but he knew more about Gemini D'Orlow Chambers than anyone else on the Tulane campus. He had devoured more than two hundred pages of biographical data as well as the Confidential file, laden with material not subject to the Bureau's usual confirmation procedures, but fascinating and truly remarkable, even if only a fraction of it were true.

He knew she was one of a long line of "God-gifted" women of the D'Orlows, a French Creole family with roots that ran deep in Terrebonne, the southern-most parish in Louisiana bayou country.

The man knew that her grandmother, Antoinette D'Orlow, was known as the Tarot Queen, the most revered woman in the parish, sought out for her wisdom and insights by mystic believers from New Orleans, Baton Rouge and all points north. They would make the pilgrimage along the single winding road through swamp and glade to the humble clapboard home where Antoinette held court.

And little Gemini was always there, her psychic talents apparent at a precocious age, honed through years at her Gran Maman's knee. Antoinette had seen the gift within her early on and chose Gemini as her princess, heiress to the Tarot throne.

She was giving full-fledged readings of her own before she started school, findings revelations in the cards that were consistently impressive, sometimes astounding.

According to the file, Gemini D'Orlow had broken into the local news for the first time at nine, when she drew a crayon-colored map that led to the discovery of a literal buried treasure, a cache of coins and jewels that archaeologists at LSU confirmed was part of the loot stashed by the fabled Caribbean pirate, Jean Lafitte.

A year later, she led the police to the door of an abandoned fishing shack where two missing toddlers had been held captive for a week. The deranged kidnapper was taken by surprise and the boys rescued unharmed. Grateful but leery, the Louisiana state cops had interrogated Gemini for two days, pressing for the real story of how she had learned of the hideout location. She never wavered from her simple declaration that she "saw it in the cards."

The section of the file covering the next few years was thin. Gemini was kept from the public eye by a family that guarded privacy like a prized heirloom. She was home schooled, not unusual for the old-line bayou clans that had low regard for public institutions. Her friends were mostly young relatives in the extended D'Orlow family and she spent most of her time with her grandmother, the two of them alone more often than not, as the girl's apprenticeship in the Tarot arts continued.

It wasn't until she was seventeen that Gemini made the news again, a few months after her grandmother passed away. She had taken over what the family called "the practice," providing the readings and interpretations for all those supplicants who had been regular visitors at Gran Maman's renowned round table. Gemini jumped from her seat in the middle of a session with a local woman seeking advice for her daughter's troubled pregnancy and ran from the room, leaving the startled woman behind. There was a storm coming, she shouted, "hellacious brew of wind and rain" that would shred the bayou lowlands like wet paper. It seemed unlikely, as the only troubling weather in the forecast was a weak tropical storm slouching east of Florida, five hundred miles away. The Weather Bureau said it was no threat, headed out to sea, but the locals had more faith in their D'Orlow soothsayer than so-called scientists. Most of Terrebonne Parish was evacuated before nightfall.

A wise choice. Within hours of Gemini's alarm, the storm was whipped into a fury by sudden Gulf stream winds, gathering strength as it spun across the Florida Keys. Hurricane Carla marched across the Gulf and slammed ashore at daybreak, rampaging through the bayou with devastating force. Damage was immense and twelve people were killed, but the local papers claimed it would have been hundreds if not for "a teenage girl in Terrebonne who saw Carla coming in a vision and sounded the alarm."

There were a dozen more stories, some embellished over time perhaps, but it was impossible to dismiss them all as fabrications or pure luck.

The Man in the Back Row was far from convinced that the Tarot cards held any magical or mystical power, but he was a true believer in hard evidence and there was more than enough that this woman possessed some genuine extra-sensory perception, and that she used her little set of colored pasteboards as precision tools to unlock those powers.

He was convinced that Gemini D'Orlow Chambers would be a great addition to his special roster. Seeing her in person, hearing her speak, he felt like a NFL scout watching a highly-touted recruit dazzle the crowd, running for touchdowns. He wanted this all-star on his team.

He knew she preferred to stay out of the limelight, and his bosses would be happy to accommodate her in that respect. As far as they were concerned, the less publicity about some of these more esoteric efforts, the better. He edged his way down the aisle already working up a scenario for making his approach. But not yet. Patience and caution were the watchwords of the embryonic program that held great promise while it offered serious risks of embarrassment for the entire Department. He would bide his time, continue to observe and assess from a distance, unknown and unseen.

She looked right at him as soon as he turned his back, watching him maneuver around the backpacks, laptops, cell phones, Blackberries, iPads, water bottles and God knows what else college students hauled around all day, like some strange tribe of high-tech nomads. She didn't know him, but it took no psychic power to know what he was.

Government man.

Sometimes they thought they were so invisible when they might as well be holding a neon sign. Blue suit, white shirt, red tie, close-cropped hair and well-shined shoes---he was government, all right. After all those years in Washington, she should know.

The Man in the Back Row was a federal agent, and he wanted something. She didn't waste time wondering what it was. She knew their ways. He would be back to tell her, and soon.

But she was wrong this time. She didn't see him again until months later, long after the course at Tulane was over. She was right about everything else. He was with the federal government and he did want something. Gem agreed to his request, adding a few of her own ideas to his intriguing proposal. Soon after, she was an active participant in Project Blue Yonder, quickly becoming the most prolific source in the program's short history. The government people were ecstatic with her work, especially Patrick Curran, the Man in the Back Row.

[]

All was well in the life and work of Gemini D'Orlow Chambers until spring of the following year. That was when it all started. One reading, one brief visit with the cards was all it took.

She was alone at her home in Naples, sitting at the old French escritoire by the fireplace. This had been her favorite work place for years, the little ornate desk was cluttered with books, photos, mail and memorabilia, a tattered red velvet pouch perched in the corner.

She removed the frayed set of cards, holding them to her, caressing them like living things. This worn and tattered deck was more than a hundred years old, passed down from her grandmother, and hers before. It resonated with layers of vibrant energies, the wisdom of generations past.

She then set them before her, closed her eyes, took one deep breath and let it go, encompassing herself in an evanescent aura of love and light.

She shifted the deck at a solemn pace, separating the cards into three stacks---past, present, future---and began the age-old process.

The Magician. Magus.

The most powerful card of all. Upright, standing tall with the potent wand in his right hand pointing to the heavens, his open left hand in perfect opposition, roses and lilacs at his feet. All the tools of his transcendent craft were displayed on the table before him---wand, cup, sword and pentacle.

She bowed in humble acceptance of the power to help mold the destiny of others, and reached for a second card.

Knight of Swords.

An urgent herald on a galloping horse; caution to the vigilant, fair warning against adversity to come. She took it as a salutation, the cards' way of saying "stay tuned for important messages to follow." Her concentration intensified as she turned another.

Three of Swords.

In the midst of a powerful storm, a heart pierced by three swords. Heartache and disappointment, loss of a loved one, clouds and water, pain, upheaval. There would be deep sorrow; but for whom? Bitter water, from what well?

She brought another into play and cringed at the foreboding image.

Eight of Swords.

A young woman, bound and hoodwinked, imprisoned by a picket row of blades. Entrapment and deceit. A crisis of great proportion loomed for this woman, dim days of jealousy and quarrel, dark nights fraught with peril. There would be turmoil and treachery, the likelihood of violence, the risk of sudden death.

Who was the woman thrust into the eye of the storm? She could not say, but Gem could feel the presence of the girl so completely, she could almost touch her fair hair. A stranger to her now, but not for long. Their paths would cross soon enough.

She was compelled to turn one last card.

Judgment.

An angel with a golden horn, calling the chosen to heaven's light, a glorious card upright. But Judgment was not upright. The card was inverted, warning of delay and indecision. Yes, Judgment would come, but it may not be swift or sure. Good or bad? Triumph or tragedy? That answer was not yet in the cards.

So much was clear, so much more remained obscure. Time would tell for this innocent young beauty, the ones who loved her and those who would do her harm. There were choices to be made, for better or worse, and all was in the balance.

Enough. She set the cards aside.

Bon chance, ma belle.

THE WORLD.

Meagan yawned as she slipped out of bed and padded to the bathroom. She rubbed her sleepy eyes as she glanced at herself in the mirror. *Not a pretty sight.*

She rinsed her face to wash away the night. Her blond hair, stringy and unkempt, sprang out in all directions. She splashed water on her fingers and tried to plaster it down. Oh, hell, why bother?

The sun was a half scoop of orange, rising beyond the palms in the distance. It was going to be another beautiful day in Southwest Florida. God, she thought, she sounded just like one of those weather forecasters who were always so disgustingly happy. But it was true. August in Naples was picture perfect. The afternoons were thick with heat and often charged with thunderstorms, but the mornings were sublime.

Meagan surveyed her appearance, squinting at the tiny wrinkles at the corner of her eyes. *Oh, well.* She was thirty-three, after all. Visions of middle age clouded her mind. Maybe Botox was the answer. *No. Not yet, anyhow.*

Ross was up.

The coffee grinder. That's what woke her. Ross was so organized in the morning. Coffee beans grinding, grinding, like fingernails on the blackboard. Good morning from your loving husband, Ross. Thankfully, Brandon, their son, had slept through it all. His door, which she had noticed in passing, was still closed.

Meagan grabbed her favorite chenille robe, the ratty one Ross hated, and trudged down the hall.

Ross was seated in his usual place at the breakfast table with a variety of morning papers all lined up in front of him. He was sipping his coffee and looked rather benign. But his innocent expression didn't fool Meagan, neither did his good looks. He was darkly handsome and meticulously dressed, one of his trade marks. In fact, Meagan couldn't remember Ross ever not being perfectly dressed or darkly intriguing although in a cynical kind of way. That was what had first attracted her to him, his dark, engrossing looks. His darkside, she called it. She could tell instantly that her husband was in a callously cynical mood that morning. She knew all the signs. She simply waited for him to speak. And it did not take long. A handsome man in an ugly mood. She could tell.

"Anything to get his face in the paper," Ross muttered as he scanned the front page of the *Naples Courier.*

"Who's that, Ross?"

"Oh," he hardly looked up, "Chase Chambers. *Now* he's going to run for Congress. I suppose he thinks it's his birthright," he scoffed. "His father was the senator, you know. And if you don't, he'll be happy to tell you."

"Do you know him?"

"We've met," Ross said. "Talked about doing some business. Never got anywhere. They think they're so high and mighty."

He put the paper down and focused on his wife.

"Enough about the Chambers---what about you, darling? Planning anything exciting today?" His voice oozed sarcasm. "Or how about constructive?"

"It's seven in the morning, Ross." Meagan poured herself some coffee. "I haven't checked my planner."

Ross didn't like her tone. He eyed her closely. Oh, that awful, war-torn robe of hers. He waited until she sat down, then spoke in his boardroom baritone, the voice that demanded full attention.

"Meagan, I've been meaning to tell you---I want you to call your friend, Eleanor, and cancel her visit."

Meagan took a deep breath. "But we made plans months ago, remember? You said no problem."

"Only because I was expecting to be at the investment seminar in London. But I had to cancel. This project with the West Coast group is taking longer than I expected. So I will be here," he declared. "And frankly, I cannot put up with that woman and her depressive disposition for three fucking weeks. And I won't."

Meagan gave her husband a furtive glance. She was afraid to face him head-on, but weary of being the Stepford wife, always bowing to his edicts. *Not this time, Ross.*

"I'm sorry, but Elle is coming," Meagan said with unusual resolve. "There's no way she can change her flights or her time off work."

"Meagan, I'm not going to budge on this."

"Then you can arrange to be out of town. Lately, you're hardly here anyway, always busy in Chicago or someplace, anyplace else but home."

Ross did not visibly react, but his mind shifted up a gear. Who was this woman sitting across from him, all feisty and full of herself? He folded his linen napkin and placed it neatly on the table, always a sign he was about to end the conversation with a closing statement.

"Yes, I am busy. Busy providing the considerable means it takes to keep you living the comfortable life you so richly deserve. All I ask for is a little support, and you can't even do that?"

That hurt. Meagan returned his stare, but hers was weaker, wounded.

"Ross! How can you say that? You know I have always---"

He glanced at his Rolex.

"I can't be late. I expect you to cancel Eleanor's visit. Put it off it for awhile, if that makes everyone feel better. And if you won't, then I'll have Stacy do it. Case closed. "

Ross walked out. No farewell, no kiss goodbye. Meagan listened to his footsteps, loud whacks across the marble floor then whispers on the carpet. The side door opened and closed sharply, just short of a slam.

⬚

Meagan heaved a sigh of relief. Thank God he was gone for the day. She lay back in the lounger, stretched her feet, wiggled her toes and reflected on her marriage and her husband, Ross. Not that she necessarily wanted to dwell on Ross. The man who had romantically swept her off her feet and married her within a mere six weeks of their meeting was a different Ross than the man that she was married to. How could she have been so wrong? Ross, the man she married, had worshipped her. At first, constantly striving to be there for her. Ross, the man she married, had grieved with her over her grandmother's untimely death due to cancer. Where has he gone, she mused. There was no doubt about it, that man was gone. Where was that Prince Charming who brought her flowers every day, lavished gifts and compliments on her, knelt at her feet and begged her to marry him? Where was the man who made love to her with such fierce passion?

Maybe he had never been. As she looked back on the events leading to their marriage, she admitted that she had been in an extremely vulnerable point in her life. And now there was no doubt that, day by day, she and her husband were drifting apart. This was so disheartening as she couldn't help feeling that some of the discord in their marriage was also her fault.

Ross worked as an international investment consultant and his work had become the most important part of his life, even to the exclusion of his wife and son. And this was bound to cause problems in their marriage. Even so, Meagan felt fairly confident that things would sort out eventually and the man she thought she had married would resurface again. He just needed time and she needed patience. She kept telling herself every day that eventually he would come around and love her the way he used to. In the meantime she put up with his control tactics and bit her lip, and constantly strived to make things work out between them. Normally Meagan would have conceded to Ross's demand and she would have called Eleanor and explained the circumstances. But, dammit, this time she was going to take a strong stand. In three weeks Eleanor was arriving and that was that!

Either way, it appeared their relationship was in for an extremely bumpy ride. She sadly shook her head, remembering back to the way it used to be.

- 3 -

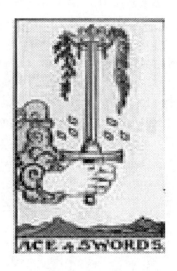

Megan and Eleanor had been best friends since their first day in kindergarten when they literally ran into each other on the playground. Eleanor, full speed ahead, not watching where she was going, slammed into Meagan. They both went sprawling. Meagan didn't cry until she noticed the empty ice cream cone in her hand, the scoop of chocolate in the dirt at her feet. Eleanor tried to pick up the ice cream with her little fingers and pat it back into the cone. The ice cream was destroyed, but it turned her tears to laughter. She and Eleanor had been laughing ever since.

Meagan smiled at the memory. Eleanor was the sister she never had. They had spent so many childhood days together, planning their lives, scrawling their dreams in notebooks. They made changes, crossed out names and wishes and added new ones as the years went by, but one thing was constant: the bond between them. Girlfriends forever.

They grew up a few blocks away and worlds apart. Eleanor was from downtrodden East Cleveland while Meagan lived in idyllic Shaker Heights with her globetrotting parents and grandmother, Amanda Payne Neeley.

Mama Neeley was hardly the sedate senior citizen. Twenty years a widow, the matriarch of the family, she was still active and vital in her seventies and not a bit bashful about speaking her mind. Her husband had been a respected judge but the family money came from her side, all the way back to her great-grandfather, one of the fortunate partners of a wily young entrepreneur.

August Payne and John D. Rockefeller were classmates at Cleveland Central High in the 1850s. Fifteen years later, Payne was a minority partner when his friend's new company issued its first shares of stock. Payne's modest investment in Standard Oil was enough to put many millions into the family coffers by the turn of the century.

Meagan never knew much about the money, or where it came from. It was just always there. Her parents were good people, but like many descendants of wealth, they waltzed through a life of leisure. Winters in Florida, summers in Europe---they loved their only child, but often from a distance. Her grandmother was the constant presence in her life. It was Mama Neeley who raised her, guided her and loved her.

⬚

Eleanor Keeler didn't have it so good.

Her father was a smart and likeable man, full of bright ideas, but plagued by demons that had him flying high one day and sullen and silent the next. A series of business failures and the emotional turmoil in his own mind finally drove him to lock himself in the garage one night and turn on the ignition in his rusted Chevy. It was Eleanor who found him the next morning.

Her distraught mother buried her grief under a torrent of anger aimed at her daughter. Eleanor was almost crushed by the burden of guilt and confusion. Drained of her optimism and self-confidence, she drifted through her late teens, a girl in a fog.

One of the only good things in Eleanor's life during those dreary years was her girlfriend, Meagan. Meagan had gone on to college at Northwestern, her father's alma mater, but stayed in contact with Eleanor by phone and e-mail. Twice a year, Meagan would send a plane ticket and Eleanor would fly up to Chicago for a weekend of non-stop talking, laughing, shopping and wild nights on Rush Street, looking for Mister Right.

Eleanor found many Misters, none Right. Meagan was too shy to try.

Back home, Eleanor worked as a waitress, trying to get herself together and find some purpose to her life.

She thought she found it in Brad.

Brad Taylor was on his way to the top of the real estate business. Brad was going to make a fortune. After his imminent divorce, Brad was going to marry Eleanor and make all her dreams come true.

Eleanor lived for Brad. Anything he wanted, she was there for him. She was his lover, his cook, maid, advisor and confidante. She quit her job to help him even more. She did his research and paperwork, checked on housing codes and tax laws, ran every errand he needed. There was never a paycheck or a "thank-you", but soon, she knew she would have the life she wanted with the man she loved. In the meantime, it was all about Brad.

But Brad Taylor was a liar.

☐

At Northwestern, Meagan became friendly with her high-energy roommate, Marsha Mills. Eleanor was still, and always would be, her "Girlfriend" but Marsha was her "Partner". Meagan and Marsha had a shared passion to start a business of their own together. Like Meagan and Eleanor who talked boys, Meagan and Marsha talked business. Endless hours of conversation eventually led to a focus on two favorite career interests: food and events.

A prodigious cook, Marsha could conjure up a seven-course meal on the rickety old range in the dorm kitchen, but she had aspirations to be more than a chef and she convinced Meagan that they could open a place of their own, a first class catering operation that would be a step ahead of the rest, providing a whole range of services to transform a party or event into something spectacular.

And Meagan loved the idea.

"First class all the way," she enthused. "That's what we'll call it-- First Class."

They agreed to launch First Class Caterers & Event Planners right after graduation. They didn't know how they would finance it, who they would get for clients or even where First Class would be located, but that didn't stop them. They made a mutual commitment to start a business. Details could be decided later.

Fate decided for them. Fate in the form of Mama Neeley.

In her eighties, the grand dame took up permanent residence at the family summer home in Naples, Florida. She had been there a year when the bad news came.

Cancer.

Meagan didn't find out until Mama Neeley flew up to Chicago for her graduation, looking fit and feisty as ever. After the ceremony, she pulled Meagan to one side and gave her the news in her usual blunt fashion.

"I'm glad I lived to see this day, honey, because your mean old grandma isn't going to be around much longer."

Meagan hugged her. "Oh, Mama Neeley, you know you'll be a hundred before you even slow down."

The old woman smiled fondly. "That's what I always said, didn't I?"

"A hundred at least, you said."

"Sweet child." She stroked Meagan's face with fragile fingers. "There's something you should know, and I wanted to tell you myself."

Meagan was caught by her solemn tone. "What, Mama Neeley, what is it?"

"I've got a cancer."

Meagan was shocked. She started to speak, but Mama Neeley held up her hand.

"I've already been to the doctors---in Naples and up at that Clinic in Cleveland---they've poked around all they're going to. There's nothing to be done."

"No." Meagan's eyes filled with tears.

"Now what have I taught you? Don't say 'no' to your grandmother."

"Oh, Mama Nee..." Meagan sobbed, her tears falling on the old woman's shoulder.

Mama Neeley had been her rock through all the years and Meagan was determined to be there for her in her time of need. She put all her plans on hold---Marsha understood—and she flew down to Naples and moved in with her Mama Neeley.

Her grandmother never said it, but that was what she wanted, to spend what time she had left with her precious Meagan.

Within weeks, the role reversal was complete. Meagan was caretaker, nurse, cook and companion. She made her grandmother's meals, administered her medications, helped her bathe and dress and in the evenings, she would take her for strolls on the beach, then back home to "sit a spell, and chew the fat".

Sometimes, she would reminisce about the days gone by, like the time the great Rockefeller himself visited the family at home. The wizened tycoon told her she was a pretty child and handed her a shiny new dime. She still had it, and she showed it to Meg---a tiny silver treasure tucked into her jewelry box with the diamonds and pearls.

More often though, she wanted to talk about Meagan and her bright future. Meagan told her of Marsha and their idea for a catering company. Mama

Neeley's eyes flashed with purpose. She insisted that Meagan go ahead with her plans.

"Time's a wasting, girl," she said. "You can't wait until your grandma is pushing up daisies to get on with your life."

Meagan said it could wait, but Mama Neeley was adamant.

"You don't have to go to Chicago, honey. Folks in Naples have to eat, too, don't you know. Now you tell your friend to come on down here, and you two get to work."

The next morning, Mama Neeley directed her lawyer to draw up the necessary papers to incorporate the business and wrote out a check to cover the start-up expenses.

Meagan called Marsha with the news. Her partner-in-waiting didn't hesitate for a second; starting plans to move to Naples before the conversation was over.

First Class was born. They were in business. Hooray!

◊

"First Class," Gemini Chambers said it aloud, holding up the card. The Two of Wands was a pleasant card; a prosperous man stands between two strong staffs, gazing over his tranquil estate, holding a globe, the world in his hands. The card spoke of achievement, a successful venture, nothing ominous or foreboding.

Yet Gemini seemed puzzled, even troubled by image before her.

"It's the only way to travel," Cole, her younger son, said idly. He was the only one in the room with her, dabbling with the paints at his easel. Youngest son and constant companion, Cole was often a sounding board for Gem while she mused over her cards.

"Not this time," Gem said, setting the card aside. "An adventure of some kind, but not a journey. Something else."

"First class? What else could it be?"

"That I don't know, Cole. The words just came to me."

"Anything more?"

Gem smiled. Cole knew the routine.

"The hint of a name. Maggie? Margaret? Meryl? Something like that. A woman---of that I'm certain--- young and pretty. And very much a presence in the cards of late. I'm sure there's more to come."

"I have a question for you."

"Yes?"

"Why is it always first names? You and all the other psychics, every one---it's always first names you come up with. Last names would be a lot more helpful, don't you think?"

"I can't argue with that," Gem laughed.

"Well, then?" Cole said with a stern face. "Let's get on it, Mother. Fine tune those psychic dials. Last names only from now on."

Gem pointed at the empty canvas. "Don't you have a picture to paint?"

- 4 -

Meagan met Ross and everything changed.

Meagan was back in Chicago helping Marsha pack up the last of her belongings left behind when she moved to Naples to set up First Class. They rummaged through the furnishings, clothes and knick-knacks in storage, packed half the stuff for Naples and hauled the rest to Goodwill. Marsha had planned two days for the task, but finished by midnight of the first. That gave Meagan a full day to shop for some special culinary items unavailable in Naples, plus a pair of Manolo Blannink shoes she just couldn't resist.

She was loaded down with bags, trying to hail a taxi on Michigan Avenue when a gust of wind knocked the bags from her arms, blew her skirt up past her thighs and left her in a mortified heap on the curb. She was on the verge of tears when a devastatingly handsome man stopped to help. He gathered her packages, lifted her to her feet and commandeered a passing cab.

Meagan gushed with gratitude and said she hoped that somehow she could repay his kindness. He said she could, if she would have dinner with him that very night.

She accepted with little resistance. How could she say no? Eleanor was the one who warned her: if Mr. Right comes knocking, make sure you answer the door. And if ever there was a Mr. Right on first impression, this was the one.

Caring, thoughtful and attentive, a gentleman in every way, Ross Hamilton was so far beyond any of the boys she had met in her school years. He was a man, strong and self-assured, exuding the confidence of one who knows where he's going, and knows what he wants.

And he wanted Meagan.

He wined her and dined her, sent her expensive flowers, Godiva chocolates and Gucci scarves.

After three glorious nights, she returned to Naples, flush with the glow of new romance.

Ross followed, pursuing her with a relentless fervor that was impossible to resist.

Six weeks later, they were married in a modest ceremony at Mama Neeley's Naples home. Mama Neeley had often spoken of a grand wedding for her beloved granddaughter, but it was not to be. Just as Meagan's romance bloomed, her grandmother took a turn for the worse. At the hospital, doctors shook their heads. There was nothing they could do to slow the ravaging fury of the disease. They warned Meagan it would be a matter of days.

At Mama Neeley's insistence, they moved up the wedding date. All she wanted was to see Meagan in her wedding dress. "If it's the last thing I ever do, that will be just about right, won't it?"

Ross flew in to meet Meagan's parents a few days beforehand. At his ingratiating best, he enchanted them with his gracious manner and sophistication, picked up the tab for an elegant dinner, and passed their brief inspection with flying colors.

Mama Neeley was not so easily impressed. He was certainly presentable and well mannered, but there was something about him---his look a little too polished, his charm a bit affected. But if Meagan loved this Ross---well, then so be it.

Ross met Eleanor for the first time, too, and that did not go well at all. The aversion was instantly mutual.

"He's so fucking full of himself, Meg." Eleanor didn't mince words. She never had. "And why aren't any of his family or friends here?"

"Parents are gone, Elle, passed away years ago. And since we changed the date, his friends couldn't make it. Prior commitments. You know."

"How convenient."

"Elle, if you only knew how sweet and kind and--- wait until you get to know him."

"God, do I have to?"

Ross was equally repelled. "I wanted to like her, darling, but it's just impossible to get past that foul-mouthed, white trash attitude."

"Ross! Elle isn't white trash!"

"All right, if you insist."

Meagan passed off the clash as temporary. Both had strong personalities. Both were protective of

Meagan. Surely that was common ground where they would meet eventually, right?

Mama Neeley was scarcely able to witness the exchange of vows from the confines of her wheelchair. It was as if she willed herself to stay alive until her Meagan was married, then surrendered to the inevitable. She died two days later in Meagan's arms.

The honeymoon was cancelled. Ross understood, and could not have been more considerate. He stood by Meagan, made all the arrangements for the funeral services, and helped his new bride through her grief.

Ross was there for her in the confusing aftermath as well, guiding her through the maze of legal formalities related to her grandmother's estate. Mama Neeley had left Meagan almost eight million dollars accumulated in various trust funds, stock portfolios and cash accounts. Ross sorted out the details and took over management of the accounts, a welcome relief for Meagan.

The next few months were a bittersweet time. While Meagan mourned the loss of her guiding light, she took comfort in the arms of her new husband. He was caring and consoling, patient and passionate. The woman she could always count on was gone, but now she had this loving man to count on, just in time.

They bought a home in West Shore, the nicest new suburb of fast-growing Naples. He carried her over the threshold of their dream house, complete with a spacious lanai and teardrop pool flanked by lush gardens, a perfect newlywed retreat.

Both were busy with their own careers. Meagan had her hands full with First Class which was becoming the number one catering and events planning company in the Naples area. Meagan and

Marsha were working almost every weekend and evening to cover all the work contracts on hand; such was their success. Ross commuted long distance to his office in Chicago for a few days each week. The hectic pace and separations only made the nights they had together more romantic. Ross always brought gifts to celebrate their reunion. Meagan welcomed him home with candlelight dinners.

All was good in the lives of Mr. and Mrs. Ross Hamilton.

But everything changed the day that Meagan discovered she was pregnant. It was hardly intended. She was on the pill, and Ross was diligent about making sure she stayed on the regimen.

She was two weeks late when she woke up one morning with a strange craving for onions and graham crackers, and she knew. Oh, my god. She was going to have a baby!

Meagan was thrilled.

Ross wasn't. He took the news like a slap in the face.

"What do you mean? You can't be! You've been on---that's not possible!"

"Oh, yes it is," she said, glowing, "and I am. I guess it was just meant to be."

They had never quarreled, never a harsh word between them, until that night. Ross questioned her---interrogated her, demanding to know how it could have happened. Did she miss a pill? Did she do it on purpose? What was she thinking?

Meagan's euphoria melted in the heat of his reaction. At one point he even accused her of lying, and demanded that she get an abortion to "solve the problem." When she refused, he turned cold. He didn't raise his voice; he lowered it, speaking in an icy whisper that gave Meagan a chill.

"You don't want to defy me, darling."

"I---I'm not---Ross, why are you acting like this? We're talking about having a baby. You should be happy."

"I told you---now is not the time."

Meagan was certain the time was right, and just as sure that Ross would come around. He would make a great dad. Everything would work out fine.

When he realized there was nothing he could say to change her mind, Ross softened a bit, but not entirely. All right, fine, have the baby. But changes must be made.

He insisted that Meagan stop working. She couldn't continue at a full-time job and be a full-time mother as well. It tore at her heart, but she didn't argue. Consoled by the fact that the business would be in Marsha's capable hands, she relinquished control of First Class and dedicated herself to becoming a first-class mother.

◻

At the same time, Eleanor was going through some dramatic changes of her own. Good things started to happen. With a renewed determination and lots of hard work, she got herself back on track. The years with Brad had not been a total waste. Eleanor had learned a lot while waiting on Brad hand and foot. She had become quite proficient at the ins and outs of commercial property transactions and used that knowledge to land a job with a top real estate firm. It wasn't long before she earned a reputation as a savvy broker. She gained a following of corporate clients who appreciated her energetic style.

Things got even better after that. Along came Nicky. Nicholas Sheehan. He was right out of those spiral notebooks where she and Meagan wrote their dreams.

Like Brad, Nick Sheehan was one of those up-and-coming masters of the universe, a big-ticket real estate specialist. Unlike Brad, Nick was the real deal.

Eleanor had met Nick at her company's Christmas party. She was just passing time, idle chatter, when Nick appeared at the door, fashionably late and drop-dead handsome. Eleanor stopped in mid-sentence, mouth open. She couldn't take her eyes off him. And Nick---he saw Eleanor across the crowded room and was drawn like a magnet. He walked over and introduced himself as if he was supposed to meet her there. He didn't tell her until weeks later that a friend had arranged a blind date for him with "a gorgeous redhead." Nick saw Eleanor and just assumed---she's the one. Nick said it was the best mistake he ever made.

From that night on, they were inseparable. Take-charge Nick was amused to find himself marching to Eleanor's tune. She just had a way with him, and he loved her for it. Nick's positive outlook revitalized Eleanor and renewed her spirit. A match made in heaven.

Their wedding was fairy tale event and Eleanor was an exquisite bride, radiant in creamy white lace and a bridal bouquet of yellow roses, Nick's favorite.

Maid of Honor Meagan beamed with joy, watching the perfect couple emerge from the cathedral as the sun broke through the clouds and embraced them with a golden light.

Who could have imagined that disaster was only two weeks away?

- 5 -

"Mommy, is SpongeBob SquarePants on?"

Brandon padded into the kitchen and gave his mother a squeeze around her bare legs.

"Good morning, pumpkin!" Meagan hugged her son's shoulders. "It's 8 o'clock, sleepy head. Show's over. Sorry."

"Oh."

She tousled his baby-fine hair. "You need to get up earlier tomorrow if you want to watch him."

"Uh-huh."

She crouched low to enjoy that cherubic face. As soon as they were eye to eye, she laughed. Just after dawn, and he already had his little black headset on, wired to the iPod strapped around the waist of his pajamas. He was carrying his Playstation in one hand, some DVDs in the other. Her little wizard. She could hardly figure out the remote for the cable TV and Brandon was already adept with iPods, Xbox 360, CDs, DVDs---the whole new entertainment alphabet. This must have been how Bill Gates started.

"What are you listening to?"

"Nemo." He smiled the word and moved closer. "Daddy gone?"

"Yes, sweetheart, your Daddy left for work a little while ago."

"Daddy yelling. You fight?"

"No, we were not fighting." Her heart went out. "Just talking. Sometimes Daddy talks loud, that's all."

Meagan guided him towards the family room.

"Now, scoot. Turn on the TV. I'll get you some breakfast."

"Cheerios, mommy. The white kind."

"You got it, champ. Frosted Cheerios coming right up."

The phone was ringing.

It was Marsha. Meagan had only a chance to say hello and then it was non-stop Marsha.

"Oh, Meg, I'm so glad I caught you. Listen, you have to do me a big favor, and, I mean, big! OK?" Marsha never waited for an answer. "I really, really need your help. A couple of the girls are sick with that nasty flu bug and I have no one else to turn to. You know the business inside out. Please, Meg, do it for me, your old buddy? Please!"

Meagan knew the business all right. Hadn't she and Marsha grown First Class from a two-girl operation to a topnotch catering and event planning company up until Brandon was born? And she still owned fifty percent of the company, one of the few facts of her financial life unknown to Ross. He didn't know and he never would. He'd kill her for keeping that from him.

"I need you. Tonight. Meg, I know this is short notice, and I know you're going to say Ross could be a problem---but you'll think of something. I know you will, and I will just die if you don't because I can't risk bringing someone else in on this, because they'd screw it up big time, and that can't happen tonight. So please, Meg, I'm on my hands and knees here---"

"Marsha! If whatever you're talking about is tonight, you better get to the point before it's tomorrow already!"

"I thought I told you. Didn't I tell you? The Chambers' estate in Port Royal. It's a fundraiser for Chase Chambers. He's the one running for Congress. Anyway, Sandra Simpson---my friend, Sandy---she talked Chase into giving us a shot at the catering! Sandy and Chase are engaged or almost or something. Lucky girl. Anyway, I need the whole crew and now I'm three short, plus Jill's son is sick, so it could be four, and there's only one person on earth who can do the job of three or four, hands tied behind her back and blindfolded---"

"You need me to work the event tonight?"

"Isn't that what I just said?"

Meagan had to laugh. "Kind of."

Meagan thought it over. She missed working with Marsha, but---

"You know what Ross is going to say."

"Oh, yeah, Ross feels you are lowering yourself to the depths of degradation by catering to others. I've heard that speech before. Shit. Now, Meagan, I know he's your husband, and I don't want to say anything bad about him, but you know I---well, then I won't say anything at all, because ----"

"You're not the only one," Meagan said faintly.

Marsha was unusually silent for a moment, struck by the change in attitude.

"In fact, I have decided, just this morning, that Ross Hamilton does not control my entire life, contrary to whatever. So, my time and talents are at your disposal tonight."

"Is that your final answer?"

"Final answer."

"Way to go, girlfriend!" Marsha screamed. "That's the Meagan I know and love. We're back in business."

"Give me the time, the address and the particulars. My watch says 12:30, as we speak."

Meagan felt good about her decision, even though she knew that Ross would blow sky high when he heard about it. On top of the morning standoff, this amounted to outright mutiny.

"Look, Meg, I'm going to make this real easy. I'll pick you up at two. Wear anything. Come as you are. Just bring your make-up bag and black heels---those Onex ones that you love. I'll take care of everything else."

"But---what about a uniform? And why the heels? We don't work in heels. And two o'clock? I've got to do my hair and get---"

"Meg, listen to Marsha. It's my gig and I'm the boss now, remember? Everything is covered. I'll explain when I get there. My battery's low, I'm going to lose you. And thanks, you're a godsend! See you at two!" Click.

Meagan hung up and stared into space. What in the world had Marsha gotten her into now? And how was she going to explain to Ross that she had decided to return to First Class for one guest appearance? Her mind was going a mile a minute. Before she had time to think clearly, the phone rang again. This time it was Stacy, Ross's personal assistant.

"Mrs. Hamilton, sorry to bother you, but Mr. Hamilton asked that I call. Something's come up on the Tannex project. He's on his way to Chicago now and won't be back until Friday. He said he'll call you tonight. He's staying in the corporate suite. You have that number, right?" Stacy was always polite, professional, and cold as ice.

"Yes, Stacy, after five years, I believe I know the number," Meagan replied. Ice for ice. "And please tell my husband I'll call if I need him."

She smiled. The gods were on her side today.

[]

The man in the short-sleeved white shirt checked the readout on the digital console and made a quick note on his legal pad: "044366---RH to Chicago. Tannex Project?" He yanked off his earphones and turned to the man at the adjoining desk.

"What's Tannex?"

The other man frowned. He was dressed in an identical white shirt and tie. Both wore the same type photo ID clipped to the shirt pocket with a name, picture and three bold blue letters emblazoned across the top: FBI.

"Never heard of 'em. Why?"

"Better check it out. Corporate name, sounds like, maybe in Chicago, could be somewhere else. Anywhere. You know our boy. He's all over the place."

"Yeah, like a virus."

"Tannex. Maybe the new big thing."

"I'll call the Chicago office and ask them to run it down. How do you spell it?"

"I don't know----T-A-N-N-E-X, I guess. All I know is, that was the secretary, and the big boy's gotta drop everything to run up there for Tannex."

"And what about the little Missus? She going?"

"Oh, no. Sounds like she's mad at him. But get this---she's going to help her friend with the catering at a big fancy reception tonight in Port Royal."

"So? That's the high rent district. Everything in Port Royal is big and fancy."

"Not like this."

"Yeah? Why's that?"

"This one happens to be at the home of Mr. Chase Chambers."

"I'll be damned!"

"You got that right. We have to pass that little tidbit on to Big Mac, ASAP. I don't think there's much that can be done about it, but he better get the heads up."

"Roger that."

- 6 -

Marsha was right on time. Marsha was always right on time. You could set your clock by the "Schedule Queen."

Marsha didn't look like a model of efficiency and self-reliance. She looked like a model, almost six feet tall with a lean body hardened by Pilates. Her chiseled cheekbones were softened by her pageboy russet brown hair, wispy and flyaway and always in her eyes.

· Her fun, high-fashion look was a great disguise for a confident and capable businesswoman. First Class was in good hands, none better. Marsha thrived on the long hours and endless demands of the job. She worked well with all kinds of people and never wilted under pressure.

In fact, Meagan mused, she used to be a lot like Marsha.

Meagan slid into the passenger seat of Marsha's sky blue BMW 325.

"So, what is going on in that devious mind of yours?"

"Just sit tight, Meg. I'll explain at Janos."

"Janos? The salon for the rich and famous?"

"You got it! We're meeting the rest of the crew there." She backed out, spun the wheel and sped off like a race driver.

"This isn't one of our normal jobs. This is special. It was Sandy's idea. They want us to be---what did she say?---unobtrusive, to fit in with the guests. So, since it's a formal affair, the whole crew will be dressing in black tie and formal gowns and nobody will wear badges or aprons or anything that signifies hired help. Is that cool or what!"

"Wow," said Meagan. Very cool indeed. "And who is this Sandy?"

"I told you. Sandy's an old friend, and she happens to be Chase Chamber's fiancée. She's the one who got us this job. She booked us all into Janos today so that Maxwell can do our hair, and Verdi is doing everyone's make-up. They've rearranged their bookings to accommodate us for total makeovers. Just think of it as Homecoming revisited."

"A total makeover? Oh, God, Marsha, how fabulous!"

They pulled up in front of Janos. A valet in a red "Janos" jacket was at the door as soon as Marsha shifted into park. Most of the girls on Marsha's crew were already gathered in the lobby, buzzing at their new sleek looks, loving the makeovers. God, Meagan thought, this gig was costing somebody a fortune!

Marsha and Meagan took seats and their makeover began in earnest. Two hours later, Marsha swiveled Meagan's chair around to face her. Meagan's hair was streaked in various shades of blonde and cut to a perfect frame for her face. Her make-up added an exotic touch.

Maxwell flittered over, hovering above them. He hugged Meagan's shoulders.

"Honey, I'm going to put you on display in the front window. You are a masterpiece."

And turning to Marsha, Maxwell gushed, "And look at you, girl. I am quitting right now. Oh, I do such a good job even though I say so myself."

They laughed and hugged him.

As they waited for the car, they stood silent, side by side in front of the floor length mirror. Who were these beautiful looking women?

"Meagan, I'm not kidding---your hair, your eyes--- you look amazing."

"You were gorgeous before we started, Marsha, just like Elle. You two always look terrific even when getting out of bed in the morning."

"Isn't Elle coming to visit soon? I'd love to see her. It's been years."

"She'll be here in a few weeks. Ross doesn't want Elle around. He can't stand her. But she is coming!"

"Wow. Where did you go for the attitude makeover?"

"Oh, Marsh. It's been coming for a while. Long overdue. I love Ross, but I don't want to be his little mouse --I just can't do it anymore. It's not me."

"Good for you, Meagan!"

"Not a word. He's in Chicago until Friday. So, for the next 72 hours, he is a non-factor. Now, where is my list of duties?" Meagan held out her hand.

"Like you need a list! We're the bosses tonight so just keep an eye on everything."

"Okay. Let's go show them what First Class is all about."

"So what's next, chief?" Meagan said as they pulled away from Janos.

"We'll stop off at my place and jump into our gowns. Then off to the castle."

"I'm so glad you called me, Marsh. God, this is so much fun! I would absolutely love to get back into the business."

They were at Marsha's condo in ten minutes, rifling through the closet like teenagers. Marsha pulled a gown off a hanger and threw it over to Meagan. She stripped off her top and jeans and slipped it on. It was a simple, black, sleeveless, stretchy crepe, a floor length DKNY gown with a provocative slit up one side and chiffon ruffles at the hem. A perfect fit. She threw on a crinkle black lace shawl for the finishing touch.

Marsha grabbed a slightly more risqué strapless mini, a red silk sheath with a short matching jacket.

They looked at one another and giggled.

"God, Meagan, this takes me back to the good, old days at school, getting ready for parties and dates. Remember, clothes all over the place? We were always tripping over each other, trying to find the right pair of shoes and fighting over the same dress. Remember?"

"Yeah. And smoking cigarettes non-stop."

"Oh, god, yes! Salem one hundreds! French inhale!"

"Please, don't make me laugh! My mascara will run and I'll look like a vampire."

The two of them howled.

"God, Meagan! Stop it right now or else find me a panty liner! You know what happens when you--- please don't do this to me now!"

"We better take some along, just in case," Meagan gasped. "You never know."

Marsha grabbed some panty liners from a dresser drawer and threw them at Meagan.

"Better safe than sorry!"

"Yep, we are definitely professional career women here," Meagan cried out. "Trying hard not to wet our pants!"

The Chambers home was set at the southern tip of the Port Royal peninsula, nestled between the Gulf and Naples Bay. The estate was an 18-acre sea of green, bejeweled with island gardens ablaze with orchids and azaleas, shaded by towering palms.

A cobblestone drive wound past the gatehouse and up a gentle slope to a palatial home with a panoramic view from the sapphire Gulf waters west to the dense stand of Virginia pine guarding the Tom's River, the wide channel that swept the bay waters south to the sea. A brightly colored caretaker's villa peeked from the pine shadows like a gingerbread house at the edge of a magic forest.

The main house was awe-inspiring. Rows of majestic columns flanked a grand entrance guarded by an imposing pair of stone gargoyles. Marble steps swept up to a wide veranda and the ornate mahogany doors beyond, opened wide in invitation.

Meagan sat in the car for a moment, unable to move, simply in awe of the majesty of the Chamber Estate. Finally she exclaimed to Marsha, "What a spectacular house!"

"Wait 'til you see inside."

Marsha and Meagan entered the elegant marbled foyer with its enormous Austrian crystal chandelier hanging from the ceiling in the center of the room. There was a stunning stained glass mural spanning most of one wall.

"Is that a Tiffany?"

"Who else?"

Marsha led the way down the cavernous hall to the kitchen.

The kitchen was also decorated with seventeenth century flare, the centerpiece being a magnificent iron and brass hanging chandelier. In fact, the whole kitchen was of iron and brass with two large islands topped with gold-flecked black granite. Huge copper pots and pans hung from the ceramic tiled ceilings over the islands. Counter space was certainly not an issue in this house. It was a caterer's dream in every way and Meagan was dying to explore it further.

The crew wore aprons over their formal attire for the frenzied, last minute preparations. All their high heels were tossed in a heap in one corner. The excitement was contagious.

One of the girls yelled over to Marsha, "Whose idea was it to do this job in formal attire, Boss Lady?"

As if on cue, a svelte blonde in a spectacular Dior gown breezed through the archway and answered her.

"It was mine! That way, if you get tired of working, join the party and have some fun. How do you like that?"

The answers forthcoming from the entire crew were unanimous.

"We love it!"

Meagan watched as this stunning woman greeted Marsha fondly, flashing a warm smile. She turned, noticed Meagan, and the smile was gone. Just like that.

The woman seemed to stiffen and draw in a deep breath as she approached Meagan, extending her hand formally, "You must be the Meagan Hamilton I've heard so much about from Marsha. I'm Sandra Simpson."

Meagan took her hand cordially.

"Hello, Sandra."

"You're married to Ross Hamilton. Am I right?"

"Yes, that's right. Do you know my husband?"

"Not really, no---well, hardly..." Sandra was not comfortable. "I met him at some charity event. I don't believe you were with him at the time...But it's nice to finally meet you." Her smile was forced.

"The clock is ticking, ladies," Marsha interrupted, sensing the discomfort. "No time to chat."

Both Sandra and Meagan looked relieved as they went their separate ways.

Meagan ducked into the pantry to gather supplies and caught sight of a heavyset man in the hallway beyond, talking into his own lapel. Security, no doubt, she thought. This is like being at the White House. This Chambers family has it all going, right down to the burly guys with sunglasses and bulges under their coats.

But why was he eyeing her so closely? Did he think she was going to steal the silverware? It made her uneasy, even a bit insulted. She tried to ignore him and plunged back into her work. When she looked up a minute later, the man in black was gone.

- 8 -

"Mac?"

"Yeah, Harry, go ahead."

"The bird's in the house."

"You sure it's her?"

"I'm sure. Pretty as her picture."

"Where you at?"

"Inside. Walking the hall. She's in the kitchen with the rest of the cooks."

"Caterers, Harry. Those are caterers."

"Whatever. You gonna tell C?"

"I don't think so. Better let sleeping dogs lie. He'll be busy all night, and it sounds like she will, too. I doubt if they'll even run into each other."

"Okay. Your call."

"But keep an eye on her, Harry. This might be nothing, but I don't buy it yet. She could be there working some angle for the hubby. Hamilton is no dummy, and if he has the slightest idea that we're on to him---"

"Okay, okay. I'll stay on top of her."

"Bet you'd like that, Harry."

"Just doing my job. Out."

[]

Marsha was a nervous wreck for the first few hours, flitting from one room to the next, an eye out for the smallest detail. By mid-evening, her concerns faded as she watched the event unfold. The cuisine was superb, the décor was delightful and the presentation was flawless, choreographed with the grace and precision of a Broadway play. The smooth music of the Jerry Bruno Orchestra provided an elegant soundtrack. But the acid test for Marsha always came down to one question. Was everybody happy? She could tell by the looks on the faces everywhere she turned. No doubt about it. The guests were relaxed and comfortable, enjoying the night. First Class had made a great first impression on the Port Royal crowd, and Marsha was ecstatic.

So was Sandy. She huddled with Marsha in the hallway, giddy with the shower of compliments for everything from the lobster quesadillas to the midnight chocolate truffles.

Meagan was circulating, providing help wherever needed. Her self-assigned tasks were to make sure the food and drink stations were replenished, keep the staff on their toes and keep an eye out for anything falling through the cracks. Presently, however, her eyes were on someone else. She saw him for the first time framed in the arched entry to the great room, greeting each new guest like a long-lost friend.

Chase Chambers.

He looked delicious, tall and lean in his fitted tux. His chiseled profile captivated her. She couldn't take her eyes off him.

She rolled her eyes, exasperated at her schoolgirl silliness. After all, she was a married woman, not so happily married at the moment, maybe, but she never contemplated straying. Not ever. Still, it didn't hurt to daydream a bit, and---

"Beep-beep! Hello! Earth to Meagan!"

She was jolted by a nudge from behind. Meagan turned to see Marsha inches away, with a knowing smile.

"Do you think I haven't noticed you ogling the man of the house?"

"Is it that obvious?"

"Only the drooling."

Meagan giggled as Marsha glanced at Chase herself.

"You think he's a hunk, huh? Everybody does. Hard to believe he used to have a brother just like him. Cameron Chambers."

"What do you mean, 'used to'?"

"Cameron died...oh, it's been more than a year now. Sad, sad story. He was with the government, way up there with the CIA or FBI. Some kind of---what do they call it---special ops, super spy stuff. He was on a mission over in God-knows-where. Killed in action."

"No!"

"Yes. Terrible tragedy. Really hit the family hard. I guess they've had more than their share."

"Other tragedies you mean?" Meagan urged her on.

"Uh-huh. Kind of like the Kennedys. Senator Chambers---the father---he was killed in a plane crash, long time ago. Then there's another brother. I think his name is Colin or---Cole. That's it. Cole. A younger brother. He's also had a rough time."

"What do you mean?"

"He almost drowned trying to save his friend, right here, down at the river, Gordon Pass. He was in a coma for a while. Finally came out of it. But he's not all there, you know?"

Meagan didn't comment. Marsha didn't wait for one.

"Chase's mother takes care of him. Dotes on him, really. And she's another story. They call her Gem. I don't even know what that stands for, Jemima? Jamaica? Gem like gemstone? I don't know. Anyhow, she's a psychic, big time. She's from Louisiana, you know, Cajun country, voodoo, all that mumbo-jumbo stuff. She's famous, works with the police sometimes and she has something to do with the university--- what's the one down there? Tulane? Yes, I guess they've got a whole psychic department there, and she's a visiting professor or lecturer or something."

"I didn't even know you could get a degree in psychic."

"Anyhow, I guess it goes way back in her family, an old Creole clan from down in the bayou. She's got the tarot cards---very big on tarot cards..."

"Interesting lady."

"Amazing, really," Marsha clarified. "She lives with Cole, ever since the accident. When they're here, they live at the caretaker's cottage. It's like this Hansel and Gretel place down by the water. That's where he works. He's an artist, a painter. Sandy says he's good. And I'll tell you something else---"

"Tell me."

"He's from the same gene pool, know what I mean? He's another to-die-for dreamboat in the looks department."

"Like Chase?"

"I've never seen him, but that's what everybody says."

Meagan settled back. "Well, these Chambers are quite a family."

Marsha continued as they reloaded serving trays. "The father was from Atlanta. Very big in politics. Senator Mitchell Chambers. I think the grandfather was a senator, too, or governor or something. It's in the blood. Now Chase is running for Congress. That's what this thing is all about tonight, working the crowd, getting the big money folks to ante up. The man is perfect for politics, don't you think?"

They both looked across the room at Chase, a movie star silhouette against the bright lights of the veranda beyond, Sandra at his side.

"I think you're looking at the new congressman from the great state of Florida."

"And his future bride."

"Sandy's a lucky girl."

"Oh, Marsh---you think?"

"Of course, it doesn't hurt that Sandy's independently wealthy. Her parents left her a lot of money. Her father was the Chambers' lawyer. The families go way back."

"So, she's beautiful, she's smart, she's rich and she's going to marry the world's most eligible bachelor. I think I hate her."

"She's really very nice. She got us this gig, remember?"

"I know. I still hate her."

Marsha grinned and they both laughed.

"I meant to tell you, keep your ears open at these things, and you hear everything, Meg." Marsha confided as she popped a shrimp in her mouth.

"You are amazing, Marsha!"

Marsha bent close, "All kidding aside, Sandy told me all of this, and it's coded information, you know."

Meagan nodded, serious. "Coded. I hear you."

"The last time we did a party here, I was going through the drawers in the pantry---looking for linens or something, I forget---and I saw this framed picture of Chase and Cameron, both in uniform.

"Sandy seemed upset when I saw it. She told me the story about Cameron. Then she put the photo away, far away, in a bottom desk drawer in the study. Anyway, where was I? Oh, yeah, the picture. I guess everybody in the family is very sensitive about Cameron. I know Sandy sure is."

"Well I won't tell a soul," Meagan promised. "And who am I going to tell? We don't exactly run in the same circles. I'll probably never see Chase Chambers again."

"Oh, never say never, Meg," Marsha shook a finger at her. "Sandy's already mentioned having First Class handle their wedding. Better start memorizing the wedding planner encyclopedia."

Meagan straightened up. "Wait, wait, wait---I'm the silent partner, remember?"

"I don't think so. Not any more."

Meagan started to protest again, but Marsha put a finger to her lips.

"Don't say anything now," she said in formal tone. "We shall discuss the matter at a later date. Now we must return to the field of battle and complete our mission."

Meagan saluted and joined her, locking arms as they marched into the kitchen together.

◊

Nine of Pentacles. She was very close.

Gemini Chambers sat by the open window at the caretaker's house in a dimly lit room, illuminated only by two candles flickering in the evening breeze and the soft glow of a half moon.

In the distance, just beyond the rise of jacaranda gardens, she could hear the sounds of music, voices and tinkling glasses, the muted cacophony of the festivities at the Big House. It warmed her with memories of evenings past. Good-natured Mitch would struggle into his tuxedo, grumbling about the endless political wing dings and "putting on the dog for the freeloaders," but Gem was enervated by grand gatherings, lifted by the rush of music and laughter.

Those were the days. Gem set her nostalgia aside and opened her mind to the new thoughts coming her way on ethereal streams.

Nine of Pentacles. *La fauconnierre*. A woman of striking beauty, surrounded by luxuriant gardens, a falcon at her wrist poised to take flight on a new adventure.

Gem saw it clearly, although she had no cards at hand. There were many times when she did not need them. Such were the innate psychic powers of Gemini Chambers. She could provide a complete reading, divine minute details of a unique arrangement of multiple cards without touching the deck, nothing before her but a blank slate, *tabula rasa*.

As it was now. It was not the physical card but a vision of the Nine of Pentacles that delivered the message. She had first caught the psychic scent in the dramatic reading that portrayed this girl in a deeply troubled light. Bound and hoodwinked then, she was strong and self-assured in this new light. Gem knew that her great burdens were not behind her, only set aside for a moment, long enough for her bright true colors to shine through.

She was so close. Right here! Gem knew she had but to stroll across to the Big House and she would find her there.

It was an inviting thought, but Gem let it pass.

"Pas le temps."

It was not the time. They would meet, but not yet. There was another rendezvous in store on this moonlit night. Gem smiled and let her thoughts drift back to warm nights long ago.

- 9 -

Meagan was sure that no one would miss her presence. The catering crew knew the wrap up routine. They didn't need her. She slipped off her heels and strolled out for a breather.

She sighed as her naked feet glided over the lush carpet of Bermuda grass. No shoes, barefoot and free.

Meagan meandered across the lawn to garden paths toward a small gazebo nestled under the flowering trees. She tiptoed up the stone steps and eased down on a carved wooden bench. As she leaned back to rest her head on the cool wooded ledge, she closed her eyes and thought, "This is heaven."

The solitude was intoxicating. She didn't want to move but took the time for soul searching. Although her feet were sore, her legs tired, her shoulders ached and her hands were raw, it had been a wonderful night. She loved being back at work with First Class. Marsha had to be happy, too. She had achieved her goals for the evening, pulled off a great event and pulled her partner back into the fold. Meagan had to admit it. She was definitely hooked again. She had missed working. She missed being productive and creative. Most of all, she missed being with people, making them happy. The urge to get back in the game was irresistible.

Yes!

She made the decision right then and there. She knew it was right, and she felt good about it. She flinched at the thought of Ross's reaction, but whose life was it anyway?

With that thought in mind, she rose to return and deliver the news to Marsha when she came face to face with Prince Charming. Chase Chambers had entered her sanctuary!

A flash of adrenaline shot through her system. Was she dreaming? No. He was here, up close and personal, standing before her. He was so close she could feel the heat of his presence and smell his distinctive scent. Her senses reeled.

"Oh God, you scared me to death! I didn't hear you. I'm sorry. Am I trespassing, Chase? I mean, uh, Mr. Chambers?"

She blushed like a schoolgirl, thankful for the cloak of darkness.

Chase was curious and pleasantly surprised. Who was this rare beauty, far from the festivities, alone in the night?

"I was going to say something, but you looked so content. And I have to apologize---you know my name, but I don't---I thought I had met everyone here tonight, but I don't remember meeting you. And I know I'd remember. Miss---?"

"Meagan," she stammered, as she took his hand.

"Miss Meagan. My pleasure."

"I mean Hamilton." She was a wreck. "It's not Miss---I mean---it's Hamilton, Meagan Hamilton."

Chase kept her hand in his and coaxed her back to the bench. "Let's sit for a minute, Meagan Hamilton."

Meagan lit like a butterfly. Chase moved in easily beside her.

"Mmm, I needed this," he said, stretching his long, lean legs. He turned to her, his voice soft, relaxing. "You must be a friend of Sandra's."

"Oh, Mr. Chase, sorry, Mr. Chambers, I'm not at the party."

He gave her a quizzical look.

"I mean, I'm here, but I'm not---I'm with Marsha---you know, the caterers. I'm not a guest. I'm a partner in First Class, overseeing this event."

"Well, that's fine. But you are a guest now, Meagan. You're my guest."

"Oh, thanks, but I really should get back and help."

She took a breath, trying to regain her composure. She felt herself swaying toward him, drawn like a magnet.

Chase gave no sign of his astonishment. *Meagan Hamilton. Mrs. Ross Hamilton!*

"Don't go yet," he said. "It's pleasant out here, isn't it?"

"Beautiful."

His eyes were glued on her. "Just what I was thinking."

Meagan Hamilton. Damn! He should have been warned, should have been prepared. He would definitely give Mac's security people an earful about this. And now, here he was, alone with her. And just what the hell was he supposed to do about it? Stand up, say goodbye, nice to meet you, and go. He didn't. He couldn't cut and run. Not his style. He would just have to play it out. Improvise a little.

"Now Meagan, let me guess---you're married to Ross," he said it easily, just making conversation.

A jolt to Meagan. "What did you say?"

"Ross Hamilton? Isn't he---?"

"My husband, yes, but how did you---?"

"I know Ross. Or I should say I've met him once or twice. Business lunch or something. He's--- he's a busy man. Lots of irons in the fire. But I'm sure you know all about that."

He studied her intently.

Meagan heard herself answer absently, hardly paying heed to her own words.

"Not really. Financial deals and investments, that I know, but that's about all. It's Ross's world, and he's very good at it. He doesn't need my help."

He caught her off guard with his next remark. "Actually, Meagan, I would like your help, if I might be so bold."

"What kind of help?"

"I have a whole series of events coming up: meetings, dinners, lunches---this political thing, you know. I'm going to need someone to handle it all, and I don't want the usual run-of-the-mill fare. It's got to be special, set a tone for the campaign. And it's obvious from tonight that you know what you're doing. I was wondering if you could take me on as a client."

"A client? Oh, Mr. Chambers, I---"

"Yes. And, please, Meagan, call me Chase. No more Mister."

Meagan relaxed a little.

"Okay. Chase. I'm sure that First Class would love to have you as a client. And I know we could do a top-notch job for you. But you really should speak to Marsha. She handles that side of things. I'm not really involved with the day-to-day business."

"Well, if I can't work with you, that is, with you personally, then I guess I'll have to find someone else. No offense to Marsha. I'm sure she's terrific, but---I don't know how else to say it---I work person-to-person, Meagan. I get a gut feeling about someone, and that's who I want for the job. It works for me, always has. I would want you to handle the account, coordinate things directly with me. So, are you interested, Mrs. Hamilton?"

Meagan knew that Marsha would kill her if she didn't grab this opportunity with both hands. It was almost too good to be true, the influential Chambers as clients.

"Chase, if you want us, you've got us. We would love to handle your account. Why don't I give you a call next Monday and we'll go over the proposed dates for the events that you have in mind?"

He shook his head. "That's not convenient, I'm afraid. I'm out of town all next week. It'll have to be tomorrow. How about, say, one o'clock, at the fishing pier, downtown Naples?"

Meagan looked puzzled. "Tomorrow? Oh, I don't think I can possibly----"

"Yes, you can....and I think you will."

Meagan didn't know how to respond to his boldness. "I will, will I?"

He stood and hauled Meagan up beside him, both hands holding her firmly at her slim waist and looked her straight in the eye.

"Yes, you will. There's no time like the present. One o'clock at the pier. I'll make arrangements for lunch. Just bring a notebook or a laptop, or whatever you use. And you might throw in a swimsuit, just in case."

"A swimsuit? Just in case of what?"

"Gotta run, Meagan. It's been a pleasure---"

He draped an arm around her and pulled her closer. She tilted her face up toward his.

He continued evenly, "---and I'm really looking forward to working with you."

Meagan said nothing, lost in his eyes.

A shrill ring tone shattered the stillness. He pulled a cell phone from his tux pocket.

Meagan was so close she could hear the voice through the phone.

"Where in the hell are you, C? The Turner people are all here on the veranda and I can't believe---"

Chase cut him off. "Hear you, Curtis. Be right there."

He slipped the cell back in his pocket.

"Who's Curtis?" she asked bluntly.

Chase swallowed hard. "Curtis is, uh, my assistant campaign manager and publicity guy. He's a stickler for details---so anal---but he's good. It's just that sometimes he thinks he runs my whole life."

"I know the feeling," she replied cryptically.

"Look, I do have to go. But I'm really looking forward to tomorrow. See you then." And with that he was off, half jogging back to the house.

Meagan stood there, in a daze. What had just happened? Had the rising star of the Chambers family, up and coming candidate for Congress, just put the moves on her, Meagan Hamilton, married woman?

No, she told herself, as she shook her head, there was no hitting on anybody. He simply wanted to hire her services with First Class. And the fact that his mere touch sent fissures of heat searing through her system--well, that was just, just crazy.

〇

Back at the Big House, Marsha packed off the last of the crew and completed a quick tour of the premises to make certain all was in good order. She had just checked off the last item on her master list when Meagan returned.

"There you are. So, what do you think? Was it a huge, four-star, best-of-all-time success or what?" Marsha gushed.

"You had this all planned, didn't you? You sucked me right in!"

"Would I do that?" Marsha smiled her Cheshire cat smile. "Listen, Meg, we're on the verge of a giant leap forward and I can't do it without you. I confess, tonight was a setup. We weren't short of people. And it was a terrible, manipulative, scheming thing to do. So, did it work?"

"Okay, it did! You win! I'm back!"

"Yes!" Marsha pumped a fist then turned to Meagan, her voice hushed.

"How do you think Ross will take it? Like, he's not going to take out a contract on you---or even worse, on me?"

Meagan waved her off.

"Oh, just the usual ranting and raving. But after a while---say ten years or so---he'll come around. "

- 10 -

"Something is wrong."

Ross Hamilton got up from the couch and walked away from the sleek laptop computer. The rows of numbers on the screen continued to scroll as he paced to the window and glanced down at Lake Shore Boulevard far below. It was past midnight, but the traffic was still heavy, serpentine lines of white winding along the black lake.

He said it again, "Something is wrong."

Stacy heard him the second time. She sat erect in the high-backed chair, glasses perched on the bridge of her nose, poring over a thick sheaf of business documents, every bit the prim and proper executive secretary, except her shoes were off and the TV on the console was on, some old Joan Crawford movie.

"Wrong with what? The accounts?"

He stared out the window.

"No, no. The numbers are right to the penny. That's what I like about the Swiss. Precision. Little watchmakers. The new statements are downloading now."

"Then what?"

He looked at her, then past her at the TV. Stacy looked very much like Joan Crawford. He never noticed it before. Slender, elegant, perfect posture, the dark eyes, the raven hair wrapped tight---Christ, she could have played the role in that nasty little movie--- what was it?---*Mommie Dearest*.

"Something, Stacy dearest. I don't know. But I can feel it."

He paced back to the laptop. A message blinked: Download complete. He hit a key and the screen went dark. A moment later it flashed back to life with a gruesome full-screen image of a well-dressed woman sprawled in a parking lot, eyes open, hair matted with blood, her face contorted in a grotesque death mask. Ross looked at it but did not react at all. He poked another key and the image disappeared. He flipped the screen closed, popped out the disk and slipped it in his pocket.

"You've had those feelings before," Stacy said.

"Yes," he nodded. "My sentinel. And it's never a false alarm."

"Maybe it's this new project." She hoisted the documents. "It's very big---the biggest ever---and very complicated."

"Maybe." He walked to the black marble bar at the far end of the room, poured a drink from the crystal decanter and took a sip. "Get the cards, Stacy."

Stacy hurried from the room and returned with a small, ornate box in hand. She removed an oversized deck of Tarot cards and placed it on the bar before him.

Ross spread the deck with a sweep of his hand, plucked a card and turned it over.

"Oh," Stacy groaned.

The Four of Swords stared up at them: a disturbing image of a knight in repose, lying atop a coffin, three swords suspended perilously above, another below. A woman and child gaze upon the morbid scene from a stained glass window.

"I told you," he said. "Something is very wrong."

Ross Hamilton did not seem like the type who would put much stock in Tarot cards. In his world, faith was a foolish word. He considered all religions nonsense, based on primitive fears and ignorance. The entire realm of metaphysics was a hoax. Psychics were all charlatans. There was no God, no devil, no heaven, no hell. In fact, for Ross, there was no good or evil; only success and failure. That was reality.

And yet, the Tarot cards were something else. He didn't consider them spiritual in any way. Rather, they were valuable tools. Properly used and construed, they tapped into some arcane power as real as electricity or nuclear energy. And just as those universal forces had been unknown for centuries, so did the nameless power linked to the Tarot remain obscure in modern times. Someday, Ross was certain, that power would be discovered and defined---by scientists, not priests. In the meantime, only an elite few had the skills required to take advantage of what the cards had to offer.

Ross considered himself one of the elite.

He had been instructed in the ways of the Tarot from an early age. His own mother was his mentor.

Every night, instead of fairy tales, she would read cards to him, laying a few on his bedside table and explaining the images. She taught him to interpret, to look past the obvious and find the subtle messages. The same woman who had passed on her contempt for all things spiritual imbued a reverence for the power of the cards.

She often reminded him that he was a direct descendant of the great Alexander Hamilton. Son of a noble father, war hero at 20, he rose to the highest ranks of the new nation, rich and respected, hailed as the wizard who crafted the new nation's financial system. Self-assured and hot-tempered, he feuded with Jefferson, John Adams, even Washington. His public rebuke of Vice President Aaron Burr as a charlatan led to the duel that cost him his life.

Ross knew the details by heart, from the courageous charge at Yorktown to the fearless final moments when Hamilton's pistol misfired and he stood there unflinching as the despicable Burr took cold-blooded aim and shot him down.

The story of his glorious forefather molded Ross, charted his course. He would be a leader, brave and bold. He would become a master of finance and take his place in the ranks of the rich and influential.

He was devastated, years later, when he learned that so much of it wasn't true.

Alexander Hamilton was born a bastard child in the Caribbean. He was not from a distinguished family. Neither was Ross. That was the biggest lie. He uncovered the truth, bound in rubber bands and stuffed under the faded family photos hidden in an old trunk in the attic. He was not a descendant of Alexander Hamilton, no relation at all. His great-grandfather was a lowly immigrant from White Russia named Herkovitz whose name changed to Hamilton at Ellis Island.

Ross's father was no hero either. A narrow-minded man of low ambition, his inconsequential life was cut short, killed in a traffic accident when Ross was two. The money they lived on after that---part of the Hamilton family fortune, his mother said---was no inheritance at all. It was the hefty settlement paid by a drunk but very wealthy driver, eager to avoid criminal charges.

His heritage was a pack of lies, inane fantasies of a devious woman. That revelation was a tipping point for young Ross Hamilton. He had already displayed some disturbing signs of deviant behavior. A petty thief, he stole toys and bikes from backyards and left them abandoned on the next block. He set fires in garbage cans and vandalized garages. He lured a neighbor's cat with a saucer of milk and choked it to death with his belt, wrapped the carcass in plastic bags and tossed it in a factory dumpster a mile away, already adept at covering his tracks.

The telltale signs of sociopathic behavior blossomed with the realization that his mother had played him for a fool. She was all that was good in his life, his love and inspiration. But from that moment, in the close confines of the attic, proof of her betrayal clutched in his sweaty hands, he despised her.

Ross did not confront her with his discovery. He said nothing, letting the resentment smolder like burning coals.

A year later, his mother was dead, drowned in her bath, another meaningless casualty of life. A tragic accident, the coroner said. Ross smiled at the memory.

Yes, it was tragic, but he was the only one on earth who would ever know it was no accident.

After her death, he was not surprised to learn that the trust fund she often dangled before him like a carrot before a dim-witted donkey did not exist. There was no money. All that he was left with were the lies, and the deck of cards.

At least the cards were real. Ross used them often. In business, they were his secret weapon, providing an edge in negotiations and decisions that his competitors could only dream of. The cards were his board of advisors, his inside traders and his spies. And unlike his mother, the cards always told the truth.

The Four of Swords was telling the truth now. But what truth was it? His eyes raced across the image like a computer scanner, absorbing every detail. He reminded himself not to jump to conclusions. A common mistake. Influenced by emotions or desires, others often fell into the trap of first impressions. Not Ross. He continued to examine and reflect, considering the recumbent knight, the swords, the woman and child.

"That's you, isn't it? That's you on the coffin."

Stacy was agitated. For over a year now he had granted her the privilege of watching him work with the cards. She was the only one. No one else knew. Not his wife, employees, business associates---no one. They wouldn't believe it if she told them. Only Stacy, and she was a good student, always attentive, eager to learn. She was nowhere near his level, but she knew more about the cards than most so-called experts by now. Her concern was legitimate.

Ross didn't answer. He only did readings for himself---his life, his future, his decisions---never for others. Why would he waste the time? He was always the central figure. Of course the knight represented him, but what did it mean?

Some things were clear. The woman and child: surely his wife and son. Might as well be photographs of Meagan and Brandon. Ross was none too pleased to see them there, looking content and unconcerned, gazing down on the prostrate figure.

The message could be related to dear Meagan's defiant behavior of late. He would have to take care of that, bring her to heel.

He focused on the card again. The woman and child were troublesome, but not menacing. They were outside, looking in. But the three swords poised above, ready to strike---there was a real threat, serious and imminent. Interpretation was critical here. What---or who---did these daggers represent? They were clearly related, one to the others, arrayed in perfect parallel and almost identical, a fraternal trio.

Three men? Most likely. The swords were obviously masculine and Ross sensed the threat was personal. Three men, then, closely allied or related, all eager to do him harm. He racked his brain but could not come up with a single possibility. Ross had more than his share of enemies, but no threesomes that he could recall.

He would do some research, check the records and files. There had to be a clue somewhere. In the meantime, he would have to be vigilant. The most important aspect of the card was the unsuspecting knight: eyes closed, oblivious to the impending risk. For Ross, so cautious and methodical with every move, that would never do. Ignorance was not bliss; it was disaster. Now, thanks to the cards, his eyes were open.

He didn't know who or what, but he knew there was danger out there, danger with three faces.

The thought did not frighten Ross---it thrilled him. He relished the new challenge. He looked forward to the confrontation, the parry and thrust. He would crush these pretenders to his throne, turn their swords back upon them, emerge victorious again.

He took another sip of scotch and strolled back to his seat in the leather chair. Everything would be fine. Something was wrong, but he would make it right.

Stacy moved to him. "So tell me Ross, please, what is the problem?"

"A threat of sorts---I'm not certain yet---but nothing I can't handle."

"Should we turn another card?"

"No. That's enough for now."

"Then what? What can I do?" Stacy implored.

Ross pulled her closer.

"I'm sure you'll think of something."

He placed his hands on her shoulders and pushed her down, steering her head toward his lap. She went willingly.

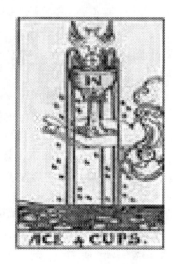

11

"Mommy's a sleepyhead! Mommy's a sleepyhead!" Brandon was shouting into his sleeping mother's ear early the next morning. She stirred uneasily and covered her head with a pillow trying to block the sound out. Her head hurt with a dull throb.

"Brandon, young man, I told you to whisper softly so as not to wake mummy up. I did not mean for you to go straight for her ears and yell softly. Sorry he woke you up, honey."

Meagan's mother, Katherine, smiled fondly at her only daughter who was still laying in a tangled mess of sheets on her bed.

"What time is it, Mom?" Meagan asked sleepily with half opened eyes, as she peeked out from under the pillow.

"About nine o'clock, darling. Do you want Brandon to wear anything special today for preschool? I just grabbed something that matched."

"What he has on is fine." Meagan stretched and pulled all her hair back from her face with both hands, then she held out her arms towards her son and said sweetly, "Come here Bran, and give Mommy a big kiss from her little man!"

She laughingly pulled her son over for a sloppy kiss as he dived on the bed with her, squirming under the covers. Then she spoke to her mother, "And thanks so much for watching him last night, Mom."

"No problem. How did it go last night? Your new hair cut looks great, by the way, even all mussed up. Did you enjoy being back in the middle of things again? Did you have fun? Did Marsha's plan work? Are you going to become active again in First Class? Well?" Katherine threw question after question at her daughter, impatiently waiting for answers.

Meagan's mother was quite aware that there was something lacking in her daughter's life. She felt that Meagan was not as happy as she would have liked her to be. It was not that she was unhappy. After all, Meagan had everything that she could possibly want: a gorgeous husband, a beautiful son and a wonderful home. But Katherine knew that these things were not the only things that Meagan needed to be fulfilled. Something was definitely missing. So with Brandon being older and not needing the constant attention from his mother, Katherine also felt confident that it was time for Meagan to get back to being involved in First Class. She felt that it was perfect timing. The big problem would be Ross's response. He was so unpredictable that it was scary. He could make things really uncomfortable for her daughter and grandson.

Meagan slowly inched out of bed and rubbed her palms against her forehead, trying to ward off the oncoming headache. She needed Excedrin. In spite of the throbbing pain in her head, she smiled lovingly at her mother.

"Yes, Mom, I'm back and Marsha has already assured me that the childcare issue is resolved, thanks to you. So glad you involved me in that important decision." She winked fondly at her mother.

"Now, Meg, I didn't mean to infringe on your life....and she can't start for a while yet---has to give notice. But you know I'll help with Brandon in the interim."

"I'm just teasing you, Mom. You are so efficient. I'm glad you took care of it for me. I'm sure I'll approve of any nanny you choose. If she got by all your questions and screening with flying colors, she must be a godsend. Now, if you could just take care of the Ross part as efficiently, I would be forever in your debt. In the meantime, could you be a sweetheart and take care of Brandon until school? I've got to get moving and grab a shower. I'm meeting Chase Chambers for lunch. He wants First Class to handle all the catering for his upcoming events. So we are going over some preliminary details regarding dates, etcetera."

"You mean, The Chase Chambers? The gorgeous guy with the political aspirations, the one who has been in the papers lately? Oh, that is wonderful! See, one night back on the job and you pick up a big-time new client! Marsha must be ecstatic. Where are you meeting him for lunch?" Without waiting for an answer, she stood up and left the bedroom to go and find Brandon who was watching television and singing along with it.

Relieved at not having to answer her mother's questions, Meagan quickly dashed into the bathroom for a quick shower. Her head continued to pound and she anxiously admitted to herself that she was really nervous about seeing Chase again.

"Nana, you color that dinosaur purple and I'll color mine red. Nana, here's your crayon." Brandon solemnly flicked the purple crayon out of the pack and handed it to his grandmother. Grandmother and grandson were intently working together over the jumbo coloring book when Meagan walked into the kitchen dressed and ready to go, waiting for the two extra strength Excedrin to kick in.

She gazed fondly at her mother and son. They both meant so much to her. Her eyes briefly skimmed over the answering machine on the kitchen counter. The green light was flickering.

"Looks like I received a call last night. It's probably Ross telling me when he will be home." Meagan focused on the blinking light as if in a trance.

"Maybe you'd better play your messages, sweetheart, instead of staring at the phone. Don't you have a luncheon appointment?"

Ross's familiar voice broke the silence. Katherine noticed her daughter wince when he started to talk. Meagan automatically muted the TV the moment she heard his voice and told Brandon to hush.

"Hi darling, it's me. Just wanted you to know that it looks like I'll be stuck in Chicago over the weekend. We are giving our Japanese clients a little party here at the penthouse Friday night. Strictly boring business, you know how it is. We'll be working day and night until it's concluded. So I will be gone until the middle of next week.

"Also, I am staying firm on the matter of Eleanor. I will not tolerate her staying with us and I mean it. Please arrange to cancel her visit immediately. I refuse to put up with her for any length of time. I'm sure you will think about it and see that I am right. I'll get Stacy to call her and cancel her visit. Just let me know how you want to handle it. See you next week."

"What a total j.e.r.k!" Katherine spelled it out so Brandon wouldn't understand. Then she turned to her grandson and said, "Brandon, why don't you go ride your bicycle around the driveway for a while?"

She glanced at Meagan. "The front driveway gate is closed, right?"

"Yes, Mom, it's closed and, Brandon, that does sound like fun. You know where your bike is. Go ahead, sweetheart. We'll be out in a minute."

Brandon dutifully abandoned the television and raced towards the side door to go outside to play. Mother and daughter waited until he was out of hearing range. Both women were silent, waiting for the other to speak.

"Now Mom, no more lectures on Ross. I married him. You didn't."

"Thank God for small favors," Katherine said under her breath scornfully.

"Cool it, Mom! Like I said, I married him so that makes him my problem. He's really not that bad most of the time."

"Meagan wake up! I've tried not to interfere with your marriage, but now I will say my due. It's past time. Ross is totally insensitive and he doesn't give you or Brandon the time of day. He is inconsiderate, insulting and rude. He downgrades you at every turn and he always puts his business before anything else no matter what is happening."

"Well, Mom, feel free to tell me exactly how you feel!"

"Now, honey," Meagan's mother interrupted. "Maybe I've said too much and it isn't my place to speak to you like this about your husband. But your whole marital situation is so frustrating for your father and me to watch."

"No, Mom, I understand your concern. And it's not that I disagree with you. However, I married the man, for better or for worse, and this is his worst. But he is Brandon's father and Brandon adores him which is hard to believe."

"When was the last time the three of you did something fun together as a family? I'll tell you when-- never! You didn't even take a honeymoon, for heaven's sake! He took you along on one of his business conventions for your honeymoon with Stacy, I might add. You know, Meagan, your father and I forced ourselves to simply sit back and observe you and Ross at the beginning. We tried to stay out of it. I mean, you were blindly in love with this man. We felt that maybe you saw something in him that we did not. You deserve so much more, sweetheart, and I feel that the time has come for me to speak out. So, that's what I am doing. Your father is going to kill me for saying these things to you. We do love you so much, honey, and we hate to see you miserable all the time." Katherine lifted her head and peeked at Meagan to gauge her reaction to the strong words just spoken.

Her daughter smiled slightly and heaved a small sigh of resignation before saying, "I know you mean well, Mom. Believe it or not, in my heart I know that you and Dad are right about Ross and at the moment it appears that he is avoiding me for some reason or another. So, I am going to do something that is totally out of character and fly to Chicago and confront him. I need to get the Eleanor situation straightened out. She is due to visit soon. Plus, I need to let him know that I am back in the catering business with Marsha as of now. I'll be surprised if he doesn't threaten to start divorce proceedings. But, I have no choice but to approach him and let him know how I feel about things. Maybe, he'll surprise me and be more accommodating about these matters. I know, I shouldn't get my hopes up, but you never know. Maybe you could take Brandon the next couple of days, Mom? I hate to ask you again at such short notice...."

"Of course, darling. That's not a problem. What are grandmothers for, after all?"

Katherine smiled fondly at her daughter. "Sorry I got on my high horse a bit ago. I guess I just needed to get it off my chest. Ross's treatment of you has been bothering me for quite some time now. So, go and enjoy yourself. Maybe if you and Ross do spend some time together, just the two of you, things can be straightened out between you."

"I'd better call Ross's voice mail and let him know I'm coming, or better still, I'll just call Stacy. She'll give him the message."

Meagan reached across the kitchen counter to grab the phone. But before she could, her mother's hand gripped her wrist firmly, stopping her in mid air.

"Why don't you just surprise him, Meagan? You know damn well that if you call him and tell him that you are coming, he'll immediately call back or have Stacy call you and try to dissuade you from coming. Just go ahead, fly up there and surprise him. Are you afraid to arrive unannounced?" her mother asked softly.

"Not especially, but he likes to feel in control, I guess." Meagan looked questionably at her mother.

"Well, maybe it's time to take that control away from him. Believe me, it's about time. Maybe, he will wake up and see you as the wonderful person that you are and not just as a possession. For heaven's sake, Meagan, do what you really want to do and fly to Chicago tomorrow morning and go shopping on Michigan Avenue all afternoon. Do this for you. You love to shop and you will need a new wardrobe since you're back to work again. Buy something fabulous that will knock his socks off and then surprise him by arriving at his little cocktail party. You know he's having it at the company penthouse. That's where he always stays. Surprise him! You are his wife! And you know all the partners in his investment group and they all adore you." Urging her daughter, she added, "Go ahead, surprise him, honey."

"You are right, as always, Mom. Okay, I'll get tickets on a flight for first thing in the morning. Then I will shop 'til I drop all day, surprise Ross at his cocktail party, tell him I've decided to go back to work full—time starting Monday, and explain to him that Elle is coming to visit regardless if he agrees or not.

Meagan glanced at her watch and exclaimed, "Shit, Mom, I've got to get going! I'm supposed to meet

Chase at 1 p.m. Get Brandon on the bus for me. Will you?" She started heading for the garage door.

"But darling," her mother yelled, halting her abruptly at the door. "You are not dressed for a business luncheon. I mean, look at you! You're in shorts and T-shirt with "Drama Queen" on the front! What kind of an example do you want to set as an owner of First Class? Don't you think you should change into something a little more classy or business like?"

"Mom, don't get started on me now. I'm meeting him at the Naples' pier for a picnic lunch as we go over tentative catering dates. In fact, I might be over-dressed."

"Don't bet on it," her mother muttered.

"Come on, Mom, don't fret over me. Go home and fret over Dad. See you later. I'll come and get Brandon later tonight. I love you, Mom," Meagan reassured her mother as she headed out the door, jumped into her silver Mercedes convertible, and zipped away.

Katherine muttered to herself as she walked out to wait for the bus with Brandon, "Casual, indeed. God, her outfit was almost indecent! What is the world coming to? Why, way back in my days......"

12

"Absolutely not."

John MacNulty was hunched at his desk, shaking his head. Curtis LaFond stood behind him, reading the one-page memo over his shoulder. MacNulty looked squarely at the man standing before him.

"You've got to cancel on her, Chambers. This is the last thing we want to do."

"I think you're wrong, Mac."

Chambers looked like a different man. The tux was gone, replaced by khakis and a white t-shirt, a casual counterpoint to the men in suits.

MacNulty wasn't used to anyone second-guessing his decisions, much less telling him he was just plain wrong. At six-six and 250 pounds, they didn't call him Big Mac for nothing. As the ranking FBI agent in the entire region and special agent-in-charge of the investigation, he expected everyone to answer 'Yes sir' and follow his orders, no questions asked. But this Chambers was a piece of work. Hell, the whole family was.

"Oh, is that what you think?"

"I just wish you'd give me a chance to run with this. The opportunity came up, out of the blue, and I don't think we should pass it up. It's a whole new angle."

Mac shook his massive head again, unmoved. "It's too risky. You could blow the whole thing wide open. We don't even know if she's in on it with him."

Curtis didn't say a word. He was clearly enjoying the exchange, but wasn't about to side with anybody but his boss. Chambers ignored him and stepped closer to the desk.

"Don't you think we should find out? And if she's not---then she's got to be another mark, like all the rest. She could be in real danger."

Big Mac paused to think it over.

"Could be. I'll give you that." He glanced at Curtis, who still had nothing to say, then slapped his hand on the desk. "But the answer is still no. Not now, anyhow. There are other fish to fry. You know the Chisholms, don't you? In Atlanta?"

"Gary and Melissa? Hell yes, I know them. Grew up with Gary. He's just about family. Same with Mel."

"Then you should be very comfortable at their fundraiser tomorrow night. We've got you booked on a late afternoon flight. That will give you time to stop in at our office in Atlanta in the a.m. for a briefing, then off to the reception."

"What are you talking about, Mac?" He stepped back, confused. "Standing around smiling all night, asking people for money? I'm not the one for that and you know it."

Mac grinned. "Oh, you're getting better at it all the time, and you gotta be at this one. Edelman's going to be there."

"David Edelman? Diane's tax guy?"

"That's right."

"I thought your people already went over everything with him."

"We did. And we got nothing. Nada. But now he says he's got something on Hamilton, something big, and he wants to talk."

"I still don't get it."

"He's the nervous type, this Edelman, and he's scared to death of Hamilton. He doesn't want his name connected to this. Nothing on the record. He says the only one he'll talk to is Chase Chambers." Mac looked up. "You get it now?"

"Yes, sir. What time do I leave?"

Mac looked at his watch. "Four-thirty. So call your new lady friend and tell her you can't make that little rendezvous. Now, are we finished playing twenty questions?"

His maverick agent smiled.

"You should be nice to me, Mac. I'm going to be a congressman soon, you know."

Chambers turned to go, then stopped and turned back. "Hey, Curtis---great talking to you, too."

13

In spite of the perfect weather, the beachfront was practically deserted. Meagan saw no sign of Chase Chambers as she strolled down the wooden pier.

"Hey, lady---got any worms?"

The man was absently fishing off the side, a rod leaning on the railing next to him, line slack to the water. His legs dangled over the edge. A worn baseball cap cast a shadow on his face, eyes masked by mirrored sunglasses.

Meagan approached him warily, still unsure.

"Is that you, Mr. Chambers?"

He pushed back the hat to unveil that perfect smile.

"It's Chase, remember. I thought we had that settled."

He scrambled to his feet and extended his hand. She took it gingerly.

"I never would have recognized you."

"That's me. Master of disguise."

She studied him for a moment. The whole act was kind of strange for a congressional candidate. He saw the flicker of concern in her eyes.

"Did I scare you? Sorry. I didn't have time to shave this morning. Quite a sight, eh? But, to be honest, this is more the real me than the stiff in the tuxedo. I prefer to go casual anytime I can. I hope that's all right with you?"

"Casual is good," Meagan affirmed. "But that hat! What is that---a Wal-Mart red-line special?"

His mouth dropped as he took mock offense and Meagan laughed. He stood there, enjoying her, as a shiver of desire crept up his spine. He knew he was entering dangerous waters with this woman. He hoped his navigational skills were up to the task. What in the hell was he doing here with her anyway? She was the wife of the prime target of the investigation, maybe in on the action herself, and here he was trading small talk with her, in direct defiance of an order from the FBI division chief.

She had not said one suggestive word or made the faintest provocative move; but the sexual tension between them was almost painful for him.

Get a grip here, he told himself, *you can handle this. Start talking.*

"Well, Meagan, you look wonderful in spite of the long night."

"You know, it's funny," she answered honestly, "but I do better with less sleep. Five or six hours a night is all I need. I was in bed by four. Slept until nine.

It was great. Usually, I'm up at seven. My son has a built-in alarm clock for his Sponge Bob cartoons."

His tanned face scrunched into a question mark. "Sponge what? What the heck cartoon is that? What happened to good old Yogi Bear and Popeye?"

"Darling, your age is showing!"

"I like that," he whispered.

Meagan faltered as the heat from his closeness rippled her senses.

"You like what?"

"I like it when you call me 'darling.'"

He stepped closer. They were face to face, inches apart. Meagan stepped back.

"Listen, Chase, are we here for business, or is this just a fishing expedition? I mean, I was under the impression that we were to discuss your pressing calendar of campaign events, and the catering skills First Class has to offer. Yes?"

That put him in his place. She was something, all right.

"Yes, absolutely. Business, that's why we're here. So, if you'll just step this way..." He gestured toward the adjacent marina where a flotilla of craft of all sizes bobbed gently in tide. "All the schedules---and lunch---are waiting right over there."

They strolled down the boardwalk.

"Which one is it?"

"Which one do you think?"

Meagan scanned the docks. There were more than a hundred boats, from tiny skiffs to luxurious watercraft, but one stood out. A majestic, three-deck Tiara yacht stretching at least fifty feet, glistening like a crown jewel among the rest.

"That one." She pointed confidently, squinting to read the name. "The *Endurance*?"

He laughed.

She confronted him, hands on hips.

"Well? Isn't it?"

"It would certainly be embarrassing if it weren't." He took her hand. "Come on."

They stepped aboard through an arched glass door into a vast white room. Oval-shaped, sloping to a domed ceiling, it was all curves with no corners, illuminated by a teardrop crystal chandelier. Meagan felt like she was inside a cloud.

Chase headed to the lower galley to retrieve lunch while Meagan stayed topside.

Remember, girl, She lectured herself, *A business meeting with a client. That's all. Even if he is the most handsome, charming man you've ever met and the two of you are all alone on his million-dollar yacht.* She took a deep breath.

Chase appeared with picnic basket laden with gourmet delights.

"Hope you're hungry. I asked Maria to throw some stuff together. So let's see what we have." He started to unpack the basket while Meagan unwrapped the food.

"This looks wonderful," she said. "Tell Maria that I'm definitely impressed by her choices. I would have made the same selections myself. In fact, I think I did!" Meagan grinned. "Aren't these from the party last night?"

"I guess I neglected to tell her not to pack any leftovers, especially yours." He blushed like a little boy. "Sorry about that."

"I'm not. I hardly had a bite of any of this last night. Too busy running around. It's nice to have a chance to enjoy it." She plucked a sliver of tenderloin stuffed with Asiago cheese from the tray. "Mmm. My compliments to the chef."

"Very funny, Chef Meagan. Look, all I can say is, we're a very frugal family. How do you think we saved up the money for this thing?" He lifted a bottle of Duckhorn Merlot from the basket, poured two glasses and handed her one. "Here. This isn't a leftover. I just opened it myself."

He raised his glass. "To our new relationship, wherever it may lead us."

"My, how profound." Meagan raised the glass to her lips for a tiny sip. "My son Brandon should see this. He's really into boats and this is fantastic. Sandy must love it."

"Believe it or not, Sandy tends to get seasick. She hardly comes near it. And you are welcome to bring Brandon aboard anytime." There was no mention of Ross. "If you want, I can get her revved up and we can motor out to the bay."

"No, this is just fine here. And we have some work to take care of, remember?"

"Ah, yes." *Time to get down to business,* he thought, *to start pushing some buttons.* "You are so diligent about work, Meagan. That must be a real asset to your husband."

"You'll have to ask him," she said with half a smile.

"Is that funny?"

"It is if you know Ross. He's kind of old-fashioned about women and work."

"Uh-oh. Sounds like I've hit a sore spot."

Meagan fidgeted in her chair. "Could we not talk about my husband now?"

He produced two copies of a list of events, with dates and details for each and moved a little closer to review them with her. Meagan took some notes and tried to answer his very pertinent questions.

Meagan was impressed. When he finally did get down to the task at hand, Chase Chambers was professional and thorough. He knew exactly what services he needed and it was enough to keep First Class going at a frantic pace until the election.

Chase took special note of the last item on his schedule: a doubleheader on election night, with hundreds expected at the campaign finale downtown and another large, invitation only crowd for a private gathering at the Chambers home.

"I think that's everything, Meagan. Now it's up to you. Can you handle it?"

Meagan took a breath. The scope of work was daunting and the election night extravaganza would surely test First Class to the limit. That will be some night, she thought. Little did she know.

"It would be our pleasure, Chase," she offered in her most professional voice.

"That's wonderful, Meagan." He took both her hands in his. "Now a more important question. Will you also take me on as a friend?"

Meagan swallowed hard. "Of course. Friends I can do. I have no problem with that." She let her hand linger in his for a moment, then withdrew.

"Chase, why didn't you list your wedding as one of the catered events? Aren't you going to have the reception at the house? It's perfect for it."

"That's, uh---Sandy's in charge of the wedding. It's not a priority."

The boundaries of their relationship had been set, off-limit signs posted. Hopefully, Chase would heed them. Heaven help her if he wouldn't.

He checked his watch. "Hey, we'd better get a move on. I've got to be at the airport in an hour and Curtis will be all over me if I'm one minute late. Come on, I'll walk you to your car."

Ten minutes later, Chase was gone and Meagan was still sitting in her car, staring out at the ocean, lost in thought.

14

Meagan stopped at her parent's home to pick up Brandon, but no one appeared to be home.

"Mom, Dad, anyone home?" she yelled as she entered the foyer area. The front door was unlocked as usual.

"Darling, we're in the den. Your father is trying to hook up that new Wii unit he bought for Brandon last week. Come on back."

Meagan breezed into the den, smiling brightly. "Hey, how's my favorite guy?" She kneeled and hugged Brandon, grin still in place.

"Well, it appears that your luncheon date, or rather your business lunch, was a success judging from your smile. Hope you accomplished what you set out to. After all, you've been gone close to three hours," her mother remarked dryly.

"Actually, Mom, it was….." Meagan searched for the right word, before giving up and simply said, "…wonderful. Marsha will be so thrilled that we now have Chase Chambers as a client. He'll definitely be one of our biggest accounts. He booked all his work with us throughout the rest of the year. I can't wait to tell her and see her reaction."

"By the way, Marsha has been trying to reach you all day. She was in such a tizzy when she called looking for you. I finally told her that you were meeting with Mr. Chambers regarding business."

"Mom, it really was a business meeting."

"If it was just a business meeting, as you say, why are you blushing and looking so happy---like the cat that ate the canary?"

"Oh give me a break, Mom. I'm just excited about getting back to work."

Her father, Robert, was sitting cross-legged on the floor with Brandon cradled in his lap as they both studiously tried to read the directions to hook up the gaming unit.

"Well if anyone would care for my opinion and, granted, usually you females don't, I am just happy to see my daughter smiling again. It's great that you have decided to go back to work with Marsha at the company."

Meagan glanced at her son, who had his iPod ear phones in and was singing along to the music. She turned back to her father and whispered, "I just hope that Ross will understand."

"Now that I highly doubt," Meagan's mother interjected. "Since when has Ross ever understood much about your needs?"

"Babe, Meagan needs our support right now, not your criticism," her father said firmly with raised eyebrows at his wife.

Katherine's lips tightened ever so slightly and she nodded in agreement with her husband of 39 years. She got the point.

"Actually, Dad, I was thinking I might fly up to Chicago tomorrow morning and drop in on Ross and surprise him. With the catered event tomorrow night at the penthouse, he could probably use my help as a hostess. And, in any event, that would give me time alone with him on Sunday to break the news that I'm back working with Marsha. What do you think, Dad? Is Chicago a good idea or a waste of time?" Meagan threw herself down on an overstuffed leather chair, waiting for his response.

"Go for it, honey. I think it's the right thing to do under the circumstances. I'm sure Ross will understand why you are going back to work after you explain it to him."

After replying, he gave his daughter a nod and a thumbs-up. He had said his piece. His attention was immediately diverted to Brandon who kept poking him, urging him to continue with the Wii installation. He automatically slipped his reading glasses back on and tried to concentrate on the confusing instructions.

"You both spoil him too much. Now, it is definitely time to get this young man home, bathed and fed in that order. Let's go, buddy. You can come over tomorrow and play the Wii with Grandpa."

- 15 -

Forty-five stories above the Chicago Loop, the view was magnificent from every window, but there was no time for anyone to enjoy it. Ross Hamilton was on the war path and every one of the twenty-six employees at the executive offices of Hamilton Securities, LLC, knew what that meant. There was something stuck in the CEO's sensitive craw, and it wouldn't come out until he had his vintage Trump moment and fired some defenseless employee on the spot.

The flimsiest reason would do or no reason at all. He was storming down the hallway now, looking for prey, his trusted companion Stacy prancing along behind, eager to see blood on the floor.

Hamilton's employees cowered in their offices, knowing it was futile. Like the sheer floor-to-ceiling glass of the exterior walls, the office partitions were clear glass as well, with glass doors that remained wide open all day. Ross insisted. The only exception was that rare occasion of a personal conference with an important client or visitor, when some semblance of privacy was required. Otherwise, all doors open. Ross wanted transparency and instant access. Nowhere to run, nowhere to hide.

He stopped at Schumacher's door. The senior securities analyst was on the phone, making notes in the margin of a spreadsheet before him. He acknowledged the boss without stopping to take a breath. It was a good pose, diligent and attentive, and it worked. Ross glared at him for a moment, then nodded and moved on, a carnivore on the prowl.

He passed Sheldon Smith's empty office without a glance. The "special assistant to the president" of Hamilton Securities worked odd hours. No one else was privy to his schedule or specific duties, whatever they might be. He was immune to reprimand for any reason.

Three doors down, Ross stopped again, peering in to see Allen Elder scattering food into the aquarium against the wall, watching the angelfish snatch it off the surface. The aquarium had been in Elder's office for years, but he should have known better. When Ross Hamilton was looking for trouble, almost anything would do. Feeding fish during work hours might be considered a capital offense.

It was.

"Elder, what are you doing?"

"Oh. Mr. Hamilton. Just keeping the fish happy."

He had an innocent smile on his face, as if he had never met Ross Hamilton before and had no idea what he was in for.

Ross stepped into the office. Stacey stayed in the hall. She liked to watch the action. "Really?" He moved closer, studying the sleek, colorful creatures as they glided through the crystal water. "And what kind of pescatorial delights do we have here?"

"Angelfish, mostly," Elder answered, "and some guppies. The big one's a trigger fish."

"No piranha?"

"Oh, no," Elder chuckled. "They'd eat the rest."

"That's too bad, because anything that doesn't serve any purpose except to take up space and divert attention from the work at hand should be eaten."

"I'm sorry?"

"Too late for that." Ross sniffed the air. He caught a hint of a fish odor near the tank. A despicable smell.

"I'm not paying you to play with fish and stink up my office!"

"But, Mr. Hamilton---"

Ross cut him off, his voice rising to a level that could be heard far down the hall, "I want you to take your rotten little fish and get out. No hurry. By the end of the day will be fine."

"Mr. Hamilton, I don't understand---"

"You're fired. Do you understand that?" Ross lowered his voice. "You can turn your papers, files and keys over to Stacy by 5 o'clock. In good order, please."

Elder stood in stunned silence. The humiliation was complete. Ross walked out, past Stacy and back up the hall.

She stayed in the doorway, watching Elder suffer. When he looked up, she gave him a consoling look and departed in her master's wake.

Ross Hamilton was already seated in the plush Tuscan leather chair at his desk. He was rifling through the center drawer as Stacy entered.

"Where in the hell is that disk?"

He pawed through the drawer for another minute then stood up, yanked out the drawer, and dumped the contents on the desktop.

"God damn it!"

Stacy could see it was good time to be somewhere else.

"Where are you going?"

She kept moving. "I'll check your briefcase."

She went straight to the dressing room at the far end of the office and opened the door to the closet where a row of custom-tailored suits stood at attention, right sleeves in regimental alignment.

Mr. Perfect had the disk out last night. Then he read the cards and had a few drinks. Now he can't find it. Who's fault is that?

There were high-security codes just to get into the disk, lots of blind passwords and firewalls and all that, but God help him if the wrong people ever got their hands on it. All codes can be broken.

Stacy picked up the briefcase, clicked the latch and flipped it open. There it was, right where it should be, tucked into the small pouch with the brass clip: an unmarked silver disk in a plain black sleeve.

Stacy waited for almost a minute before returning. Ross didn't look up until she was standing right before him at the desk.

"Well?"

She shook her head.

"It's not there."

16

As the early morning United flight took off from Ft. Myers, heading directly for Chicago's O'Hare, Meagan dropped her head back against the head rest and closed her eyes. The first class section was fairly comfortable and practically empty. She was reasonably sure that she would be able to relax, something that she hadn't done for days.

But apparently that was wishful thinking on her part. Disjointed thoughts kept flitting through her mind---thoughts of Ross, thoughts of Brandon, and unsolicited thoughts of Chase. Now why Chase? Probably because she had spent nearly two hours on the phone with Marsha, going over the booking dates for Chase, in order to be able to fully accommodate every one of them in plenty of time. In fact, the next catered event for him was a small dinner party for the city councilman next weekend at his home. Men only, interesting enough. He had given her carte blanche to serve whatever she wanted.

Marsha could not believe that Meagan had pulled it off. It was quite a coup signing Chase Chambers as a client. "The Client", rather. From now on, Marsha declared, Chase Chambers was to be referred to reverently as "The Client." She had been trying to get his work for almost a year now, ever since he had moved down from Atlanta. She had been working through Sandy, thinking that Sandy naturally had some pull with her fiancé. Most fiancées would, but in this case, it was to no avail. She absolutely could not believe that Meagan had pulled it off all on her own.

Now Ross. Why was she so anxious about seeing him in Chicago? She wanted his face to light up. She wanted him to rush to her, take her in his arms, and embrace her like he used to.

The manner in which she confronted Ross would be critical to the whole issue of whether he accepted her decision to go back to work. She wanted to ensure that she did not handle that confrontation carelessly, as she had so often in the past. She needed to be in control of the situation from the very start, and to handle it professionally through to the end.

But she was nervous, almost afraid. Why? She felt confident that she could deal with Ross's high handedness. And surprisingly, her self-esteem was now at an all-time high and a lot of that was due to Chase. Somehow, he had triggered her defenses and helped her to level the playing field between Ross and herself. And that's what counted. She was just as good as Ross.

She finally drifted off to a fitful sleep, her last thoughts of Chase, not Ross.

The flight landed at 8:30 a.m. Meagan grabbed her small carry-on from the overhead compartment along with her dress bag and was one of the first to exit the aircraft into the mid-morning rush at O'Hare. She hailed a cab to take her to the penthouse on Michigan Avenue to drop off her bags before setting off on a day of serious, heavy-duty shopping. She had pulled out the spare set of keys for the penthouse that Ross always kept in a drawer at home.

The traffic was horrendous at that time of the morning. But finally after almost an hour's ride into the city, they arrived and she grabbed her things and started up the steps of the apartment block.

The doorman spotted her as soon as she hopped out, grinned and reached down to hold the door for her and help her with her bags. She smiled brightly at him, "Just hold the door for me, George. I've got a firm grip on the bags. Thanks. And George, you are looking really well these days. How are your wife and grandkids?"

"Just fine, Mrs. Hamilton. Thanks for asking. You staying a few days?" he inquired hesitantly.

"Mr. Hamilton doesn't know I'm here, George. I thought I'd surprise him and drop in for the weekend. He is here at the penthouse?" She stopped abruptly and looked directly at George. God, what if Ross wasn't here?

"Sure thing, Mrs. Hamilton, they're here alright. I mean, Mr. Hamilton is in residence. That's what I mean." George quickly smiled, mumbled something, and lowered his gaze to avoid her eyes. "Guess there's gonna be a large party here tonight. I have orders to bring in the valet guys for the parking and everything."

"That's what I understand, George. You know how Ross loves his parties, top notch and first class all the way! See you later, George."

She crossed into the spacious lobby and headed for the brass elevator doors. She glanced back at George and gave him a brief wave. He was acting rather strange and seemed almost guilty, she thought. Oh well, it must have been her imagination. And with that thought, she accessed the elevator with her master key and punched in the "P" level.

17

The company penthouse on the 30th floor overlooking Lake Michigan was spectacular. Contemporary décor mixed with traditional furnishings complimented each other. The living room was elegant in beige and black leathers with ornate Persian rugs. Huge, silk-fringed pillows were strategically placed for accent. It had always seemed a little too cold for Meagan's taste, but Ross loved it. And, considering it was the clients who frequently used it and liked it, it was more than adequate.

Since it was the only unit on the top floor, the elevator opened directly into it. Surprisingly, as she stepped out, the double stained-glass entrance doors were standing wide open. Meagan glanced around, saw no one, and entered the suite dragging her bags behind her. She sighed deeply when she saw that the catering crew was hard at work, setting up in the kitchen area.

Quickly, she made her presence known so as not to unnecessarily alarm them. "Hi, I'm Meagan Hamilton, Ross's wife. Please don't mind me. I'm just here to drop off my bags, then do some shopping. How does everything look for tonight?"

She addressed one of the older women in the kitchen, the one who seemed to be issuing the instructions and fielding the questions.

"Everything is coming along just fine, Mrs. Hamilton. We just thought that since the suite was not occupied this morning, we would get a head start on the set-up. That's what takes the most time, you know. Mr. Hamilton didn't mention that you would be here this morning."

The older woman was wiping her hands on a dishcloth as she spoke to Meagan. Then she promptly reached out and offered her hand. "I'm Michelle Morgan. I think I remember you from a previous job a couple of years back. Mr. Hamilton uses us exclusively for all his business parties here in Chicago."

Meagan smiled as she shook the woman's hand. "Well, then you must do an excellent job. Mr. Hamilton can be a hard taskmaster and demands only the best. Nice to meet all of you. Also, I would appreciate it if you didn't mention that I'm here to anyone. I want to surprise my husband later at the party. So, you never saw me, okay?"

Meagan glanced inquiringly at the people assembled there in the spacious kitchen and they all nodded their heads in response.

Michelle responded decisively, "I understand completely. You have our cooperation on that matter.

We haven't seen you today. Enjoy your shopping. You definitely picked a good day for it." And with that, Michelle turned back to the tasks at hand.

Meagan eagerly grabbed her bags and headed for the master bedroom, located in the back wing. Glancing towards the formal dining area, she noted gorgeous fresh flower arrangements were grouped together on the table as centerpieces. Apparently, Ross was going all out for this party. It must be for some of his more important clients. The cleaning crew was busy vacuuming the Persian rugs in the living room. She continued down the foyer hallway, her heels clicking on the marble floor.

She came to an abrupt halt when she spotted an elderly woman walking towards her, mumbling to herself. She appeared to have a permanent scowl on her lined face.

"Rosie, Rosie DiFranco, is it really you?" Meagan rushed over to the older, black woman and embraced her warmly. "Rosie, I'm so glad to see you! It's literally been years. I thought you had quit your housekeeping job with Ross and retired a while ago. I'm sure that's what he told me. It's so good to see you. It's been too long."

Rosie enthusiastically patted Meagan's back as she hugged her fondly.

"Meg, darlin', how are you doing? What brings you up this way? Mr. Ross never even made a mention that you'd be arrivin'. Drat that man! Wait till I get my hands on him. You're looking gorgeous as ever." Rosie stepped back examining Meagan from head to toe, her hands still warmly grasped in Meagan's.

"Oh, it's a surprise. Ross has no idea that I'm here. I thought I'd fly in, shop all day, and then surprise him at the cocktail party he is having here tonight."

"Cocktail party? Heaven forbid Mr. Ross would be content to throw a simple cocktail party. No my dear, the party is a full sit-down, seven-course affair. I tell you, I never thought that I'd see the day when we would put in so much effort to entertain a bunch of foreigners. These Japanese are definitely a different breed, a different culture altogether. Everything has to be just so-so."

Rosie shook her head with exasperation and then exclaimed, "What is this world coming to anyway? And, I did give up my full-time housekeeping position with Mr. Ross. But somebody had to oversee today to make sure the cleaning crew stays on schedule. Plus, the florist keeps coming back with more floral arrangements. For heaven's sake, it looks like a funeral parlor around here. So, here I am, just back for the day to lend a hand. Tell me, darlin', how is little Brandon?"

"Brandon is just fine. He's staying at his grandparent's for the weekend, happily driving them crazy, and not me, for a change. I'll send you some recent pictures of him, I promise. He's gotten so big. He's a darling. And, Rosie, remember you can't mention to Ross that I'm here. I knew he'd be at the office all day. So, I thought I'd come back after shopping, clean up, slip on my little black dress, the one the Ross loves, and *"surprise"*. I'll be his hostess for the night. So, you won't say anything, will you, Rosie?"

"Not a word, dearie."

Meagan grabbed her bags and steered Rosie towards the master suite.

"Look, I just have to hang some clothes in the closet and then I'll be off, out of your hair. Maybe tomorrow we can get together for brunch? We need to catch up, Rosie. After all, you worked for Ross here in Chicago for years. How you ever survived that ordeal, I will never know!" Meagan squeezed Rosie's arm teasingly, pulling her along.

Rosie appeared dazed, stumbling a bit as they walked down the hall. Then she abruptly stopped, snapping her head back toward Meagan, eyes wide.

Meagan tilted her head and looked at Rosie. Why was she acting so strange, almost panic stricken?

"Look, Meg, darlin', give me those bags and I'll hang everything up for you. You just go on now, do your shoppin' thing. I'll have your things hung up and pressed by the time you get back. All in perfect shape. That's my job. And then, we'll have some tea and a chat."

Rosie, ripping the carry-on from Meagan's arm, marched through the double doors into the master bedroom, slamming the door sharply after her. Meagan was left standing in the hallway looking at the closed doors, totally perplexed by Rosie's strange behavior. Oh, well, Rosie was Rosie...

Meagan smiled fondly at Rosie's attempt to be helpful and turned around to leave. Suddenly, she remembered that she needed to change her shoes. Her flats were much more comfortable than her heels.

Not giving it a second thought, she entered the master suite. "Wait, Rosie, let me grab another pair of shoes from my bag...."

Meagan froze in mid-step. She closed her eyes tightly, hoping maybe that the whole scene would simply fade away. She had to be dreaming. This couldn't be real. She opened her eyes and reality hit her with a vengeance.

Brightly colored articles of women's clothing were strewn haphazardly everywhere. There was a black lace thong laying across the tangle of pristine white sheets, right next to a zebra stripped teddy. On the floor beside the bed, a pile of women's shoes and fashion magazines were bulging out of a black patent leather Prada duffel bag. On top of one of the crushed pillows at the foot of the unmade king-size bed was a pair of men's silk boxers, inside out. They were the ones that she had given Ross for Valentine's Day, the ones with giant red valentines that spelled "I Love You."

Rosie was in the walk-in closet and had not heard Meagan enter. One side of the closet was stuffed full of brightly colored female clothes, casual wear, business suits and formal dresses, none of which belonged to Meagan. Lots of pinks and yellows, stripes and dots.

Meagan was in shock and felt herself start to crumble, backing into the wall for support. "What the hell..."

Rosie turned around sharply and a veiled look descended upon her face when she spotted Meagan. Rosie threw down the clothes she was hanging up and rushed to her side.

Shaken by the sight of another woman's things in her husband's bedroom, she turned to Rosie and demanded in a quivering voice, "You knew, didn't you? God, Rosie, how long? How long has this been going on?"

Meagan was surprised that she could even speak, overwhelmed with such utter disbelief. "I just can't believe this is happening. Not with Ross and me. Why

Rosie, why? You know Ross better than anyone. So, tell me why?" Silent tears were streaming down her face.

"Come along, dearie, let's get out of here."

Rosie gently took Meagan by the hand and guided her to the study. She pushed her silent form down into Ross's over-stuffed black leather lounger. Meagan recognized the scent of her husband's favorite cologne immediately. She cringed. Anger, in its rawest form, was quickly erupting to the surface, taking precedence over the shock.

"Now, darlin', looks are deceiving. Maybe it's not what you think," Rosie said softly, eyes downcast.

"Not what I think? Oh, no, Rosie. Don't even try to get him out of this mess. Quit protecting him. I know what I saw. I saw pink and yellow dresses, loads of them, hung up on my side of the closet. And none of them are mine."

Meagan stood, confronting Rosie face to face.

"Obviously, they've been at this for awhile, considering how full my closet is."

"Now, darlin', calm down..."

"And, if I had to guess, I would bet that it's Stacy's stuff, right?"

"How'd you know?"

"Instinct, I guess...plus, I recognized a couple of the outfits of hers in the closet. And, Rosie, did you see the condition of that room? A total mess! Ross is such a neat freak at home, always demanding that I keep everything in its proper place. Apparently that rule doesn't apply to Stacy! What a fool I am! What an asshole he is! "

Meagan rubbed her forehead hard with the tips of her fingers, continuing, "Stacy's always acted proprietarily towards Ross, like he was her territory.

Now I know why. Was I ever blind or what? Dumb, blind, and stupid. Come on, Rosie, how long have they been sleeping together?" Meagan focused on Rosie.

"Now, Meagan, you settle down," Rosie urged, feeling decidedly uncomfortable. "It isn't my place to tell tales. I do care about Mr. Ross and I do care about you, too. Remember that Mr. Ross and Stacy grew up together. They were like brother and sister, practically raised together. That's why he hired her, because she knew him so well."

"Well, they're not like any brother and sister team I know. And they obviously know each other very well, too well for my liking. I have been so stupid!" Meagan exclaimed, throwing her hands up in the air.

"Mr. Ross doesn't want to hurt you."

"Too late, I'm hurt."

Meagan started to pace, back and forth across the paneled study. "How long, Rosie? Please, just tell me."

Meagan's tear-stained cheeks touched Rosie's heart. She felt that Meagan deserved to know the truth. Rosie took a deep breath. "Mr. Ross and Stacy have carried on together, off and on, since college. Being next door neighbors made it very easy for them."

"Since when? Oh. My. God." Meagan threw her head back in despair, and stared at the ceiling, trying to get her bearings. How could Ross have done this to her? But more importantly, why? Why not just marry Stacy years ago? Why go through the subterfuge of a marriage with her? What was the point of it all? If there was one thing that Meagan had learned about Ross, it was that he never did anything without a valid reason. He was meticulous in that sense.

"Meagan, listen to me. Mr. Ross swore to me that this thing with Stacy was a harmless fling, meaningless, stupid. I really thought it was over until I arrived today and saw the bedroom. I'm just as shocked as you are. And I'm extremely mad at Mr. Ross. You deserve much better. I am so sorry, Meg, darlin'."

Meagan pushed her hair back behind her ears with both hands as she tried to regain her earlier composure.

Rosie crossed her arms. "So now that you know, what are you going to do? There is Brandon to think about. You can't deprive a son of his father. That's it! You should have more children. An only child is no good."

"You are right about that, Rosie. Ross is an only child and look at him. He's no good! As for having more children, that's so not a possibility since Ross took it upon himself to have a vasectomy hours after Brandon was born. No more children for us. Period." Meagan then whispered under her breath, "No more Ross for me either."

Rosie patted Meagan's shoulder softly, hating to see her suffer. "I'm so sorry, darlin'. But things have a way of working out. Just you wait and see. Maybe this thing with Stacy is just temporary. Maybe we've misread the whole darn situation."

"Don't go there, Rosie. You and I both know what is going on here. Their affair of some twenty odd years is not temporary. It's permanent. While my marriage of five years appears to be quite temporary. Honestly, it's kind of funny in a way. For years Ross has preached that I needed to be home with Brandon to ensure stability within the family. And I agreed. I became "Susie Homemaker" because that was what Ross wanted. He said I needed to be there for Brandon's sake and I needed no outside job to interfere with my motherly duties. I mean, Ross really had me under his thumb. He always knew where I was and what I was doing. What a control freak! And where was Ross during all Brandon's formative years? Secretly screwing Stacy. Never at home with Brandon and me. To think that I was actually scared to tell Ross of my decision to go back to work at First Class. Well, as of this moment, he has definitely lost control of me. From now on, I am in control of my life and I will live it as I see fit. Ross will just have to cope with the outcome. He no longer has a choice."

Rosie continued to let Meagan rant, listening to her vent her frustration. She knew it would be good for her to get it all out.

"So what are you going to do about Stacy?"

"Stacy? Stacy is not my problem! She is Ross's problem. And he's welcome to her. As far as anyone is concerned, I am totally ignorant of their affair. Do you understand, Rosie? This is how I am going to play this. I flew up here and rushed in. You conveniently unpacked for me and I quickly left to do my shopping. Honestly, right now, I just feel numb. Not mad, not furious, almost relieved. I'm sorry that I'm putting you in the middle of it, Rosie."

Meagan embraced Rosie warmly. "I know your loyalties lie with Ross and I appreciate you confiding in me. Please, don't feel like a turncoat. I love Ross. After all, he is the father of my son. But at this point, I'm no longer "in love" with him. I refuse to be the other woman in my husband's life. I'm worth more than that. Maybe divorce is the answer. Who knows? I don't. I do know that forgiveness on my part, right now, is not in the cards. I'll get through this mess one day at a time."

The phone rang loudly on the desk next to Meagan. Rosie quickly reached over to grab it.

"No, Rosie, allow me," Meagan whispered as she pulled it out of Rosie's hand and answered, "Hamilton residence."

"Rosie, this is Ross."

"Ross, darling. Hi, it's me, your wife, not Rosie. And you just caught me. Oh, there goes my big surprise. Guess I shouldn't have answered the phone. Actually, I just walked in this very minute. Rosie was just being her kind self, taking my things to our room to hang them up. I need to do some shopping and I thought we could spend the weekend together, just the two of us. I was going to surprise you tonight at the party and be your hostess. Are you surprised, darling?" Meagan stopped talking and waited. His answer was long in coming. It took him a full minute to reply.

"Umm.....sure, darling. This is quite a surprise. I wish you had told me that you were coming. I could have made the arrangements for you. The party is at....uhmmmm... 6 p.m. sharp. I'm busy until then with work. You know how it is with my job, conference call after conference call. Will you be okay on your own? Feel free to use my house charges at all the department stores. You know the ones."

"Why, Ross, how nice of you, so considerate. Well, I'd better be off now. See you later, darling, at the party," Meagan purred softly, holding her disgust at bay. Her voice remained steady.

Rosie applauded her performance. Maybe Meagan was made out of firmer stuff. She was going to have to be strong in order to stand up against Mr. Ross. He was not used to losing on any level.

Ross replied in a brisk tone, "Yes, I will see you later. Put Rosie on the line, would you? I need to talk to her for a minute about tonight's preparations."

Yeah, right, Meagan thought to herself, like Ross would be involved in the preparations for the party. He must want something else from Rosie.

Rosie hesitated before taking the receiver from Meagan's shaking hand. "Yes, Mr. Ross?" She nodded her head several times. "No problem at all. Yes, your wife is leaving directly to shop. Yes, sir, I'll take care of it. Goodbye." Too embarrassed to make eye contact with Meagan, Rosie put down the phone slowly.

"Well, let me take a guess. You are instructed to pack up all of Stacy's things---hide the evidence--- and someone will pick them up shortly?" Meagan questioned with a look of satisfaction, halfway enjoying herself, in spite of the circumstances.

Rosie simply clucked her tongue, "You know, you two really do know each other inside and out."

Meagan grabbed Rosie's shoulders, hugged her gently and kissed her soundly on the cheek. "Thanks, Rosie. Please don't fret. Things do have a way of working out. See you later. I'm out of here. I need some air and space to think this through."

Meagan reached for her purse and walked out of the penthouse, forgetting to change her shoes. She reached the elevator, when suddenly the elevator doors swished opened and Sheldon Smith stepped out. She should have expected that Ross would send the company trouble-shooting chauffeur right over, but his appearance caught her off guard. She was still a bit shaky.

"Good day to you, Mrs. Hamilton," he spoke solemnly. "Mr. Hamilton asked that I come over to drive you around town. Shopping day, is it?"

Meagan automatically stepped back with an instinctive loathing as Sheldon stepped in front of her, halting her movement. He was purposely crowding her. Built more like a bodyguard than a chauffeur, his aggressive behavior gave her the creeps. She made a quick decision.

"Actually, Sheldon, I appreciate the offer. However, my plans have just changed, much to my dismay. Please go in and grab my two bags. Rosie knows where they are. I just talked to my mother and it seems that Brandon has developed a secondary asthmatic infection."

Meagan rambled on to Sheldon, lying effortlessly, knowing every word would be repeated to Ross verbatim. Hell, he was probably recording her. "I need to head back home immediately to be there for Brandon. If you don't mind dropping me off at the airport, I'll catch the next flight back to Florida. I'll meet you out front by the limo, okay?"

Meagan slipped past Sheldon, jumped into the opened elevator, and stabbed the Lobby button.

As the doors started to close, she caught Sheldon's droll reply, "I do not know what Mr. Hamilton is going to say about your change of plans."

The elevator doors swished close with Meagan inside, cutting off any further comments from Sheldon.

Upon reaching the lobby, she waved a quick goodbye to George. "Brandon is sick, so I'm headed back home." She hurried out the door.

As she rushed over to the parked limo, she heard George yell, "Have a good trip, Mrs. Hamilton. See you next time." George deftly tipped his hat and waved.

"Doubt that there will be a next time, George!" she exclaimed quietly under her breath.

Sheldon caught up with her and put her bags in the trunk of the limo.

"Now, was that O'Hare or Midway?" Sheldon asked politely.

"O'Hare, Sheldon, please." Meagan sighed as they smoothly pulled away from the curb. She dropped her head back against the seat cushion and, looking out the tinted windows, she contemplated her untenable situation.

What exactly was happening here? Ross had been flagrantly cheating on her for years. With Stacy, no less. So why was she so calm? Why wasn't she crying and screaming? Didn't she care anymore? That was it. The level of caring had shifted without her even noticing. She almost felt relieved and that confused her.

She was reassured by the fact that she still had her Grandmother's trust fund, and most importantly she had the unconditional support and love of her family. She was free to be Meagan. Just plain Meagan. Not an appendix to Ross, not Ross Hamilton's trophy wife. She was no longer going to give Ross the power to sanction her decisions. She was free to start back to work. She was free to explore new, fun possibilities that life had to offer. She was free to pursue her own worthy goals and free to be true to her inner self. She had only herself to count on and it felt damn good. She smiled with great satisfaction and heaved a big sigh of relief. She was, in one simple word, happy for the first time in a long time. It made no sense whatsoever. She smiled again.

"I need to call Mr. Hamilton, Sheldon," she said politely.

"Go right ahead, Mrs. Hamilton," Sheldon replied. He raised the sound proof panel up to give her privacy.

She speed-dialed Ross's private line and was immediately placed into voice mail. No surprise. She started her explanation, keeping it brief and to the point. No reason to arouse his suspicion. No reason to yell and scream at him for his adulterous behavior with Stacy. No reason to ever yell and scream at him for anything, anymore, ever again.

Smiling, she lied to him flawlessly, "Ross, I just wanted you to know that I checked with Mom and Brandon has developed a secondary asthmatic condition due to the head cold that he had last week. So, needless to say, I am heading back home to give Mom a hand. Sorry about screwing up the whole weekend thing. Hopefully, you can have Stacy play hostess tonight. Let me know when to expect you back. There's no hurry. I can handle everything at home."

[]

Ross digested the message, trying to fathom his suddenly unpredictable wife. He slammed the phone down.

"Shit! Now she's leaving! Why? What is this stupid game?"

Stacy tried to mollify him. "You heard her. Brandon is sick."

"She's lying. I know she is. She's found out about us and didn't feel up to confronting me. So she's running back home. "

Ross rubbed the back of his neck to ease the tension. He didn't need this.

"So? Let her go, Ross. Let her run home. It's almost time to cut her loose anyway."

"'Almost' is the operative word, Stacy. Don't you see that? It's too soon! She could ruin everything."

"Ross, you know her. She may suspect, but she doesn't want it to be true, and she'll make herself believe that it's not. She couldn't take the consequences---her perfect little world tumbling down around her."

Ross raised an eyebrow. "Meagan's a little more than you give her credit for. She may be naïve, but she has good instincts. She might even be a little psychic. I wouldn't underestimate her. She's not stupid."

"No, but she is predictable." Stacy stood and moved behind him, massaging his neck and shoulders. "And that means that you can control her. You always have."

"Yes, you're right. I have, and I will. She's like all the rest. She wants to be taken care of … and I'll take care of her."

He grasped her hand. "You're such a help."

"That's what I'm here for, darling."

"I know." Ross smiled and squeezed harder.

- 18 -

"I've got the GDC on four."

The VICAP operator spoke in a matter-of-fact voice, like an air traffic controller on a quiet shift. He had the same state-of-the-art headset and pin mike, and the same kind of illuminated, interactive map on the console before him. This one was even more sophisticated; a precision-detailed U. S. map that spanned the wall of a large room with a kaleidoscope of color-coded lights indicating active contact points in real time.

The operator spoke directly to Patrick Curran, Supervisor of Investigations, the FBI agent-in-charge for linked multiple-victim homicide cases: serial murders.

VICAP. The Violent Criminal Apprehension Program was the official name of the fabled Profilers, the special FBI unit that investigated the most horrific crimes and pursued the most vicious criminals. The Profilers made a big splash when they debuted thirty-five years ago.

Starting with a small collaborative team in 1967, the Profilers have come a long way since, adding a range of specialists from varied fields of science to provide technological insight and develop advanced theories of criminal behavior. This six-man special unit had become a full department with two hundred VICAP personnel involved in the ongoing investigations of more than 60 active serial murder cases.

Patrick Curran was the supervisor in charge of them all. As a rule, he didn't have time to get personally involved in specific cases, but this call was an exception. Anytime the "GDC" was on the line, it was an exception. It sounded like something official---GDC. General Director of Cases? Government Defense Counsel? Maybe something to do with Washington, DC? That was the joke. Only Curran and a few others at VICAP knew what the acronym signified.

Gemini D'Orlow Chambers.

Curran was always eager to talk to the soft-spoken lady from Louisiana low country. She had no valid credentials in criminology and no official standing with the FBI, but this wasn't some old hag stirring a pot of jambalaya down in the bayou. Mrs. Chambers was the widow of a famous U. S. senator, a guest professor at Tulane University, matriarch of a distinguished family and a widely respected clairvoyant.

Still, Curran had to wonder sometimes. He had to admit that it was kind of strange to be dealing with a woman who provided information to VICAP based on what she garnered from reading Tarot cards.

Maybe it was crazy, but the VICAP people were not kidding when they said they were going to employ every conceivable means to solve the highest priority criminal cases. Even Curran wasn't sure how they first became aware of her, but he did know that she had an amazing record since he first recruited Gem Chambers for the Project Blue Yonder team at Tulane University two years ago. She had been involved in five cases since then. All those cases were solved; five vicious killers brought to justice, three imprisoned two dead. The information and insight she provided was rated from "valuable" to "critical" in the final report on every case.

Stranger yet, they didn't assign any of the cases to her. She called them. She picked up something in those cards of hers, dialed in on the special line, and opened the conversation with whatever insights she thought might be relevant.

The first time, it was slow going. They struggled with her abstruse symbolism and the metaphors. But these were very smart people and it didn't take long for them to tune in to her wavelength. By the third contact, they were linking GDC's input to case files in less than 48 hours.

She wasn't very good with names---she hardly ever came up with one---but she was dead on with all kinds of other information: places, times, victim types, perpetrator motives and M.O.s, and occasionally a specific prediction of when and where another crime might occur. "Might"---she always said that. She constantly reiterated her mantra that nothing was certain. There were variables to human behavior. Outcomes always depended on choices made.

Once, solely on a tip from Gem, they caught a Most-Wanted predator in the act, leaving a truck stop in Mississippi. She told them the time, described the general location and cautioned them about a "one-eyed monster." He was a scruffy little man with two good eyes, but he was driving a big rig with one headlight out. He had just picked up a 14-year-old runaway and was only five miles from the same desolate area where he had killed three others. The duct tape and butcher knife were under the front seat.

They had no idea how she did it, but her impressive history was reason enough not to keep her on hold for long. Curran picked up the phone.

"Hello, Gem, how are you?"

She insisted they just call her Gem.

"Fine, Mr. Curran. And you?"

"Fighting the fight, and it doesn't get any easier, except when you call. And what do you have for us today?"

"Disturbing news, I'm afraid."

"We're used to disturbing news around here."

She spoke with genuine sympathy.

"That must be hard on you. I'm sorry."

Curran smiled. She was a nice lady. He was about to tell her that when she started right in. She never wasted time when she called.

"The cards tell me about a man---it's always a man, isn't it?"

"Almost. Not sure why. Must be that testosterone thing."

"Perhaps. This man is like the rest in one way. He has killed before, but it did not satisfy him, only made him stronger, bolder."

"Know the type," Curran nodded.

"Ah, but in every other way, he is not like the rest. He looks different, acts different, everything is different with him."

"Different how, Gem? Strange-looking? Scary?"

"Not at all. He looks very respectable. Handsome, even."

"We've had a few like that."

"Not like this. He is accomplished, successful. He's not a loner either, this one. Not quite famous, but well known and respected."

"Interesting."

"And he is not so erratic like many. Organized, very much in control. For him, there is truly a method to the madness."

Curran thought it over. "He's dangerous."

"Very."

"Do you have anything about where he is?"

"That is an enigma. He is everywhere. Up north, down south, out west ... I don't understand."

"Anything about the victims, patterns---anything else?"

"Mostly women, but not all. And they are everywhere as well. And here is something else that's different---he changes: different means and methods. No two are the same. And he may have help, a partner in his bloody crimes, maybe more than one."

Curran scribbled notes.

"Is he a sexual predator? Rape? Assault?"

"Never. With him, it's something else."

"Do you know what that is?"

"I think so. He does it because he is filled with hate and rage; he has to punish them. And there is one more thing."

"Yes?"

"He does it for money."

19

Sheldon pulled up to the first United gate at O'Hare and offered to walk Meagan in. She declined politely and disappeared into the terminal.

The first available flight had a connection through Atlanta with a lengthy layover. Meagan didn't care. She booked it without another thought and made her way through security to the departure gate. Once on board and seated comfortably in first class, she allowed herself to relax or, rather, to collapse. Before the plane taxied away from the gate, she pulled out her cell phone, reminding herself that she better call her mother.

Her mother answered promptly on the first ring with a brisk, "Hullo."

"Hi, Mom. Believe it or not, I am on my way back home from Chicago through Atlanta. Just wanted you to know that I'll be home later tonight."

"But, darling, what happened? Wasn't Ross there? Why are you coming back so soon? Didn't you just get there? What happened to your shopping spree?"

"Oh Mom, it is a long and disgusting story. And believe me, if I go into it now and tell you what's happened, everyone on this plane will weep for me!"

Meagan stopped for a minute to gaze around to see if, in fact, anybody was listening. Then she continued. "Just kidding, Mom. I was trying to add some humor into a horrific situation. But really, I can't talk about it now. It's too fresh in my mind. I'll tell you all the details when I get home. You won't believe it! I hardly believe it myself, but surprisingly, I am fine. Could you please keep Brandon over night since I don't get in until very late and I'd rather pick him up tomorrow?"

"Well, of course, darling, you know we will. We were planning on having him for the whole weekend anyway. Did you tell Ross that you're going back to work? Was he so mad that he sent you home?"

Meagan sighed softly, stifling her tears. Her mother heard the sigh and her heart ached for her daughter. Katherine could tell that something was definitely wrong by her daughter's tone of voice. Something had happened. However, Katherine didn't force the issue, knowing her daughter would tell her in due time. But she would bet that it had something to do with that bastard husband of hers.

"Actually, I never saw Ross and really don't care if I ever see him again."

"I didn't catch that last part, Meagan. Speak louder, darling," urged her mother. "Just what is going on? Are you ill?"

"Mom, I'm fine. Like I said, it's a long story and I gotta go. We are just about to taxi out to the runway. See you tomorrow. Please don't worry and give Bran a big kiss for me. I love you."

Meagan pressed the END button and slumped down in her seat for the journey home, her thoughts chaotic.

She turned her cell on as soon as the plane touched down in Atlanta.

There were three messages, the first from Marsha. Meagan was cheered at the sound of her bright happy voice.

"Hey, kiddo, it's me. You know, Marsha? Marsha Mills? You remember, your partner? Where the hell are you? It's about noon Friday and Chase Chambers---you know, THE Chase Chambers---has been trying to find you. Called *me* twice. Don't know why---you know why? Anyway, he left his number. The man's got an 800 cell phone number. Is that cool or what? It's 991-0550. He wants you to call him ASAP. Anyway, call me."

Meagan jotted down his number on her ticket folder. Marsha was so…Marsha.

The second message was from the man himself. Meagan's heart rate picked up.

"Hello, Meagan Hamilton. Chase Chambers here. I've got a whole new set of dates … event dates, that is. In politics everything changes daily. And did I tell you how much I enjoyed our lunch? Even if it was leftovers. Please, call me when you get a minute. Thanks, Meagan Hamilton."

It was simple, completely innocuous and thrilling to Meagan. Somehow, the fifteen-second message seemed highly erotic. His voice, his tone, the way he said "Meagan Hamilton"---It was close to pure phone sex. She was still enjoying it when she was rudely interrupted by Stacy's voice. Third message. She couldn't believe the bitch had the nerve.

"Mrs. Hamilton." Stacy, cold as ever. "This is Stacy. Mr. Hamilton requested that I fax you the schedule for his return next week. It should be at your home when you get there. I hope Brandon is feeling better. Goodbye."

Meagan pressed the button hard to erase Stacy, leaving Chase's number on her cell phone readout. She pushed Send.

"Good afternoon, Mr. Chambers' office. May I help you?"

Meagan blinked at the sultry voice.

"Hello, uh, my name is Meagan Hamilton. I'm returning Mr. Chamber's call. Is he in?"

"Meagan? Hi, this is Sandy. Chase's secretary had to step out for a minute. So, here I am. Substitute host. How am I doing?"

"Great by me."

"Chase said you might call. He's not here but I'm supposed to transfer you to him right away. Where are you calling from anyway? What's all that noise?"

"It's a long story, Sandy. I'm on a layover in Atlanta right now. I was in Chicago with---with my husband. But something came up, so I, I..." Meagan felt very tired. "Sandy, I can talk to Mr. Chambers tomorrow or whenever. Would that be better?"

"Oh, no, he really wants to talk to you," Sandy insisted. "He just checked in to see if you had called. Hold on, I'll patch you through."

He answered at the first ring. "Chambers."

"Well, hello, Mr. Chambers."

"Sandy?"

"Yes, Lover Boy, and I've got Ross Hamilton's honey on the line. Do you want her?" she asked with a breathy flourish.

"Cut it out, Sandy. Where is she?"

"Well, it appears that your Meagan was in Chicago with the dear hubby, but there might be trouble in the Hamilton household because she's on her way back home right now. And, what do you know, at this moment, she is sitting in the Atlanta airport."

"Atlanta?"

"That's what I said. And I'm sure you'll do the right thing with this good fortune, so I'm going to put you through now. And remember, I'm a very modern fiancée but I draw the line at flagrant cheating. Watch your step."

"Very funny. Please, Sandy, connect me. Now."

Click.

"Meagan?"

"Hello."

"I'm glad I caught you. Sandy tells me you're in Atlanta."

"Kind of, just a layover on my way back home."

"I was hoping we could get together for another meeting, as soon as possible."

Meagan couldn't help but think she might have a lot more open time on her schedule.

"We could do that."

"Great!" He launched into his spur-of-the-moment plan. "Meagan, listen. Please go down to Exit Area 3---it's the middle one---and a man by the name of Rodney will be there shortly, holding a sign with your name on it. Rodney will bring you to me."

"What?" Meagan was stunned.

"Didn't Sandy tell you? I'm in Atlanta fundraising for a very worthwhile project---me. Some old friends of the family are doing me a favor."

"You're in Atlanta?"

"Yes. And I think you should join me for dinner tonight---or would you rather spend the next several hours sitting in the airport, bored to death?"

Not a sound.

"Meagan? You still there?"

"Oh yes, I'm here, or maybe I'm in the Twilight Zone. I'm not sure yet."

Chase laughed. All she needed now was a little push.

"Come on, Meagan, go with it. There are several things I want to talk to you about, and we can have some fun."

"And Sandra thinks that's a good idea?"

"Fine with her. Just a chance encounter between business associates...and friends."

Meagan muttered under her breath, "What is happening to my life?"

"What?" Chase couldn't make out what she said. "Listen, if you don't have anything to wear, I'll have Rodney stop at Lennox Square and you can pick out something for tonight. My treat."

"No, that's not a problem. But Chase, I just don't think..."

"Don't think! Do! The fates have thrown us together."

"Drop the fate stuff, Chase," she replied.

"Look, Meagan, Sandy won't mind at all. She's the one who suggested it when she heard where you were."

Meagan bit her lip. This Sandy was something.

"Now we're wasting time. I'm here. I need an escort tonight. You're here. It was meant to be. So, go to Area 3. Rodney will be there any minute now. Please don't keep him waiting. That's rude, you know."

"Chase Chambers, you were so sure, weren't you? You sent that man to the airport before we even spoke? Do you think your wish is my command? I hardly know you! If I wasn't trying to make it through the rest of one of the worst days of my life, I would come over there and---"

"So you'll come, then? Pretty please."

My, he was persistent.

"Yes." She couldn't believe she said it.

"Just two friends and business associates, right?" Meagan added.

"I couldn't agree more. Cross my heart and hope to die." Might as well make a total fool of himself.

He clicked off. He didn't want to give her a chance to change her mind.

Ten minutes later, she was in the back of stretch Lincoln limo, Rodney at the wheel, streaming through the Atlanta traffic, headed to Chase Chambers.

[]

He was on the phone again as soon as he hung up with Meagan, this time on a secure line to Naples.

"This is C. Put me through to MacNulty."

A gruff voice come on the line.

"MacNulty."

"Mac. There's been a little change in plans, and I wanted to give you a heads up."

"Don't tell me you missed your flight."

"No, I made it. I'm here in Atlanta."

"Good."

"It gets better. Meagan Hamilton is here, too."

"What are you talking about?"

"She's here in Atlanta, alone. She just called me."

"Well, isn't that a coincidence."

"That's exactly what it is, and a perfect setup. It gives me the chance I need to check her out, one-on-one."

"Aw, for Christ's sake. You are playing with fire."

"Listen, Mac, I know how to handle this. If there's any sign that she's part of this whole thing, I'll cut and run. And if not---well, then we're golden. We'll be inside the castle. Mac, you've got to green light me on this."

"You don't give up easy, do you, Chambers?"

"I never give up."

"Okay. Shit. Go ahead. Just be careful. And don't go sleeping with the enemy."

He grinned. "Thanks, Mac."

"One more thing."

"Yes, sir?"

"Why do I have the sneaking suspicion that you already talked to her and set up the whole god damn agenda for the evening before this courtesy call to me? Am I just getting paranoid in my old age?"

He almost laughed, but managed to hold it in.

"Sorry, Mac, you're breaking up. I'll be in touch."

20

Ross and Stacy were in the now infamous bedroom, dressing for the dinner. The bed was made, the room clean, all evidence eradicated.

After years of being with Ross Hamilton, Stacy had become an expert at handling his moods. He could be impossible when his feathers were ruffled. They were definitely ruffled tonight. The Meagan episode had thrown him into a rage.

She tried to sooth him as she applied her makeup. "Really, Ross, it's nothing. If she asks about my things in your room, you deny. You are completely innocent.

"You can tell her that you stayed somewhere else Thursday night, a seminar or something." She glanced over as she finished an eyebrow. "And, gentleman that you are, you let me use the master suite. No big deal.

And what she saw---maybe I had a friend over, you know?"

Ross measured her with a look.

"Aren't we the clever one? Stacy had a friend over? That's good. Very creative."

Stacy arched toward the vanity mirror, inspecting. "Or you can just let her go a little sooner, that's all."

Ross finished the Windsor knot of his tie, pulled it tight, then scowled at the mirror. The narrow end hung slightly long. He unraveled it and started over again.

"I can't get rid of her yet. The investments, the trust fund---we're only halfway home. It takes time."

"But Ross, you have all you need to clean out all the accounts right now. The waivers and consents, all the access codes. I don't think---"

"That's right, Stacy, sometimes you just don't think. If we try to accelerate the process--look what happened with Diane! We can't rush things now. Same pace. Same routine."

"It's not the same routine. You didn't marry Diane or any of the others. Only Meagan. It added complications."

"It had to be done that way. I told you. I took everything into consideration."

"Including the boy?" Stacy was so smug.

"That wasn't my mistake," he snarled. "That was hers." He pulled up his tie, perfect this time.

"We're about two months away," he said. "At least. It'll take that long to finish the transfers without any red flags."

Stacy watched herself pout. "Whatever you say."

"And Stacy, let me give you a little more breaking news: If we don't find that disc, we are----how can I put this?---totally fucked. All the data for Meagan and everybody else, everybody---it's all on that disc. And nowhere else."

"Nowhere?"

"No copies. I sure as hell never put it on the office hard drive."

Stacy stared at the mirror, wheels turning. "Maybe she has it."

"What?"

"Maybe Meagan has the disc. Maybe that's why she came up here."

Ross stepped to the bathroom sink and turned on the water. The hotter, the better.

〇

Rodney delivered Meagan to the main entrance of the Ritz Carlton in Buckhead, the affluent northern suburb of Atlanta.

The double doors to Suite 600 were wide open. The bellman entered, deposited her bags and departed, shaking his head as she offered a tip. *Taken care of, ma'm.*

Meagan caught Chase's distinctive scent in the air before she saw him. He was on the phone, pacing as he spoke. He had not noticed her yet. His broad back was turned. As she drew closer, two things caught her attention. First, she noticed he was dressed in a dramatic black on black tux that fit his muscular build like a second skin. Second, he was speaking on the phone in a harsh voice. And this was the first time she had heard him agitated.

"Listen, I am doing this my way, get it? So, why don't you just stay out of it? Of course I do... It makes perfect sense... Yes, I will... Listen, you tell him everything is covered on my end. All right. All right, Sandy, goodbye."

He was talking to Sandy like that?

He spun around to see her there, unable to hide a trace of guilt as he realized she had over heard his conversation.

Meagan was mortified. She felt like an eavesdropper caught in the act. Her cheeks flushed.

"Maybe this wasn't such a good idea." She lifted her bags. "Look, I'll get a cab back to the airport. I can still catch my flight if I hurry."

"Stop." Chase headed her off with a few long strides. "You're staying. End of story. Forget what you heard. It's not what you think. Erase it. It doesn't matter."

While Meagan stood there trying to decide what to do, he reached out and gently brushed a strand of hair from her eyes, an intimate and unexpected gesture.

"Now, how fast can you get ready? I can't be late for a dinner where everyone is coming to say nice things about me and give me money."

"All right, I'll stay. And I'll come to your dinner. But the rest? Count me out."

"What do you mean?"

"I doubt if I'll say nice things about you, and I'm definitely not giving you money."

He reached for her bags. She let them slip from her grasp. The tension eased.

"I need twenty minutes to get ready, give or take, if you leave me alone," Meagan said. "No talking."

"Okay, you've got 20 minutes flat. The bathroom is through there and there's a dressing room and bedroom on the other side."

Minutes later, Meagan stood naked in front of the dressing room mirror. Arms raised, she slid the expensive black silk sheath over her slim frame. The thigh-high slit up the side accented her tanned bare legs. High-heeled strappy Jimmy Choo sandals completed her ensemble. She slipped on Tiffany silver hoop earrings and several sterling arm bangles, all different designs. She liked the bangles for . the shimmer and the sound. They jingled and jangled as she waved both arms. Meagan felt in control.

She glanced at the clock. Nineteen minutes. Not bad. She took a deep breath and headed for the lobby.

Chase broke from a conversation to greet her, transfixed by the blonde vision shimmering in silver and black. His eyes roamed over her curvaceous body.

"Hi, I'm Meagan, I'll be your escort for the evening, sir."

He burst out laughing. "You look absolutely gorgeous."

As the waiter handed her a glass of champagne, he continued to eye her and taking a glass from the tray, he raised it to her.

"Here's to tonight. To us. Together."

"Chase Chambers," she scolded quietly. "There is no 'us' in the personal sense. I am married to Ross, remember? And you are getting married to Sandy, right? Or did those facts slip through the cracks of your mind?"

"God, you sound just like Curtis."

"Please, Chase. I don't want to regret this, and I don't want it to interfere with the work we're doing for you---First Class, that is. It means so much to Marsha, and we're going to be a big help to your whole campaign. I truly believe it."

"I do, too. And you don't have to worry about that."

"Well, I am worried. I hate to think I messed it all up with one bad choice. That would be stupid. And no blonde jokes, please."

"Right. Like you're a real blonde anyway?"

"Just for the record, I am!" Meagan spouted. "Not that you'll ever find out."

[]

After they settled in the limo, Chase gave Meagan a quick lowdown about their hosts for the evening.

"I grew up with Gary. Best buddies. My brother, Gary and I were the Three Musketeers. And Melissa was a little pest who followed us around and tattled on us all the time. Gary was the only one who would put up with her. He still does. They've been married about six years now, and she's still running him ragged."

"What do they do?"

"Gary owns an IT company, does a lot of proprietary government software. Smart guy. Mel's a child psychologist and author, published a couple books. And she's great fun. You'll like her. And Gary's the best. True blue, solid as a rock. I would trust him with my life."

He edged closer. "Now, tonight---I hate to say it, but remember tonight is all about me."

She laughed. "Isn't that special?"

"I know. It's embarrassing. But in politics, that's the way it works. You've got to do it. Officially, tonight's event is sponsored by the ACF, the Atlanta Community Federation, and I am being honored with their annual citizenship award."

"But you don't live in Atlanta."

"I was born and raised here, but I've been gone ten years now."

"Well then, why---"

"This is their national award, for stellar contribution to the community somewhere else, could be anywhere in the country."

"And you won that? That's great, Chase."

"Yes, except I don't deserve it."

"Oh, you're being modest."

"No. I really don't. It's all political. Gary and some old family friends---we still have strong roots here---they got me nominated, and made sure I won the award."

"Why would they do that?"

"Because they want to help me get elected. And the award is a good excuse for this party, and all these rich folks in Atlanta will show up, and---oh, by the way, how about contributing to Mr. Chambers' campaign for Congress in Florida? We'll pick up about a hundred grand to spend on TV ads. That's why."

"Well, at least you're honest about it," Meagan said. "I like that. I like it that you say whatever's on your mind."

He looked at her intensely, as if he were about to say something important.

Meagan picked up on it. "What?"

He changed his mind.

"Nothing. It's just---It's just that I'm really glad that you are with me tonight. And you will enjoy yourself, I promise."

Dammit, he thought, he was here to do a job and that did not include lusting after a married suspect. He needed to focus, keep himself under control. Hell, he had been the catalyst for this investigation and he was determined to follow it through. Ross Hamilton was a marked man. He was going down. The question was whether Meagan deserved to go down with him?

The limo turned into a narrow, winding drive between rows of weeping willows leading to a white, plantation-style mansion.

"What a beautiful home," Meagan murmured.

"It's been in Gary's family forever, since before the Civil War. It's a special place to me, too. We had a lot of great times here."

"Anyone in particular that you want to tell me about?"

He grinned. "I'd better not."

"You don't have a southern accent, Chase. I would have never guessed that you grew up in Atlanta."

"There's a lot that you don't know about me, Meagan," he said. "A whole lot."

21

As soon as the limo came to a halt, the car door opened and a huge man with curly red hair and beard to match stuck his head in. He looked like a bear in a tuxedo.

"Chase, you old dog! C'mon up outa there."

The two men grasped each other in a fierce hug.

"Gar, it's been too long, man. You look great."

A slim woman in a white lace halter dress stepped out on the veranda above them, her raven hair drawn into a sophisticated French roll, a few strands framing her exquisite face. Meagan thought she looked like Demi Moore.

"Chase!"

She raced down the flagstone steps and hurled herself into Chase's arms, kissing him on both cheeks. Then she stood back and looked him over solemnly.

"What's the matter, Melissa? Have I changed that much?"

"Oh, Chase. I haven't laid eyes on you since Cam---since---It's so good to see you."

She hugged him again, warm and consoling.

Chase drew Meagan to his side with an easy grace.

"Melissa, Gary, I want you to meet Meagan Hamilton. Meagan's working with the campaign. I just found out she was in Atlanta, so I asked her to join us tonight."

Gary bowed. "My pleasure, Meagan."

"I hope it's all right," Meagan said, a hint of red in her cheeks. "It was definitely a last minute arrangement."

"Those are the best kind," Gary said with a wink.

"Welcome to our home, Meagan." Melissa eyed Meagan warily.

"It's beautiful, Melissa. It looks like it's out of *Gone With the Wind*."

"Thank you. It's not Tara, but it is almost as old, and we love it." She took Meagan's arm. "Come on, I'll show you around. These two bad boys, they're going to want to go off and smoke cigars and tell lies for a while."

The men traded looks. She knew them too well.

"They're not lies! They're true stories!" Gary protested as his wife led Meagan away.

[]

Melissa was cordial but slightly distant as she led Meagan on a tour of the home, every room restored to perfection. Meagan said nothing. Melissa knew Sandy, no doubt, and probably saw Meagan as some scheming vixen trying to get her claws into Chase. She was relieved when they arrived at the whitewashed kitchen with the old-fashioned pantry. Familiar territory. A bevy of caterers were hustling about. Stacks of dishes and platters of food covered the counters.

"Wow, Melissa, this is quite a spread." Meagan took stock of the ample quantities, running the numbers in her head. "How many people are you having, like two hundred?"

"That's exactly right." Melissa was impressed. "How did you know?"

"Oh, it's what I do. Catering. We're handling events for Mr. Chambers in Naples."

"Really? Well then, maybe you should stay and keep an eye on this motley crew while I get myself ready for this gala."

Meagan brightened. "I'd love to help out if they'll let me. You go ahead."

"Oh, I was kidding," Melissa fluttered. "You can't do that. You're our guest."

"Please," Meagan persisted. "Let me help."

"Well OK," Melissa warmed to her sincerity. "If you insist. Jeanette?" she called to the tall black woman inspecting the serving dishes in the pantry, all business.

"Ma'm?"

"Jeanette, this is Meagan, my new friend and catering consultant. She's here to make sure you guys don't steal the silverware."

Jeanette's serious look softened. "You're too late--- it's already in the truck."

Meagan smiled back. "Can I give you a hand, Jeanette? I'll work for food."

"Grab an apron. Welcome aboard."

Melissa leaned to Meagan, "Are you sure you're okay with this?"

"Couldn't be better. You go on, now. Let me make myself useful."

◻

Melissa made her way to the study where the men were hiding out. She marched straight up to Chase.

"All right, Chase, what in the hell is going on here?"

Chase exhaled slowly, watching the cigar smoke curl to the ceiling.

"What are you talking about, Meli?"

"You are on my turf now, so cut the crap," Melissa said, hands on her hips. "I'm talking about Meagan Hamilton."

"Yes, Meagan. Nice lady."

"Chase Chambers, you look at me when I'm talking to you. Is this Meagan related to Ross Hamilton?"

"She's his wife," he answered through a smoke ring.

Her eyes widened. "His wife! Oh my God! Well, isn't that nice and cozy. And did she agree to turn on her husband before you slept with her or after?"

"I am not sleeping with her," he said evenly.

"Oh, then she's the innocent bystander here? And does she know that you're out to destroy Ross Hamilton---ruin his life, and probably hers, too?"

"Melissa, you have it all wrong. This isn't---I like Meagan. Forget that her last name is Hamilton and give her a chance. Ross doesn't even figure into this equation."

"No? And how does Sandy figure in? Does she like Meagan as much as you do? Are you two into threesomes lately?

"You always did speak your mind, huh, Mel?" Chase put his hand on her shoulder. "Look, I don't think Meagan knows about my, uh, history with her husband. I believe she was kept in the dark completely."

"So what's the deal here?"

"There is no deal."

"Whatever. I know that you blame Hamilton for Diane's suicide. You always have. And, here you are, with his wife? Excuse me, but---what's wrong with that picture?"

Chase ran his fingers through his hair.

"Yes, I hold Ross Hamilton responsible for Diane. He is a thief, a con man and maybe a lot worse. He's got to pay for that and I'm going to make sure that he does. For Cam. I know that's what he would want. And I'm going to tell both of you something that cannot leave this room. There is a federal investigation going on, right now, aimed right at the black heart of one Ross Hamilton. He is going down, all the way down."

"With your help?" Gary asked.

"I guess you could say I'm playing a part in it."

"With the FBI? My god, Chase, what have you got yourself into?" Melissa was aghast. "What about this—what about Congress? You can't be out playing G-man and still find the time to get elected. It's crazy."

"No, it's alright. I'm not doing that much, just helping Uncle Sam a little."

"Yeah," Melissa scoffed. "And look what happened the last time you guys decided to help your good old Uncle Sam. Cam never came back."

"Mel!" Gary spoke up sharply. "That's enough."

"That's okay." Chase held up a hand. "I am working with the FBI, and Ross Hamilton is the target. But Meagan wasn't on the radar screen. I didn't even know who she was when I ran into her. It just happened. Now it's my job to evaluate her---I mean---god, I don't know what I mean. Look, truth is, I like Meagan, and I don't think she had anything to do with any of Hamilton's bad acts. But I have to be sure. "

"We're with you, Chase," said Gary. "Just tell us what you want us to do."

"I want you to put her at ease," he said. "I want her to feel comfortable, let her guard down. Then I think she'll open up."

"In more ways than one." Melissa rolled her eyes. "Chase, I can't---what about Sandy? I just can't believe you would---"

"Sandy knows all about this," he said. "In fact, she helped set it up."

He stood to face Melissa. "You know I would never betray Sandy, but tonight, you've got to let me do this my way. And you've got to back me up."

Melissa was confused and upset, but she believed in this man.

"All right, Chase," she said finally. "If that's what you want. I'll be Meagan's best friend for the night. I just hope I won't be sorry in the morning."

"Thanks, Meli." He kissed her on the forehead. "I knew I could count on you."

Gary glanced at the mantel clock. "Hey, our guests are due right now, folks. The pre-game strategy session is over. Understand, Mel? Let's put on our happy faces."

22

For the next two hours, Chase made the rounds with Meagan at his side, introduced as "campaign assistant" or "event director" as Chase showcased his political charm, making friends feel welcome and strangers feel like friends. Meagan enjoyed watching him work the crowd. More than once, he would excuse himself with a whisper and stroll off to the study for a private chat with special guests. He spent five minutes with the state party chairman, five more with two trials lawyers from Tallahassee, then a full ten minutes with another senator. He was back with Meagan when the little man in the dull gray suit approached, sweating profusely.

"Mr. Chambers?" He offered a limp hand.

The good candidate clenched it firmly. "Hello, how are you? Thanks for coming tonight."

"Yes, yes. Mr. Chambers. Herb Edelman."

Meagan noticed that Chase did a slight double take. It was the first time all evening she had seen him caught off guard. He bounced right back.

"Of course! Herb! Great to see you, my friend. Come on, we've got to get caught up on things..." He steered him toward the study with an "I'll be back" nod to Meagan. She shook her head. Politics.

▯

Edelman began complaining as soon as the door was closed.

"I really shouldn't be here like this."

"Mr. Edelman, I was told you asked for this meeting."

"Yes, but not like this." Edelman wiped his brow. "There are too many people here. Some of them know me!"

"Didn't they tell you it was a fundraiser?"

"I thought it was just a few---never mind. It doesn't matter now. I just have to go, as soon as possible."

"Whatever you want. Look, we appreciate what you're doing. Tell me how to make it easy for you."

Edelman withdrew a slim envelope from his pocket.

"I just want to help put this bastard away," he said, handing the envelope to Chase. "And this might do it."

Chase opened the envelope and glanced at the pages of numbered printouts.

"What is this?"

"You'll see. It's all in there---summaries of all the accounts."

"Diane's?"

"Yes, and the others."

"There were others?"

"Three more that I know about, clients of mine at one time or another."

"And you think there are more?"

"I would bet there are, and I'm not a betting man. How many? I don't know."

"But these are summaries," Chase said, patting his pocket. "That's not evidence. What about the actual records?"

"Mr. Chambers," Edelman frowned. "I am a CPA, an actuary and a lawyer. All the filings and account numbers are listed. They will reflect my summaries exactly. As for access to the originals, I trust your people are capable of handling that."

"I'm sure they are," he said. "The only other thing we'll need is testimony in court, from you and these other women, verify the evidence."

Edelman gave him an odd look. "That can't be done."

"Why not?"

"Because they're dead, Mr. Chambers. Didn't you know that? All the women are dead."

He was stunned. "But how---?"

"Accident, suicides---all sudden, all unexpected--- like Miss McAlister. Strange coincidence, wouldn't you say?"

Chase didn't answer.

"I'm an accountant, Mr. Chambers. I don't believe in coincidence. I can't prove it, but I believe Ross

Hamilton is the reason that none of those women are alive today."

"That's all the more reason we are going to need you to testify," Chase said quietly.

"It will be my pleasure---but only after you have Hamilton in custody. He is a very treacherous man. I wouldn't put anything past him."

"You let me take care of that." He shook Edelman's hand. "Listen, Mr. Edelman—Herb---I won't keep you, but I want you to know that you've been a tremendous help. This is exactly the break we needed on this case. And if there's anything we can do---"

"Just one thing."

"Name it."

"I'm going to go now, and I'd like to leave alone. No offense, but I'd rather people didn't see us together. If Hamilton had any idea that I was providing information to---"

"No offense taken," Chase patted him on the back. "You go ahead. I'll wait here. And thanks again."

Edelman slipped out the door. Chase took a minute to study the summaries he had provided. Mac would be pleased, he thought. It was a map to a treasure chest of hard evidence, perhaps enough to make their case and convict Ross Hamilton on several counts of fraud, conversion, maybe even tax evasion.

He smiled. It had been a very worthwhile trip to Atlanta already and the night was still young. There was a fair-haired woman in a black dress waiting for him in the next room and he had promised her a good time. He planned to keep his promise.

- 23 -

The ballroom band moved into an old standard. A strong hand nudged Meagan's elbow and she looked up to see Chase at her side. Without a word, he took her in his arms and moved onto the dance floor. She trembled as she felt his breath in her hair.

"Are you cold?"

"No, no, not at all. I'm fine. I feel good."

"Yes you do." He nestled her closer. "You know, I could get used to having you in my arms."

"That's an interesting thought. Sandy on the left, me on the right..."

He pulled her tight and she melted into him as he steered an effortless course across the floor. Meagan felt as if she were afloat on the music, drifting in a sensuous fog.

His hand glided ever so slowly down her bare back, fingertips grazing her skin. The feeling was exquisitely erotic.

"This is crazy," she whispered.

Chase steadied her. "Works for me."

She looked up, eyes glistening. "I'm scared, Chase. I think I'm in over my head here. I just can't handle all this. It's all too much."

"Too much good or too much bad?"

"Too much good, but too soon. I need to think," she stammered, "I've got to---"

Meagan caught sight of Gary watching them through the branches of a ficus tree like a predator in the woods, ready to pounce on unsuspecting prey.

"Your friend Gary doesn't look too happy."

Chase executed a neat twirl, turning to see Gary, brow furrowed in concern.

"Uh-oh," Chase paused. "I better talk to him before he gets the wrong idea."

"He's not the only one," Meagan mumbled as he released her and hustled off to huddle with Gary.

Looking for safe harbor, Meagan was relieved to see Melissa approach with open arms and a friendly face.

"C'mon, girl!" Melissa hooked her arm and marched her off. Meagan fell in step with her new friend, no idea of their destination but grateful for the rescue.

"The party's over," Melissa said, steering Meagan through the back of the house to the patio, grabbing two bottles of champagne off a serving buffet without breaking stride.

"Follow me. We've got a local after-party custom that I think you'll like."

▯

Gary lit up the expensive Havanas; first Chase's, then his own. He took a quick puff and leaned back to gather his thoughts.

"I'm on your team, buddy. You know that, don't you?"

"Sure I do, Gar, never doubted it for a second."

"Then why don't you let me in on the game plan?"

"What?"

"Hey." Gary pointed the cigar at him. "I know you. At least, after twenty-five years or so, I think I do. And I watch you out there with that little filly, Meagan, and I gotta wonder---is Sandy getting kicked off the roster?"

"No, God, no!" He shook his head. "I told you, I'm part of---"

"I heard what you told me, but I've got eyes. I can see. The way you are with her. Now that's no act. And it sure as hell ain't part of no FBI rule book. There's something you're not telling me here. Now are you going to give me the low down or leave me hanging?"

He stared out the window. "I can't."

"You can't what?"

"I can't tell you everything. You're right. There's more to the story, and I wish I could get into it, but I can't. And I won't lie to you either. I won't do that. You've just got to ride with me on this. Okay?"

"Okay, pardner, if you say so." Gary didn't hesitate. "I just hope you know what you're doing. Reckon you know that politics and sex is a dangerous mix. Highly combustible."

"Tell me about it," he answered ruefully.

"All right," Gary said. "The scientific explanation goes something like this: politics and sex are relatively harmless in isolation, but when combined, especially during a hotly contested election, they can blow up in one's face---namely yours."

"Thanks for the lesson."

"Enough said." Gary nodded. "Let's go find your woman."

"My woman?"

"You want to deny that, too?"

"I'm not---" He gave up. "No, I won't deny it. I care about her. Too much, maybe."

"And Ross Hamilton?"

"Hate his fucking guts."

"Well now, I guess you have gotten yourself between a rock and a hard spot, Chase Chambers."

[]

Meagan and Melissa were chatting like old school pals when the men found them. An hour had passed, along with two bottles of Dom lying empty nearby. The girls were sprawled in the Jacuzzi, immersed in the water frothing up to their chins.

Gary saw them and elbowed Chase. Both men stood silent in the shadows. Chase noticed Meagan's dress draped over the chaise lounge. Well, he thought, this should be interesting.

Neither woman was aware that they had guests until Melissa caught a whiff of cigar smoke.

"Hey guys---come out, come out, wherever you are."

Gary and Chase stepped from the shadows, caught like schoolboys.

"How dare you spy on us!" Melissa splashed water over Gary's black leather shoes. He jumped back out of range.

"Hey!" Gary yelled. "We weren't spying. We started a search party to find two lost girls. Have you seen them?"

"Wondered what happened to you two. I'm just telling Meagan about some of your escapades, Chase. Hope you don't mind. Of course, it is a little too late if you do, because she knows all your innermost secrets now!"

"I don't mind. But I'd better stick around to make sure you get the details right."

"Come on in, the water's fine." Melissa leaned over drunkenly and whispered to Meagan, "Don't worry. Won't happen in a million years. Not Chase. He's way too shy."

Meagan watched him peel off his tuxedo jacket, place it on the chair and start to unbutton his shirt. Her eyes widened as she turned to Melissa.

"Well, he's a pretty good bluffer."

"This is not like Chase. Not at all! I don't know what's gotten into him."

Chase continued, nonchalant, stripping down to boxer shorts. Gary shrugged and started to shed his clothes. Might as well join the party. It was suddenly quiet in the hot tub, the murmuring bubbles of water the only sound.

"What's the matter, girls? Change your minds?" Gary teased.

Meagan looked at the men, then back at Melissa. "Maybe it's time that I got out. There's probably not enough room for---"

"Oh, Meagan. Let them come in," Melissa giggled. "We've seen it all before."

"Maybe it's like old times for you all, but I've never---I mean, look, they're actually getting naked! Right now!" Meagan squeaked and covered her eyes.

Chase dropped down to her side. "Naked? You want us to come in totally naked? Don't you girls have anything on in there? Like underwear?"

"Underwear?" Melissa purred, glancing sideways with a saucy grin. "Meagan darlin', did you keep your panties on?"

Meagan sank beneath the bubbles.

With a flick of the wrist, Chase was out of his boxers. Gary followed suit. Both men eased into the water.

"Oh, my God!" Meagan gurgled, thrashing around in embarrassment.

"You shouldn't have dared us." Gary pulled his wife to him and gave her a sloppy kiss on the forehead. "You brought it all on yourself."

"But the Chase I know is so shy," Melissa said. "I mean, I can still remember that night in high school, after the prom, when Donna-what's-her-name---Donna Clough, remember her?---when she tried to---"

"Ahem!" Chase interrupted.

Gary took his cue. "That's enough, babe. No more stories. You're slurring your words. Let's get you out of here before you turn into a prune."

Gary jumped out, grabbed a towel for himself and draped another over his wife. They headed for the house, weaving slightly.

"Night, kids." Chase waved. "Thanks for the party! We'll see ourselves out."

"Hey, Chase," Gary called out. "The guest house back yonder is open. I don't think the Ritz would appreciate you sloshing through their lobby at three in the morning. You hear me, buddy?"

Gary steered his wife to the patio doors.

"Do you really think that's a good idea?" Melissa whispered.

"Safer than you think."

☐

Chase glanced at Meagan. Her head was back, resting on the tile ledge with her eyes closed, a winsome smile on her luscious lips, water lapping at her breasts.

"What's so funny?"

Meagan opened her eyes. "God, I feel so good."

"Sure it's not the alcohol talking, Meagan?"

"Nope. My head may be spinning, but I do know how I feel." She turned towards him. "And just how I do you feel, Mr. Candidate?"

Laughing, Meagan reached out to touch his shoulder, her hand drifting down to the thick curly hair on his chest. His whole body tensed. He had to be careful here. Meagan seemed to hold some sensual power over him that he couldn't resist. He didn't want to hurt her---nor himself. Both were at risk.

"I feel good, too, Meagan. Too damn good, if you want the truth. We're walking a fine line here."

"I think it's too late for me," she whispered. "I've already crossed the line."

She leaned into him, surrendering. Chase caught her chin in his hand and ran his thumb over her soft lips, eyes glued to hers. They remained like that for a long moment, captivated by each other, no words to speak.

With little thought, the walls came tumbling down. Chase molded her naked body to his. He stroked her skin, soft, smooth and wet. She arched up, frantic with anticipation. They forgot where they were, who they were. They were lost, drowning in desire.

Chase couldn't help himself, couldn't stop, didn't want to. He cupped her breast and brought it to him, licking tiny droplets from her nipple, dark in the bubbling heat. Meagan strained toward him, wanting more. He explored her, hands skimming down her back, across her belly, between her legs.

She began to moan at the tantalizing touch of his fingertips. It was magic. Her thighs parted as he probed deeper, slow and gentle, stirring the heat. She was ignited, on fire for him.

Chase felt her push against him, separating them. They moved apart, breathing hard, reflecting each other's lustful gaze.

"Chase, I'm so sorry. I'm---I'm so confused."

"You are so beautiful," he whispered.

She saw her desire mirrored in his eyes.

"Chase, I want you to know that I'm not...I don't care about tomorrow. I want you to make love to me. Tonight. Now. That's all there is in the world right now. Just us."

He embraced her, surrounded her with his passion. Meagan was swept away in his sweltering warmth.

- 24 -

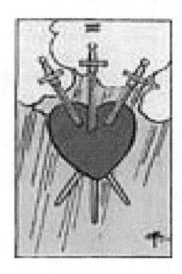

Chase climbed out, secured a towel around his hips and held another for Meagan. Grazing her face with a tender kiss, he folded his arms around her naked body and led the way to the guest house.

Inside the spacious room was a four-poster bed bathed in moonlight from the single window above. He eased her across the room, slowly, languidly, a dance in the dark.

He could feel the heat of her as he gazed into her smoky green eyes, aching to fulfill her every fantasy.

"You're overdressed," he said, unwrapping the towel to reveal her, a goddess in the moonlight. "That's better."

She moved in, pressing against him. "How many hours until morning? No, never mind---don't tell me.

Don't spoil it for me. Just hold me please? For the rest of the night."

"My darling."

Chase swept her up and placed her on the bed, stretching out beside, warming her with his embrace.

He palmed her breasts with smooth, tender strokes until her nipples were warm and taut, begging for his touch. She gazed into his smoldering eyes, caressing his face with her fingertips. Meagan smiled as she felt him quiver against her.

His kissed her face, her shoulders, her arms, moving towards her feminine core.

She moved uncontrollably as he laid siege to her senses, slow kisses on her thighs, tongue flashing as he rose to worship at her sweet altar. He licked at her, savoring her taste. As she groped for the pillow she buried her face to muffle her screams. She moaned as he lavished her with pleasure and then cried out as she came.

He paused for a moment then renewed his torrid assault on her senses, kissing her hard on the lips as his fingers swirled between her legs, working their ruthless magic once again, bringing her back to the edge. Her fists clenched the sheets as she soared higher.

It was too much. A complete overload. She called out his name as she slid into ecstasy.

"Chase! Chase!" Meagan gasped as she surfaced from her sexual haze. "Stop! God, please! "

He would not be halted in his mission to overwhelm her with his fierce passion. Once again she felt his lips skimming her tender breasts. Her body was throbbing at his ardent touch.

He moved to conquer her again. His powerful legs straddled hers. He slipped into her, probing slowly, then out, teasing her higher and higher. She screamed, begging for mercy. He thrust, complete in her, swift and sure, again and again, plunging them into a blazing vortex of unequivocal pleasure.

- 25 -

"Then we have a deal, Mrs. Tan?"

The room fell silent as all eyes turned to the tiny woman at the head of the table. She set her glass down and stared straight ahead. Ross waited. If this were a gathering of American executives, the passing seconds would be considered an uncomfortable silence, but Ross knew better. In Japanese culture, it was not necessary to fill every gap in a business conversation. A long pause was considered a mark of wisdom, serious consideration and respect. Ross had been at meetings with Japanese businessmen who would remain perfectly still and silent for five minutes before responding to a simple question.

He waited for Mrs. Tan.

She finally spoke.

"You are most persuasive, Missah Hamilton. I must point out there can be no contract, no deal as you say, until there is ink dry on paper. I believe we are on the threshold now, tonight, and the door is open. We will review all documents you provide. If all is in order---"

She raised her glass. Every one of her associates scurried to join her, hoisting glasses. Ross grabbed the moment, raised his glass high.

"Here's to crossing the threshold."

There were oohs and aahs and murmurs of agreement all around. Stacy watched with admiration from her place at the corner of the table.

Formal farewells were exchanged as the last of the guests departed. Stacy shut the door and leaned against it. Finally, the long night was over. The sting was in. Time would tell whether they had pulled it off. It had been touch and go there for a while, especially with that awful woman, but Ross could turn the charm up a notch when he had to, and it looked like he had won over Mrs. Tan before she departed with her entourage, all happy, bowing and smiling.

She turned to look for him. They had hardly had a chance to speak all evening. Stacy had been exchanging pleasantries with all the Tan Group men while he focused on the Queen Bee. She knew Ross would want to talk now, review the game plan.

He had been right beside her a moment ago, now he was nowhere to be seen but she knew where he was. Just to make sure, she went down the hall to the master bedroom, stopped in the doorway and listened. Yes, she could hear the shower.

She went back to the kitchen and told the three caterers they could go before grabbing her purse and heading for the computer in the den. She took out Ross's precious disk from an inside zipper pocket, slipped it in the slot and began entering the six separate codes needed to enter the system. She knew them all.

The screen came to life with a navigation page in outline form: three sections, multiple sub-sections each in rigid, symmetrical columns. This was Ross Hamilton, all right, good order for evil purpose. She clicked on Accounts.

All the banks, all the deposits and current balances, and all the Hamilton Securities records were there, in sequence and up to date. She didn't have time to study all the numbers, but scanned through enough to get a good idea of the total on hand: more than fifty million dollars. No surprise to Stacy. She had been around for the maneuverings that provided most of the money, deeply involved in several. It was somewhat more than she would have guessed, but she knew Ross well enough to figure he had been moving the money like a chess master, making it work, probably in hedge funds and futures markets, in and out for hefty, short-term gains.

She closed the Accounts Section, navigated back to the Home Page and clicked on Photographs. She had to know. Would he dare?

· The full-color images were arranged in three rows, chronological sequence. Ross was so precise, even when it came to this. It took her breath away.

[]

Ross stepped out of the shower, pulled on a white terrycloth robe and dried his hair briskly with a thick white towel. He felt clean and in good spirits. Once again, he had risen to the occasion. Mrs. Tan was formidable, but no match for his persuasive powers. The evening belonged to him.

He buffed his neck with the towel as he ambled down the hall. Stacy was sitting at the computer, back to him, engrossed in something on the screen. What was she...?

Ross moved in silently and peered over her shoulder to see recent data on the Tan Exports group scrolling past. Good girl. Doing her homework. Waste of time, though. The company was privately held, wholly owned by Mrs. Tan and her close relatives. They were fiercely protective of every shred of information about income, investments and net worth, family secrets, everything.

"You won't find anything worthwhile about the Tan Group on the Internet, Stacy."

She spun to face him. "Maybe it's a long shot, but I wanted to try. Might help."

"No," Ross dismissed her. "It won't."

He walked to the window on the north side, speaking to her like a child while he gazed at the bright lights below.

"And completely unnecessary. Didn't you see? I won them over. They were enthralled. The inscrutable Mrs. Lu Ong Tan and all her astute advisors are in the net. The speculative markets in precious metals can be made to look most attractive, especially to those who aren't satisfied with reasonable profits. Greed is a wonderful thing. It's a done deal. Agreements will be signed. Checks will be forthcoming. And then---" He shrugged his shoulders with a satisfied look. "Things will happen."

- 26 -

    In the cottage, two lights burned in the early hours of the morning.

    Gem had risen from her bed an hour before dawn, gone right to her cards in the study, and had turned up the Two of Cups and the Nine of Wands. She knew that was enough. Whatever the message, it was present and whole in this oddly matched pair, although she was not clear as to exactly what it was.

    Gem looked away and looked again. She had learned the process through many years and countless readings. First impression was important. The subliminal mind was so attuned, responding in a visceral rush before any conscious recognition of the card. The process of translating the sensations to thoughts and words was ponderous and time-consuming. Is it this or that? Be careful. Think twice and think again.

She knew there were times, many times, when the connotation of the card was present at first sight, obvious and complete. But that was the exception, not the rule. Patience, caution and humility were the bywords of the true masters of the Tarot, a lesson lost on so many who read the cards in haste, presuming too much, too soon.

Not Gem.

Two of Cups. Nine of Wands. She absently stroked the cat while she studied the cards. Ursa had joined her as a silent partner, crouched like a sphinx at her side.

She focused on the Nine of Wands, an ominous presence. A young sentry stood calm but alert before a palisade of staffs, one in hand. She had seen the card a thousand times before and always seemed to divine its meaning promptly, but it was elusive and perplexing now. The young man was not a sentry but a warrior. The staffs were his arsenal of weapons. What troubled her most was the juxtaposition to the card on the left. The warrior's menacing gaze was transfixed on the handsome couple of the Two of Cups.

Two of Cups. No mystery there. There were lovers somewhere, touching for the first time, the heat of their passion bursting into full flame. The image brought wistful memories of her own first night with the only man she ever loved.

"Mon amour," she whispered. "I miss you so."

Her nostalgia was shattered by a raucous commotion that shook the walls.

[]

The corner room where the light was best had been converted to a studio for Cole. He had been in there all night working feverishly. Now he scowled at the large canvas before him.

He wasn't happy. The painting was an intensely colored landscape, an impressionist view of the abundantly flowered south border of the Naples estate. He toyed with the paint on his easel and dabbed at the canvas, then pulled back. He tossed the brush aside, chose another and poked again. No good.

He snatched a thick brush, swept up a glob of red and slathered it across the painting, back and forth in wide swaths, vandalizing his own art. He gouged the brush straight through like a dagger then grabbed the frame with both hands and smashed it against the easel, ripping a gaping hole top to bottom. Out of control, Cole pounded the frame against the wall again and again until the wood splintered in his hands. Then he sagged to the floor as ragged shreds of canvas fluttered down around him. He sat there, breathing hard, frustration spent.

He looked up to see his mother standing in the doorway, managing a weak smile as he held up the largest remnant.

"I'm working on my performance art."

Gem took in the destructive scene in a glance, saying nothing. She would not judge. She would not lecture. Let Cole work it out himself.

"It was awful. Trite. Meaningless. It was a painting for a Holiday Inn." Getting back to his feet, he said, "I couldn't stand to look at it any more, so I put an end to its suffering."

His mother shrugged, still silent. *All right, if you say so.*

"You know, it's really not the painting, it's me. I'm not an artist, not a painter. I'm a joke. I'm--I'm like an old man---no, a zombie. That's what I am." He turned to face her. "I was dead, and you should have let me stay dead."

That was enough. Gem stepped into the room.

"Sit down, Cole."

He didn't argue, collapsing in a chair.

She walked over, stood behind the chair and patted his shoulder.

"I wish your father could have been here for you."

"I guess that wasn't meant to be."

"No, that's not it," Gem said. "What have I always taught you?"

"The fates are strong, but the will is stronger." Cole grinned. "See? I listen sometimes. But a strong will wouldn't have helped Dad. The plane crashed. There was nothing anyone could do."

"There was something I could have done." She turned away. "It was my fault."

"I don't believe that."

"It's true."

"I wasn't around then, but I can read. The plane went down in a blizzard, a mile from Dulles Airport. You were five hundred miles away, Mother."

She got up slowly, moved closer and sat next to him.

"I never told you the whole story, or your brothers. I was too heartbroken, too ashamed. Now I think you should know. Your father meant the world to me. He was the only one, my only man. I married your father when I was seventeen---did you know that? We were never apart after that, not for a single day in sixteen years."

"What about when he went to Washington, to the Senate?"

"I went with him. We kept our home and we had an apartment in Georgetown. Even when he went overseas----a conference in London, fact-finding mission to Africa---I always went along. He insisted. 'Can't go without my good luck charm,' he'd say."

"But you didn't go on ...on the last trip."

"I was too pregnant. The doctors wouldn't let me fly."

"That wasn't your fault."

"No."

"Then why would you blame yourself?"

"I knew. Don't you see? I knew the plane would crash, and no one would survive."

"From the cards?"

"From the cards. From my dreams. I knew."

"And you didn't tell him?"

"Of course I told him. I begged him not to go. But he wouldn't listen."

"Why?"

"He was a headstrong man. Like your brothers. And you, Cole. All the Chambers men have that stubborn streak. He said he had to go; it was important, and that was it."

"I don't get it. He had to know about you and the Tarot cards."

"He wasn't a believer. He believed in me, but not in the cards. His family was old school Christian, Pentecostal. They thought the Tarot cards were the devil's tools. Black magic."

"That had to be rough on you."

"It wasn't easy. I never stopped with the cards, but I kept them out of sight, to keep the peace. And your father never knew what a blessing they were for him."

"For him? What do you mean?"

"So many times, so many decisions, he would ask for my opinion, my advice, and I would go to the cards and come back with an answer. He thought I was so smart, but it wasn't me."

"The cards. But I still don't see why you think it was your fault when he---you tried. You did everything you could."

"I should have done more, whatever it took. Lock him in the closet if I had to. Lay down in the front of the plane. But I didn't. He resisted and I gave up. My will was weak. I let him go...to his death."

Cole saw the tears well up in his mother's eyes.

"I know how you feel. I was weak, too, with Andy?"

"Cole. You risked your life for that boy. You were a hero."

"I wasn't a hero. I was a coward."

"Don't say that."

"It's true. Yes, I dove in, I went after him and I wanted to save him, but I got scared---the water pulling me down---scared to death. I wasn't thinking about Andy anymore. I didn't want to die."

"There's nothing wrong with---"

"Let me finish. I got there, I caught up to him, and he grabbed at me. I went under and I panicked. I fought him off---"

"Cole---"

"And then I pushed him down, climbed on him to stay above water. I let him die so I could live. That's not what heroes do."

"No one could blame you."

"I can. And I do. And I always will, every day, as long as I live."

Gem pulled him close. They held each other in the dark, tears falling. It was a long time before Gem spoke.

"We'll get another chance, Cole. Both of us. And we'll make the right choice."

Dawn arrived too soon.

Meagan woke to find her limbs entangled with the slumbering Chase, his arm across her shoulder, leg between her thighs. The sight of his splendid body flashed memories of the endless ways they had made love. She tried to slide out from under, careful not to wake him. Wide awake, he watched her in amusement.

"Hello, beautiful." He kissed her on the forehead.

She smiled at the kiss but was reluctant to look him in the eyes. Their magical night was over. The morning light brought reality back with a vengeance. This was no fairy tale. She was no Cinderella. She was a married woman in a bed with another man. The thought of her broken vows turned her stomach.

"Meagan," he said sensing her discomfort. "I want you to know that last night meant--"

"No, Chase---stop right there." She couldn't take any morning-after endearments. "Last night is over."

"Don't say it's over. Last night was only the beginning. We can make this work."

"Make it work? Are you crazy! I'm married! You're engaged! There's not a chance in the world that we---" She looked up in despair. "My God, what am I doing here?"

"Meagan, come here." He reached for her. "The chances are better than you think. I really believe that and there will come a time when you do, too. But for now, this is between us. It's our secret."

"I'm not good at secrets." She tensed, shaking her head. "I'm not. I'm not good with lies, or sneaking around having affairs, or adultery. I hate it."

He held her. "It's not like that. Don't make it like that."

"I can't talk about this any more. I hurt too much." She slipped out of his grasp and escaped to the bathroom, shut the door and leaned against it, hyperventilating.

He called her name, once, twice. The only answer was the shower on full blast.

[]

They made the trip to the airport in gloomy silence.

What a mess, he thought, wondering if the magnificent night had been a colossal mistake. Maybe she would understand when all was said and done. Maybe not. He tried to tell himself that there was no sense agonizing about it now. There was nothing he could do until he finished the job he had to do and put an end to the charade.

This forced him to think about another problem. MacNulty. He would definitely have some explaining to do. It was not going to be easy.

Still, it had been worth every glorious minute.

Meagan looked sideways at Chase. She still craved his touch, his taste, his smile. Her own thoughts startled her. She expected that the most spectacular night of her life would eventually fade but she could not stop herself from reliving every word spoken, every caress, over and over. And in between the flashbacks, she couldn't stop telling herself what an awful, despicable woman she was. She had betrayed her husband and her family. She was a cheat, disloyal. How could she?

It was that man, Chase Chambers. He lured her into his sweet trap, tricked her with his hypnotic smile and his wily charms and---

Wait. No, he didn't. She knew what she was doing. Lounging around naked in a hot tub drinking champagne in the middle of the night wasn't the kind of behavior that would discourage advances from a man on a mission, was it?

Yes, she had yielded to temptation. Yes, she was ashamed, appalled at her own behavior. But she wouldn't have traded last night for anything in the world!

◻

The car cruised out to the tarmac and halted next to the open hatch of the waiting Lear. Rodney had the luggage in the storage compartment beneath the fuselage before the two passengers were up the short ramp and on board. He offered a farewell salute as he closed the hatch, then a thumbs-up to the pilot. The jet rolled down the runway and they were airborne for Naples.

Meagan stole another glance. She couldn't help it. In a simple navy blue suit, white shirt, sky blue tie---his "political cookie-cutter outfit," he called it---he looked like he walked right off the cover of *GQ*. What do they say? The clothes make the man? With Chase, the man made the clothes. The image of him naked flashed before her eyes.

Stop this.

She squeezed her eyes tight, trying to erase the picture and opened them at the light touch on her arm. He flashed a smile and handed her a small slip of paper.

"Here's the name and number of the best divorce attorney in Florida."

She stuffed the paper into her purse without a glance.

He pressed on.

"Look, my schedule this week is crazy. I don't have a minute to breathe. But I'll be in touch. I'll find a way. Count on it." He squeezed her arm.

"Mr. Chambers, message coming in for you up front," the co-pilot announced.

"There's a little problem," Chase said, returning from the cockpit with a disconcerted look. "We'll just have to make the best of it."

"Problem?" Meagan felt a tingle of fear.

"Curtis called. Somebody in the media got wind of us together last night in Atlanta, and they're looking to make something of it. They're camped out at the Naples airport, ready to pounce."

"Oh, God! You mean, news people?"

"Yes. And TV, like Fox and CNN. They smell scandal. You know---'Congressional hopeful and married woman: Details at eleven.' They love that stuff."

Meagan gasped. "What do we do?"

"We pounce right back on them."

"We do?"

"Here's the way we'll play it. Curtis will be at the airport. He's bringing Sandy. We will step off the plane together just to let 'em know there's nothing to hide. Make sure you're holding papers. You're on my staff now, remember?"

Meagan shook her head. "I can't do this."

"Sure you can. We joined forces in Atlanta to work on the campaign. No big deal. "

"Maybe you can do the spin doctor stuff," she said. "But wouldn't it be better if I hid in the bathroom until they all go away?"

"That's the worst thing you could do. These media people, in a group, they're like a pack of dogs. If they sense fear or weakness, they'll attack; but if you handle them right, they'll just whimper and go away."

"Handle them right?" Meagan was near panic. "Chase, I am scared to death!"

"Relax. Sometimes you have to pet them, and sometimes you have to smack them on the nose. But whatever you do, don't let them see you sweat. We can do this, Meagan. Don't worry."

Meagan said nothing.

"Look at me, Meagan." She looked up reluctantly.

"Last night wasn't just some casual encounter for me. I know there are complications, for you, and me, complications I can't even tell you about. But I want you to know that last night meant the world to me."

"Oh, Chase," she gripped his hand.

"And no matter what happens, no matter what you hear or what you think of me---"

Meagan was hanging on every word, but he never finished. A booming voice over the intercom cut him off in mid-sentence.

"Final approach to Naples," the captain announced, "Y'all better batten the hatches and buckle up back there."

The engines whined as they started their descent.

Chase buckled her seatbelt, then his own, shouting over the noise, "It'll be OK. Remember, follow my lead." He leaned over and kissed her quickly as the jet touched down.

Showtime!

The cabin door swung open. Meagan took one step into the light and was besieged by a pack of reporters. Cameras flashed. Video cams whirred. Meagan winced but Chase held her arm, steadying her.

Curtis elbowed his way through and up to the steps, a welcoming smile plastered on his face. He spoke through clenched teeth, "Okay, let's look a little happier here, kids." He tugged at his candidate's sleeve, pulling him closer. "FYI, your fiancée is anxiously awaiting your return. Sandra's her name. You call her Sandy, remember? And you are oh-so-thrilled to see her."

Chase muttered through a smile of his own. "I'll try to remember that, Curtis."

Sandy ran to Chase's side and kissed him. She was poised and self-assured as the reporters surged in, pelting them with questions.

Meagan stayed back, trying her best to be invisible. Then the inquiring questions started coming her way.

"Do you have a statement, Mrs. Hamilton?"

"What is your relationship with Mr. Chambers?"

"Why isn't your husband here to meet you?"

The questions came faster as they moved in for the kill. Cameras and microphones poked at her like knives.

Curtis stepped in front of her, both hands in the air. "Hold it! Let's take it easy here. The lady is new to all this hoopla.

"Mrs. Hamilton's company has signed on to manage events through the election, and, I might add, will also handle the planning and catering for the upcoming wedding between Mr. Chambers and Ms. Simpson. That's it. End of story. "

"Hey, man, let the lady talk for herself."

"What are you scared of?"

"Tell us the real story, Mrs. Hamilton!"

Meagan tried to say something but no words would come out. She thought she might faint when Chase appeared at her side like a gallant knight, pulling her to his side. His strength calmed her. She straightened.

"Look, people, you'd better get used to seeing Sandy and I with Mrs. Hamilton in the future because, believe me, between the campaign and the wedding, there's an awful lot of work to do, and Mrs. Hamilton's company will be involved with all of it. "

"That's right," Sandy joined in. "We're lucky to have her. So don't start trouble. If we lose Meagan because you scare her off, I'm holding you all personally responsible."

The reporters laughed. Sandy was good. She slipped a supportive arm around Meg. Smiles all around. It was just the photo op Curtis wanted.

"Come on," he coaxed. "There's your picture." Cameras clicked and whirred.

"Show's over, folks!" Chase announced with a wave. "Thanks for coming, and don't forget to vote."

The press crowd began to disperse, disappointed at the lack of fireworks.

Chase turned to Meagan and gave her hand a perfunctory shake. "I'll---we'll be in touch with you directly. Thanks."

Sandy and Chase climbed into the waiting car, leaving Curtis behind with Meagan, the two of them alone on the tarmac.

"I think that went very well, don't you?" Curtis asked.

Meagan didn't answer, watching the car drive away with Chase and Sandy.

"Mrs. Hamilton?"

"I'm sorry. What did you say?"

"I don't think we've been properly introduced. Curtis LaFond---I'm the assistant director on the campaign."

"Meagan Hamilton," she said wanly, her eyes still following the car.

He studied her. She looked like a lost little girl.

"Is there anything I can do for you, Mrs. Hamilton? Take you somewhere?"

"Home. Please. I just want to go home."

- 28 -

As the car pulled in her driveway, Meagan saw the lonely figure huddled on the front steps, head resting in her arms, long red hair spilling every which way. She looked up at the sound of the car.

"Oh, my God, it's Elle!"

Meagan flew from the car and raced up to the steps. "Elle! I'm so glad to see you!" Meagan embraced her. "But why are you---are you OK?"

"God, Meg, I'm so sorry," Eleanor gazed up contritely. "I just----I mean, you're always home on the weekends. You're always here and Ross is never here. So I thought that Saturday would be a good day to pop in. God, tell me he's not here. He's not, right?"

"No, you're safe for now," Meagan said. "And I love it that you're here, but you're about two weeks early. How did you finagle that at work?"

"I quit."

"You---?"

"I tried to call you the last couple of days---I wanted you to tell me it was okay---but there was no answer. So, I just did it. Fired myself. Put everything in storage, sublet my condo. I just had to get out of there, Meg."

"Are we all right here, ladies?" Curtis loomed above.

"Oh, Curtis." Meagan was on her feet. "I'm sorry, I---this is my friend, my best friend, Eleanor Sheehan."

"A pleasure." Curtis bowed, ever the gentleman.

Elle looked him over with interest.

"Great suit. Must be Italian?"

Elle smoothed his lapel. "Love the fabric."

Curtis basked in the attention. "It's a Brioni."

"Okay, enough fashion talk." Meagan took over. "Curtis, thanks for the ride."

"My pleasure." Curtis saluted. "Your bags, madam."

"Maybe we'll see each other again," Eleanor chirped. "Curtis, was it?"

"I'm certain of it, Eleanor." He tipped a finger.

Eleanor watched him amble back to the car and drive off. Interesting character, this Curtis, and he had a nice butt, too.

"Bet there's a story there, eh?"

Meagan rolled her eyes. "Oh, there is. Wait till you hear."

"He's so cute, Meg, but don't you think he's a little young for you? What is he, twenty-eight? Thirty? He's a baby."

"Oh, I don't know. I've always thought younger men are the way to go, especially at our advanced age."

"Come on. You wouldn't date somebody that didn't have an AARP card when you were in college! Always the older guys. Look at Ross, for Christ's sake. He's old enough to be your father."

"I don't want to get into specifics, but he's only eleven years and one month older than me. Please, Elle, let's not talk about Ross. Ross can go to hell."

"Oh. My. God. Did I hear that? You are so not Meagan."

"Let's get inside. I'll tell you all about the new me. We can relax, break out some wine, and order a pizza. How does that sound?"

"You know me and pizza," Eleanor confessed. "Better than sex. You can order it the way you like, you're never disappointed, and the only conversation is, Thank You, Sir."

"And---" Meagan giggled. "It comes in twenty minutes."

"Even if you get the works."

They howled.

"You want me in the cabana, right?" Eleanor grabbed her bags. "Like last time?"

"Whatever. I'd just as soon you stay in the house."

"No, no, the cabana is fine. It's so private. You won't even know I'm here."

"That's where you are wrong, Elle."

"Well, I don't want Ross to think I'm going to overstay my welcome."

"It doesn't matter what he thinks. I doubt there will be a Ross and me anymore. "

"Meg, is it that serious? Shit, I had no idea! "

Meagan went to the kitchen and called in the pizza. The phone's digital readout blinked with twelve messages. Meagan ignored them. She had been gone for one day and it seemed like a month. So much had changed. She grabbed two wine glasses, some blue chips and hot salsa dip. Eleanor plopped on the couch with a bottle of Camus Select.

"So, tell, tell, tell…"

"Elle, it's over. My marriage is over." Meagan launched into the story of the Chicago fiasco, Ross and Stacy, and the telltale lingerie in the bedroom.

She grasped Meagan's hand. "Oh, honey, how awful for you!"

Meagan leaned back against the thick leather cushions. "Didn't the last five years mean anything? And Brandon---what about him?" A single tear cruised down her cheek. Eleanor wiped it away.

"Don't you cry, Meg. Don't you dare! He's so not worth it. And you're the winner here because you have Brandon. Without Ross, no Brandon. He gave you the joy of your life." Her face went serious. "Now get a tough lawyer, take him for everything he's fucking got, and throw the bum outa here."

"Wait," Meagan said. "There's more to the story, like the most incredible twenty-four hours of my life."

She explained about Atlanta and Chase Chambers---leaving out some critical details---and concluded with an account of the media assault at the airport.

"Wow," Eleanor said. "You have been a busy girl."

Meagan sat up. "Chase gave me the name of some lawyer. He's supposed to be the best. I'm going to call him…I guess."

"Are you in love with him?"

"Right now, I'm just numb. I don't know how I feel about Ross anymore."

"Not him, Meagan. I mean Chase Chambers."

Meagan was jolted upright. "Why would you say that?"

"I know you pretty well, remember?"

"God, I don't know. I just don't know anything right now? But, Elle, I'll tell you, that man is so---he just ignites something inside me. I don't have the words for it."

"Sounds like a past life connection to me."

"Maybe. But there can't be a connection in this one. He's engaged."

"Shit." Eleanor almost spit out her red wine.

"He's getting married in the fall to this wonderful girl. Plus, running for Congress. On top of all that, he's a client. Big client."

Eleanor sank her chin in her hands. "Damn, we got some complications going here, girlfriend."

"Uh-huh. So explain to me how I can possibly fit into the picture, because I just don't see it. There's no future for us. But yes, to answer your question. I do care for him. A lot. Love him? I don't even know what love is anymore."

"Wait, wait, you lost me. Go back. Chase is a client of Ross's?"

"No, mine. I'm back working with First Class. Didn't I tell you?"

"Good for you!"

"Oh, I'm so glad you're here, Elle. I want you to stay forever."

"Ha! In his house? Won't Ross love that? Shit, he'll kill us both! No. He'd hire an assassin. That's more his style. Wouldn't want to get his fucking hands dirty."

Eleanor made a disgusting face and wiped her hands on her jeans.

"It's not his house," Meagan protested. "I paid for this place with money from my grandmother's trust fund. It's mine. And mi casa e su casa."

"Thank God for Mama Neeley."

"So enough of my problems. What about you, Eleanor Marie?"

Eleanor put on a brave face. "I'm fine. Good. Great. Never better."

"I don't think so," Meagan said softly.

"You know, Meg, I still miss Nicky so much." She started to cry. "I'm sorry."

Meagan turned to wipe her friend's tears. "We're a couple of cry babies. So what?"

Eleanor started to tell her friend how she decided to get herself out of her rut. She put her condo up for lease and took the first offer. On the same day, she gave her notice. She had to get out of Cleveland and away from everything that reminded her of Nick.

"So, here I am, jobless, homeless and helpless. Financially, I'm set for a little while, at least. I just need to get my head screwed on straight. Again."

Meagan hugged her. "You came to the right place, girlfriend."

The phone rang. Meagan answered with a low "hello," afraid of the voice she might hear. *Please don't let it be Ross.*

"Meg, it's me, Marsha. Don't you check your voice mail, for God's sake?"

"Sorry, Marsh. Elle showed up today and we've been catching up."

"Well, we've got a problem. Monday I have to be at The Bar Association seminar. That means someone, like you, has to cover that planning session at Chambers'."

Meagan gagged at the thought. What if Chase is there? And how could she face Sandy? "Oh, Marsh, I don't think---"

"Hey, you're back on the team, remember? And it's your account."

"OK, OK." Meagan looked to Eleanor. "Maybe I could drag Elle along. I'm thinking of asking her to come on board, help us out. Is that alright with you?"

"With the workload we have now? The more the merrier. Ten o'clock sharp. Be there." Marsha hung up.

"Please, Elle, come with me," Meagan beseeched. "I need the moral support."

"Not to worry, Meg. I'll go. I'll protect you from that old son of a bitch, Chase Chambers." Eleanor scowled. "Even if I have to get physical with him."

"I'm trying to make you a bona fide job offer here, and I'm not talking about being a bodyguard. We want you to work with us at *First Class*---supervisor, coordinator and chief assistant cook and bottle washer."

"And I'm fucking trying to say, 'Yes, thank you, I'll take it.'"

◻

"Mommy, Mommy! Are you home?"

"In here, Brandon." Meagan braced as he came barreling into her arms. "I really, really missed you, sweetheart. And, guess what? Your Aunt Ellie is here."

"Auntie Ellie!" Brandon swerved and hurled himself at Elle.

"Brandon Hamilton, where did my little boy go? Look at you! You're too big!" Eleanor held him up.

Brandon grinned at her, nose to nose. "Your eyes are dirty, Auntie Ellie."

He wiped a little finger beneath her eye where the mascara had run with tears and showed it to her.

"Thanks, buddy. I love you, too."

Brandon turned back to his mom. "Daddy called! He's bringing me present!"

"Did you speak to him?" Meagan asked her mother, who was hugging Eleanor hello.

"No, Brandon answered the phone. They talked a bit, they did."

"He says it's a surprise, Mommy. Yippee!"

Eleanor hissed under her breath, "Maybe, we'll have a few surprises for Daddy, too."

- 29 -

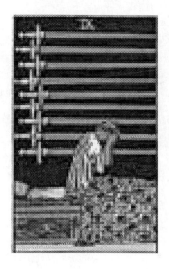

"You know, Meg, I'm your friend." Eleanor slipped off her sunglasses as they cruised down to Port Royal. "I mean, I am, right?"

"Of course you are. You're my best friend."

"Okay. Then I have to tell you what's on my mind."

"I know what you want to talk about." Meagan sighed. "And I want to hear what you have to say, I really do, but do we have to do it right now?"

The Dixie Chicks were singing "Earl Had to Die." Meagan turned up the volume, lyrics blaring about the wife determined to rid herself of a lying, cheating, abusive husband. At the last line of the chorus, both friends joined in singing.

"...And Earl had to die!"

Eleanor laughed, "That song is a sign from God."

"So you think I should kill him?"

"No! For Christ's sake, Meg. I'm not talking about killing anybody...Well, maybe that whore, Stacy."

"Oh, I love you, Elle."

"I love you, too, but I'll say this---you don't love Ross. That is so fucking over."

"I know I don't love him anymore. But I do remember loving him. I can't erase all that. And I can't erase our family...Brandon. And then there's this thing with Chase looming on the horizon. I mean, I'm just as bad as Ross. I cheated on him, too, you know."

She glanced at Eleanor, gauging her reaction.

"Sure you did, and I can't wait to hear the sordid details, one by one."

"Oh, Elle. I can't believe all this is happening. I feel like a train wreck waiting to happen."

"I'll tell you what you are going to do. You are going to call that attorney."

"Before I talk to Ross?"

"Yeah, I mean right now! You have to get your fucking ducks in a row. For example, are you absolutely sure that the house is still in your name?"

Meagan hesitated. "Well, I assume---"

"And that's a mistake, like assuming that bitch was just a secretary."

"The house must be my name. It's part of the trust." Meagan gnawed at her lip, trying to concentrate as she maneuvered through the morning traffic.

"And how much is in Granny's trust fund?"

"I'm not sure, I think---"

"And who would know? Ross? That motherfucker has control of your trust fund? Please say it's not true."

"He doesn't have control, Elle. He takes care of the paperwork, that's all. That's what he's good at---money and paperwork."

"Yeah. Too goddamn good. Meg, get on your cell this minute and call that attorney. Pull over. I'm fucking serious."

"Elle, calm down. I left the number at home. I'll call him later. Ross isn't running away to Rio today with all my money. That's crazy. He has plenty of his own. He doesn't need mine. And he has a thriving business. He's not going to walk away from that. And well, he couldn't even do it. I mean, legally he couldn't, could he?"

"Don't you get statements every month showing where the money is invested and how much?"

"Yes, but I never---Ross handles all that. So I don't have to hassle with it, he says."

Eleanor grimaced. "You're probably fucked."

"Now you are really scaring me, Elle."

Meagan put her foot on the gas and darted through an intersection as the light turned red, narrowly missing a van. A blaring horn chased her down the street.

"Meg, watch the god damn road. You're all over the place. You want me to drive?"

"No. Right now, I just want you to shut up. If you want to get there in one piece, I think we should finish this trip in absolute silence."

Eleanor didn't say another word until Meagan turned up the winding driveway to the Big House in Port Royal.

"Holy shit... Who lives here---the President?"

[]

Meagan stood at the door with Eleanor, heart pounding. She had no idea what to expect. Sandy had been quite amicable at the airport, but she'd had forty-eight hours since then to pry all the gory details out of her fiancé. Horrible thoughts flashed through her mind. Sandy could greet her with a cordial smile or a slap in the face. Caught in a tangled web of guilt and emotion, Meagan was resigned to simply face the music.

Sandy opened the door, all sunshine. "Meagan, good to see you!" She hugged her like an old friend. "No Marsha?"

Meagan returned the embrace gratefully. "Marsha was tied up this morning, Sandy. This is Eleanor Sheehan. She's going to be helping us with the events."

"Glad to hear it." Sandy extended a hand. "Welcome, Eleanor."

This is one classy lady, Meagan thought, feeling more ashamed by the minute.

Sandy led them to the library where calendars, schedules and notebooks were spread on a large oak table and wasted no time in getting down to business. She was focused and quick, running through the details on her checklist like a drill sergeant. They were finished in an hour and as they were leaving she called out toward the stairs. "Chase? Are you still up there?"

Meagan froze in her seat. Oh, no! She wondered if Sandy could hear the loud thumping in her chest.

No answer.

"Maybe he left," Sandy said. "I know he's got to be in town at noon."

Meagan sagged back in her chair, relieved until she heard the footsteps. All eyes turned to Chase

Chambers, the leading man making a confident entrance to the stage.

"Did you call me, darling?" he said, slipping a coat over his shoulders. "Oh---hello, ladies."

"Chase. This is Elle, and you know Meagan, of course."

"Yes, yes. Good to see you again." He took Meagan's limp hand and nodded to Eleanor.

"Are we having a beauty contest here or what?"

"Now don't start flirting," Sandy scolded. "These are professional women here to plan the next few months of your life, so you better behave."

"I'll try."

He smiled but Meagan didn't see, staring at her hands on the table. She couldn't bring herself to look at him.

Sandy watched Meagan with veiled eyes, then spoke up, "I need a word with my elusive fiancé before he escapes for the day. Can you excuse us for a moment?"

"You two go ahead. We'll find our way out," Meagan said, eager to escape. "I think we've covered everything, and we have another appointment downtown."

"We do?" Eleanor blurted. "Oh, that's right...we do."

Chase waved as Sandy hooked his arm. "Take care, ladies."

"Wait here a minute," Meagan said to Eleanor the moment they were gone. "I've got to use the bathroom."

Meagan stepped down the hall and closed herself in the marbled bathroom. She looked at the dejected face in the mirror and whispered, "God, Chase, please explain the rules to me because I absolutely don't know what's going on here."

While Meagan was in the bathroom, Sandy had steered Chase into the study but before she could speak, he placed his hands on her shoulders and nuzzled her neck.

"I made reservations at Bistro 21 tonight. Just us."

"No entourage?"

"I think we need some quality time alone together, don't you, to get some things straight." Chase kissed her softly.

"Starting now." She arched her back, rising to him.

◻

Meagan emerged from the bathroom and headed back up the hall, stopping at the sound of Chase's voice behind the closed study door.

"Yes, dear. I get your point. I'll be nice to Meagan. But just how nice, I wonder?"

"Chase, this isn't funny. It's not right to---"

"Hey, I think you need to talk to somebody else about that."

Meagan fled. She found Eleanor admiring the décor in the dining room and herded her toward the front door, ignoring her raves.

"This place is so freakin' unbelievable! And Chase? God, is he ever a hunk and a half," Elle said. "But you know, Meg---and I hate to say this---he seems totally attached to Sandy, like at the hip."

"Tell me about it..."

As they left the house, neither one noticed the figure watching from the shadows of the upstairs window.

Gem stepped away from the window in the master bedroom which she rarely used. It was still intact, as it had been years before, when she shared it with her husband, Mitchell. The bed was made and ready for two, but it had slept only one in twenty years. When she did spend the night in the Big House, Gem would slip into the left side of the bed, leaving Mitchell's space undisturbed, his pillows untouched.

The room was crowded with memories, walls lined with favorite photographs, cabinets stacked with mementos. There was the wedding picture, and there, the boys as toddlers. Over there was the young senator, right arm raised in solemn oath, Gem at his side, his first day in the Capitol. And there they were with President Carter, and again with Reagan.

"Our young woman in the storm has come," Gem said as she shifted the cards and placed them on the desk. "Let us see what shelter we can offer."

Her hands moved swiftly, revealing a full display, ten cards in the classic pattern.

She took careful note of the Significator first: the Five of Wands, a jumble of staffs crossed by vigorous boys in mock battle. She knew there were times that this could be a playful card, but not here. There was much deceit and harmful intentions.

Her eyes moved to the Page of Wands. Strange. His single staff put him in the game with the others, but apart, rising above. This figure was more man than boy, and he struggled here, caught between loyalties.

Other cards vied for her attention. The Three of Pentacles told of a difficult plan in process. The inverted Four of Cups warned of discontent and disappointment. To the right, the immutable Emperor stared at her from a stark throne.

And above them all, the Wheel of Fortune seemed to glow, spinning before her eyes, changing form with every revolution: a clock, a disk, a steering wheel, a yellow ball, a shadowed moon, a baby's face, a black hole, a golden coin---

"Mais non!" She cried. It was too much. The forces at play in the life of this young woman were coming from many directions at once, all so intense. This was a woman in a storm, all right, a potent storm that threatened to change her life forever.

Gem gazed out at the perfect blue sky and the sun-dappled gardens where the day lilies and irises posed, still as a painting, unmoved by a whisper of wind. But she knew. The storm fronts were converging just beyond the horizon, gathering momentum.

"Toute pour une raison," she said. *Everything for a reason.* She was part of this now. With the gift came the obligation. This young woman had come into her life and she must heed the call. She would not be deterred, not even by the ominous message delivered by the last card in the set before her.

The King of Pentacles reversed. The simple meaning was bad enough: perversion, malice and greed added to the already turbulent mix. The monarch was surrounded by the trappings of his kingdom, opulently attired, clutching symbols of wealth and power, but still unsatisfied, wanting more. But there was something else, an impression of the character portrayed that she had never seen with such clarity before.

The King of Pentacles was a very handsome man.

- 31 -

From his penthouse office, bright and early Monday morning, Ross surveyed the Chicago skyline, cup of steaming black coffee in hand. It was a magnificent view, from the Sears Tower to the south, across the mighty assemblage of high rises along the boulevard to the vast expanse of dark blue water stretching east to the horizon. It usually gave him a sense of power and superiority. An affirmation that he was in control and all was well in the world.

But not today.

He was tense and restless, sensing danger lurking like the billowing gray clouds creeping over the lake. Ross had a sixth sense and like a cunning animal it was pulsating now, warning him to beware.

Sheldon Smith stood at the door, a soldier waiting for a command. Ross spoke with his back to him.

"Do you remember Diane?"

"The woman in Atlanta?"

"Yes. Gone but not forgotten, I'm afraid."

"Sir?"

"Her accountant has raised his ugly head. Edelman. I met him once. A weak little man. He has Diane's financial records, tax returns, bank statements, all of it."

"Is that a problem?"

"Not by itself, no. But if someone had those and could decipher the records of my transactions with Dianes —that could be…embarrassing."

"You have always covered your tracks."

"Covered, yes, but not erased. It would take someone very good to find them, and even then it wouldn't be easy to put it all together. But it could be done."

"Sometimes it is better to let sleeping dogs lie."

Ross paced at the window, hands clasped behind his back.

"I have been informed that Edelman met with Chambers last week in Atlanta. Behind closed doors."

Smith waited, silent. Orders were coming. Ross picked up an index card from his desk and held it out.

"Edelman's not just awake; he's barking. You know what to do with a barking dog, Sheldon?"

The man shrugged. "Put him to sleep."

32

Eleanor waited in the lobby of Stein, Rashoff & Bernstein, while Meagan met with the attorney Chase had recommended. Meagan's nerves were quickly eased by the attorney's gentle manner.

"Now, Mizz Hamilton, y'all just relax, you hear? Sitting down with a lawyer is worse than going to the dentist for most folks nowadays. Talking about all kinds of personal stuff, some of it mighty painful--- nothing easy about it. But I want y'all to know that what we discuss here is gonna stay right here in this room. You have my word, and folks around here'll tell you that's worth something, even for a scruffy old lawyer like myself. So, what say I get you a nice cup of tea and let's get started?"

Arnold Bernstein seemed more like an old, coun-try doctor than a tough divorce lawyer, kind and patient, listening carefully as she told her story, taking occasional longhand notes with an old-school fountain pen. Before the session ended, Meagan was certain he was the right lawyer for her. She offered to pay a retainer on the spot.

"No need for that, ma'm," Bernstein said. "Y'all need some time to think here, and we need some time to do our homework. We're gonna check on your accounts an' all---get the lay of the land to make sure there's nothing improper going on."

"Oh, I don't think Ross would do that, would he?"

"I doubt it. I truly do. But it's better to be safe than sorry."

With the residual of her grandmother's trust, stocks and investments, Meagan's assets exceeded seventeen million dollars. She was comforted by Bernstein's interest in making certain they were secure. After completing a lengthy checklist, the attorney sat down next to Meagan.

"Now, Mizz Hamilton, it's going to be a few days until we get up to speed with all this. In the meantime, there are a few things we're gonna need y'all to do."

"All right."

"First off, I want you to think long and hard about this."

"Mr. Bernstein, I came here because---"

He held up his hand, "I know how you must be feeling right now, but I'm here to tell you that I've seen this a thousand times, and it's always hard. The end of a marriage is a lamentable occasion. There's no getting around it. Bonds are broken. Lives disrupted. I tell all my clients, and I'll tell you---if there is any way on God's green earth you can save your marriage, then you oughta think about doing just that."

"I'm afraid that can't be done."

"Well now, that may rightly be so. And if it is, so be it. But you're angry right now, all out of sorts. All I'm saying is, you want to think this through, cool and calm, and make sure, absolutely sure, that it's the right course. Will you do that for me?"

"Yes. Yes, I will."

He patted her shoulder. "Good. That's fine, then. And one more thing."

"Yes?"

"I told you that everything we know and everything we do here will be kept completely confidential. While you're thinking and we're getting to work, I want you to know how important it is that you do the same."

"I don't know what you mean."

"I mean that this is no time to antagonize your husband. If he gets a whiff, if he finds out you've taken the first steps down this path, he might well take some of his own, and that could be very detrimental."

"You don't want me to tell him that I've talked to an attorney?"

"Absolutely not. Don't tell anyone else, either. If you decide to proceed, then he will be duly informed in a timely manner. Until then---well, I believe it was Lao Tzu who said 'that it is most unwise to announce your battle plans to the enemy'."

"I understand. I won't say a word."

By the time she emerged from his office, Meagan was spent. Eleanor took one look at her, wrapped an arm around her shoulder and took the car keys from her hand.

"C'mon, girl. Let's go. And leave the driving to me."

Meagan slept all the way home.

33

"It's worth the price."

Stacy was talking about the Prada purse she bought on the day trip to New York, but she might as well have been talking about Ross. He could be a difficult and diabolical man, but here they were, winging their way back from Manhattan on a Gulfstream 5, a silver bullet in the sky with a veteran pilot at the helm and a dutiful flight attendant at their beck and call. Only two passengers, Stacy and Ross. Only one class, and that was luxury class.

The bankers in New York had been so obsequious, fawning over Ross. It really was fun to watch, but even better to be part of, as his second in command.

Like the purse, Ross came with a high price tag, taking a toll on her psyche and her soul, but he was worth it. Oh yes, a bargain at the price. She glanced at him, unaware of her thoughts, more important matters to attend to, all caught up in himself as usual.

Ross was hunched over the white table, studying the Tarot cards arranged in a cross and triangle before him. He had been at it for more than hour, trying to make sense of the patterns and correlations, but it just wasn't coming together.

Stacy had been asleep, curled up on the white leather couch which was part of the Gulfstream's luxurious furnishings. The only sound was the throb of the engines as the pilot throttled back. They would soon be landing at Midway in Chicago.

They were running out of time.

That's it, he thought---running out of time. That's what was evident in the three-card triangle. But he knew that. He had been in end-game mode for weeks, making all the moves to set things up for the grand finale. Nothing to worry about in that area.

Or was there? Was this a warning that the schedule he had so carefully planned was not fast enough? Perhaps he could accelerate it? He would have to think that over.

Back to the signature card at the bottom of the cross, the one that had plagued him so much.

The High Priestess.

"Who is the High Priestess?" he said aloud. He stood up, eyes still on the card. "A very powerful woman. Wired. Friends in high places. Likes to get involved. A meddler. And she's meddling with me? Who does she---?

"Meagan? No---not Meagan. Older, much older. And wiser. Thinks she's on a higher plane. Maybe Tan? Is she playing me? No. Why would she? Who, then?"

He paced away and back again. "Who the fuck is the High Priestess?"

Stacy stirred on the couch. "What? What's the matter?"

"I'm sorry," he said, sarcasm oozing. "Did I wake you from your beauty sleep, princess?"

She sat up and looked at the table. "Still with the cards?"

"They're being difficult today."

"Maybe you're trying too hard, seeing things that aren't there."

"More likely, I'm not seeing things that are. You see that?" He pointed. "The High Priestess, opposing me, defying me! Now who do you suppose that is, Stacy?"

He looked down at her. "Is it you?"

His tone disturbed her, but she didn't show it.

"I hardly think so. I'm on your side, remember?"

"Of course you are."

Stacy looked out the window. "Are we landing soon?"

"In about five minutes."

Stacy hurried back to the rear of the plane and slipped into the lavatory. Out of Ross's line of vision, she opened her new purse with a snap and removed the disk like it was hot to the touch. She stepped across the aisle to the open closet, empty except for Ross's suit coat and briefcase, stooped to slide the disk into the middle of a folder of papers and walked briskly back to her seat. It was less than a minute, start to finish.

Ross never looked up from the cards.

"What were you doing in the closet?"

It was a jolt, but she didn't flinch.

"I was looking for my other shoes. It's a long walk through the airport and I'd rather not wear these heels."

"And?"

"Not there. They must be in the suitcase."

"What a shame. Maybe we can get one of those airport golf carts they have for handicapped people."

"I'll make it in these."

"I hate to see you suffer."

"I'll be fine."

Ross turned back to the cards and resumed his staring contest with the High Priestess. She didn't blink. He snapped down another card.

The Hanged Man.

Stacy was jarred by the disconcerting image of the figure dangling from the cross, his rigid body inverted at odd angles, but the card seemed to soothe Ross and brighten his mood.

"I don't get it," Stacy said.

"Oh, I do." Ross was smug. "It means good news is coming, problems are resolved and everything works out fine."

"Hm. It doesn't look that good."

"Well, not for everyone."

34

David Edelman was at the end of his tether.

September was second only to early April at Edelman & Associates, as well-heeled clients lined up for his highly regarded advice on third quarter tax returns and last-chance adjustments before year's end. Edelman was looking forward to the morning after when he would depart on his annual vacation to Puerto Vallarta and not look at a tax form for two glorious weeks. He double-checked the numbers on his spreadsheet, put his distinctive check mark on the bottom of the page and tossed it in the stack. Two more to do, and it was already five-thirty. He had just started on the next folder when his receptionist's voice came over the intercom.

"Mr. Edelman?"

"Yes, Helen?"

"I just wanted to remind you. I'm leaving now---
Jennifer's recital at school."

"That's fine."

"Do you want me to lock up? No one else is here."

"No, that's all right. I'll take care of it. Good night,
Helen."

She slipped the cover over her console, gathered
her purse and departed. As she disappeared into the
elevator, a hulking figure emerged from the men's
room down the hall. His rubber-soled shoes didn't
make a sound as he approached the door marked
"Edelman & Associates" and he turned the knob. It
was unlocked. Sheldon Smith walked in.

Edelman was annoyed to see a stranger at his
office door. "Can I help you?"

"I am looking for Mr. Edelman?"

"That would be me, but the office is closed now
and I really don't have time to---"

"This will only take a minute."

"Look, I don't want to be rude, but I don't even
have a minute to---"

He saw the gun, an automatic with a long barrel.
Edelman didn't know anything about guns, didn't
recognize that it was a silencer extending the barrel
length by half.

"We don't keep any money here. I---I've got a
wallet, some credit cards."

"I do not want your money. I want you to make a
phone call. If you do it right, I will be gone and you can
forget I was here. If you make a mistake, just one little
mistake--"

He looked at the gun in his hand then placed a
folded sheet of paper on the desk.

"Read it. That is your script. It must sound right. Authentic."

Edelman picked up the paper and read the brief paragraph. His heart raced.

"Hamilton sent you."

"Do not think too much, Mister Edelman. It is not good for you." He waved the gun at the paper. "The number is at the bottom. You can dial it any time you are ready."

Edelman thought of his wife, and how she looked sitting by the pool just beyond the terrace door in Puerta Vallarta. Every suite in the hotel had its own private pool. That's what she loved. That's why they returned every year. Same hotel. Same room. It was the only time, the only place in the world she would traipse around, posing for him in her sexy little outfits, or sometimes no outfit at all. God, he loved her. She was his life.

He set the paper down and pushed it away.

"You're going to kill me if I make that phone call."

"No. But I will kill you if you do not." Smith nudged the paper back. "Once you make the call, I do not have to kill you. Why should I? You are on the record. You can say anything you want, but it is your word against yourself. No one will know what to believe. Doubt, confusion---that is good enough."

Edelman wouldn't look at the paper or the gun, holding his stare on Smith's poker face.

Smith looked at his watch.

"I will leave here in two minutes, one way or the other. It does not matter to me. You make the choice."

35

He entered the Northern Trust Bank Building on Park Shore in downtown Naples, and took the elevator to the third floor. He knocked on the door marked "ROSSCO." That was Mac's little joke. The FBI investigation was so secret that the code name could use a transparent acronym for the target suspect, list it in bold letters on the office door and no one would be the wiser. A tiny video cam stared down at him from the corner of the doorjamb. A buzzer released the lock and he stepped inside.

Mac, Curtis, Harry Black and two agents he had never met were gathered at the small conference room table, grim faces all around. Mac's greeting didn't do anything to lighten the mood.

"We're fucked."

"What happened?"

Curtis drew a photo from the pile on the table and held it out. "Your friend put a bullet in his head last night."

He looked at the gruesome photograph. It was David Edelman, head down in a crimson pillow of blood-soaked papers on his desk, gun clutched in his right hand.

"Holy Christ."

"It gets worse," said Mac, picking up the small cassette player in the center of the table and placing it in front of him. "He left a farewell message before he departed for the next life." He pushed the button. The voice was uneven but clearly Edelman's.

"This is for Mr. Chase Chambers. I---I'm sorry I deceived you, but the, uh, the information I gave you---that---that was---that wasn't right. Ross Hamilton didn't---he didn't do anything wrong as far as Diane McAlister and the others...I---uh---it was me. I needed the money. Hamilton is innocent...I'm sorry. I didn't mean to---I'm so sorry."

"I don't buy it," he said. "The whole thing stinks."

"Agreed," said Mac. "But these are the guy's last words---final declaration of a dying man. That's hard to get past."

"I'm telling you, it's bogus. Did you have your own CSI guys there or did the locals handle it?"

"What do you think---I'm a rookie?" asked Mac. "Our people were there for three hours. Went over everything. Took pictures, prints---the whole shebang."

"And?"

"No sign of a struggle, no forced entry, no other marks on the body, nothing. Powder burns, angle of entry---everything checks out. Only Edelman's prints on the gun. I'm not saying he wasn't set up, but if that's the way it went down, whoever popped him is a real pro."

"Somebody got to him. Hamilton."

"Yeah, maybe," Mac replied. "But which one?"

Chambers glared at him. "What the hell does that mean?"

"It means that Ross Hamilton was in Chicago all week," Curtis said. "But Mrs. Hamilton was in Atlanta, at that fundraiser---with you. She could have seen Edelman talking to you. Probably did. She could have dropped a dime on him, tipped her husband. And she was in town---she could have gone to Edelman's office herself."

"Meagan? Are you joking?"

Mac grumbled in exasperation. "Oh, so it's Meagan now."

"We're trying to look at all the logical possibilities," Curtis justified.

"And you think Meagan's a murderer?" He leaned over the desk. "That's logical?"

"I don't think it was very logical for you to have been there with her." Mac stood up. "I don't know if she was involved, but I do know that Edelman's dead. The evidence we got from him is worthless now, and we're back to square one on this whole goddamn thing."

36

"Oh, you're killing me."

Meagan was doubled over in the booth at Ben & Jerry's.

"No, I'm serious," Eleanor continued like a stand-up comic. "They got the greatest thing going, this god awful-looking hunk of cheese that smells like absolute shit---I mean, that's what it smells like---and they're getting seventeen bucks a pound for it."

Meagan couldn't stop laughing.

"And the worse it smells, the more it costs. And then---how about this for balls? They take this shit and they roll it in cigarette ashes, and they charge you even more."

"Stop!" Meagan sputtered. "It's not cigarette ashes."

"Oh, okay. From a fireplace then. What difference does it make? Ashes are ashes. You get shit rolled in ashes and you're paying like it's filet mignon. That's a nice racket."

"Aunt Ellie said a bad word," Brandon said to his mother.

"Oops...sorry 'bout that, Bran. Better eat your ice cream, though, before it melts," Elle pointed out, trying to distract him from listening to their conversation.

"Oh, you are something, Elle!" Meagan wiped her eyes. "But you have it all wrong, and you've got to learn this stuff if you want to be a First Class caterer. That cheese at Minnillo's is the finest you can get anywhere in the world. And that ash coating is a special process. It braces the flavor, adds a hint of texture."

"Whatever you say. I'll learn it, but I'm not buying it. You'll never catch me putting that crap in my mouth. I'll take Velveeta any day."

They had spent two days on a catering crash course for Eleanor, with Professor Meagan as head of the class, filling the curriculum with field trips. They spent an hour at Pier 19, lectured by Meagan's pal Tony on the finer points of pescatorial preparation as they trudged past display booths stacked with grouper, red snapper and yellowtail. Eleanor, a fast learner, took it all in without cracking a joke.

Brandon held his nose the whole time. "Can we go? The fish are looking at me funny."

They spent the afternoon at the Sixth Street Market, wandering through the cornucopia of fresh produce, fine meats and delectable pastries. They intended to go to dinner after, but they were all so stuffed with tasty samples of everything from stuffed mangoes to death-by-chocolate torts, they could barely drag themselves home for a long nap to recover.

◻

The next afternoon, when Brandon was busy at the zoo with his grandparents, Meagan introduced Eleanor to her secret catering weapon---the affinage at Minnillo's. Hardly bigger than a closet, it was the only one in Florida. Specially constructed and cooled to exactly 48 degrees, the affinage provided just the right environment for the magnificent cheeses from France, Belgium and Italy that were aged to perfection and offered to select customers, like First Class.

Eleanor was duly impressed, but didn't stop her ranting.

When the laughs died down, Meagan found herself completely exhausted. Again today. It happened yesterday, and the day before. She couldn't keep her eyes open. She handed the keys to Eleanor and curled up in the passenger seat for the trip home.

"I should get one of those peaked caps," Eleanor said as they merged into highway traffic. "I'm a goddamn chauffeur now."

Meagan didn't hear a word, already fast asleep.

◻

Eleanor saw the black Mercedes parked in the driveway before Meagan woke up. Ross was back. She pulled in and sat there for a few minutes before shaking her friend by the shoulder. Meagan opened her eyes.

"Are we there yet?"

"Yes, we are."

"Thanks for driving." She yawned. "I don't know what got into me. I was so tired."

"It's called stress-related fatigue syndrome, I think." Eleanor turned off the engine. "Pills might help."

"Right, that's all I need."

"Either that or a good, stiff drink. You better brace yourself. It appears that Mr. High-and-Mighty is in residence."

Meagan sat up and looked out the window. "Ooh." She said as she slid back into her seat.

"Maybe we could leave and come back tomorrow?" Eleanor offered.

"I wish. But that just puts off the inevitable."

"Hey, I'm all for putting off the inevitable. Why not?"

"I've got to face him, Elle. Might as well get it over with. At least you're here with me. Safety in numbers. Like Girl Scouts, remember?"

"All I remember is I got thrown out of Girl Scouts for kissing Boy Scouts."

Brandon burst out of the front door, running to the car. "Mommy, Mommy! Daddy's home! And he brought presents!" He held up a bright yellow vinyl doll. "Look, look! It's SpongeBob SquarePants! Cool, huh?"

Meagan crouched to admire his prize. "Wow. Very cool, Bran."

"Daddy has more presents for me, inna beefcase!"

A shadow fell over them. Meagan looked up to meet the stern eyes of her husband.

"Meagan, what is going on here?" he started right in. "I come home to find my son home alone."

"Oh, Ross. My mother has been watching him. "

"Katherine is not *his* mother. Then I learn that my missing wife is out working---just as she promised not to do---working as hired help."

"I am not hired help, Ross, I am---"

"And then, to top everything off, there's a stack of luggage in my home, and, low and behold, it belongs to a Mrs. Eleanor Sheehan."

He glared over at Eleanor in the car. She refused to acknowledge him, looking straight ahead, hiding behind dark sunglasses.

"Have you lost your mind?"

Meagan set her son down. "Go on inside, Bran. We'll be there in a minute."

As Brandon raced up the steps, yellow doll in tow, Ross grabbed Meagan's arm. "Come with me, my dear. We need to have a little talk."

Ross hustled her toward the house. Stumbling to keep pace, Meagan mouthed, "I'm okay" to Eleanor, but she didn't look too convincing. Eleanor sat there for a minute, unsure of what to do, then followed them in.

She stopped in the hallway. Meagan and Ross were nowhere to be seen, but there was Brandon sitting on the stairs, his father's briefcase in his lap, the vinyl doll sitting against the wall next to him.

"I got presents, Auntie Ellie. I got this doll, and Daddy said two presents."

He fished through the briefcase, pulled out some papers and shoved them back in. He probed another pocket and came up with the shiny disk that Stacy had slipped back into Ross's briefcase on the plane. His eyes brightened.

"Bet it's a movie! A new one for me!"

"That's great, Bran." Eleanor was distracted by the loud voices upstairs.

It sounded like a heated argument, but not out of control. No screams, no thuds or crashes. Yet.

"Mommy and Daddy are fighting," Brandon said, more to the doll than to Eleanor.

"Don't worry, Bran." She stroked his blonde head. "It's OK."

"Listen. Daddy is yelling at Mommy."

Elle turned the doll's face her way. "Hey, isn't that Bob something?"

"Yeah. SpongeBob."

"Is he a friend of Nemos?"

"No, silly. He's not."

"Oh, that's right."

⧠

In the bedroom upstairs, Ross whipped Meagan around, fingers tight on her arm. She winced and pulled away.

"I guess you really put me in my place, huh, Ross? Are you going to hit me now?"

"The woman has a temper. Will wonders never cease?" Ross looked at her with disdain. "Well, listen closely, *my dear*, because I am not going to repeat myself."

I can't believe I married this man.

"First, there is no way that you are going to get back into that First Class crap. I won't allow it! My wife is not catering for other people. Your job is to cater to me!"

She glared at him.

"Second, there's Eleanor---"

Meagan finally spoke. "Elle is my friend."

"She's not mine. I want her out of here."

"No."

He surged at her. "What did you say?"

Meagan stood her ground. "I said no. You're being totally unreasonable."

Ross eyed Meagan, daring her to continue arguing. Meagan only stared as if she were seeing her husband of five years for the first time.

Ross tilted his head. A new Meagan, bold and defiant? Interesting. Put some steel behind that perky optimism. That would make her a worthy adversary, like a---

The thought struck him. High Priestess? Sweet little Meagan? Was it possible? It did not seem likely, but it gave him pause. He would have to find out, give her some rope. He switched tactics.

"I know why you're upset Meagan," he said calmly. "And I want you to know, it's not what you think."

Meagan didn't budge.

"Just to set the record straight, I let Stacy and a friend of hers---a male friend, I believe---use the penthouse Thursday night. I had to go to New York to meet with the bankers on the Tannex deal. The bank dropped the ball; the whole thing was coming apart." He snorted in contempt. "They are so incompetent. I had to sit there for six hours, walk them through it, get them back on track. I stayed at the Waldorf. Came back Friday morning. I've got the receipt downstairs if I need to prove my case to the jury."

It was a good mix of fact and fiction, just enough to blur the lines. Meagan faltered. He sounded sincere, so real---so like the old Ross.

"Meagan, I'm sorry about any misunderstandings. I love you. You know that. And I'm sorry I've been---the pressure has been brutal lately. The thing is---like right now, I just got the word. I have to go to L.A. Today. Last dance with Mrs. Tan." He was taking clothes from the dresser as he spoke, laying them neatly in his overnight bag. "I'll be gone a few days." He zipped the bag. "Elleanor can stay and keep you company."

She blinked in surprise. Quite a concession.

"And we can discuss everything when I get back."

"All right," she said, relaxing her guard.

He hoisted the carry-on to his shoulder. "Oh, and Meagan---have you seen a computer disc around here, no label? I may have left it in the house somewhere."

"No, haven't seen it...nothing like that, but I'll look for it."

He looked at her squarely. "Yes, do. That would be very helpful."

He kissed her lightly on the cheek. She smelled good, clean and fresh. And something else, something---he couldn't quite say.

"Now you take care, Meagan," he said. "We'll work all this out. Everything is going to be fine." He gave her a reassuring hug. "Just fine."

A minute later he was gone.

Meagan flopped on the bed, her head whirling and her life spinning out of control.

The tears came again, and this time she let them flow unchecked.

37

It seemed right for Gem to have a cat around, but not this one. Gem was beautiful, serene and close to regal in her manner. The cat was beautiful, too, a gray Persian with blue marble eyes, but she was very big for a Persian and walked like an alley cat, all muscle and swagger. And she acted like a guard dog around Gem, growling at anyone who dared approach her mistress. Gem named her for Ursa, the bear in mythology and in the heavens. This Ursa was her bearcat. Ursa's eyes glistened like sapphires in the candlelight, watching Gem with her cards.

The Eight of Wands. A wild card, full of action and danger, difficult to decipher, easy to misinterpret. The simplicity of the card enhanced its power: a squadron of staffs hurtles through air, aimed at an unknown target. Nothing else to enhance or elucidate:

no person or symbol; nothing in the sky above, only a tranquil countryside below.

"Sacre, what now?"

It could be that many of those close to her were destined to be involved in a single event. Or perhaps the traditional interpretation applied: an imminent change of location, for herself or others. But she was drawn to the crème-de-la-crème meaning: put all intuitive powers on high alert. Gem accepted the mandate to persevere.

She turned another. The Knight of Cups.

"My Cameron."

In so many family readings, Cameron shone forth as the Knight of Cups, handsome and strong, riding a powerful steed that bowed to his commanding grip. His winged helmet attested to many travels and battles won. He held his golden cup aloft, looking to the future, seeking the ultimate conquest. Here was another reminder that he must be alive. She knew, had never doubted, not even when the officers came to her home to tell her they had stopped the search and given up hope. *We're so sorry, Mrs. Chambers.* They said they had information from a most reliable source.

She had reliable sources of her own and they assured her the government was wrong this time. She returned to her cards.

Three of Cups, reversed. Three lovely maidens toast one another in a bountiful world. Inverted, the message was not joy, but consternation, turmoil and danger.

"Look out, girls." Gem stroked the cat pensively. "All is upside down."

On an impulse, she slid three cards off to the side and flipped them together. It was not her way, but she felt compelled to do it. When she saw the cards, she understood.

Two of Pentacles. A rendezvous does not go well. An angry stranger brings a swift solution to a problem for one, at great cost to others.

Ace of Wands. A new endeavor leads to unanticipated consequences.

Ten of Swords. Many complications increase the chance for catastrophic results.

It was a separate set, unrelated to the reading, like a bulletin from beyond. She thought of the words they use for breaking news on television: "We interrupt this program to bring you an urgent message ..." This message was instantly clear to Gem.

She picked up the phone and dialed the special number. A minute later, she was talking to Patrick Curran at VICAP.

"Yes, Gem?" Patrick Curran was on the line at VICAP.

"The one we spoke of---the handsome man?"

"Yes, I remember. We've been on it. Nothing yet."

"He has killed again."

Currant picked up his pen and pulled a legal pad closer.

"What else can you tell me?"

"A man his time. He killed a man. An innocent man."

"Breaking the pattern? Is he losing it?"

"Not at all. Still part of a plan, a grand plan. He is still in control."

"Makes no sense."

"It makes sense because this one is not from the rage. It's because of the money."

"I get it. Listen, Gem, I'm going to go with this, double up on it, but I could use a little more direction? Is there anything about where, when, names, descriptions, details---any details? Anything like that?"

"Water. Fast and deep. Yellow roses. One is two. Two are one. "

Curran frowned. "Meaning?"

Gem was quiet. She did not know.

"Listen, Gem, you know how much I value your—your services, all that you've done. But this, I can't put it together. Water, yellow roses, two, one, one, two? The only thing I can think of is the song, you know, 'Yellow Rose of Texas.' Does that ring a bell? Is this guy in Texas?"

"No. Not Texas. They're real."

"What?"

"The yellow roses. They don't mean something else. They are right there. I think they will be there when you find him."

"All right. That's something, anyhow."

"More will come, but there is much darkness now, only slivers of light and many more choices to be made on both sides, good and bad."

"Good. More will come. That's good. And the yellow roses are real. I can work with that. The yellow roses are real."

38

Meagan, Eleanor, and Marsha met for lunch at Silver Spoon at the Waterside Shops. In season, there was always a waiting list for the great food at unpretentious prices. They sat outside on benches in the shade waiting for a table.

"I'm starved," Eleanor announced.

"Ask me if I'm surprised," Meagan chuckled.

"Can we get down to business while we wait?" Marsha didn't wait for an answer. She opened her leather folder and started ticking off open items on her agenda for the "Men's Night" gathering, now only four days away. Her biggest concern was the oversized crowd. The "Hold 'Em Poker Tournament" that Eleanor came up with was a clever enticement that had pushed responses to more than twice the original estimate. That would be good for the campaign coffers, and double the amount of work for First Class. Thankfully, Eleanor had an answer for Marsha's every concern. This was Eleanor's first shot at handling an event from start to finish, and she was running with it. Meagan was happy to see her getting excited about something again.

"Hey, Meg? You going to be there Saturday night, right?" Eleanor asked.

"What did I tell you? I wouldn't miss your First Class debut for the world." It took some effort for Meagan to sound cheerful about it. She was wary of being at the Chambers and still felt very awkward around Sandy. "But I don't think you need me for anything, Elle. You have all the bases covered."

"And pretty well at that," added Marsha. "I'm impressed. Meagan said you were good, Elle, but I had no idea how good! Especially with this men's thing."

"That's the key word. Men. That's my specialty."

"Always was, huh?" Meagan winked.

Elle gave her an elbow. "You should have taken better notes."

Marsha laughed. Those two---what a kick! "Now remember, you have to go back to Chambers', drop off the stuff, go over the checklist with Sandy and get her to sign off. That way, no surprises and nothing falls through the cracks. "

"Is she always this bossy?" asked Eleanor.

"Get used to it," Meagan said. "I've tried to tell her to get professional help for her obsessive-compulsive behavior, but no."

Marsha pointed at the menu. "Here's the last order I'm giving today, Elle. Order the spinach and goat cheese pizza. It's to die for."

"Yes, boss."

The PA system squawked, "Mills. Table for three."

"That's us. Let's go."

As Meagan rose, a flicker of light caught her eye. She focused on the flash of the sun reflecting off mirrored sunglasses in time to see a husky man slip into the shadows of the entrance to the Walgreen's across the street.

It looked like Sheldon Smith, Ross's chauffeur-assistant-factotum from Chicago. She felt a chill at the thought. There was something about the enigmatic Mr. Smith that made her uneasy. He had never said anything offensive but she was never comfortable with him around. Seeing him in Naples was downright scary. He never came here. Why would he be here now?

She tried to shake it off. Wasn't him. Looked like him, but it wasn't him. Couldn't be. No way.

As they walked to their table, Meagan giggled. Now, along with the nausea, she was having little bouts of paranoia. Swell.

"What's so funny?" Elle asked.

"Nothing," said Meagan. "Nothing at all."

- 39 -

"I will kill her."

Ross Hamilton said to Sheldon on the phone. Stacy could see he was seething.

"She got herself a lawyer, eh? What's his name?"

Ross scribbled on a note pad and tore off the sheet.

"… Bernstein … No. I've heard of the firm but I've never met the man."

Stacy tried to get his attention but he ignored her.

"I want to you get in there, see what he has. Whatever documents she gave him, whatever he got on his own, you get them. I want them all. And see if he has that fucking CD. Maybe she got her hands on it somehow and gave it to him. I need that disc."

"I cannot do that."

"What?"

"It cannot be done."

"Sheldon. Do I have to remind you that---"

"It is only the truth. With the lawyers, you cannot get the documents back. They lock them. Safes. Security. And they make copies, many copies, of everything."

Ross stewed for a minute. Sheldon waited.

"All right. Fine. Maybe we can't get to him. But we can get to her, and if he starts causing trouble, that's what we'll have to do."

"That is not a problem. Do you want me to---"

"No. Not yet. You stay down there. Stay on her. I want to know every move she makes. And if she gets out of line---"

"I will take care of it."

"No, don't. If our little Meagan needs, uh, correction, I'll come down there and take care of that myself."

Stacy caught his eye, pointed at the door. Ross nodded.

"I've got to take this meeting. Keep me posted."

He clicked off and turned his attention to Stacy.

"Chase Chambers is here," she announced, breathless.

"Well. Let's not keep the candidate waiting."

At first, it was polite small talk. Candidate Chambers spoke in a disarming tone, but his mind was elsewhere, trying to absorb every nuance of the office and the man.

Ross was doing the same. What did Chase Chambers want from him? What did he have to offer? And why would he come all the way to Chicago for a meeting?

Ross made the first surprise move. "I understand you met Meagan?"

It caught him off guard.

"Did I? Oh, Mrs. Hamilton, yes. At the fund-raiser."

"She said you were very gracious. I'd say she was very impressed with you---as a candidate."

"Please tell her that's very kind. It was nice of her to be there. "

He should have stopped there, but he couldn't help himself.

"She's a beautiful woman, your wife."

Ross blinked. "Well, thank you. You really think so?"

"Yes. Yes, I do. You're a lucky man."

He decided there was no future in further conversation about Meagan.

"Ross, I have to get on a plane back to Naples---can't get many votes in Chicago---but I wanted to meet with you, face to face, about this campaign project of ours."

Ross leaned back and folded his hands as Chase continued.

"People we talked to---down in Florida, in Washington at the DNC---they all put your name on a short list. You come highly recommended."

"I'm honored."

"And frankly, I share that opinion. But what do I know, I'm just the candidate."

Ross smiled. Funny.

"We call it the Double Project. Very simple, really. Can I give you a few figures?"

"Please do."

"We have about three million in the bank, more or less, and I need at least five by October, when they roll out the media blitz. Six would be better."

"TV's expensive, isn't it?"

"Ridiculous, but we need to go wall-to-wall there at the end. That's key."

"And you want me to help raise the money?"

"Not exactly. We've gotten about as much as we can from likely donors."

"Can't your family make up the difference?"

"You've heard the saying, 'Any lawyer who defends himself has a fool for a client?' Well, that goes for politics, too. Anyone who pays for his own campaign has a fool for a candidate."

"I would say that's wise. Then what can you do?"

"I was hoping you could answer that question."

"Me? How so?"

"They tell me you are a very savvy investment broker. The best. Isn't there some way we could put money into some short-term fund and double up by October?"

"I don't know, maybe. A hedge fund or a hot IPO, if you had an inside track. It's possible, but risky. And tell me---is it legal to use campaign funds for investments?"

"No."

Ross studied him. This was getting interesting.

"That makes it a much bigger risk, and I'm not sure it's one you want to take."

"This is politics, Ross. No-holds-barred. Down and dirty. I'll do what I have to do. I just don't want to get caught."

"It's awfully hard to move that kind of money without leaving a trail."

Ross was circling the bait. Now if he could just get the hook in his mouth.

"I was hoping you might know of a way to do that, even in this oppressed economy."

"Oh?" Ross thought a minute. "I might, but you would still need serious front money from someplace else, not the campaign. Can you get that?"

"How much?"

"A million would do the trick."

"That could be done, on a short term basis. You use that for the investments, and then we yank it back and flip the profits to the campaign. Is that how it works?"

Ross's eyes narrowed. This Chambers was a player.

"Something like that."

"Good. And make no mistake, Ross. If you can get this done, the entire Chambers family account is yours from here on out."

"I would welcome that opportunity."

"And it won't hurt to have someone in Washington, watching your back."

"Won't hurt a bit."

Time for the close.

"We have a deal then?"

Ross shook hands hard, eye-to-eye.

There was a wire, a tiny microphone embedded in the American flag lapel pin, but it wouldn't do much good if Ross didn't say something---anything---to confirm.

"I just need one more thing, Ross."

"Name it."

"I need some kind of guarantee that you'll get us the money, and that the deal never leaves this room. I don't ever want to read about it in the papers."

"I don't know what kind of guarantee I can give you, Chase. After all, we're breaking the law here, and I don't think you want that on a piece of paper."

"Your word is good enough for me."

Ross relaxed. That was easy.

"You have my word, my friend."

My friend. That was more than enough, he thought. It was awfully nice of Ross Hamilton to admit he was breaking the law, in so many words. It should play very well in court.

- 40 -

THE HIGH PRIESTESS

"Mizz Hamilton?"

"Yes?"

"Arnold Bernstein, I apologize, ma'm. I don't like to call folks at home late in the day. I hope I'm not a nuisance."

"Of course not."

Brandon was sprawled on the family room floor, listening to music on his iPod, kicking his spindly legs to the beat, playing with his Transformers.

"I'll get right to it then. My people tell me you are no longer the owner of record of your home in Naples. The county recorder's office confirms the title was quitclaimed over to your husband last year. Did you sign your home over to him?"

"I didn't sign anything like that. Why would I?"

"Are you sure?"

"Positive."

"That means someone forged your signature on the quitclaim deed. It was notarized and witnessed by one Stacy Lynn Sullivan. Do you know her?"

Meagan felt light-headed. She swayed and bumped the counter. A stack of spoons clattered to the floor. Brandon came running out to the kitchen to see what happened.

"Mizz Hamilton? You still there?"

"Yes...sorry. Ahmm, I know her all right. She's my husband's, uh...assistant."

"Mommy made a mess," Brandon decided, hands on hips.

Bernstein continued with the alarming litany. "It also appears that your trust is dwindling. Why are you withdrawing funds every week?"

"But I'm not. I haven't touched the trust account."

"I think it would behoove us to freeze those accounts," he said. "Immediately."

"You're scaring me, Mr. Bernstein."

"I hate to be the bad news bear, ma'm," the lawyer said. "But y'all are being handled, Mizz Hamilton, and I'm not goin' to just sit here and let that happen."

"There's got to be some mistake."

"I s'pose that's possible, but I believe the prudent course is to make sure your assets are secure. Then we can verify the facts. We've got to stop the bleeding first."

"I just can't believe he would do----not Ross, not like this."

"Any other important, financial documents in the house?" Bernstein asked.

"I'll look. Ross keeps most of them at his office. The only account I'm familiar with is my cap account at Wachovia here in Naples. Is that still all there?"

"Yes, ma'm. Hasn't been touched in months. Completely intact."

"Why wouldn't he drain that, too?"

"Might not be wise, considerin' you'd notice right quick."

While Meagan tried to digest the news, Eleanor came in the kitchen door, weighed down with bags of groceries. She plopped them on the counter.

"Is this a beautiful day or what? So how you doing, Meg?"

Meagan didn't respond.

Eleanor cheerfully answered her own question.

"I'm fine, Elle, thanks for asking." She headed back out for more.

"Listen, we're gonna lock this down," Bernstein reassured her. "And we're gonna track down every penny that's gone and get it back for y'all in short order. You hear?"

"Yes." Meagan sighed.

"All right, then, don't you fret. I'll be in touch."

Eleanor returned with more groceries. Meagan grabbed her with both hands.

"That was my---oh, my God---Elle! I've been robbed!"

"What? Here?"

"Yes. My husband."

"Oh, sweetie." Eleanor put an arm around Meagan's shoulder. "I told you---Earl has to die."

"It's all about choice."

Chase Chambers' voice rang out over the speakers, crisp and clear. "I am not going to criticize my opponent. He is a good man with good intentions, and I respect him, but I have to take issue with him when he says he is the only candidate with experience, and we have no choice but to send him back to Congress. "

He stepped away from the podium, closer to the audience.

"Experience is important, but not just in politics. My opponent has spent his entire career in Washington. Maybe he's forgotten that there's a whole world out there beyond the Potomac. That's where I've been, getting a wide range of first-hand experience in the military, in business, in the community. I think that will serve the people of this district better than the same old politics, year after year. I think we can do better, and my experience will help make that possible."

Chase walked back to the podium and slipped the mike back on the stand.

"That's for you to decide. But I know one thing: my opponent is wrong when he says you have no choice. You do have a choice---Old ways or new? Business as usual or a fresh start? A Washington perspective or one from right here at home in Florida? That choice is your right, your duty, and I hope you make the right one in November. Thank you all."

He acknowledged the warm applause with a wave, shaking hands left and right as he waded through the crowd.

A reporter in a seersucker jacket elbowed his way forward. "Mr. Chambers, did you have a private meeting with Mrs. Hamilton on a yacht at the Naples marina?"

Chase frowned at him. "I don't know what you're talking about."

More reporters joined the barrage.

"Where's your fiancée?"

"Is Mrs. Hamilton with you today?"

"Is the wedding still on?"

Chase raised a hand. "Hold on. One at a time, please." The uproar subsided. "But first, let me ask one---do you all work for the *National Enquirer*?"

No answers.

"What about the economy? Terrorism? Taxes? The deficit? There are a lot of important issues in this election, and all you want to hear is gossip column stuff? That's a game I won't play. I don't think it serves the voters well. So, if there's nothing else---"

He nudged the ornery reporter aside and made his way to the side door, pushed it open and melted into a bright slash of midday light. Outside, a black limousine with dark tinted windows pulled around the corner and stopped at the curb. The back door opened and Chase ducked in as the limo slid into a quick turn down a side street.

Inside, all was cool and quiet except for the whoosh of the air conditioner. Chase loosened his tie and looked around. There was Curtis in the jump seat. Agent MacNulty filled his share of the front seat. Harry Black was at the wheel.

Chase looked to his left. Except for the clothes, it was like looking in a mirror. The man in the t-shirt and khakis had the same features, the same sandy blonde hair with the cowlick on the right, same water blue eyes, same cleft in the chin, same tiny dot of a mole just above the jaw line.

Sitting there shoulder to shoulder with Chase was his twin brother, Cameron.

Mac turned in his seat, looking from one to the other. Unbelievable. He had spent many hours with each of them separately, but never side by side, not until now.

"Ah, the Chambers brothers, together at last."

"Remarkable," Curtis piped in. "Like a double exposure, isn't it?"

"Take a picture, why don't you, Curtis," Cameron grumbled.

"It's good to see a Chambers in a suit and tie," Mac said to Chase. "Your brother has an attitude about that."

"Oh, he's got attitudes about all kinds of things."

"Don't I know it?"

Cameron shifted in his seat. "Hey Mac, you want to get to the point? Chase and I can have family reunions on our own time. "

"I can do that," Mac said. "Meagan Hamilton is the point."

"Love her outfits," Curtis said to no one.

"I'm handling that end, Mac," Cam declared.

"Not anymore. Harry's got a Q & A with her tomorrow."

"With Meagan? I don't know if I like that."

"You should," Mac said dryly. "He's doing you a favor. He's gonna give her the run down on the Mister, chapter and verse, let her know what a creep this guy is."

"Why? I thought she's still a suspect."

"Not according to you. So, Harry's gonna find out if she'll come to Jesus. If she's in the dark on all this like you say, and she gets pissed off enough when she sees the dirt, maybe she'll want to help us out, work with us. Just like you wanted."

"OK. Good. But it should be me. I should be the one to talk to her."

"You're the last one I want talking to her---about her husband, about this case, about the weather, for Christ's sake."

"But, Mac---"

"No buts this time. You keep crossing the line and you'll end up getting this whole case bounced. The lawyers will scream entrapment and Hamilton will take a walk."

"It's not helping the election, either," Curtis chirped. "All the reporters want to talk about is Meagan. It's turning into a soap opera."

Cameron was adamant. "I should be the one."

Mac turned to Chase. "Can't you talk some sense into your brother's head?"

Chase shrugged. "Not so far, and I've been trying for about thirty-eight years now."

- 42 -

Sandy was there when the girls arrived at the estate, the day before the event, directing them around to the port-au-cochere to unload the equipment stuffed in the back of the SUV.

Meagan took a deep breath. Okay. She could do this. God help her, she was getting used to Sandy's consistently friendly attitude. As long as Chase wasn't around---and he wasn't expected all day---she would set the guilt and confusion aside. She was determined to behave professionally in Sandy's presence.

As they stepped from the car, Eleanor spied two figures walking across the wide lawn. There was a woman, dressed head to toe in vivid purple, and a tall young man ambling toward the cottage together.

"Who's that?"

"That's Gemini, the queen mother of the Chambers family," Sandy said, "You should meet her."

"I'd love to," said Eleanor. "But I meant that hunky guy with her."

"You mean Cole?" Sandy asked.

"Cole who?"

"Cole Chambers is the younger brother," Meagan interjected. "He's the one that almost drowned trying to save his friend."

"Oh." Eleanor squinted into the sun, trying to get a better look.

"Not almost," Sandy clarified. "Cole died that day."

Eleanor and Meagan stared at her.

"It was just over a year ago now," Sandy started telling the story. "Cole and Andy---that was Cole's best friend---were fishing down at the pier, here at the estate. They were horsing around on the dock and the shrimp bucket got knocked in the water. Andy, ignoring the posted "Dangerous Currents" warning signs, jumped in to save his bait. He came up with the bucket but continued swimming around in the water."

"So?"

"You don't swim in that channel. Ever! The currents and undertows are brutal. Anyhow, Cole yelled at Andy to get his ass out of the water and the next thing he knew, Andy was screaming for help. The current had carried him further down river and he was moving fast.

"There was no time to run for help. Cole kicked off his shoes and dove in after him."

"Uh-oh. I think I know where this is going."

"Gem was back at the house. She couldn't have heard anything---it's too far---but somehow she knew something was wrong. She went out and called for Cole.

When he didn't answer, she ran back and called 9-1-1. The Coast Guard got there fast---it couldn't have been more than five minutes before they spotted them."

"Oh, no." Elle moaned.

"They hauled them on board, tried mouth-to-mouth, but they weren't breathing. Tried Andy first. Nothing. It was too late. Then Cole. They finally got a heartbeat on the fourth or fifth try. Kept working on Cole all the way to the hospital. They said his heart stopped two more times."

"And then he was all right?"

"I wouldn't say that. He was in a coma for six weeks. Nobody thought he'd come out of it. The doctors said there wasn't much chance. Gem never left his side the whole time. She had all these psychic healers in there, laying on hands. And one day, he opened his eyes like he was waking up from a nap, sat right up, and spoke to her."

"What did he say?" Eleanor was breathless.

"He said..." Sandy looked away. "He said he was sorry."

"Sorry for what?"

"Sorry he let her and the whole family down. You have to understand---the Chambers come from a long line of heroes, and he felt like he came up short."

"Poor guy," said Eleanor. "How about now? Is he okay?"

"He's not quite all there, you know? Kind of half in this world and half somewhere else. Doesn't talk much, except with his mother. Not too sociable, a real loner. He's an artist. A good artist. So he paints, and paints some more. And waits."

"Waits for what?"

"For his second chance."

- 43 -

It was going to be a long day for Marsha and Eleanor.

They were at the Big House just after dawn setting up for the Men's Night event. By noon, Port Royal sweltered under a September sun and the place was smoking. On the sprawling patio, there were five coal caldrons fired up, five more ready to go, with chefs in Waldorf whites standing by.

First Class had constructed a boardwalk with an assortment of waterfront areas---barbeque, burgers, shrimp, and bars--- pre-fabricated shacks with graphic art to dress them up. It looked like a Hollywood film set. And it was smart. The boardwalk drew all the food and drink traffic outside, keeping the inside clear for the Texas Hold 'em tournament play.

It was almost five o'clock when Eleanor and Marsha joined up for a final inspection, walking through the house, out to the boardwalk and back around in a full circle.

"You're a genius," Marsha said as they completed the tour.

"Please," Eleanor blushed. "I'm just a lowly worker bee. But it does look damn good, eh?"

Marsha smiled. "We have got to get ready."

"No kidding. I need a bath *and* a shower."

"I'm going upstairs."

"Go ahead, I'll be right up."

After ten hours of non-stop preparation, Eleanor decided it was time for a personal moment. She slipped out the back and sprawled on the grass like a kid, flat on her back. She closed her eyes and fell fast asleep, only to be awakened by a lilting voice.

"Ah, the Queen of Cups has come."

Eleanor found herself being observed by a woman with the most exquisite amber eyes she had ever seen. She had a radiance about her which transported Eleanor. She felt lifted, lighter. She basked in this woman's glow for a moment and then suddenly realized who it was.

"I'm sorry---"she stammered, scrambling to her feet. "I'm Eleanor, Mrs. Chambers, I was just---"

"Eleanor," Gem took her hand. "A lovely name, a queen's name. Never a coincidence, *cheri'*, *tu comprends?*"

"I'm not sure I---"

"You must take your part in the story now, Eleanor. *C'est le temps.*"

The woman was captivating, and impossible to understand.

"I'm only here to work on the---" Eleanor started.

Gem placed a finger to her lips. "You're here because you're here. That's enough."

Eleanor was captured by Gem's eyes. Time slowed.

Laughing voices broke the spell. Sandy and Meagan approached, both dressed in classy knock-offs of 1940s WAC uniforms. All the hostesses were wearing them as part of Eleanor's grand plan. From a distance, they looked like Lana Turner and Ava Gardner strolling through the grass.

"Elle, the place looks awesome!" Meagan called out.

"Fabulous! Love the military theme," Sandy added. "So, I see you've met the matriarch of the family."

"Kind of."

Sandy turned. "Meagan, this is Gem Chambers."

Meagan was struck by her presence and ageless beauty. She had the bearing of French royalty. Meagan was tempted to curtsy before her.

"Hello, Mrs. Chambers."

"Meagan, what a pleasure to meet you at last." Gem looked at her fondly. "And it's Gem. Just Gem." She spread her arms wide. "And aren't we blessed here, in this moment? Three angels, here with me in this lovely place. And all that will come revolves around you three." Gem pointed to each in turn. "You, you, and you."

"Eleanor." She turned to her, eyes flashing. "You will be the first. The opportunity you thought had passed comes round again. Embrace it."

"Where are we?" Eleanor whispered to Meagan. "Down the rabbit hole with Alice?"

"Hush," Meagan said. "She's the real thing. I can feel it."

"Easy, Gem," said Sandy. "They're not familiar with your ways. They may need time."

"Ah, but Sandra," Gem said. "Time is the luxury we do not have. You go with Meagan, Sandra. You two should spend time together. You may have more in common than you know." Gem looked to Eleanor. "Come with me a while."

Elle balked. "Oh, no Mrs.---Gem---I have work to do. I couldn't possibly----"

"Go ahead, Elle," Meagan urged. "We're all set for tonight. And you can't pass up an invitation from the lady of the house."

"Yes, go, Elle," Sandy insisted. "There's always a reason."

"A very good reason," Gem confirmed. "There's someone you should meet. I think it will be good for you and good for him as well."

"Him?" Eleanor perked up. "Well, all right. I mean, what the hell, can't be any worse than those Internet chat rooms."

⬚

Meagan and Sandy retreated to the wicker rockers in the shade of the veranda. Launch time was still an hour away. They took advantage of the lull, swaying gently.

"So, what's up with Elle?" Sandy asked. "Marsha said there was some tragedy in her past and you were the only one who knew the whole story."

"She's been through the mill all right."

Meagan told Sandy about Elle and Nick Sheehan, how their romance blossomed, the perfect wedding and the blissful honeymoon.

"Sounds like a fairytale," said Sandy.

"It was. It really was." Meagan nodded. "But then, it was the night they came back from Hawaii, Nick went out for his run. That was his thing, like six miles a day. He was only gone half an hour, but she had a bad feeling. She went out, hoping to meet him on his way back. She found him a few blocks away. Almost made it home."

"Almost?"

"He was lying in the street. Hit by a car. Hit-and-run."

"Oh my God!"

"Her beautiful Nicky. He was all---it was awful! One week after the perfect wedding, Elle was a widow, planning Nick's perfect funeral. Yellow roses again. Just like the wedding. Nick brought her yellow roses on their first date. And the second. And forever. Brought them or sent them every day. Sometimes one, sometimes a dozen. Yellow roses for his Eleanor."

"Poor Elle. Did they ever find out who did it?"

"Not a clue."

"How long has it been?"

"It happened April last year."

"Bad month. That was when Cole almost died. And Cam---" Sandy stopped short.

"Cam?" Meagan ventured. "The other brother, Chase's twin, right?"

"Uh-huh." Sandy looked away.

"Was that when he was---" Meagan groped. "Was that when Cam---?"

"It's something the family doesn't like to talk about at all, and I don't want---I'm sorry I brought it up."

Sandy stood and pulled Meagan to her feet.

"C'mon," she said. "There's work to do, and when I'm working, I keep my mouth shut and stay out of trouble."

They walked down the front steps arm in arm, like good friends.

The illusion was shattered when Chase pulled up in the driveway and Sandy took off, racing to lean in the driver's side for a kiss.

Meagan's stomach churned. So much for good friends, she thought. It could never work with her and Sandy. She rushed back to the kitchen and leaned against the counter as the queasy feeling in her stomach rose to a full wave of nausea.

Great, she thought, just seeing Chase could be hazardous to her health.

She drew a glass of water at the sink and gulped it down but it only made her feel like she might throw up all over the spotless counter.

Got to get out of here.

Meagan scribbled a note for Eleanor and made a hasty exit. She drove home, feeling awful, soaked in a cold sweat by the time she rushed inside to collapse on her bed. Thank God Brandon was with her parents that night.

Still nauseated, she thought of the meeting with the FBI that Bernstein had arranged for the following morning. They wanted to interview her about Ross and her attorney strongly recommended that she cooperate. Why were they coming? What did she know, for heaven's sake?

"Nothing," she murmured, drifting into a restless sleep. "I don't know anything at all."

"It went great, Meg. You should have been there to hear the raves. They loved it! Elle did such a great job, and Sandy really stepped up when you flew the coup."

"I'm so sorry, Marsh. I don't know what happened to me. I was perfectly fine, and then I was so sick. I barely made it home."

"Oh, man. Are you okay?"

"Yeah. I am now. I'm just sorry I left you guys short-handed."

"No problem. We pulled it off. Another First Class job!"

"I'm so glad." Meagan heard the doorbell. Time for her FBI appointment. "I gotta go, Marsh. Later."

Harry Black was no-nonsense, suit and tie, full FBI. No sunglasses. He extended his badge for ID.

Meagan waved it away. She just wanted to get this over with. They sat down across from each other with the coffee table between them as a token buffer. Meagan took a nervous breath. She could do this.

He opened his brief case on the coffee table and took out some papers. He glanced around. "Beautiful home. How long have you been here?"

He reminded her of an insurance salesman. "Five years."

"Since you were married?"

"That's right."

"Mrs. Hamilton, if I can ask, just what is your relationship with Mr. Chase Chambers?"

"What?"

"Chase Chambers," Black said blankly. "I believe you are, uh, familiar with him?"

She sat straight, suddenly alarmed. What was going on here?

"I was under the impression that this meeting was about my husband, Ross?"

"Please, Mrs. Hamilton, just answer the question."

Her anger pushed away the nausea. "Mr. Black--- is it really Mr. Black? Is that your real name?"

"Yes, ma'm. Harry Truman Black."

"Your parents must have been Democrats."

"Nope. Republicans. My father's name was Harry and my mother's maiden name was Truman. My folks never voted for a Democrat, not even Harry Truman."

"Well, Mr. Harry Truman Black, my attorney told me to answer your questions regarding my husband. I'm willing to do that. But anything beyond that is off limits."

Black leaned over the table. "This *is* related to your husband, Mrs. Hamilton."

Meagan returned his persistent look with one of her own. "I don't think so. Now, I'm not really feeling up to arguing with you. So we can call my attorney right now, if you want, and I'll let you talk to him."

The FBI man leaned back. One for Meagan.

"We don't have to do that. Let's get to Mr. Hamilton. How well do you know your husband, ma'm?"

"Excuse me? He's my husband."

"Well, did you know him a long time before you were married? Childhood sweethearts, something like that?"

"No. Just the opposite. Whirlwind romance. We were married six weeks after we met. Is that a crime?"

"Not at all. Very romantic." Black wrote something down. "And do you work with your husband?"

"I have my own business."

"Right. The, uh, catering thing."

Meagan resented the way he said it. "Yes, the catering thing."

"What I mean to say is, are you very familiar with your husband's business?"

"I know he's a financial adviser and broker. He has his own company, Hamilton Securities, offices here and in Chicago. And I know he's very good at what he does."

"Maybe too good. Are you aware that complaints have been filed with the SEC?"

"Against my husband?"

"Some. Others against partnerships and holding companies he's involved with. A lot of people have lost a lot of money."

"I know how they feel."

"Ma'm?"

"Let's just say that I'm learning first hand about my husband's financial strategies."

"I'd like to hear about that."

"It's personal, and private. I don't want to get into details."

"But that's what I'm here for, Mrs. Hamilton. The devil's in the details. For example, did you know many of the complaints have been filed by executors or probate courts?"

"What does that mean?"

"It means a lot of those folks who lost money are dead now."

"What are you saying?" Meagan gasped.

"Maybe nothing." Black shrugged. "Most of the deaths were natural causes, at least on the record. Some were suspicious. More than a little. Were you acquainted with Diane McAlister in Atlanta?"

Meagan's jaw dropped. "Diane McAlister! I know that name. Melissa mentioned her. She, she was---how was my husband connected to her?"

"He was her investment adviser. He managed her money, and a charity trust fund, after they became, uh, close, I guess you could say."

"Close? How close?"

Black didn't answer.

"Was Ross having an affair with Diane?"

"That's not material to---"

"It's material to me!"

Black said nothing, but the look on his face told Meagan all she needed to know.

"God, this was a year and a half ago? And I had no---Excuse me, please."

Meagan ran to the bathroom and threw up in the toilet. She fixed her face and brushed her teeth before returning with a cold resolve. Any last spark of feeling that she had felt for her husband was gone forever. He wasn't worth any emotion, love or hate.

"All right, Agent Black, I think you've accomplished your mission. I get the message. My husband is scum and I'm a fool. Now, is there anything else?"

"I'm in a delicate position here, ma'm, telling you confidential information about the investigation. I'm not supposed to put the Bureau at risk like that, but I think you deserve to know. And I think I can trust you. Now I'm hoping you'll help us out."

"Me?" Meagan was baffled. "What do you want me to do?"

Black dropped the bombshell. He told her she had to forget all she had been told and pretend that she loved him, that all was well in their marriage. She had to play the role of the subservient wife to keep Ross Hamilton relaxed and unsuspecting, give the FBI time to wrap up an airtight case against him.

"I can't do that!" Meagan was appalled. "I'm not an actress, Agent Black."

"You can do it, and you've got to. It's the only way."

"You don't understand. I can't even look at him anymore. Our marriage, our---he's ruined everything!"

"And he's not done yet. Don't you understand that? You could be in real danger, Mrs. Hamilton. You and your son."

"Brandon? Please, Agent Black, you have to promise me you won't let him---you won't let anything happen to my baby."

"We'll be here, watching and protecting. Your son will be safe. I promise...But you need to do this."

Meagan felt she had no choice. She nodded.

Black explained the details. She should tell Ross she had quit First Class and that Eleanor had departed---everything he wanted. They would move Eleanor into a hotel and give her a new cell phone with a secure line so Meagan could stay in touch.

Monitored by the FBI no doubt, Meagan thought. How very generous of the government to allow her such a concession.

Black said that there were still documents they were looking for, and a computer disc that was very important.

"That's the Rosetta Stone," he said. "We think he has all his private data and the most incriminating records on one CD. He might keep it somewhere in the house."

Meagan signed a consent form for access to anything in the house or her lawyer's files. She knew nothing of the computer disc but remembered Ross mentioning something about it a few days ago. What was on that disc?

Black did not tell her that there would be bugs placed strategically throughout the house and on the phones. A judge had already signed the court order. He did say that the FBI would provide round-the-clock surveillance of her home, starting immediately. No one could slip in unnoticed. Meagan raised her head at that.

"Not that anyone would," he said, deadpan.

"I'll send some people over to clear out your friend's things and I've programmed my cell number into the speed dial on your cell. Just push '9' anytime."

"How---when did you do that?"

"When you were throwing up in the bathroom," he said as he shook her hand. "Thank you, Mrs. Hamilton. We're confident that you can do this. We're counting on you, and we'll be here to back you up a hundred percent."

"Glad somebody's confident. What if I can't keep up this charade?"

"That's not an option."

"So I don't have any choice here, do I?"

"No, ma'm. Not anymore."

Two men came by an hour later, flashed their credentials, and packed up all of Eleanor's things. They proceeded to search the house top to bottom, including the attic, basement, even Brandon's room. They seemed disappointed when they left with two boxes of documents and records. They had found some things of interest but not what they were looking for. No mysterious disc. The Rosetta Stone was still missing.

- 45 -

"That can't be right."

Ross was on his cell in the car, driving home from the Naples airport. It was almost six but he knew the staff would still be in the office in Chicago. They better be. He had called to check on the status of the Chambers money. The first $100,000 had been received, as promised by Chase, and the scheme was underway. Not the one he had agreed to with Chambers to buttress his campaign funds, but a much better and more lucrative plan, with all the benefits accruing to Ross Hamilton.

Ross chuckled. Chambers was a fool. Did he really think Ross would put himself at risk to assist in Chambers' political aspirations? Whatever for? No. He would take the money, move it around a bit, slip it through his own carefully constructed laundry system, then make it disappear. When the time came, he would regretfully report that the markets took an unexpected turn. Futures were volatile and unpredictable. Nothing he could do. Wipe out.

And what recourse would Chambers have? Call the police? Sue him for failure to commit campaign fraud? The plan was flawless.

And now this. A fly in the rich ointment. He called to confirm the check had cleared and been deposited, only to learn that there was a problem. The check was not from the Chambers campaign fund, nor from any Chambers family account. It had been issued by a small investment firm in Naples, Rossco Corporation. And Stacy had just informed him that they could not find any information on Rossco aside from confirmation of a single filing for incorporation in Florida. There was no history, no records, nothing.

That was odd, a little too odd to Ross. Was Chambers just being careful, using a front company to cover the money trail? Was he more sophisticated at financial legerdemain than Ross thought? Or was there something amiss in the whole deal, something rotten in Rossco?

He would have to find out, and there was no one in the office he trusted enough to take on that task. It would have to wait until he could do it himself, and that wouldn't be for a few days, at least. At the moment, he had another issue to deal with, another carefully planned scheme plagued by unanticipated complications.

Meagan.

Ross pulled into the garage at six o'clock sharp.

He propped his briefcase on the kitchen counter and walked through the house, gazing about with his inspector's eye. Everything was neat as a pin, scrubbed and polished. He nodded, a king pleased with his castle.

Ross stopped at the foot of the stairs and called out.

"Meagan?"

She came down on cue. Like the house, she was fresh and sparkling.

"Ross, it's so good to have you home. It seems like you've been gone for ages."

"No rest for the wicked."

It was rare humor for Ross. Meagan didn't laugh.

"I'll hope you'll be home for a while. Brandon missed you."

"A few days, at least." He studied her closely. There was something new, something different. Hair? Makeup? Clothes? No, none of the above. Something else. Whatever it was, he didn't like it.

"Where is Brandon?"

"He tried to stay up, but he couldn't keep his eyes open. I just put him to bed a little while ago. You ought to go up and say hello. He wanted to see you so much."

"I'll see him in the morning." Ross flipped through the stack of mail, tossed the envelopes on the counter and stepped to the sink to scrub his hands. God knows what he picked up on the flight.

"I made dinner, darling. Are you hungry?"

Ross sniffed the air. "What is it?"

"Your favorite. Beef Wellington."

"As long as it isn't overcooked. You know how I hate that."

Meagan was trying hard to stay in character, sweet and compliant. *God, what a jerk!*

"Of course. It's very rare, just the way you like it."

He ate the sumptuous dinner, presented by Meagan like a servant girl. Ross devoured the meal while she picked at her plate, moving the food around to disguise her lack of appetite.

Meagan cleared the table and set a steaming cup of black coffee before him.

"So, fill me in. What has my lovely wife been up to?" He patted the chair next to him. "Sit here."

"Quite a bit, really," she said. "I think you'll be glad to hear that I gave notice."

"Gave notice about what?"

"I told Marsha I won't be working with First Class any more."

"You did?"

"Yes. You were right. With Brandon and all, I don't have the time. We worked a big event two nights ago, and I told her, that was it for me. No more."

"Well I'm proud of you. Family first. I'm glad you've seen the light."

"And you don't have to worry about Elle anymore, either."

"Eleanor? She's gone?"

"She's still in Naples, but she won't be staying here. She left yesterday."

"Will miracles never cease?" Ross beamed.

"I just want us to be a happy family, that's all." She hated herself for saying that. She knew she was supposed to play the part, but she didn't have to over do it.

"That's all I ever wanted." Ross topped her.

His reply diminished her guilt. She was lying to him, but he had been lying to her for years and he was lying now. He was much better at it.

Meagan retreated to the family room after dinner. The flat screen TV was on, an old movie with Sandra Bullock and Hugh Grant, but she paid little attention to it, burying her face in a magazine.

Ross sauntered in, coffee in hand and joined her on the couch.

"It's been too long since we've had time alone together like this."

Meagan bridled when Ross came over to her and began to massage her bare feet. His hand crawled higher. She retracted her legs and tucked them under.

"Ross, I think that I have a touch of the flu or something. I ache all over."

Her eyes were glued to the magazine. She didn't want to look at him.

"Meagan. I need you tonight. Come here." He reached for her.

"Please, Ross---" She withdrew. "I really feel like I'm going to throw up."

☐

"And she's not kidding you, pal," Black said under his breath.

He was sitting in the FBI ROSSCO office, his feet propped on the desk next to the speaker. Relayed from the panel truck parked a half block from the house, the sound was clean and clear, pure as a movie sound-track. The volume was loud enough for Cameron and the five others in the office to hear. They were all busy, acting like they weren't listening, although they all were.

It was painful for Cameron. He didn't want to hear, but he listened intently as Ross spoke, a hint of irritation in his voice.

"What's the matter?"

"I'm not---I---maybe it was something I ate." Meagan sagged on the couch.

"Something you ate? What could that have been?" He pressed her. "It wasn't dinner. I had the same dinner. I feel fine. What else did you have today?"

"Just give me a minute," Meagan begged. She felt miserable.

Ross caressed her shoulder. "I want you, Meagan. Right now. Do you hear me?"

He held her firmly, slipping one hand down between her legs.

"Ooh." She flinched at his touch. "Ross, you're hurting me."

He released her. "You're my wife," he spat the words. "Remember?"

"Ross, I just can't----I'm sorry. I have to lay down." She scurried to the bedroom.

◻

In the FBI office, the only sound was the muted chatter on the Hamiltons' TV. A few minutes later, that ended with a quiet click. Ten minutes passed without a sound. Harry yawned and stood up, ready to pack it in, when the voice-actuated speaker came to life once more. The sound was barely audible. It was Ross, whispering on a cell phone.

"...Nothing I can't handle."

"And how's the little woman?"

"Meek as a lamb. Quit the job. And Miss Eleanor is out of the picture."

The agent in the panel truck fiddled with dials and switches; the voices came clear.

"Doesn't that seem just a little strange to you?"

"Not really. She does what I tell her to do."

"Ross. Have you forgotten? She hired a divorce lawyer last week. "

"She went to see a lawyer. That's all. Now it looks like she had second thoughts. She decided the best course was to be a good girl, try to make her marriage work."

"That's not how she's been acting."

"That was an aberration, probably brought on by a sudden attack of the dreaded Elle from hell. But she came to her senses. We're back to normal mode, Stacy."

"I hope you're right."

"I'm going to stay here for a couple days just to make sure. I can work out of the Naples office. I'll be back in Chicago by Friday."

"I don't know, Ross. She knows too much, even if she doesn't know she does."

"Listen, if I ever thought she was that kind of risk, I would not hesitate. You know that. I would take care of her."

"Take care of her how?"

"I can handle her, one way or another. I always have."

◻

Cameron looked at Black.

"Don't worry, we'll keep her safe," Black said earnestly.

Cam's reply had an edge, "I'm counting on that. And I'm holding you responsible, Harry."

"Listen, Chambers," Black raised his voice. "I've been doing this for twenty-six years and I've never lost a witness yet. And I'll tell you something else---" He pointed a finger, not quite at Cameron, but almost. "I like her. She's a good lady, she doesn't deserve to be in this mess, and I'll do my best to keep her out of trouble---but I gotta wonder if that doesn't include you."

Cam recoiled. "You think I'm putting her in jeopardy? Is that what you think?"

"What do you think?"

"I sure as hell---" He stopped short. "I don't know, Harry. I really don't know."

PAGE of CUPS.

Two agonizing days passed for Cameron Chambers. He felt like he was handcuffed to the chair in the office. On direct orders from Mac, he was limited to monitoring the conversations in the Hamilton home as they were relayed from the site. Even that was redundant. Harry and the others could manage that task quite well without him.

Cam needed to do something, anything besides sitting there like a perverted Peeping Tom, eavesdropping on the mundane activities of Meagan's private life. The only good thing about it was hearing her voice, and the way she talked to her son Brandon. She was a good and caring mother. On the other hand, he couldn't help notice that Ross hardly paid attention to the little guy. Even when he was in the house, which wasn't much, he was an absentee dad.

When Curtis told him that Chase would be out of action for at least a day with a hoarse voice, Cam thought he saw a chance and grabbed it.

"Laryngitis? Chase?"

"I've seen it many times, working security on campaigns. The pace and all the speeches and interviews---wears them down. The voice goes. Can't talk, can't campaign. It's that simple. He'll be all right in a day or two."

"What about tomorrow?"

"We cancel everything. It's no big deal. There was nothing crucial."

"You don't have to do that. I can cover for him."

Curtis looked skeptical.

"How noble. I thought you hated the campaign folderol."

Cameron looked around the quiet room.

"Compared to this, it's a day at the beach."

Curtis shook his head. "Why are you always trying to get me fired?"

"Curtis, please, get me out of here for a day. You can pick me up tomorrow morning."

"All right, all right, but I've got to get Mac to sign off first or it will be my head on a platter."

Cameron raised a hand in a stop sign.

"I'll talk to Mac. You better get over to campaign HQ to make sure they don't blow off the schedule. I'll be waiting at eight. Best behavior. Promise."

"This is a federal election campaign, Mr. Chambers. I'll be there at 6 a.m. sharp. Wear a good suit, and you better let me pick the tie."

"What---you don't like my ties?"

"They're...they're very nice. We just want to stay away from the ones with the little brown doggies or the golden golf clubs on them."

◻

Cameron was waiting out front, dutifully attired in a conservative tan suit with several ties in hand when Curtis pulled up at six a.m. Curtis picked the navy one and left the rest draped over the mailbox.

"What did MacNulty say?" Curtis asked as Cameron climbed in.

"Nothing."

"He must have said *something*---what?"

"I didn't talk to him yet."

"Sweet Jesus, Cameron Chambers!" Curtis pulled over with a screech of brakes. "This is not the Post Office we work for. It's the FBI. You can't do that! He'll go through the roof."

"He doesn't have to know. Don't be such an old lady. Let's just get to the first---"

"Oh, no." Curtis shook his head. "We're going to the office right now, and you are going to march in there and make a formal request for permission. And that's final."

"That's a total waste of---"

"You have to be a man, Cameron," Curtis chided as he made a u-turn.

◻

Big Mac didn't look surprised to see him.

"By God, Cameron---you do look good in a suit."

"How do you know it's me and not Chase?"

274

"Curtis just called to warn me. So you're going to play candidate for the day?"

"Thought I might as well help as long as---"

A voice on the intercom interrupted. "Sir, you have a call."

"Take a message."

"It's Agent Black, sir, says it's urgent."

He picked up. "MacNulty."

Mac listened, expressionless for a minute, then glanced at Cameron before he spoke.

"How the hell---I thought we had real time sur-veillance, Harry."

He listened again.

"What hospital?" MacNulty frowned. "OK, OK. You get over there. And I want to know as soon as you do."

Cameron stared at him as he hung up. "It's Meagan, isn't it?"

"Yeah."

"God damn it, Mac, if that son-of-a-bitch laid a hand on her, I'll---"

"Calm down, Chambers. We don't know much yet."

"I knew something like this would happen."

"We don't have any details. We'll find out and we'll handle it."

"Oh, no. I'll handle this myself."

"Stop right there. I'm in charge here, and I'll decide who handles what. Got it?"

Cameron was in Mac's face.

"You can't stop me because I don't exist. I'm dead, remember? Cameron Chambers, MIA. And you can't fire me because I don't work for the FBI. My name's not even in the files. I'm just a god damn ghost."

Cameron shook his head in disgust.

"You know what, Mac? It's time for me to come in from the cold. I'm rejoining the living."

"You go off like a loose cannon, man, and you're going to fuck up this whole thing!"

"It already is! You've got enough to pick up Hamilton right now, but you keep pissing around, putting the wrong people in the line of fire---like Meagan."

Mac was working hard on his self-control.

"You know, it's my fault. It is. I let you talk me into it. Remember when you called from Atlanta? I knew it was asking for trouble, and---Don't you get it? She's the one that's got you all---"

"She's the one?" Cameron was furious. "She's in the god damn hospital!"

"Be reasonable, will you? You can't bolt on us now."

"Watch me."

☐

Cameron crossed the street to the car in a few long strides.

Curtis was in the driver's seat with the car idling, listening to a Barry Manilow song. He watched Cameron approach, his face taut.

"So, how did it go?"

Cameron yanked the door open.

"Get out, Curtis."

Curtis didn't argue. As soon as he stepped out, Cameron jumped in, shifted into gear and sped off. Curtis stood at the curb and watched him go.

"Not that great, I guess."

- 47 -

Time crawled by as Meagan suffered through two days with Ross, doing her best to be sweet and compliant while her true feelings raged beneath the surface. She could hardly conceal her relief when Ross booked an early flight to Chicago after another call from Stacy. Meagan thought she heard him mention the name *Chambers* and held her breath. *Couldn't be.* He said nothing after, only that there were some loose ends with his all-important Tannex deal and he had to get back to his Chicago lair.

Meagan's joy didn't last long. She was out of bed as soon as Ross left the house, eager to get in a full day free of the burdensome charade. The dizziness hit her as she started down the stairs. Next thing she knew, Meagan was in an awkward heap, her leg bent painfully beneath her, Brandon staring down fearfully from the top of the stairs.

"Mommy! Mommy!"

She tried to get up and sagged back again, still woozy.

"It's okay, honey."

"Mommy hurt bad!"

She spoke with some effort, trying to soothe her son.

"I'm all right, Bran. Mommy's fine," she continued. "Don't worry. But I need you to bring me the phone, sweetheart. Get the phone and bring it to Mommy."

Meagan called Eleanor instead of 9-1-1.

"Elle. Oh, thank God."

"Where've you been?"

"Never mind, it's where I am right now that's the problem."

"Yeah, trapped like a rat in the house with the cat."

"No, he's gone back to Chicago."

"That's not far enough, if you ask me."

"Elle, will you listen, please? I've fallen, and I can't get up."

"What are you talking about?"

"I don't know what happened. My head started spinning, and I fell down the stairs, like a stunt man, top to bottom."

"No fucking way!"

"I'm lying here like an old lady who fell out of her wheelchair."

"Don't fucking move. I'll be right there."

And she was. Eleanor to the rescue.

▯

Three hours later, they were back at the house, after a harrowing morning at St. Vincent's Hospital. Meagan was poked, prodded, x-rayed and scanned, then lectured by a stern nurse about how to behave when pregnant.

Watch those stairs.

Pregnant. The word reverberated in Meagan's mind as she nodded obediently.

Hours later, she was home, resting on the sofa. She was fine and so was the baby, but Eleanor was a wreck.

"Why the fuck didn't you tell me?"

"I didn't know. Well, I had an idea, but I wasn't sure, and I was going to tell you and then things got crazy."

"Does he know?" Eleanor didn't even ask who the father was. She knew.

"No."

"You've got to tell him."

"I don't know...I don't know how...But, I've got to see him...today...now."

"Call him at home?"

"No way---what if Sandy answers the phone?"

"His cell?"

"No answer, and I don't want to leave a message."

"Well, hell, call your friends at the FBI. They know how to get a hold of him."

Meagan sank her chin in her hands. "I've got to think about that one. His name already came up with them once, and they didn't seem too happy about it."

Eleanor jumped to her feet.

"Oh shit. It's almost noon. Marsha will kill us both if someone doesn't show at that meeting."

"You better go then." Meagan shushed her out. "Brandon's in the front yard waiting for you to drop him off at Mom's. And thanks, Elle, for everything."

As soon as the door closed, Meagan snatched the phone, speed-dialed Harry Black and told him she wanted to see Chase.

"Sorry, ma'm, he's unavailable---speeches, meetings---political stuff. You know."

"Look, Harry---is that all right if I call you Harry, or do I still have to say Special Agent Black all the time?

"Call me whatever you want, ma'm."

"Thanks. Now Harry, I have done every thing you asked me to do, everything you said I had to do, and your favorite perpetrator---isn't that what you FBI guys say, perpetrator?"

"Yes, ma'm. Perpetrator, perp…"

"Okay, fine. The perp's gone and now I am at the end of my rope."

"Mrs. H, you are doing a good job, a great job---"

"Then, you've got to do something for me, Harry."

"Anything you want."

"I want Chase."

"That I cannot do."

"Yes you can, Mr. FBI man. You could get the president here if you had a mind to."

"I don't think so. Not him and not Chase Chambers."

"Well, you better get one of them over here---say, within the hour—or else."

"Or else what?"

"I don't know what! Quit asking me questions!"

"I'm sorry."

"Harry."

"Ma'm?"

"I have to see him. It's important. Crucial."

Black didn't ask why, didn't say anything. Meagan took that as an encouraging sign.

"You can do this for me, Harry."

"Let me make a call. I'll get back to you."

"Work your magic, Harry Black."

[]

Twenty minutes later, Chase slipped through the sliding glass door from the patio, holding a finger to his lips. He went to the kitchen sink and turned on the water full blast, flipping on the disposal for extra measure.

"You okay? Ross didn't...?"

"No, no, he didn't touch me---just a silly accident. I fell. It was nothing. I'm fine, really. Better now that you're here."

Chase ran his eyes over her, just to double-check. Meagan leaned into him. She was amazed that Harry had been able to round him up so fast.

"Get dressed. And hurry. We're playing hooky. Grab your car keys."

She didn't say a word, just opened her robe and bared her breasts in all their naked glory.

"Holy---!" He raised a hand as if blinded by the light. "Get going before I---" He gave her a light whack on her bottom to send her on her way.

God, she would be the death of him yet.

[]

The yacht drifted aimlessly in the gentle swells of the gulf waters, waves lapping against the hull. Meagan's stomach stayed intact, much to her delight. She had always been prone to the seasick side on a boat, any boat, but now that she had bouts of nausea almost daily on dry land, she found herself steady as a rock at sea, not a twinge of discomfort. Being pregnant was funny that way. She had never liked green olives either, but she had several on her breakfast cereal.

Meagan lay on her back, warmed by the sun, caressed by a hint of breeze. He climbed through the hatch and flopped down next to her.

"Ah, this is heaven." Meagan sighed. "I could stay here forever."

"Sounds good to me."

"If only ... How long do we have?"

"The rest of our lives," he said it like he wasn't kidding.

"Really---how long can we stay out here?"

"The rest of the day, anyhow. You tell me."

"What about the campaign, Chase? Don't you have to be about a hundred places, spend time with the voters?"

"Uh, not today," he scrambled. "There was a break in the schedule. Besides, you're a voter, aren't you? I'm spending time with you."

- 48 -

Back at the Big House, Eleanor was actually making progress with the reluctant Cole.

Gem watched, trying to conceal her delight.

"Come on, Cole. Get your butt over here," she demanded.

Eleanor jumped nimbly from the pool and plopped down on the lounge chair, almost tipping them both into the water. Cole grabbed her for support, hands molded to her shoulders. She broke free and dove back in, beckoning him to join her.

He moved to the pool's edge. Eleanor swam away, rising up to splash him. He leaned to dodge the spray, then slid in, standing waist deep in the shallow end.

Gem could not believe her eyes. Cole had not been ankle deep in water since Andy drowned.

Cole pulled her under in retaliation. Eleanor squirmed away and leapt on his broad˙ shoulders, straddled him like a horse and rode him down. He reared up to grab her.

"Gotcha!"

He plunged down with her, disappearing in a swirl of foam. They emerged with Eleanor gasping.

"Just you wait, buster. Payback's a bitch!" She splashed him again.

He grasped her arms and looked in her eyes. "I want to paint you."

"You do? You mean like put some day-glo color all over my naked body?"

"No, I want to paint your portrait."

His eyes held her. She couldn't look away.

"That's a great pickup line. Do they teach you that in art school?"

Gem laughed. Eleanor was an angel sent to heal Cole's soul. With one last glance, she left them to their reverie, departing for the cottage.

[]

She set the cards in three stacks, past, present and future and turned one to begin.

Death.

The Death Card upright. The Grim Reaper in full armor astride a white stallion, riding past the fallen king on a barren battlefield. It could mean something else---transformation, change of life, a seismic shift on a life path---but not this time. This was death and nothing else. Someone was going to die.

But who?

Another card, the Nine of Pentacles, reversed. A pretty maiden, serene in her luxurious garden, an exotic bird perched on the back of her hand.

Gem knew. This was Meagan. Paired with Death and inverted, the card told of a bad decision made some time ago. The bill had come due and the cost would be high.

Gem pressed on.

The Strength card, present, upright. The lion on the prowl was an unruly force that could bring ruin if left to run wild but a powerful ally to champion Meg's cause if she could rein him in, use the force to her advantage. Which would it be? Gem's hands moved again and two cards came up together, dealt as one. Two as one...one was two. She set them side by side.

Knight of Cups, bold and full of promise---who else but Cameron?

Knight of Wands, a revered leader, thoughtful and considerate. Chase, of course.

How could her sons be entangled in Meagan's nightmare?

She went to the third stack once more and unveiled the Star card, upright. A night sky filled with celestial lights above the lovely maiden who straddles the abundant land and flowing water, replenishing both from her twin vessels. One glorious star rises above the rest, illuminating all, turning darkness to light.

Cole, her shining star, here on the brink of a defining moment. He would be tested to the limit, perhaps beyond. Risks and rewards were both extreme. It was both disturbing and exhilarating for Gem. She feared the danger, but embraced the chance for Cole's redemption.

Chase, Cameron, Cole---somehow Meagan's crucible involved all her precious sons. Each had a role to play in her drama and all were in peril.

"C'est foncé, c'est lumière." *There is darkness, there is light.*

Find the path to light.

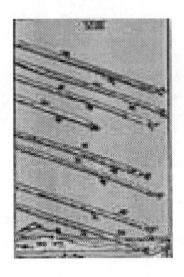

"Gem?"

"Hello, Agent Curran."

"How did you know it was me? Was that psychic precognition?"

"Nothing of the sort. I recognized your voice."

"Gem, I think we may be getting somewhere with your Handsome Man."

"Who?"

"The case we've been talking about. That's the file name."

"I see. Yes, the Handsome Man."

"We've done a lot of cross checking on the computers, looked at a lot of cold cases."

"I hope I haven't led you down the wrong path. His aura is so foggy. It's hard to pinpoint exact traits."

"We think we have some good data on this now---possible victims list and some suspects---persons of interest, that is. We profiled them based on what you told us."

"How can I help? I don't have any new information. I would have called."

"I'd like you to take a look at what we have. See if you pick on up anything, get a gut reaction."

"That's an excellent idea."

"I can come down there, bring the files. I could be there Thursday afternoon?"

"I'm sorry. I won't be here. Cole and I are going to Cassadaga Thursday."

"Cassadaga? Is that in Mexico?"

"No, it's right here in Florida, about three hours from Naples. Just a tiny town, but it is home to more spiritualists than anywhere else. It was started for that very purpose more than a hundred years ago."

"Psychic City?"

"Something like that. I'm speaking at a seminar there."

"Gem, I don't think this can wait. You're the one who said this guy is very active right now."

"Yes. I believe that's true."

"Would it be all right if I met you there, in Cassadaga? I promise it won't take long."

"Certainly. We'll be at the Cassadaga Hotel in the middle of town."

"I think I can use all my investigative skills to find the place. I'll be there by four."

Another shock wave pulsed through Gem as she put down the phone. Like tremors before an earthquake, they were increasing in force and frequency. This one surprised her. Curran, the VICAP cases---they were completely unrelated to her family concerns. Why would such a premonition take hold of her after talking to Agent Curran?

Pas de chance. Nothing is coincidence.

- 50 -

He stretched out next to Meagan on the upper deck. The low October sun dancing on the waters. A light breeze toyed with her hair and caressed her sun-kissed skin. He hadn't felt this comfortable with a woman since Diane.

"Chase?"

"I'm right here." He ran his fingers over her bare arm.

"Talk to me."

"What do you want me to say?"

"Tell me about your brother, Cameron, and Diane."

It was like a bucket of cold water. He jerked up.

"How did you---What brought that up?"

"Please, Chase, humor me. I know it's hard, such a tragedy, but I keep hearing these bits and pieces about those two. I'd like to hear the whole story. For you, it must be so---have you ever told anyone?"

"No," he said quietly. "No, I haven't."

"I wish you would tell me. Can you do that?"

A moment of silence.

"Diane." He started slowly. "Diane was a very special woman. Cam loved her. Funny, she wasn't anything like him, wasn't his type at all. She was sweet and shy, both feet on the ground. She was like an anchor for him, safe harbor in the storm." He looked across the water. "And he made her laugh. He made her life more exciting, and she made his complete."

Meagan sat up. "Did she work with him---you know, in the government?"

"Hell, no. She hated that stuff. Diane was into the arts. She wasn't an artist herself, but she had a great eye, knew her stuff. She worked with the museums and the foundations as a consultant, especially working with children's exhibits, education, special programs--- she loved art and she loved kids. She wanted to have about ten of her own."

"Why didn't they get married?"

"They were going to that summer, but Cameron had to go overseas first. Special ops. Cam was always---" His voice was thick with regret. "She didn't want him to go and he didn't have to. He wanted to. One last time for the team. It was stupid."

Meagan cringed. Chase was being too hard on his twin.

"Don't say that. He did it for his country. He was a hero."

"No, Meg. He did it for himself. He always had to prove he was the best, the bravest, the toughest. You wanted the real story. That's it. It was a mistake, a selfish mistake. He never should have left Diane."

He was agitated now. "He was in hostile territory, no communication allowed. Diane was alone and vulnerable. She was easy prey when---"

"Enter the evil villain, Ross Hamilton."

"You said it, not me."

"But that's what you think. He swindled her?"

"Took her for everything she had."

"I still can't believe it. You know, Ross has made a lot of money for a lot of people."

"Yeah, I know. And then he cherry picks the ones for his scams. Always women. Always with the charity angle to lure them in. He's dirty, Meagan."

"But he's not a murderer. He didn't kill anybody. He didn't kill Diane." Meagan said it more for herself than for him. She needed to believe.

He crouched next to her. "That's enough talk for now, okay?"

"But I really want----"

In one swift move he pulled her onto his lap, straddling him. "I know what you really want."

"Think so?" she teased.

He kissed her hard, his hands stroking her bare legs then wandering up to caress her thighs, exploring higher, slipping under her cut-offs to delve into her dewy softness. Meagan buckled as his fingers beckoned her to pleasure.

She arched back, every muscle taut, then screamed and surrendered with a gush of heat, collapsing into him.

"Oh, too much. Too much."

"Too much is not enough."

He grabbed her shorts, yanked them down and slipped them off her feet. Her legs opened to welcome him as he knelt to her, bowing before the sweet blond patch. He lavished her with kisses, slow and wet. She groaned as the heat rose to engulf her again. His mouth moved up to meet hers. She tasted herself on his lips, felt his need. She wanted him now, all of him.

He could wait no more. He reared up like a stallion and mounted her, driving deep, filling her with a single thrust. He stopped there, both of them on the brink of ecstasy, and whispered in her ear.

"I love you, my Meagan, I love you."

The words took Meagan even higher. She sobbed blissful tears as she came in his arms.

51

"Good morning. Chase Chambers, please."

Curtis handed the phone to Chase, standing beside him, opening mail at the kitchen counter. Chase took it absently.

"Hello."

"Chase. I'm glad I caught you."

"Uh-huh."

"I wouldn't call you at home, but I said I would keep you up to speed on anything serious, and---well, this is serious."

"Right." Chase slowed to a stop with the mail. "And this is?"

"I'm sorry." Ross looked at the phone. "It's Ross, Ross Hamilton. Is this line secure?"

"Sure is," Chase said. *Securely bugged*, he thought. Ross Hamilton? Why was he calling here?

"Good," Ross continued. "We had a little setback in the futures market. We're down some. I'm sure it's only a blip on the screen, but we'll need more in the meantime, a booster shot."

"I'm sorry, I can't get into that right now," Chase said, fuming inside. Christ, what the hell had Cam gotten into with Hamilton?

"Is there some problem at your end?"

"No. No problem," Chase said evenly. "I'm in the middle of a meeting here, and the schedule's backed up all day. I'll have to call you back when I get a chance."

"All right. But Chase, please keep in mind---you know how time-sensitive this is. The sooner, the better."

"Right. Don't I know it. Thanks for the call."

[]

Ross clicked off, unsettled. The conversation was all wrong. Why would Chambers treat him like some door-to-door salesman? Mr. Fancy Candidate had come crawling to him, begging for help, and now he was too busy for him? Call you back? Ross had been wary of the Chambers deal from the start, now he was certain. There was poison in that well.

The brief conversation was enough of a red flag for Ross to make an instant decision: pull the plug. The investment deal to compound Chambers' campaign funds was over. Terminated. He would send a check, return the money---minus a service fee for his efforts, of course---and wash his hands of the matter. But it didn't end there. That's what troubled Ross. Chase Chambers made the approach, feigned interest and respect, and tried to game him. Why? Ross could understand if it had been the late brother, Cameron. That one was ill-tempered and volatile, and the Diane episode was ample reason for bad blood there. Ross had not been sorry to hear of the man's untimely demise last year.

But he had never met Chase Chambers before. Why would he go out of his way to tangle with Ross, and what was his real agenda? Ross would have to find out, and when he did----

You want to play games with me, Mr. Chambers?

◊

Chase pushed the unopened mail aside.

"What in the hell is Cameron up to now, for God's sake?"

"He's your brother." Curtis was no help.

"That was Ross Hamilton talking to me like we're old friends, and now it sounds like we're partners on some kind of---Curtis, find him for me. Now."

"That won't be easy. He got into it with Mac this morning and he took off like a crazy man. He's not answering his cell, or the pager. I have no clue where he is."

"I can give you one---Meagan."

"Don't you think I tried that? She's MIA, too. Incommunicado."

"Curtis, you're the FBI agent. If Cam wanted to be alone with Meagan, somewhere no one could see them, couldn't call, and couldn't bother them---where do you think that might be?"

The light went on for Curtis. "On the boat."

Chase pointed to the door. "Go!"

52

After their passion had been spent, Chase slipped on shorts and golf shirt and returned to the high deck cockpit. Meagan emerged from a quick shower to join him, wrapped in a towel, bearing a silver tray with Dom Perignon, two glasses poured.

She curtsied. "For the captain."

Chase took a glass. "Mmm. You are a fine first mate---and I love the uniform, or lack thereof."

Meagan giggled. He put his arm around her.

"How did you get to my house so fast this morning?"

"I heard you were in the hospital. I was worried."

"Who told you?" She held her breath. Did he know about the baby, his baby?

"Uh…a friend of mine called me."

"Harry Black?"

"Yeah, Harry. How did you know?"

"He's a friend of yours?"

"Yeah. We go back a long way, Harry and I."

"What---You two work together?"

"Not exactly."

"Meaning---you do?"

He steadied her arm as the boat plowed through a choppy wake. She was rigid.

"If you mean---do I know what's going on with you and Ross and this whole investigation? Yes, of course, I do. They talked to me. They had to."

"The FBI talked to you? Why?"

"Because I---because you're working for me, remember? And I'm running for Congress. And---and that's their job, cover all the bases."

God, he hated this, hated the lies. He wanted it to end, wanted to come clean.

"What did they tell you?"

"The FBI? I think they told me everything, including that you are cooperating with them in your husband's investigation, and I think that's good."

"You know what they want me to do?"

"I know it's important you do what they say. This is serious business, Meagan."

"So, Chase, let me get this straight. I am supposed to kowtow to Ross, keep him happy, do anything he asks, right?"

"Right. It won't be for long, but that's the way it has to be right now."

"So, if he says, 'Let's make love,' I say, 'Sounds good to me.'"

"Jesus, Meagan!"

"Answer me! Am I suppose to act like nothing is wrong or not?"

"Not! Make up an excuse. You're a woman. Think of something."

"That's easy for you to say, but you don't know--- it's not so---"

"I know, I know. But you can do it, Meagan."

"What makes you so sure?"

"Well," he said it without thinking, "According to your dossier---"

"My dossier? You have a dossier on me?"

She jumped back. The towel dropped. She stood there stark naked, eyes blazing. "Did you memorize it so you could seduce me?"

"Wait, you've got it all---"

"Did it tell you how I like it? Suggest any favorite positions?"

She stabbed a finger at his chest. "You're just like Ross, you know. You're both controlling egomaniacs!"

He caught her arm. "I am nothing like Ross Hamilton!"

"This is so----" She pushed him away. "This is crazy. My whole life is crazy. My husband is some kind of criminal. My money's gone. I've got the FBI in my house..."

She pointed at him. "And you---you are playing me for a fool, Chase Chambers!"

He opened his arms wide, pleading.

"I'm not."

"Oh? You're not playing me?"

"I'm not Chase Chambers." There. He said it.

"What did you say?"

"I'm not Chase. I'm Cameron."

She stared at him in stunned disbelief. "That's a lie. Why are you lying?"

"It's the truth. I'm sorry, but I had to do it. It was the only way to get to Ross."

"And me!" she croaked. "You put on this charade so you could fuck me?"

"Meagan, I didn't even know you when this started." He reached for her. She dodged away. "None of this was planned. I was on a mission and I was captured---they thought I was dead, but I got out. When I came back, it was all classified. No one knew I was alive except the CIA and the FBI---"

"So, you are with the FBI?"

"Not really. I was Special Forces, but after the debriefing, I stayed in D.C., to work with the FBI anti-terror people. That's when I heard about this Ross Hamilton investigation, and I wanted in on it."

"Because of Diane?"

"God damn right, because of Diane. I told them I knew Hamilton and how he operated. I wanted to help. And it would be better all around if he didn't know I was alive."

"So, you conveniently stayed dead, and the government let you?"

He nodded.

She shook her head. "I don't believe you. It doesn't make sense. "

"It does make sense. It was the only way I could get actively involved. Ross wouldn't go near Cameron. But as Chase---I could get to him, maybe do some business with him, get inside his operation---"

"And seduce his wife?"

"That wasn't part of the plan, Meagan. You've got to believe that."

"I'm supposed to believe a liar? And a spy? You were spying on my husband."

"That's the idea. And it was working. He was taking the bait. And then I met you."

"And you worked me right into the act, Chase — Cam---whoever you are! Damn you both!"

◻

Cam steered to the dock. As soon as he switched off the engines, an angry Meagan appeared top side, dressed. He clutched her.

"Meagan, I---"

She pulled away. "I'm getting off this roller coaster."

"Wait!" He grabbed both her arms, then winced as he looked over her shoulder. Curtis LaFond was scurrying down the dock.

"One day. Just one---that's all I wanted," Cameron muttered. "How did you find me?"

"Your brother said---Oh, hello, Mrs. Hamilton, hope I'm not interrupting."

Meagan perked up. "Your brother?"

"...err, Cole." Curtis tried to cover. "Your brother Cole told me you might be on the boat."

"You're a little confused aren't you, Curtis?" Meagan scoffed. "You mean his brother, Chase, don't you?"

"But Chase is right here with---"

"You don't have to work so hard to make a fool out of me anymore, Curtis---if you really are Curtis--- and I don't give a damn anyhow. I'm through with all of you."

Curtis gave Cameron a worried look. Meagan saw it.

"That's right. He finally let me in on the joke, and it's on me. Imagine that?"

"Don't say that," Cam pleaded. "It wasn't a joke. We couldn't tell you what was going on until we were sure you weren't---"

"Weren't what? A criminal?"

That was it. She marched down the dock, struggling to complete her dramatic exit as her stomach started to churn. Wouldn't you know it? Solid as a rock in the rolling sea, and now, back on dry land---seasick.

She made it to her car and collapsed in the driver's seat.

Curtis scratched his head. "I take it there's a problem with Mrs. Hamilton."

Cameron didn't answer.

"Well." Curtis shrugged. "At least MacNulty will be pleased, and you don't have to quit now. Everybody's happy."

Cameron's gaze was fixed on Meagan's car.

Inside, Meagan was sobbing, her head buried in her hands.

"I know it's hard," Curtis said. "But maybe it's time that you let her go."

"Not in this lifetime, Curtis. I won't let her go until I die."

- 53 -

THE DEVIL.

Ross Hamilton watched the shadows move in across the lake. One by one, the rectangles of light in the city towers went dim, a patch or two remaining. Dark was closing in and the game would soon be over.

It wasn't just the money, although he would happily take it and find a pleasant place to enjoy the rest of his days.

It wasn't the killing either. He didn't like that part of it, certainly not the hands-on kind. He had done it more than once, but it was filthy, messy. There was no sexual stimulation, no thrill at all except for the empowerment.

But that was enough. The satisfaction of ruling the game, seizing the right to decide who wins and who loses, who lives and who dies. It was transcendent, almost divine.

And why all the women? He wasn't sure. There will be those who will try to make something out of that when they tell his story---which they surely will someday---but that will be mostly psychobabble. He didn't hate his mother, although she could be quite despicable at times, and perhaps there was a cinder or two smoldering in him about her, but it was not a driving force. And he didn't hate all women. He didn't hate the women he killed. He wasn't concerned about them one way or another. It was business. He determined that they should die. It was in his best interest. Simple as that.

His reflections ended when Stacy entered without knocking, a slim leather folder tucked under her arm.

"Ross---I have to talk to you."

"Apparently." He folded his hands on the desk. "What's the problem?"

Stacy took a seat across the desk from him. "It's not a problem; it's a solution. Or a resolution, I should say."

"Resolution of what?"

"You and me, Ross, darling." She placed the folder on the desk. "It's all in there."

Ross looked at it with distaste. "What is this?"

"A full accounting of everything we've done---together."

He opened the folder and scanned the first page, feeling the heat begin to rise.

"That's interesting, Stacy, but you needn't bother. I know what the numbers are."

"I just wanted to be sure we were on the same page."

"On the same page?" He was on his feet. "On the same fucking page? Who do you think you're talking to?"

She had braced for this but it was still intimidating. She pressed on.

"I just want us to be clear. I've done everything you've asked and more. I've been a part of all this. I think I'm entitled to--"

"You're entitled? You're a fucking secretary. You're entitled to what I say."

"One third of the money. That's fair. I'm your partner, Ross. You must know that."

"You can be my partner in hell!"

Stacy cringed as he seized her throat. "Ross, no!" She clawed at his hands.

He squeezed. He could kill her right now, right here in this room. He could--

The intercom voice broke the spell.

"Mr. Hamilton---Mrs. Tan on two."

He released her, hands recoiling. She collapsed on the carpet, gasping.

"Put her through," Ross said, with a warning glance at Stacy.

"Missah Hamilton?" The sing-song accent chimed over the speaker.

"Mrs. Tan. How are you?" Ross was back on good behavior.

"I am fine. And you?"

"Very well, thank you."

"And your family?"

"All is well in our home."

It was her way to go through a litany of pleasantries---inquiries about family, health, weather---but she moved to her point quickly this time. It was a bad sign.

"Missah Hamilton, we have difficulty with agreement. I do not want attorney to inform you. I call myself."

The hair rose on the back of his neck. "Mrs. Tan, if there is any problem with the contract language, I'm sure it can be resolved without---"

"It is not contract," she interrupted. Mrs. Tan never interrupted. "It is you."

"Pardon me?"

"Yes, it is you," she said. "Problems in the past with other clients, and the American government. This is not acceptable."

"I have no idea what you are talking about, Mrs. Tan."

"We do diligence," her voice was cold. "This is reliable source."

Ross and Stacy exchanged worried looks. "Mrs. Tan, I assure you that is false information." He moved closer to the speaker. "I have to believe this is some devious attempt by a competitor to disrupt our relationship and dismantle an agreement that is very rewarding for all of us, very lucrative for you, and very secure." Ross was at his best now, calm and reassuring. "You know that. We've gone over the numbers many times."

"Character more important than numbers." She was unyielding.

"Mrs. Tan, please." Ross was starting to sound desperate. "I can refute---these are lies! Who told you this? Who would say such things? You must give me a chance to---"

"My people are acquainted with the Chambers family there. I believe you are also."

The name staggered Ross. "Yes, I know the Chambers. And I think you should know that they have a hidden agenda here, Mrs. Tan, a self-serving agenda that is not in your best interests, or mine."

"How is this so?" There was a hint of doubt in her response. A glimmer of hope.

"It is complicated, Mrs. Tan. I would not want to pursue it on the phone, but believe me---I have documented proof."

"You must send me this."

"I can do better than that." He paused for effect. "I will be on the first flight tomorrow and bring it to you myself. All the proof you require. We can work this out, Mrs. Tan. We've worked too hard to let it fall apart because of meddling malcontents."

"I look forward to seeing you tomorrow."

Ross clicked off and turned to Stacy.

"Would you like to go out there and clear up this mess before the whole deal goes up in smoke---partner?"

She touched her neck gingerly. "You almost killed me," she said in a raspy whisper.

"Oh, please, Stacy, don't be melodramatic. It wasn't that close." He leaned back, not a care in the world. The mood swings were getting bizarre, Stacy thought. "I just had to teach you a lesson---Don't fuck with me."

Stacy squirmed in her seat. "I'm sorry. I thought it would be best for---"

"I'll decide what's best for both of us...darling. Don't ever forget that again."

"What are you going to do about Mrs. Tan? You don't have any documents."

"I will by tomorrow morning," he said confidently. "I've got four months and a quarter million into this, and twelve million on the table. I'm not walking away."

- 54 -

"Mac, you gotta see this." Harry Black huffed up to MacNulty's desk, shaking the papers in his hand. "Higgins copied us on the bulletin from VICAP yesterday..."

"VICAP? In Quantico? That's the Profilers."

"Uh-huh."

"So what does that have to do with us? Those guys, they're heavy duty---serial murders, that kind of shit. I don't even like to think about what they get into. Con men like Hamilton don't even show up on their radar screen."

"Yeah, well he does now."

"What?"

"They're working on this case---Higgins says it's the strangest one they've ever---nine females, all over the country, all dead in the last five years."

"That's too bad, but it happens all the time now, Harry. It's a jungle out there."

"These weren't hookers who got picked up at a truck stop, Mac. All wealthy women. I mean, serious money."

"That's a new one. But I still don't see---"

"All of 'em lost a bundle in scam investment deals, fraud, securities theft---the grand total is at thirty million, maybe a lot more."

"And are you going to tell me---"

Black held up the papers. "It says here, at least three were involved with Ross Hamilton, one way or another."

"Hmm," Mac chewed on it. "I'm not sure how much that means. All his clients are wealthy, and he's had a lot of them over the years."

"There's more," said Harry. "Along with the nine females, there's two male victims."

"That's another twist. The psychos usually go one way or the other."

Harry gave him the punch line. "Both connected to Hamilton. "

"I'll be damned."

"One was a financial guy in Cleveland, Nicholas Sheehan, did some real estate deals with him." Black took a breath. "The other one was Edelman."

"Why the hell didn't we know about this?"

"They just started putting it together. Most of them weren't listed as homicides---accidents, natural causes or suicides, like Edelman. The MO's are all over the place."

MacNulty grabbed the papers and started reading as Harry continued. "Hamilton's name didn't come up until last week. You know how he works. He's got all these layers---venture capital outfits on top of LLCs on top of holding companies."

"Christ, Harry, we're trying to take this bastard down on a fraud rap," Mac stood up, hands on hips. "And now you're telling me he's a mass murderer."

"I'm not saying that, Mac. It's not concrete evidence. But it's a mighty strange coincidence."

"I don't believe in coincidence."

"They don't either. That's why they want all we've got on Hamilton."

"Fair enough. You tell 'em it's on the way. And tell 'em we want everything they've got, too, on Hamilton and all the victims."

Harry nodded.

"And where the hell is Chambers? He's gotta know about this."

"I'll have Curtis track him down." Harry stood to go. "But you better talk to him yourself, Mac. He's going to go ballistic."

"What do you mean?"

"Look at number seven on the list."

MacNulty read the entry aloud. "'Diane McAlister.' Oh, shit."

55

As the campaign momentum continued to build, the family home in Port Royal was transformed to election central. The staff had taken over the great room, now cluttered with phones, printers, and computers. Rows of TVs and fax machines converted the library into a media center. Even the pantry had been commandeered by First Class for planning and staging.

Sandy had managed to salvage the kitchen as a private island, off limits to all but family. She and Chase were grabbing lunch with Gem before heading back on the campaign trail. Chase's mother had spent the morning conjuring up a hearty meal of crawfish stew and cornbread. Gem watched them devour it with maternal satisfaction.

"Slow down, son," said Gem. "Those crawdaddies won't jump out of the bowl."

Chase grabbed another hunk of cornbread. "Where's Cole? He loves this stuff."

"Your brother is working on a portrait and he doesn't want to be interrupted."

Sandy nudged Chase. "Elle's posing for him."

"Oh, great, I hope the reporters don't get wind of this." Chase winked at Sandy. "I'm trying to win this election and Cole is doing nude paintings of the campaign staff!"

"Chase, hush." Gem scolded. "It's not a nude. And Eleanor is hardly campaign staff. It's a fabulous work, maybe his best, and it's good for Cole."

"She's been great with him," Sandy said. "He comes alive when she's around."

"Yes," Gem nodded. "There's something special there. I've seen it in the cards."

"Gem," implored Sandra. "Will you do a reading for Chase and the election?"

"I don't need the cards to tell me he's going to win." She patted Sandra's shoulder. "And I can't now, dear. I'm going to Cassadaga for a few days. "

"Cassadaga?" Sandra perked up. "Oh, I'd love to go there sometime. They say it's amazing."

"It truly is. There are so many gifted ones living there. It's a magical place."

"Cole's going with you, right?"

"No. He's staying here."

Chase and Sandy exchanged glances. "Whose idea was that?"

"Cole wants to stay and finish his painting."

"And Elle---"Chase grinned. "Will she be staying at the cottage, too?"

"He may be your little brother, but Cole is a grown man, Chase. He can make his own choices. Now you go on, take care of your business, and let Cole take care of his."

"Yes, ma'm." Chase bowed. "C'mon, Sandy, let's get going before I get myself grounded."

56

Ross Hamilton thought he picked up a hint of cheerfulness in Sheldon Smith's voice and he didn't like it. The man was never cheerful. Ross liked him that way, never wasting time on inane pleasantries. This new congeniality was faint, but it was there and it seemed to mock Ross with a hint of contempt. Smith droned on with his report.

"...It was about four when they came back in, the two of them. If there was someone else on board, they never came up on deck."

Ross nodded. "And what was she wearing?"

"Cut-offs and blouse, I guess. Towel around her shoulders."

"What about him?"

Sheldon shrugged. "Shorts, shirt."

"Did he touch her?"

There it was---the trace of a smile on Sheldon's placid face.

"I did not see that." Sheldon shook his head. "In fact, it looked like they had words. The little man that works for him was there to meet them. He said something to Chambers. Chambers spoke to her, and she does not like it."

Ross looked out the window. "A lover's quarrel, perhaps?"

"I do not know."

Ross swiveled in his chair.

"So what do you make of it, Sheldon? Is Chambers fucking my wife?"

"I could not say. I did not see any---"

"I know that! But just tell me, for a change---what do you think?"

Sheldon answered with no expression in voice. "Yes, I would say probably yes."

Ross laughed. Sheldon Smith didn't get the joke.

"Well, well. Chase Chambers is not only involved in some sort of investigation into my business and interfering with my operations, he's having an affair with my lovely bride. He's getting to be somewhat of an issue, Sheldon, hmm?"

No comment.

"He's going to take my money, get me arrested, fuck my wife, ruin my life---and he thinks he can do that to me? With impunity?" He turned from the window. "We're not going to let that happen, are we?"

"No."

"Kill him."

Smith stood impassive.

"He's the one. Just like his brother started the problems with Diane. Fucking twins. I should have known. Asking questions, sticking his nose and his cock in where they don't belong. Well, his brother's dead---and if he hadn't gotten himself killed, I would have done it. And this one needs killing, too."

"That will not be easy."

"Maybe not. But it's got to be done. I can't imagine why, but he's behind all of these, these complications. I know it. And he's fucking my wife. Can you believe it, Sheldon? Chase Chambers is fucking my wife."

"What about her?"

"Meagan? Oh, no. Not yet. I'm not finished with her yet. But her time will come. First I want Chambers. I want him dead."

"I do not know how you can get close to him. He is an important man, candidate. He has many people around him all the time."

"But that's just it, Sheldon, don't you see? He's in politics, and politics is a dangerous game. There are people out there---crazy people. They shot the Kennedys, didn't they? And Reagan. Some lunatic killed the mayor of San Francisco. Another one killed a congressman in New York. Happens all the time."

"Easy to say, hard to do."

"You don't have to get close. One shot with a rifle. A hundred yards. You'll be gone before he hits the floor. And they'll never know who, or why."

"I do not think---"

"Haven't I been good to you, Sheldon?"

"I am not complaining. I am telling you, you cannot just kill this man and walk away. He has big friends. The family is wired. Media, FBI---they would never let it go."

"How much?"

"That is not it. It is not the money."

"It's always the money, Sheldon. Doesn't matter who it is or what it is---it's always the money. Now, just tell me. How much?"

"A hundred thousand dollars extra up front."

"Done. I'll have Stacy deposit the money today." He smiled. "See how easy that was?"

Smith thought he should have said more.

57

There were two hundred people at the seminar, an eclectic assortment of psychics, spiritualists, mediums and seers, real and imagined. Gem had spoken for an hour then answered questions for most of the next. She was warmly received, revered by many in the audience. Still, she was relieved when it was all over, impatient to return to the hotel. Agent Curran was due to arrive and she didn't want to keep him waiting.

And there was something else. Gem was plagued by a growing discomfort, a sense of unease. She didn't know what the problem was but her intuition told her it was not to be taken lightly. As she entered the Victorian lobby of her hotel, she saw the man sitting patiently near the front desk, a thick briefcase at his side. She knew at a glance that it was him.

"Mr. Curran?"

"Mrs. Chambers?"

She tilted her head in a disapproving look and he corrected himself.

"Gem." He took her hand. "I hope I'm not too early."

"Not at all. I hope I'm not too late." Gem gestured toward the closet-sized elevator with the old-fashioned brass grill. "Please..."

They rode up to her room in silence.

Curran placed his briefcase on the table.

"Can I get you something?"

"No thank you, ma'm. I appreciate you letting me come down here like this on short notice and I don't want to take up any more of your time than I have to. I'd just as soon get started on this right away, if that's all right with you."

Curran removed a thick manila folder.

"Now, Gem, I've got to tell you that a lot of this is hard to look at. I don't even like carrying it around with me, but if you're going to be able to help us with this it doesn't make sense to censor it first."

Curran opened the folder. "With apologies in advance, here we go."

He placed the first photograph in front of her, an image of a woman, slumped against a brick wall, her throat cut and her head twisted at an obscure angle.

·"These are some of the victims. Possible victims. We don't know anything for sure. They're from cold case files that match up to what you have told us."

Gem studied it without expression.

"Take your time. This lady was in New York. You never mentioned New York. It doesn't tie in to anything else. It could have been a random---"

"It was him."

Curran nodded and placed another picture on the table: Two Illinois state troopers stood by the wreckage of a car in a ditch. A dead woman in the driver's seat.

Gem ran her hand lightly over the glossy surface. "I'm not---he didn't do this. An accident of fate. Meant to be. It was her time."

Curran did not comment, placing another image on the pile. It was a woman in a jogging suit, face down on the asphalt, her body broken and misshapen, reddish hair matted in a dark pool.

"*Mon dieu*," Gem whispered. "This poor girl."

"What do you think---was he involved in this one?"

"Yes, oh yes, but he was not the one who killed her."

"Sorry?"

"There was someone else, another man, a dark man with a long shadow."

"So our man has an accomplice? Is that it?"

"I think so. Yes."

"And the other one, he's African-American. Am I getting that right?"

"I don't know."

"You said he was a dark man."

"There is a darkness about him."

Curran looked a little perplexed as he paused to write a note.

"I'm not being very helpful, am I?"

"No, don't say that. We know it's a long shot. And if one thing clicks, just one---would you like to see the suspect photos?"

Gem sat up straighter. "All right."

Curran took a set of 8 x 10's from the folder, placed on the table and turned one up.

Like the cards, Gem thought.

The picture was a headshot of an older man, wild-eyed and disheveled.

"Anything?" Curran asked.

"Nothing."

Curran took it from her. "OK."

Gem picked it up. "Wait! He is not the one, but he is not innocent. He has hurt people. Children---I hope I'm wrong, but I think he killed a child."

Curran looked at her in wonder. "You're not wrong, Gem. He did. We know all about it." He took the picture from her hands. "Let's move on."

He gave her another photo, a dark-haired man in a neatly tailored suit. The picture was slightly out of focus, taken with a telephoto lens.

Gem gasped. "That's him."

"How do you know?"

She answered the question with a look of certainty.

"Gem, can you give me more to go on. This isn't just some lunatic living under a bridge. This is a respected man. He's got money, connections, he runs in high circles. I need more to go into court ---"

"Why is he a suspect?"

"He's had business dealings with some of the victims and he's the target of a separate investigation---fraud and theft---but that's a far cry from murder."

"Is it? Or is it all one? I told you this one was different. I told you about the money."

"Yes you did. But in my business, we have to have evidence, and without that, we're nowhere. Do you think that you've seen him somewhere else?"

"I've never seen him in my life."

"Maybe not. Or maybe you don't remember?"

"Why would you say that?"

"He lives in Naples, Gem." Curran could see he had her attention. "And we believe he may have been involved in some business with one of your sons."

"Chase?"

"They've met at least twice."

She rose abruptly and walked across the room. Curran watched her, puzzled.

"Now where are you going?"

"I can't give you any evidence, but I might help point you in the right direction."

She took the velvet pouch from her suitcase, removed the cards and set them on the table. Curran stared at them.

"So these are the famous Tarot cards."

Gem was already into her routine, sitting straight, eyes closed, taking deep breaths. The cards moved as if by rote, shifting back and forth, bottom to top. She squared them in front of her and rolled one over.

The Devil.

The bug-eyed beast with the head of a goat, wings of a vampire bat and the sharp talons of a bird of prey, he squats on a cold stone throne, his scepter a phallic torch pointed to hell, his right hand raised in grim greeting to the damned. Surrounded by darkness, marked with the inverted pentangle of despair, he peers down with scorn upon his woeful subjects, a naked man and woman, saddled with horns and tails, chained by the neck to an altar of lust and degradation. The Devil was the most repulsive image of the Tarot, always a warning of serious danger, often violent, sometimes inevitable.

Gen flipped two more cards in rapid succession, then rose up from her seat as if she had seen a ghost.

"What?" Curran said. "What's the matter?"

"I must go home," she said. "Back to Port Royal. I have to be there in time---to try to stop it."

"Try to stop what?"

"Death. Death walks in the fifth house, the house of my children."

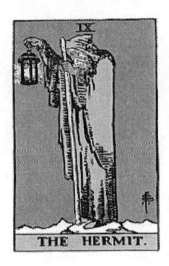

58

Meagan was alone, and she didn't like it.

Her mother had taken Brandon to the beach for the afternoon.

Ross was still in Chicago or L. A. or God knows where. He hadn't even bothered to call for two days and Meagan was fine with that. She curled on the bed and closed her eyes, but sleep would not come; too many jumbled thoughts going through her mind.

She had been to the doctor's office the previous day, only to confirm what she already knew. She was eight weeks pregnant. Dr. Tasse delivered the news with hearty congratulations.

She had not gained any weight yet. In fact, she had lost some, and her appetite was not improving. She had dark shadows under her eyes but the nausea had subsided somewhat.

And now the TV was mocking her. The local news was on, and there he was---Chase Chambers, walking through the crowd, smiling and shaking hands with Sandy at his side. He looked so confident. Sandy, too. Both of them beaming. The TV reporter was saying something about a surge in the polls when Meagan clicked it off.

[]

Cameron was alone in his office at the FBI outpost in downtown Naples. He was reviewing the Edelman file trying to find the key to put Hamilton on the hot seat for murder.

It was hard to focus on the work. He was thinking of Meagan. Where was she? What was she doing? Was she OK? The last time they had spoken had been the debacle on the boat---what a fool he'd been to mention the stupid dossier. All he could think of was seeing her again and making things right between them.

And there was something else. He was worried about her, a feeling that wouldn't go away. He didn't put too much stock in premonitions, ESP or Tarot cards. He loved his mother, and that included a profound respect for the psychic talents that had amazed him many times. But he was much more like his father when it came to Gem's gift. He tipped his hat and kept his distance, assured that his mother had good standing in that mysterious world and fairly certain that he did not. He was far more comfortable in the reality of here and now.

This time he wasn't so sure. He couldn't get the anxious thoughts of Meagan out of his mind. Or the dreams. Lately, Meagan filled his dreams, alluring and fragile, always surrounded by a confusing cluster of symbols, light and dark. He groped through the dream maze---What did it all mean? The answer eluded him. He had to do something about it.

Pulling Harry Black aside that afternoon, Cameron told him of his concerns. Harry had seen it himself, up close. Everything was taking a toll on Meagan. So Harry invited him outside to join him for a cigarette.

"I don't smoke," said Cameron.

"Neither do I," Black replied with a wink.

[]

"It's not your imagination. She's not doing so great --- she's taking a pounding."

"It's got to end. We've got to get her out of this, Harry."

"We're the ones that got her into it."

"Don't remind me."

Black sat down on the bottom step and took a bent cigarette from a rumpled pack.

"I thought you didn't smoke."

"I don't," he said, lighting up. "Only when something gets on my nerves."

"How often is that?"

"Four or five times a day, I guess."

Black dropped the butt and crushed it into the pavement with the sole of his shoe.

"Tell you what, Chambers. You didn't hear this from me, but I think you ought to see her, face-to-face. I know it's not in the game plan right now, but I think it might help."

"Tonight?" Cameron asked.

"No, not tonight, and you can't get anywhere near her place again. That would be a mistake." He stroked his chin. "Here's what we do. We'll get her out to Port Royal on Tuesday night."

"That's election night, Harry."

"You think I don't read the paper? Look, it'll be packed out there, wall to wall people. You're not on the schedule---that's one night your brother has to handle himself. She's got an excuse to be there--- First Class is doing the catering. What's to say you can't be in the vicinity, step in when Chase goes downtown for the formalities?"

"That's perfect," Cameron said. "Tuesday night, then. Thanks, Harry."

- 59 -

Eleanor's life had gone through so many changes she felt like a different person. In but a few weeks, she had gone from real estate broker in Cleveland to an event planner in Naples, from living alone to living with Meg and now in a hotel. It was wild. It was crazy. She loved it.

For Marsha, Eleanor was a godsend. The complications in Meagan's life had made her less available, but the campaign would not wait for anyone. Marsha was grateful that Eleanor was there to pick up the slack.

First Class had virtually taken over a guest room at the Chamber's home and had converted it to an on-site office. Eleanor was spending ten hours a day there with Marsha and the staff, coordinating details for the remaining events, including PR and publicity. And it was no small task. But her remaining hours were spent with Cole at his studio.

Eleanor had hardly had a chance to talk to Meagan in a week but she had been thinking about her a lot. As much as she hoped it wasn't true, she was convinced that Meagan's relationship with Chase Chambers was doomed. She'd had a ringside seat to watch Chase and Sandy together as she had practically been living at the Big House. It was clear that Sandy and Chase were a perfect couple. And in spite of her undying loyalty to Meg, she had come to like both Sandy and Chase. They were good people who were decent and considerate to everyone, including her. She couldn't figure out why Chase was playing with Meagan's emotions. Everything told her he wasn't that kind of man. She racked her brain but couldn't come up with an answer.

"Could you lift your head, just a little?"

Cole's voice brought Eleanor back to the moment. He was at his easel, paintbrush in hand. Eleanor had been sitting for him for hours since Marsha had shooed her out insisting she comply with Cole's request.

"Every girl ought to be an artist's model at least once in her life," she said with a wicked grin. "Go on."

Now here she was with this curious man in a gingerbread house by the river, Cole half-sitting on a stool at his canvas. She couldn't help noticing that his frayed jeans were tight---too tight.

"Elle, don't look down. Keep your head up high. That's it. Perfect. Hold it there."

"For how long?"

"For as long as I say... Chin a tad higher. Shoulders down. Don't slump."

"I don't slump and I need a fucking break."

"In a minute...don't move."

330

Cole mixed the blobs of paint, red and white in with a twirl of pink, a dot of yellow, and a pinch of azure.

Eleanor watched, fascinated. "What are you doing?"

"Screwing this up. I'm trying to find the right shade for where the light catches your cheek."

"Oh."

"It's a beautiful color, but I'm having trouble getting it."

"Come closer."

"What?"

"You can see it better if you come closer. "

Cole moved in, brush in hand.

"Break time," Eleanor announced, abandoning her pose. She pulled him close and kissed him. His lips lingered, eager for her.

The brush dropped to the floor.

〇

Eleanor and Cole were asleep on the couch by the fireplace, when the cottage door opened and Gem appeared.

Eleanor slowly raised her head. Wide awake in an instant, she jumped off the couch, mortified, holding the top of her loosened gown against her chest.

"Mrs.---Gem! Oh my God. We were just---we weren't---oh, shit. I'm sorry."

Her face red, she pulled the straps up and rummaged on the floor for her shoes. Cole remained asleep and unaware.

"Darling Elle." Gem looked at her son's tranquil face. "No apologies."

"Well, then..." Eleanor grinned. "It was good for me, too."

"You stay," Gem said. "He'll need all you can give him---strength and courage."

Gem said no more and departed, closing the door behind her. Eleanor fell back on the couch, bewildered.

"Don't start thinking too hard," Cole spoke up, "My mother can do that to you."

"You're awake. Oh, you---" She poked him hard.

"Hey!"

"Your mother talks in riddles. Sometimes I don't know what to make of it."

"I do," Cole said. "The cards say you should make love to me, right now."

He pulled her back into his arms.

◻

At the Big House, Curtis paged through his ever-present notebook while Chase and Sandy slumped on the couch, weary from another 14-hour day.

"Great answer on that question about the military budget and the base closings in Florida. You hit a home run, Chase."

"But I fouled up the one on prescription drugs. They didn't care for that at all."

"Maybe. It was just the truth. Too much money."

"Tell that to the old woman eating dog food so she can pay for her medicine."

"Not me. I'm not running. You are. I'll say this, though, I'm starting to get the hang of this politics thing. If you win, I think I might take leave from the Bureau and sign on as your chief of staff."

"You're certainly welcome to submit an application."

Curtis dropped his pen. "An application?"

"We already have a few dozen," Sandy tossed in. "All female, I'm sorry to say."

"If you think for a minute I'm going to compete with a bunch of groupies for the---"

"Chase, I need to talk to you."

Gem stood in the doorway.

Chase scrambled to his feet.

"I thought you were out of town."

"I came back early. Please, call your brother."

"Isn't Cole at the caretaker's? He was---"

"Cole knows what he has to do. I need to talk to you ... and Cameron."

Gem had never been told that Cameron was alive. It had been decided on the highest levels, as soon as the plan was formulated, that Cameron's escape, his return, and his very existence must be on a need-to-know basis. The twins had agreed, convinced that telling their mother would only put her at unnecessary risk.

Now she talked as if she had known all along.

"Mother, I don't---"

"There's no time to waste on secrets anymore. I know there were good reasons, but it's time for me to be with my sons again, all my sons. I have good reasons of my own."

"I'm right here, Ma."

She turned at the sound of Cameron's voice. He rushed to embrace her.

"I missed you, Ma. I'm sorry I couldn't---I know it wasn't right, but we had to---"

"Shhh." She patted him like a baby. "It's all right. You had a mission ..."

She stood back at arms length, still holding him. "Now I have a mission, and I want you and your brother to listen to what I have to say."

60

Meagan was cleaning out the huge closet off the family room on the first floor, the catchall utility room that served as a repository for everything in her home that didn't belong anywhere else. It was the one place that was always cluttered, always on her to-do list for a complete overhaul. Stuck in the house with too much on her mind, today was the day. The process of discarding things helped her clear her head. Out with the old, make room for the new. Every thing must go!

Harry Black found her curled up on the floor, surrounded by piles of clothes, mounds of toys and stacks of boxes.

"So this is how you spend your spare time, huh, Mrs. H?"

"Yep, this is my life. Take a look. Knee deep in useless, out of date garbage."

Pulling out a drawer full of papers and receipts, she dumped all the pieces in a waste paper basket.

"I swear, men are such pack rats," she muttered.

Black crouched beside her, grabbing the wastebasket.

"Wait! Maybe there is something here worth---"

"It's trash."

"Yeah, but it's his trash. Notes, receipts---from when? Where?"

"I don't know, a year or two ago," Meagan shrugged.

"Save it all. It must be checked and categorized, piece by piece, and you're the best one to do it. You can tell us if it's regular stuff, or...? Look, I'll help you go through it, if you want."

"OK, but it's just junk."

"One man's junk is another man's evidence."

Black pulled on a pair of latex gloves and gave another pair to Meagan. "Here. This means you are deputized. You're an official G-man."

She slipped them on and they started going through all of Ross's suits, checking the pockets. Every scrap of paper was packaged in a plastic bag and set aside. It was nice for Meagan to be doing something worthwhile. She felt like an active participant, not just a pawn in the game.

"God, I never knew men's clothes had so many hidden pockets. No wonder you guys don't carry purses. You don't have to," she said as she explored the pockets of another suit.

"Who said I don't carry a purse?"

Meagan laughed. Special Agent Harry Black was an okay guy.

He picked a short stack of computer discs off one pile.

"How about these? Are they his?"

Meagan looked. "No, those are Brandon's DVD's. You know, games, cartoons, movies---all that stuff."

Harry Black paged through the disks, reading the titles. 'The Incredibles,' 'Harry Potter,' 'Aladdin II'--- you know, when I was a kid, we had crayons. That was it."

"That was a long time ago, Mr. Black."

"Back when dinosaurs roamed the earth." He stopped and looked closer at one of the disks. "Hey. Why doesn't this one have anything on it? No title."

"Let me see."

He handed it to her. She checked both sides and gave it back.

"I don't know. That one was mixed in with Bran's but it's not one of his. He tried to play it, but it wouldn't work. I don't know where he got it. I was going to throw it out."

Black took it back and studied it. "So, this could be his?"

Meagan shrugged. "Could be."

"Let me take this downtown, let our guys take a look at it. OK?"

"Sure."

"No chance there could be anything embarrassing for you on this, right?"

An insulted look from Meagan. "Harry Black, what are you implying?"

"Sorry," he said sheepishly, "Strike that. We'll take a look at it. Maybe there's something there."

He slipped it in the inside pocket of his suit coat.

"You know, Mrs. H, you're going to make it through this okay. But here's just a little word of advice. Take it for what it's worth. Chambers. He's a complicated fellow. You oughta be careful. I don't want to see you get hurt. That's my job, you know. To make sure you don't get hurt."

"I'm afraid you may be a little late, Harry. Between my husband and your Mr. Chambers, I think I already jumped from the frying pan into the fire."

"Hey, don't get me wrong." Black looked right at her. "Chambers is not like that. He's a little wild, kind of a maverick, maybe, but he's a good man, and he cares about you. It's just that---well, sometimes, things just aren't what they seem. People aren't who you think they are." Black paused to scratch his head while Meagan gave him a blank look.

Harry Black frowned. "I'm not making much sense here, am I?"

"Not really."

Black laughed at himself. "I never was the Dear Abby type anyhow."

Meagan touched him lightly on the shoulder. "Harry, I appreciate what you're trying to tell me, I really do. And I want to tell you something: I know a lot more than you think. I'm not sure if I'm OK with it, but at least I'm not in the dark anymore."

"Then I guess I ought to shut up."

Meagan's cell phone rang. She checked the readout. "It's Elle," she mouthed, and flipped it open.

"What am I doing? Well, right at the moment, I'm in the closet with an FBI guy."

"In the closet? Must be Curtis, eh?"

"No, silly. Harry Black."

"Shit, I didn't know he was gay, too."

338

"Good-bye, Elle. Gotta go." Meagan snapped the phone shut with a grin.

Harry Black acted like he didn't hear.

"I'm supposed to give you a message. Tuesday at Chambers? Are you part of it?"

Meagan froze. "I wasn't planning on it. You know the rules."

"Better change your plans. You-know-who wants to meet you there."

"Oh, really? And what if I don't want to? Who does he think he is anyway? Or should I say, which one does he think he is? I'm not sure if he knows himself."

"He says it's important, Mrs. H. That's all I know."

"I get the message."

"Well?"

"I have to think about that, Harry."

He nodded. "Fair enough. You do that."

Meagan asked him boldly, "What do you think?"

"I don't know. Honest to God, I don't." He gave her a weary smile. "But I'll tell you this, whatever choice you make, I think it'll be the right one."

61

It was raining in Chicago. The entire lakefront was draped in a bleak gray shroud and it was just as gloomy inside the suite.

Stacy was packing the clothes and the selected items they would take with them when they made their exit. Ross had provided a list, of course. He wanted nothing more and nothing less than what was on his neatly typed sheet of paper.

She took stock. There must be a couple hundred thousand dollars worth of furnishings and art they would leave behind. When they abandoned the suite and the office in Chicago, it had to be swift and sure, with no hint that they would ever return. She understood about the furniture, but the art---some of her favorites weren't on the list, including the Braque lithograph and the small jade Buddha she loved. All of Ross's pet pieces made the cut.

"Fuck him."

She took the Buddha from the mantel, wrapped it in a thick cashmere sweater and stuffed it in a suitcase.

By the time she had completed her assignment, there was a small mountain of suitcases in the foyer ready to go. They had to be hauled out for shipment by private carrier to the storage location in Florida. The plan was to pick them up on the final leg of the trip to the airport, and then Ross and Stacy would fly away to Never-Never Land and live happily ever after.

"Like that's going to happen," Stacy said aloud.

In spite of what he said and all she had done---she didn't even like to think about all the things she had done for this man---it was all too obvious that Ross had other plans. She didn't know when, and she didn't know where, but she knew her happily ever after was going to have an abrupt and unhappy ending, not unlike Diane and the others.

"Not this time, Ross." She was not Diane. She was not Meagan. She didn't plan on being the one to go flying. She checked her purse. Yes. The shiny little revolver was tucked in the corner, fully loaded. She snapped the purse shut and returned to her work.

She wanted to summon Sheldon to start hauling the ton of luggage down to the loading dock in back, but he was nowhere to be found. Neither was Ross. She hadn't heard from him since he left for L. A. and the summit with Mrs. Tan. She would have to do the heavy lifting and make all the arrangements herself.

"That's all right, Ross, honey," she muttered as she hefted a suitcase. "I'll just put it on your tab."

Her cell phone rang. Ross.

It gave her a chilling thought. Was it possible? Could he read her thoughts from a thousand miles away? There was a hint of fear in her Hello.

"I have the check."

"Ross?"

"Did you hear me? I said I have the check."

"That's wonderful!"

Double relief. No, he couldn't read her thoughts and yes, he closed the deal, their biggest score ever. "Unbelievable!"

"Believe it. Everything. The whole twelve million."

"Ross, you are the best! The fucking best."

"There were some, uh, complications. Mrs. Tan decided to be a bit recalcitrant at the end and I had to be firm with her. Very firm."

"Nothing serious, I hope."

"Serious enough that we're going to have to accelerate the time table. I'm on my way back now. I expect you to have everything on the list shipped out today and everything else ready to go early tomorrow."

"Tomorrow? But Ross, I can't---"

"Yes you can, and you will. You don't want to let me down on this, Stacy."

"I'll find a way."

"That's the correct attitude … partner."

Click.

62

Mac tossed the manila folder on the desk.

Cameron paged through the stack of 8 x 10 police photos of a drowning victim, a woman being fished from the water. Uniformed men on a Coast Guard vessel watched as others on a smaller boat marked "LAPD" hauled in the body. The picture was date and time stamped only twelve hours earlier. A handwritten notation under the stamp read "Zuma Beach." There were more photos of the same sequence as the body was recovered, including close-ups of the woman, the color drained from her Asian features. Her face was bloated and gray, a small bruise on her forehead.

"And why would we be looking at pictures of some Chinese lady, a floater off Malibu?" Cameron asked.

"She's not Chinese, and she's not just some lady. That happens to be Mrs. Lia Tan, president and CEO of Tan Exports, one of the wealthiest women in Southern California."

Curtis shook his head. "Tan Exports. Oh, my. We've been trying to track down Tannex for weeks. Heard it on the wiretaps. We knew he was working something there, but we couldn't find a Tannex anything, because there is no Tannex. Its---"

Cameron grimaced. "Tan ... Ex."

"I'm embarrassed," Curtis confessed.

"She was last seen on Tuesday morning, leaving her bank with a certified check for twelve million dollars made out to an investment firm." Mac picked up the story, "Her Blackberry listed a meeting with the firm's CEO at the Beverly Wilshire Hotel."

"Don't tell me."

"You got it. Our man Hamilton. LAPD would love to get his version of what happened at their little rendezvous, but they can't to seem to locate Mr. Hamilton."

"What about the check?"

"Cashed. Money transferred to an Illinois account, and already out of there to God knows where--- Switzerland, Caymans, whatever."

"Jesus Christ, Mac---what more do you need? Let's get him!"

"Hold on, Chambers. We can't jump the gun here."

"Jump the gun? He killed that woman. You know that! How many more people are we going to let him waste before we put a stop to this maniac?"

"I know how you feel, but we can't operate like that. First of all, this Mrs. Tan---this is not a federal case yet. Officially, we're not even involved. It's local, LAPD's jurisdiction, and it's not even a homicide until the coroner rules. Second, they have enough to pick him up for questioning---he's a person of interest---but not to charge him. The check was made out to his firm, remember? Why shouldn't he cash it? And why would he want to kill a lady who just gave him twelve million bucks?"

Cameron shook his head impatiently. This was all crazy.

"And finally," Mac continued. "He's out of L.A. by now, most likely, and there's nothing we can do until there's a confirmed sighting of Ross Hamilton somewhere on the planet.... So, unless you have some bright idea that we haven't thought of?" he continued. "By the way, aren't you supposed to be doing something important for your brother at this home stretch of his campaign?"

63

It was the last major speech before the election, and Chase made it count. It was eloquent and sincere before the capacity crowd at the Ritz Carlton. Curtis broke through signaling it was time to go. Three young staffers ran like blockers for a running back, leading Chase to the elevators.

"Thanks, Curtis," said Chase. "I thought I was never going to get out of there."

"Don't thank me yet. I finally screwed up," Curtis said sheepishly.

"Why, Curtis---I thought you were perfect."

"So did I. But I'm afraid I double-booked you for tonight. You have to be at the Rotary Club at seven. Very important. All the small business people."

"Okay…"

"And you can't miss the Jenning's Assisted Living Home. You need the grannies, and these are the most important ones---the leaders and activists."

"What time is that?"

"Seven. On the dot. You know those old folks---right on time."

"Great."

"I told you, I screwed up."

"I guess we have to blow off one of them. You pick."

"Oh, no. We can't do that. Not with three days to go. These are both crucial."

"But Curtis, I thought you said---"

"Yes. I screwed up, but nothing I can't fix. I've got it covered."

"I hope you're not thinking---"

"Already done. Your alter ego is on his way. And he wants to do it, Chase. I think he's starting to like this political stuff."

"You're going to get us all into trouble, Curtis."

"Good. Then we'll take the Rotary and give the old folks to Cam." Curtis checked his watch. "You've got seven minutes to change. I'll meet you at the front desk."

The elevator doors closed between them. Chase stepped out on the twelfth floor into a trio of ambitious *Naples Tribune* reporters who had pried the candidate's suite number from the front desk clerk.

"Mr. Chambers----"

"Just one question---"

"Give us a break, we've got a deadline."

"Not today." He nudged past. "And you're not getting extra points for cheating."

"C'mon, two minutes, we just---"

"I don't have two minutes. Look, there's a press conference tomorrow and you can have the first questions. Best offer." He moved on. "I've got to go."

Chase entered the suite as he loosened his tie and grabbed a bottle of water from the granite bar. He drank half of it in a few gulps on the way to the bedroom. A fresh shirt, suit and tie were laid out on the bed. He nodded in appreciation of Curtis's efficiency as he sat on the bed to slip off his shoes.

[]

Cameron huddled with Curtis in a private conference room on the lobby level, reviewing the outline of Chase's proposed speech for the Jenning's Home.

Cameron was sitting quietly, a good pupil listening to instructions from Curtis. Suddenly, he jumped to his feet.

"Where's Chase?"

"He's changing in the suite upstairs."

"I've got to go up there---now. What's the number?"

"You can't do that," Curtis squawked. "Somebody might see you together. Besides, you have to----"

"Curtis!" Cam shouted. "The number?"

"I think it's 1203, but I'm telling you----"

Cameron sprinted out the door.

[]

Chase heard a noise at the door. He moved towards the sound and stopped abruptly. A thickset stranger was standing inside the suite.

"Hey! What did I say?" Chase pointed at the door. "No more today. And you're going to get yourself in trouble coming in here like this. You can't just---"

He gave the man a closer look. He wasn't from the group in the hallway.

"You're not a reporter," he said cautiously.

"No."

"What are you doing here?"

"I do not report news. I make news. And you are the headline tomorrow."

"What?"

"I have a message from Mister Hamilton."

"Ross Hamilton? Listen, I don't know who the hell---"

Smith had the gun out from under his jacket, shiny black barrel leveled at Chase.

"Hey, hey, wait---Why? Why would you---"

Chase raised his hands, backing away.

"Because you must die. Because you are the one who is making the trouble. You hurt his business. You fuck his wife."

He raised the gun, aiming at Chase's heart.

"No. That would be me."

Smith spun around at the sound of the voice. Cameron stood in the open doorway, the mirror image of his brother, in the same suit and tie. Startled, Smith looked back to Chase. The moment of confusion was all Cameron needed.

He pounced, slamming his forearm into Smith's extended arm, knocking it upward. The gun fired harmlessly into the ceiling with a muffled pop as Smith stumbled back into the window ledge. Before he could aim again, Cameron was on top of him, landing two powerful body blows.

Smith doubled over, but came up fighting, charging like a bull, throwing Cameron against the opposite wall. Cameron broke free and lashed out with two short jabs to the face, then a roundhouse right to the side of his head that sent him reeling. Dazed and bloodied, Smith backed away, swinging the gun around.

He only made it halfway. Chase was on him now, both hands clamped on the gun, wrenching his wrist, turning the gun in on the shooter.

Smith howled in pain and clawed at Chase with his left hand, fighting for control of the weapon. They lurched toward the window, locked in a deadly dance.

Sheldon Smith looked up too late to see Cameron coming full speed, hunched over, shoulders plowing into Smith at full force.

With a guttural groan, Smith tumbled back. His head struck the window shattering the windowpane, the momentum carrying him over the sill through the falling shards of glass. His eyes bulged in fear as he groped the air in desperation. He caught Cameron's wrist and held onto it like a vice as he dangled from the window.

Braced against the ledge, Cameron and Smith locked eyes. Cameron didn't pull back or pry the man's fingers loose but he didn't try to help either, watching Smith flail with is free hand as he strained to reach the ledge out of his reach. His shoes scraped against the brick as he struggled in vain to climb the sheer wall. Cameron watched making no move to help. Smith's grip began to shake, then slip, one finger at a time.

As Cameron leaned out he spoke two words. "Remember Diane."

He thought he saw a hint of recognition in Smith's eyes as his grip broke free and he plummeted thirteen stories to the pavement below.

Standing in the wreckage of the window, Cameron's shoulders heaved as he looked down at the body on the curb, a dark pool of blood spreading from beneath it. Chase wrapped an arm around his brother's shoulder.

"That's some payback, brother."

"Not hardly enough."

[]

The suite was bedlam. Staff, police, hotel security, EMS crews---at least a dozen people filled the room. MacNulty and the FBI crew were there so fast, Chase thought they must have been in the building when it happened. They weren't, but they got there in record time after Curtis had called them. So many unmarked cars racing through the streets with sirens blaring that some downtown bystanders thought there had been a terrorist attack.

Mac took charge. "I want the cleaners in here......now! Nothing in the paper, nothing on TV. I want the lid clamped down so tight on this!"

"I don't know if we can do that, sir," said Curtis. "There were a lot of witnesses. I can't even guess how many people have seen the body."

"All right, all right..." Mac paused to take stock, then laid it out for them. "Here's the story. John Doe. Despondent male jumped to his death from his hotel room. A businessman---make it boring---an insurance man from Illinois. Police have not released the name pending notification of next of kin---the usual bullshit. Just another jumper."

Make sure NPD has it down, chapter and verse. And keep our office out of it entirely. They'll only ask more questions if it comes from us. Who's our guy over there?"

"At Naples Police? Jerry. Jerry Rivers."

"Okay, give it to him. By the time he's done, I want it to be a nothing story, paragraph on the back page. Follow me?"

"Jerry is good. He'll do it."

"Make it happen." Mac turned his attention to Chase and Cameron. "Now we gotta get you two out of here. Chase, you're walking right out the front door with the whole entourage, everybody happy, just another day on the campaign trail. You don't even know what all the ruckus was about on the other side of the building. Got it?"

Chase nodded as Mac focused on Cameron.

"And you—" Mac tried to look stern but couldn't stifle the grin. "Nice going."

"Thanks. My pleasure."

Mac inspected the demolished window. "Looks like you got a habit of being in the wrong place at the right time." He folded his arms across his massive chest. "But you gotta disappear now. Get out of those clothes and get out of here before the reporters show. Even those idiots can figure out that one and one makes two."

Cameron saluted.

Curtis cancelled the Jennings Home's speech.

64

Time was running out. He had to hurry. God, what a hellish week! Just a few more days and he would be out of the country, with seventy million dollars in cash, bearer bonds and negotiable securities. Untouchable.

And then Stacy. Ah yes, dear Stacy. Well, that could wait. First things first. Meagan. He had plans for little Meagan. Very special plans.

And he needed that fucking disk.

Right this minute, there was another problem. Sheldon Smith. Good old reliable Sheldon. He had not heard a word from him in sixteen hours. The last message, confirming the timetable from the execution of Chambers to the rendezvous on the boat at midnight, had been on the Blackberry, precise and on time. Sheldon should have called again by now to say,

'I'm sorry, wrong number,' and then hang up. That meant that Chambers was dead and everything is on schedule. But Sheldon had not called. Nor had he heard any reports of a sudden death in the Chambers family. He had the office TVs tuned to the news networks, certain there would be a break-in bulletin within minutes after the fact but there was nothing so far.

He had called Sheldon's "hot line," the cell phone reserved for Ross that he kept with him twenty-four-seven. No answer. That was not good. Sheldon always picked up on the second ring, anytime, day or night. He was so consistent that Ross sometimes wondered if the man ever slept. Now it just kept ringing. Ross hung up and considered the possibilities. None were good. His only reassuring thought was that the worst-case scenario was unlikely. If Sheldon had been caught in the act, that was sure to be breaking news as well.

Ross was fairly confident that everything was still on track and there would be good news from Florida soon enough but he didn't care for the suspense.

Now he had a choice to make. Stacy had everything packed and ready at the suite. They had the charter plane standing by at Midway, checked out for the flight in 45 minutes. He had to make the call now, tell the pilot they were good to go or call it off.

On an impulse, he reached in his drawer and pulled out his cards. He snatched one from the middle of the deck and slapped it down.

Knight of Swords, charging into battle, lethal sword held high. No time for indecision. He who hesitates is lost. Ross made the call.

"We'll be there on schedule. I want the engines running, in the air at six."

"Right, Mr. Chase."

That's how Ross had introduced himself the one and only time he met pilot Jimmy Lee. At that brief encounter, Ross paid him, cash in advance. Jimmy didn't ask any questions.

"But I gotta tell ya, when I filed the flight plan, I got the reports, and there's gonna be some real bad weather up there tonight."

"Can you fly in it?"

"Me? Shit, I can fly in anything. I've flown through enemy fire, missiles, flak---a little rain don't bother me none."

"Then why are we talking? I'll see you at five-forty-five."

"Alright, then. I just thought you'd wanna know 'cuz the winds are gonna get up there---like gale force---and that means the winds aloft---"

The pilot stopped when he realized that there was no one at the other end of the line.

65

"All I know is, if Chase Chambers loses this god damn election by one vote, I'm going to be pissed."

Election Day. It was mid-afternoon and Eleanor realized there was no chance she would get to the polls to cast a ballot. She was already overdue at the Big House to help Marsha with the last First Class catered event, but Cole insisted that she stay at the cottage and maintain her pose until the portrait was complete.

"I'll finish it today if it's the last thing I do, I swear to God," Cole promised.

He was so adamant that Eleanor didn't dare argue. She wanted to suggest they put it off for a day--- but a glance from Gem told her to stay the course. She remained quiet and kept her pose.

Another hour passed. Her neck hurt. Her back ached. Her eyes burned from the thick haze that hung in the room from Cole's incessant smoking. Without moving a muscle, she glanced over, hoping for a rescue from Gem, but the lady of the house was as engrossed in her cards as Cole was in his painting. Eleanor couldn't take it any more.

"Cole, I'm dying here."

He didn't look up but set the brush aside. "Not a minute too soon then."

"That's it?"

He stepped back to gaze at his creation.

"That's it."

Gem was there at his shoulder, the first to witness his masterpiece. "So beautiful."

It was more than a portrait. It was Eleanor, vibrant and vulnerable, framed in verdant shades of the Port Royal gardens standing at the water's edge, cradling a spray of wildflowers and a single yellow rose.

She broke from her pose. "Let me see. I want to see it!"

Cole bowed and offered it to her.

"Oh my God. Cole." She melted into tears completely overwhelmed.

Gem left the two of them and returned to her cards. She turned one and crossed it with another. "Six of wands," she announced. "The time has come."

"Uh-huh." Eleanor was hardly paying attention.

"Three of Swords," Gem continued. "The cards tell of rain."

"Kind of like a weather forecast?" Eleanor said absently.

"Not the weather outside, Eleanor, but inside. A pierced heart and the rain of troubled times, tears and blood---" She looked at Eleanor. "Falling on a yellow rose."

Eleanor caught her breath. "What does that mean?"

Gem returned her stare, "What does it mean to you?"

"Yellow roses mean a lot to me. They mean too much."

"*Je sais, ma belle*," Gem said. "I know."

"But how?" Elle asked. "How can you know that?"

"It's in the cards...and in your eyes," Gem said softly. "I know."

66

The hurricane that had pounded the Bahamas had spent its fury, dissipating as it wandered into the Gulf, but the remnants still had enough left to soak the entire Florida coast with torrential rain. Every local TV station carried the warning.

The weather wasn't the only danger. Harry Blacks's orders were to keep a 24-hour guard on Meagan until Ross was in custody in Chicago, and no one was sure when that would happen.

The FBI had stormed his office in Chicago shortly after the attack on Chase. They had all the evidence they needed, including the handwritten directions on the back of Ross Hamilton's business card found in the bloodied pocket of Sheldon Smith. And they had him cornered. The camera and audio surveillance pegged him in his office with Stacy. They heard their voices in conversation only moments before, as the agents were on the way up. It was over for Ross Hamilton.

But he wasn't there.

There was no response to their insistent knocking and shouts. They broke through the door and rushed down the hallway to Ross's office. He was gone, that sixth sense working for him again. He and Stacy must have taken the service elevator down and out past the loading docks before the agents finished searching the floor. An all-points bulletin was relayed to the Chicago police with their descriptions, but they had no idea where to look. His car was still in the lot. The police at the airport, at Amtrak, the Greyhound station, and in the suburbs were all on alert. But for the moment, Ross Hamilton was on the loose.

Harry Black checked in with the second shift team on watch at Meagan's house on his way in. He passed a large, steaming coffee through the open window to Miller, in the unmarked car on the street in front, then circled around to the end of the cul-de-sac where he had a clear view of the back of the house. It was a dim view in the heavy rain, but still visible under the row of lampposts that stretched from the lanai to the patio.

Satisfied that all was well, Black pulled into Meagan's driveway, clicked open the garage with the remote, parked inside and closed the door. He let himself into the house through the breezeway, calling out as he stepped into the kitchen.

"FBI! Anybody home?"

Black was a regular at the house now. Brandon came running to greet him.

"Mr. Harry! Mr. Harry!"

"Come here, you." Black fished in his pocket. "I found this somewhere. I think it belongs to you." He opened his hand to reveal a giant Hershey bar.

Brandon grinned. "Is it mine?"

"Not mine, so it must be yours."

"The whole thing---all mine?"

"Tell you what, Brandon. Half now, and save half for tomorrow. Deal?"

"Deal." Brandon pumped his hand.

"And where is the lady of the house?"

"Mommy is all dressed up, Mr. Harry, there in the living room," Brandon called out. "She's pretty like a movie star."

"I'll bet she is."

Meagan was in a fitted satin bodice with a tiered lace skirt skimming her knees and a diamond pendant at her neck.

"Are we going now to the Big House?"

"Not yet."

"I thought we were supposed to be there---"

"Yeah, yeah, I know, but this whole election thing is dragging. Problems with the computers. The results are coming in slow. All the campaign folks are going to be there for a while. You don't want to go there in the middle of that."

"Yes, I do."

"I say we stay here for a while."

"Why?"

"You're both safe here, that's why," Harry Black said, like a parent to a child. "And the weather out there is for shit."

67

The controlled chaos of election night was underway. The TV cameras and reporters were camped out at the official campaign headquarters at the Ritz Carlton. Several hundred were expected there, but the real place to be was Port Royal, where all the candidate's family and friends gathered. It was invitation only, off limits to all media.

Chase and Sandy planned to stay there until enough precincts were in and counted to make the outcome clear. Then they were off to the Ritz for the perfunctory thank-yous and a brief speech---victory or concession. Chase was ready either way.

There was plenty of security on hand, two restless agents in a remote corner of the top floor of the Big House, Curtis LaFond standing at the upper window, watching cars pull into the drive, valets with oversized umbrellas providing escort to the house.

"It's a do-or-die election night, we've got a houseful of Naples finest here, and there's a hurricane coming. Should be interesting," Curtis noted. "So tell me, Cameron, what are we doing up here in the attic looking like old furniture?"

"This is bullshit, that's for sure, but there's nothing I can do about it." Cameron paced the room. "Chase is down there now and I can't show my face until after he goes downtown, after the speech, after everything. It'll be midnight at least."

"At least," Curtis echoed. "Good thing you're a patient man."

"There's no reason you can't go down. There's only one of you. Go on, Curtis--- go mingle with the voters."

"No, I think I'll just stay up here." He forced a smile. "Where it's nice and quiet."

〇

Eleanor had been in the thick of things ever since arriving at the Big House late that afternoon where she had been franticly working with Marsha and the crew. She was still basking in the reflected glow of Cole's magnificent portrait.

"What's up with you, Elle?" Marsha asked. "You look like you won the lottery."

"Something like that," she sighed, wiping her hands on her apron.

"I'm thinking Cole is in on this somehow. He's got the same silly grin on his face."

"Oh, Marsha, you wouldn't believe me if I told you."

"I'd love to hear all about it, but that can wait. Right now, I think you better hang up that apron and go hook up with your new man for the big night."

"I'm not going to leave you in the lurch with everything that---"

"We're on automatic pilot. Go on---don't make me throw you out of the kitchen."

"Thanks, Marsh."

She tossed her apron on the counter and hurried off to join Gem and Cole in the downstairs library. It was quiet there except for the muted drone of the TV sets arrayed against one wall, four channels of election coverage and one for weather.

The weather lady was smiling but the forecast wasn't good. She pointed to an ugly blotch of purple on the giant map. Hurricane Jane was weakened but still wicked, swarming up from the south with one last wallop aimed at Naples.

"I'm sorry to say our high pressure front has collapsed," she apologized to the anchorman as if it were her fault. "Jane is pushing everything north."

"And does that mean we're in for it?" The anchor played straight man.

"I'm afraid so. The driving rain and strong winds have already started and I think it will only get worse tonight. Some of the wind gusts may get up to ..."

Eleanor stared at the screen. "Is there really a hurricane coming?"

"Yes, tonight," Gem said pleasantly, like it was a long-awaited guest.

68

Mac received the call that Ross had dodged the bust in Chicago and disappeared. Shit! Where was he now?

Mac could barely hear. Lightning flashed and static scratched at the words.

"Agent MacNulty? Borchert on GPS. We got your boy fingered now. He made a cell phone call we traced on satellite. He's on the move, back toward the residence."

"In Chicago?" Mac was glad to hear it. They still had a stakeout at the penthouse. They would have cuffs on Hamilton before he made the elevator.

"No---" came the reply. "He's in Naples. Don't know how he got down there---charter flight or something, I guess. But he's in a car now, moving southwest."

"Naples? Damn it!" Mac was out of his seat. "You get that word out! Tell Cam, for Christ's sake---out at the Chambers' place."

"I'll call him right now."

"And call Harry---never mind, I'll call Harry---you get a hold of our crew. I want Naples PD all over this. Priority suspect. Stop on sight. Shoot the son of a bitch if you have to."

Mac clicked Harry's speed dial number. After the third ring, the voice mail: "Special Agent Harry Black; leave a message."

"Wake up, Special Agent Harry Black," Mac growled. After the beep, he barked into the phone. "Harry. Emergency. Hamilton is here in Naples. Call me now."

Mac yelled at the nearest agent. "I want a vehicle description and a license number on Hamilton, and I want it five minutes ago!"

Mac hit redial. Still no answer. "Where the hell is Harry?"

- 69 -

PAGE + WANDS.

Harry Black had stepped out in the rain to make his security rounds. It was coming down so hard that he couldn't see Miller in the car posted out front. He could hardly see the car. He had talked to Miller on the handset twenty minutes ago but Harry was old school. He liked to check every hour, just to make sure.

Harry grabbed an umbrella. The storm was getting fierce. He had to hold the umbrella at a hard angle to keep from being pelted by the wind-driven rain. He edged down the drive until he was close enough to see Miller in the car, then backtracked through the lanai and full circle around the house. Satisfied that all was well, he ducked inside the back door. He never heard his cell phone ring.

[]

The big blue Lexus slowed to a stop next to Miller's car and the lady in the passenger seat of the Lexus caught his attention. She waved for him to put his window down, like hers, then shouted her questions through the rain. Pretty lady, very polite and very lost. Miller could barely hear her.

"Is this Bishop?"

Miller shook his head, and pointed. "No---two lights over. East. Two lights east."

She didn't get it. "Two lights---which way's east?"

Miller pointed again. "To your right. Take a right at the stop sign."

She smiled. "Thanks so much. Sorry to get you wet."

Miller smiled back. "No problem. I'll be okay." He didn't hear the click of the latch on the far side of her car.

[]

Meagan hurried to answer the door, peered through the peephole and saw Agent Miller, his hat pulled low against the rain. She flipped the deadbolt and started to turn the knob when the door burst open.

Meagan saw Miller standing in the open doorway, arms slack, head lolling to one side. He pitched forward, face first, landing at her feet. She stared in stunned silence.

"Hello, dear." That chilling voice.

Meagan could not believe her eyes. Ross stomped in like a wild animal, rain-soaked hair plastered on his forehead, dark eyes blazing. He stepped over Miller's body like litter on the floor and moved in, waving a gun.

Meagan could not move.

Harry Black was up off the couch like a young athlete going into the game. He grabbed for the gun under his jacket as he leapt to his feet. The adrenalin was making his mind work fast and clear. If he could get to a solid stance, with his weapon up, he could drop this creep before he----

Harry Black was only one second away from making his move, when Ross angled the gun away from Meagan and squeezed off two quick shots. Black's weapon clattered to the floor as he was thrown back on the couch, his arms and legs going limp. Meagan screamed and lunged at Ross, ignoring the gun, clawing at his head and face. Ross pushed her away. She fell hard to the floor.

"You killed him! You--" she shrieked as he leveled the gun at her.

"That's right. Stay right there or I swear to God, I'll kill you, too." He dabbed at the scratches on his cheek and saw splotches of blood on his fingers. "Bitch."

Meagan stared in horror at the mayhem: Harry Black shot on the couch, Agent Miller dead by the door.

The front door opened again. Stacy peered in and entered, triumphantly walking past Miller's body to join Ross.

"Good work." Stacy looked to Meagan with contempt. "Now what about her?"

Meagan got to her feet slowly, her mind racing.

Ross's eyes narrowed. "Give me the disk, Meagan."

"What?"

"No more games. The computer disk. I need it. Now!"

"I don't know what you're talking about."

Ross gave her a menacing look.

"Don't make me—" He turned, distracted by a groan from across the room.

Harry Black stirred, his eyes still closed. Ross frowned. He had put two perfectly placed shots in the center of his chest. What was the problem? He stood over Harry Black and flicked his coat open with the barrel of the gun. He could see the gray Kevlar shell of the bulletproof vest through the holes in his shirt.

"Now that's cheating," Ross smirked.

He put the barrel of the gun flush against Harry's forehead.

"No!" Meagan screamed.

Ross pulled back.

"Well, well, what have we here?"

A computer disk peeked out from Black's suit pocket. Ross snatched it from him.

"The key to the vault." Ross held up the disk. "Mission accomplished."

"Not quite." Stacy grabbed Ross's gun and fired.

Harry Black fell hard against the sofa, blood streaming.

Meagan rushed to him. "Oh, no, no!"

His eyes were open, but he was fading fast, the color gone from his face. He tried to speak and Meagan leaned close.

"What? What? Harry? Tell me what to do!"

He pulled her closer, whispering, "Speed...dial 1."

As he spoke, he slipped his cell phone in her hand. She tucked it in her skirt's pocket as he grabbed at her with one last effort, pulling her close.

"Never lost a witness..." he said with a feeble smile. "Don't let me down."

The smile faded. Meagan sobbed, her head against his chest.

"Where's the boy?" Stacy said coldly. "I want that boy."

Meagan's eyes filled with rage. "You're not going to touch him!"

She rushed Stacy, knocking her to the floor. "Not---my---son!"

Ross let it happen, watching Meagan pound away at Stacy. Meagan grabbed her by the hair, ready to smash her head when she heard the small voice.

"Mommy---"

Brandon stood on the landing in his pajamas, clutching his SpongeBob doll.

"Oh, honey." Meagan rushed to him, comforting him, "It's OK. Everything's OK, baby."

Stacy struggled to her feet, her face swollen. "Give me the gun," she said thickly.

Ross dismissed her, "Forget it, Stacy. They're coming with us. Both of them."

"Take me if you want," Meagan shouted. "But not Brandon. Ross, please. You don't want to hurt him."

"No, I don't. Now I'm only going to say this once. Take Brandon and get in the fucking car, or---I guess I'll have no choice."

Brandon started to cry. Meagan grabbed his blanket from the banister, wrapped it around him and started moving. "Shhhh, baby, it'll be okay."

"Daddy's mad."

"Yes, Brandon," Meagan glared up. "Totally mad."

- 70 -

The Big House was teeming with people where two hundred hopeful celebrants had gathered. It was both exciting and nerve-wracking, with a palpable sense of optimism, a feeling that Chase might beat the odds and pull out the victory, but they all knew it was going to be very close. The minutes ticked by with no relief in the suspense. There were glitches at the Election Board delaying vote counts and certification. The early totals gave Dawson a slim lead, but not enough to mean much with only ten percent of the precincts tallied.

On the third floor of the Big House, political junkie Curtis monitored a TV, a laptop computer with a live Internet feed and a portable radio. Cameron paid no attention as he paced wall to wall, his footsteps making a wooden drumbeat on the hardwood floor.

"Excuse me? Mr. Chambers?" Curtis was trying to be polite. "I'm trying to follow this---your brother's election. Could we---?"

"What difference does it make?" Cameron snarled. "We can't do anything about it. The votes are all in now, they count 'em, and it's going to be whatever it's going to be."

"Yes, but---" Curtis couldn't think of a good argument. "Okay. So?"

"So when can I go downstairs? Meagan's probably down there by now."

"You know the deal. You've got to wait until after Chase goes to the Ritz---"

"Well, why doesn't he get the hell going?"

"---And when the TV coverage is over, all over. The people here can't be looking at you and watching him on TV at the same time. Am I right?"

"You know, Curtis, this is getting stale." Cameron sat on the large sofa in the middle of the room. "I mean, I could go down there right now and say hello, it's me, Cameron, how's everybody doing? There's no reason we can't tell them now that I'm alive. The election is over. Let's end the charade now. What do you say?"

"Are you insane? Do you know what MacNulty would do if you blow the cover on this thing without his OK?"

"Maybe he'll be pissed." Cam shrugged. "But what can he do---put me in jail?"

"You and me both." He shook a finger at Cameron. "He would have my head on a platter, that's for sure. I know that doesn't mean much to you. You're going to charge ahead and do whatever you please, but I'm telling you---"

Curtis was interrupted by the ring of his phone. He looked.

"It's him. His ears must be burning." He answered, "Yes, sir."

Curtis listened and Cam waited. "What is it?"

Curtis held up his hand, still listening intently. "What? But that's not----no!"

"Curtis?"

"But she was---Yes ... Yes, sir, I understand.... Yes, sir, I will."

He set the phone aside and looked at Cam.

"What?" Cameron demanded.

"She's gone."

Cameron grabbed him by the shirt. "What are you saying?"

"That bastard! Ross has her---He---he killed Harry!"

"Harry's dead?"

"Poor Harry---oh, Jesus---and Miller, he killed them both---and he took Meagan. Cam, he's got Meagan and the boy in his car."

"Where? Curtis! Did they say where?"

"They think---they have him on GPS---he's on 41, going north, toward the city."

Cameron eased his grip. "Let's go."

Curtis had to run to keep up as Cameron bolted for the stairs.

In the front hall, Cameron caught sight of Chase in a gray pinstriped suit and crimson tie, standing with a half dozen people near the TV monitors. He was wearing the same outfit. That was the plan for later when Chase was supposed to depart so that Cameron could appear for his reunion with Meagan.

The plan was history now. Cameron made a beeline for Chase. The crowd parted like the Red Sea, stepping back in amazement as a second Chase Chambers virtually ran across the room. Chase did a double take as his brother approached.

"Cameron, what are you doing?"

"I'm sorry to ruin everything, but you've got to know---" Cameron ignored the people around him. "The whole operation is blown. We've got two men down and Meagan's been taken hostage. I've got to get to her, Chase."

"Oh no! Do you know where they're taking her?"

"I think so."

Chase fished in his pocket and handed Cameron a set of keys. "Take the Lincoln, the campaign car. It's the fastest thing out there."

Whispers fluttered through the crowd as the twins huddled.

"What the---"

"That's Cameron! That's his brother!"

"It can't be!"

"It is! It's Cameron! He's alive!"

Cameron took the keys in one hand and gave his brother a quick hug. "Thanks."

"Go!" Chase said. "Just tell me what to do. Where do I send the cavalry?"

"Call Mac." Cameron was moving. "Whatever he says do, but don't take any chances."

"Cam!" Chase called out. "Be careful. I don't want to lose you twice!"

[]

Cameron and Curtis were lashed by wind and rain as they made their way through the maze of cars parked bumper to bumper, until they reached the white Lincoln. Curtis jumped in the driver's seat as Cameron slipped the keys in the ignition.

"Go! Go! Let's go!"

Curtis slammed into gear. The Lincoln sideswiped a Cadillac as it careened away from the parked cars.

Cameron's phone rang. "Yes?"

"He's still northbound on 41."

"Mac---what about---"

"Wait---wait a second...Okay, listen. You cut down Branson. If you hurry, you can intercept close to Grove and 41. Get there, Chambers. I want this fucking creep."

"We're on it. But Mac, you gotta tell me---what about Meagan. Is — Is she--?"

"She's in the car. And the kid. They're in the car. That's all I know."

"Shit." He slammed his fist on the dash. "C'mon, Curtis! Move!"

Curtis bumped another SUV as he weaved down the driveway coming across two more parked cars which were completely blocking the entrance. He pulled over to the side and roared across the lawn, leaving ribbons of mud as the car jumped the curb and raced down the street.

Cameron listened to the urgent voices on Mac's end.

"OK. NPD's got a pair of cruisers in hot pursuit. They can be on him in about two minutes."

"No! God damn it! Pull 'em off, Mac! They'll get her killed! If he sees---for Christ's sake, Mac, let me do this!"

"All right, all right, but you gotta hurry. We can't let him get into the city. We could lose him. We've got people on the bridge at the river, roadblocks at the north end. And that's the end of the line for this bastard. He's not getting past that."

"Roger, Mac. See you at the river." He threw the phone on the seat and yelled, "Step on it, Curtis! We have to stop him before he gets to the river!"

◻

Meanwhile, Meagan was still in shock at seeing Harry Black die before her eyes, as she numbly obeyed as Ross herded her through the rain to the car, Brandon in her arms.

She opened the back door, shielding Brandon from the rain, slid him into the seat, clasped his seatbelt and started to climb in next to him. Ross pulled her back.

"No. You get in front. With me."

"I've got to---"

He gestured with the gun. "Get in, Meagan."

She did what she was told as Stacy climbed into the back. Ross already had the car moving before the doors were slammed shut. Meagan caught a glint of something in Stacy's hand, but turned too late to stop her from injecting Brandon with a hypodermic needle. She tried to lunge over the seat but Ross held her.

"Stop---it's just a sedative," he said, pulling her back.

"We don't want the boy to suffer, do we?" Stacy oozed, stroking Brandon's hair as his eyes began to close.

"Stay away from him!" Meagan screamed, lunging back over the seat towards Stacy.

She continued to struggle with Stacy until Ross slammed on the brakes, reached out and whipped the back of his hand across her face landing her a stunning blow.

He then calmly put the car back in gear, pulled ahead and turned toward the highway.

Dazed and deathly afraid, Meagan breathed in strength, thinking of the child behind her and the tiny one inside, their lives in her hands. She was the only one who could protect them from this monster. She had to find a way.

Think, Meagan, think!

"Murderer! You killed him!"

She lunged, catching him off guard, clawing at his face and neck. He raised his arms as she flailed at him. Driving blind, Ross slalomed off the road. As the car lurched, he grabbed her hands and pulled her close.

"You stupid bitch!" he screamed. "Do you want to get us all killed?"

"For God's sake, Ross," she gasped, pulling back. "How can you---Brandon is your son!"

He steered up the ramp, in control again.

"He's not my son." Ross stared straight ahead. "Do you think I don't know that?"

Meagan's mouth dropped. "What?"

"I know about Chase Chambers. I know that you're a whore."

Meagan was stunned.

"I don't know if the lucky father was a one-night stand or a long-term engagement, but I know it's not me. Why don't you admit it?"

A single tear coursed down her cheek. Meagan watched him out of the corner of her eye. He had a look she had never seen before. His eyes were glazed; his pallid skin had a sickly sheen. He looked manic, out of control.

Do something. Say something before he's gone completely over the edge.

"He is your son, Ross. Your flesh and blood. Look at him. Can't you see?"

Ross glanced at the innocent face of his son in the backseat. As soon as his eyes shifted, Meagan fumbled for Harry's cell phone tucked in her skirt and pushed a button. She didn't know who the call would go to or if it would connect at all, but it was worth a try.

Ross turned back to her. "Brandon will be fine, as long as you do exactly as I say."

"Ross, my God, think what you're doing."

"I know exactly what I'm doing, sweetheart," he said, the words dripping. "You wanted out of this marriage, so I'm taking you out."

Stacy leaned forward. "I think we better get off the main highway. The police will be---"

"I know, I know." He jerked the car to the right, then back left at the first cross street and raced down the two-lane road parallel to the highway.

◻

Cameron grabbed his cell phone at the first ring.

"Yeah...?"

Nothing.

"Hello?...Hello?"

Still nothing. He was about to click off, but he heard something, a faint hum and a rhythmic clap-

clap-clap. What was that? Windshield wipers. It was someone calling from another car, driving in the same rain. Meagan? He pressed the phone to his ear, hoping to hear a voice, a sound, anything…

Curtis kept his eyes on the road. "What, Cameron? Who is it?"

"It's from Black's cell," Cameron said, eyeing the number. "Shhh. I think it's her." Cam pressed the volume button. Meagan's muffled voice came through, the connection distorted by the storm. He strained to hear. "Shit, it is Meagan!"

"Ross,   you…   why   are… turning…Tamiami…you… Tamiami …"

"They're off the highway, Curtis, on Old 41---they're taking Tamiami to the bridge!" He pointed to the exit sign looming ahead. "Get off---right here. Get off!"

Curtis swerved across two lanes to exit, a chorus of horns chasing him up the ramp.

"Come on, Curtis, hurry!"

"Hey, I'm an analyst, not a wheel man. I'm doing the best I can."

"You've got to do better!"

Curtis cinched in his seat belt and floored it, ignoring the red light ahead. The Lincoln flashed through the intersection, narrowly missing two more cars.

"Okay."

॰

Meagan tried to think. What do you do with a mad man? Pull him back from the edge or push him over?

"If I'm a whore, what are you, Ross? What about you and Stacy?"

"Can't you make her shut up?" Stacy screamed from the backseat.

Ross ignored them both.

Meagan thought fast, hoping that the conversation was being picked up. "Why did you kill Diane McAlister?"

Ross stomped on the brakes. The car sluiced off the pavement to the shoulder.

"Why did I kill Diane? Because she defied me. Me! Threatened to run to her soldier boy---the other Chambers. They were going to file charges. And now they're both dead!" Ross laughed savagely, then turned cold again. "Who told you about that?"

Oh, the hell with it, Meagan thought, *trump him with the truth.*

"Cameron Chambers. He's alive, Ross, and he's been working with the FBI to put you away in a cage where you belong."

"Do you expect me to believe that?"

"And I've been working with him, helping the FBI, doing everything I can."

He stared at her, eyes burning with rage.

⬚

Curtis squinted through the rain-blurred windshield. The storm had taken out the power. Even the streetlights were off, the whole area soaked in darkness. Only pairs of car lights dotted the road ahead.

"Look! I think that's them, Cam. See the taillights of the Lexus pulling off?"

"Got to be," Cam said anxiously. "Get up there, but not too fast. Don't spook him."

☐

"You don't want to play games with me, Meagan," Ross spoke calmly, the manic mood swinging back again. "Not unless you want to join Diane."

"Diane wasn't the only one, was she?" Too late for Meagan to back down now.

"Hardly," he said with a satisfied smile. "You would be surprised."

"Nothing would surprise me anymore."

"No? Then I suppose you know all about the unfortunate Mr. Sheehan."

"Nick Sheehan?" Meagan bolted upright. "You killed Nicky? You killed Elle's husband?"

"And you all thought it was a drunk driver. Surprise, surprise."

"Oh God, Ross---you----you had no reason! You hardly knew him."

"I knew him well enough. We did one deal, remember? The real estate trust in Cleveland. And he had to make it...problematic."

Meagan stared out the window, at nothing. "You killed poor Nicky."

"He brought it on himself," Ross shrugged. "Said there ' were improprieties---had to be disclosed. I couldn't let him do that. You understand."

"Diane, Nicky..." Meagan shook her head. "And there are others, aren't there?"

He didn't answer.

"Whatever made you---who was the first? Who was that, Ross---your mother? Did you start with her? Did you kill your own mother?"

"Shut up!" He lashed out, grabbing her by the throat, his nails piercing her skin.

"Ross! Look!" Stacy exclaimed. "There's a car, someone's behind us...closing in fast!"

Ross saw the headlights in the rearview mirror. He released Meagan and slammed on the gas, spraying the intruder with wet gravel as he cut back into traffic. He looked to Meagan as the car gained speed.

"It doesn't matter who was first. All that matters is---you shall be the last, my darling, as I always planned."

71

As the bridge came into view, Ross pulled to an abrupt halt.

"End of the line, Stacy. Take the boy and get down to the boat. I'll bring the bags."

Stacy squinted through the darkness. "I can't see a boat, Ross. I can't see anything. Are you sure it's there?"

"Sheldon said the boat would be there, it's there. It's not going to have neon lights on it. Now go. Here, take this---"

He handed her the gun. Stacy took it, reaching to release Brandon from his seatbelt.

Meagan reared up. "No! You can't!"

Ross yanked her back. "Go Stacy---now."

Stacy scooped up Brandon, dazed and dozy from the drug, barely staying on his feet as she tugged him along.

Ross held Meagan.

"Get hold of yourself. We're going right along with them."

She tried to fight him off. "You're not taking him anywhere!"

"Stop it!" He pinned back her shoulders. His face was inches away, foul breath in her face. "When are you going to learn? We're going to do what I say. We're going to do it my way. And I swear to you, Meagan, if you try anything else, I will kill that boy."

Her shoulders sagged. She surrendered.

"That's a good girl."

He released his grip. Meagan didn't move. Ross studied her for a moment. Satisfied that she would stay in line, he popped the trunk and opened his door, stepping out to retrieve the two valises stuffed with cash and bonds, his pot of gold. He had one foot on the ground when Meagan made her move.

"Not this time!"

She stretched a leg over, pushed the gear in drive, and slammed on the accelerator. The car rocketed forward. Caught half in and half out, Ross grabbed at the door frame as his legs flew out from under him. The Lexus slashed along the concrete, picking up speed. The front tires popped as the car jumped the curb and tore through the guardrail, sparks flying. Meagan closed her eyes as the Lexus went airborne.

[]

Cameron heard the crash reverberate through the cell phone.

"Oh, God, that's the river! They've gone in the river!"

Curtis veered onto the shoulder and pulled up at the bridge. They scrambled from the car as Cameron shouted into the phone.

"Meagan! Meagan, we're coming! We'll get you! Hang on..."

[]

Stacy stood at the water's edge with Brandon. Illuminated by an arch of lights, the stretch of water beneath the bridge was sheltered from the rain and completely deserted. No boat. No Sheldon. Nothing. Stacy's frustrated scream echoed beneath the bridge. She ran back up the embankment, tugging the reluctant half comatose Brandon, and hid under the bridge.

Racing for the bridge, Curtis slowed to a halt as he saw the two figures huddled in the shadows. He recognized Brandon in the clutches of the woman.

Curtis called to her, "Come out of there or I'll shoot!"

"Get away!" Stacy shouted. "I've got the boy!"

Brandon whimpered, struggling against her hold.

Curtis opened his arms wide.

"Look, lady---there's nowhere to go. You can't---"

He ducked as the shot rang out. He heard the ricochet as the bullet pinged off the retaining wall behind him as he hugged the wet ground. Stacy emerged from the shadows, gun in hand, holding Brandon like a shield, her face drawn in desperation.

"Stay back! Stay away from the car! I swear I'll kill him if you move!"

Curtis came up slightly, hands half raised.

"Let him go. Let the boy go and you can---"

Stacy was less than thirty feet away now. She looked toward the bridge and the raging river, then ahead at the empty Lincoln, lights on, engine running, doors open. Only Curtis blocked her path. She made her choice; raising the pistol to take aim at Curtis who was an easy target framed in the car lights.

A shot rang out. Curtis cringed and closed his eyes, waiting for the pain but feeling nothing. He opened them to see Stacy's body go limp. Her eyes rolled back as she teetered, standing for a moment, and then fell like a rock, leaving Brandon crouched all alone in the rain.

Curtis turned around to see Cameron standing behind him, arms extended in a marksman pose, focused on Stacy. He slowly lowered the gun.

"She would have killed you, Curtis."

"I know," he said, brushing off dirt and mud. "She's already ruined my best suit."

Curtis ran to Brandon, hoisting him in his arms.

"I want mommy," Brandon whimpered.

"Me, too, Bran. We'll go and get her for you. I promise."

72

The Lexus blasted through the corrugated metal with an ear-splitting screech and shot through the air, hitting the water in a jarring nosedive.

Everything went into slow motion. Meagan's seatbelt held her fast as she pitched forward. The airbag burst open rushing forward and knocked the breath out of her. The shock of the car breaking through the guardrails and hurtling through the darkness into the raging river would be forever seared into her mind.

She groped for bearings as the car hurtled through the water, landing head first as the strong raging currents swiftly carried it downstream.

And then it started sinking and the water started to form pools at her feet. She was held tightly in her seat by her seat belt. She started to take check of her body to see what damage had been done. Her head hurt, her body ached, but she didn't think she had any broken bones. Her legs were crushed, but she could move them slightly. She was covered with cuts, but none too deep. It didn't look good---trapped in a shipwrecked car in the middle of a raging river---but with some luck, she just might live through this, if only she could release her legs.

Ross was not so lucky.

Hurled out of the car by the crash, Meagan had watched in disbelief as she saw his lifeless body, rushing past her, disappearing face down in the churning water.

Ross is dead.

Meagan felt neither joy nor sorrow. It had all been too much. Her emotions were spent. She sat in the car, staring at the water swirling about her like some disaster movie. She was in total shock. But not for long.

She was jolted into action by the water lapping past her ankles. She released the seatbelt to give her space away from the airbag and felt the first tinge of panic as she realized she was still trapped. Her right leg was wedged in the corner of the car where the frame had been pushed in by the collision. She tried to pull it out, but it would not budge. She shifted her weight to work another angle but there was no room to maneuver. She could still see the dashboard and headlights glowing, but she couldn't think of any way to escape. The water was rising, edging up past her shins.

Random thoughts coursed through her head. She remembered the stories: the hiker trapped in the rocks who cut off his own arm; the farmer under a tractor who amputated his leg. That's what she should do, she thought---cut off her foot.

Then she realized she couldn't do it if she wanted to. She didn't have a knife, or anything like one. And she didn't have enough time. And even if she did, she didn't think she had the courage to do it.

She renewed her determination. She pulled and wrenched at her leg. Stuck fast. The water lapped past the seat, intensifying her panic. Desperation seeped in.

〇

Cameron shielded his eyes from the rain, straining to see out over the pitch black water. He caught sight of two cones of light in the distance. The headlights were still on, turning and twisting as the car danced down river.

"Meagan!" he shouted into the phone. "Talk to me! Please, God, say something!"

He heard a few garbled words. "Cam...my leg...I can't..."

Lightning flashed and the phone crackled with static. Cameron listened. Nothing. He could still see lights but they were dim stripes now, fading into the distance. Police in rain gear lumbered toward him from the roadblock at the end of the bridge, guns drawn.

"Stop right there! Police! Don't move!"

Cameron ignored them, hoisting himself up on the concrete rail, as Curtis struggled up the bridge toward him with Brandon in his arms.

"Cameron, wait!"

Too late. Cameron was in mid-air, a dark silhouette against the heavy rain. He plunged in, disappeared beneath the churning foam and emerged down river, swimming with the current. Curtis turned to the cops, holding his badge high.

"FBI! We need help!"

The uniforms holstered their guns. A cop with sergeant stripes stepped forward.

"What the hell's going on? Was that Hamilton?"

Curtis pointed. "No, that's---that's one of our guys. We've got to---"

"Where's Hamilton? You got him?"

"He's in the river. And...and his wife. I've got her son here---he's OK, I think. We need to get him to a hospital." He patted Brandon's shoulder.

The sergeant pointed to Stacy's body. "What about that one?"

"That's the other perp, with Hamilton. She's---" Curtis looked at the lifeless form. "She's not going anywhere."

The cop pushed the button on the radio at his shoulder.

"This is Lawler, at the bridge...."

A dispatcher's voice crackled back at him. "Go ahead, sergeant."

"We got a 10-19 here, one suspect down, and one vehicle overboard, with---"

"Say again, sarge."

"I said we've got a car over the bridge, in the river, two occupants. One is the prime---Hamilton, Ross Hamilton. The other is Mrs.---"

"Meagan," Curtis prompted.

"---Meagan Hamilton." The cop continued, "Car in the river."

"Can you get to it?"

"How the hell are we gonna do that? It's moving too fast with the current, south away from the bridge. I mean moving. We need help, now."

"A boat, a helicopter if you can," Curtis said urgently. "We've got to move fast."

The sergeant nodded. "Any chance of the helicopter?"

"No can do. The bird is grounded. I say again: The bird is grounded, and no boats on the water. Nothing's moving until this weather lets up."

The sergeant looked at Curtis with regret. "Roger that."

❑

Curtis was already moving toward the building adjoining the bridge, a Quik Stop store and bait shop with a narrow dock jutting into the river. A stripped-down skiff with an outboard motor was tied to the dock, covered with a snap-on tarp. Curtis sprinted for it. As he yanked the tarp loose, an old man emerged from the bait shop.

"Whaddya think you're doing there, pal?"

Curtis worked the tarp free. "I need this boat!"

The man in the slicker hustled toward him. "You can't take it, god damn it!"

"I'm a federal agent. This is an emergency! I need to---"

"That boat ain't goin' nowhere."

Curtis pulled the cord feverishly, again and again, but the motor wouldn't catch, sputtering to silence. "I need it---I'm sorry, but I've got to---" He pulled again. Nothing.

"It ain't goin' nowhere, I tell ya! Damn thing's broke!"

Curtis released the cord in despair.

"Listen, you have to help me. There are people in the river---They'll die if we don't---Is there another boat? Anything?"

The old man scratched his head. "That little Whaler at the end of the dock runs, but I sure as hell wouldn't take it out in this. 'Sides, that's Grady's. He ain't here, and I ain't got keys. You gotta hot wire that sucker to fire her up."

"You know how to do that?"

"Maybe," he eyed Curtis. "Lemme see what one of them FBI badges looks like."

◻

Back at the Big House, the election was all but forgotten in the confusion about Cameron's astonishing appearance and hasty exit.

Chase and Sandy retreated to the library to join the family, Chase clutching a phone to his ear, trying to get through to MacNulty. He finally made the connection.

"Mac! This is Chase. Cameron told me what----"

"Where are you, Chase?"

"At the Big House."

"Thank God somebody's where they're supposed to be. Listen, I'm knee deep in this shit right now and I can't talk. But I want you to know we're on it, okay? And I want you to promise me you will stay there."

"But, Mac, Cam might need me to---"

"We've lost enough good men tonight, God damn it. You stay put, you hear me?"

"OK, Mac, but you've got to keep us in the loop."

"I'm going to keep this line open just for you, and as soon as I hear anything, you'll be the first to know. Now let me do my job."

0

The TVs were still on in the library, but the volume was off. A sumptuous tray of food was untouched on the table. Ice melted in a silver bucket next to empty glasses. Eleanor was leaning against Cole on the sofa, her hand clasped in his. Gem was near, but her gaze was miles away. Chase and Sandy slipped into the room. Gem could see the trouble on their faces.

"What is it, Chase?"

"We've got a major situation. Ross Hamilton---"

Eleanor sat up. "What about him?"

"He ambushed the agents guarding Meagan---killed them both---and took off with Meagan and her boy."

"Oh, no!" Eleanor cried. "He'll kill them!"

"He can't get far. The FBI, every cop in the county---they'll get him."

"What about Cam?" Cole asked. "Does he know?"

"Cam?" Eleanor queried, confused. "Isn't Cam..."

"He's gone after him, too." Chase glanced outside. "And Ross better hope that Cam doesn't find him first."

"What can we do, Chase?" Cole was on his feet.

"The FBI wants us to stay here. They want to be certain that we're safe."

"No, they want to make sure that you are safe. The candidate. That doesn't apply to me." He spoke with more self-assurance than he had for a long time. "I'm going."

Eleanor chased after him. "Cole, what are you doing?"

"I'm going out there. Maybe I can help."

"Now? In this?"

"I have to."

He stopped to rummage through the bureau drawer. "I'll probably need a flashlight." He found one, clicked it on and off, and slipped it in his pocket. "All set."

Cole opened the door and stepped across the threshold into the raging storm.

"Cole, stop!" Eleanor grabbed his arm. "Are you out of your mind?"

"Elle, it's all right," Gem called out. "Let him go."

Eleanor looked at Gem, then to Cole. She released him.

"Goodbye, Elle," Cole said as stepped into the darkness. "I love you."

"I love you more," Eleanor whispered after him, heart pounding.

73

Special Agent Curtis LaFond stood at the helm of the 16-foot Boston Whaler, squinting through the low-rise windshield, puttering at low speed, steering a zigzag course to dodge the tree limbs and other flotsam that crowded the river.

He was muttering to himself as he weaved the boat through the turbulent waters. He couldn't believe it, any of it. He had been involved in a high-speed car chase, was almost killed in a shootout with a maniacal woman, rescued a kidnapped child, witnessed a two-ton car take a nose dive off the bridge, and watched Cameron dive after it. Now he had stolen a boat to risk his life in a hurricane.

"Everybody's crazy including me," he said to no one.

▯

Meagan was still trapped in the car with the water now up to her shoulders; the last pocket of air was dwindling fast. Her foot was still wedged in the crumpled corner where the seat was bolted to the frame. She tried again, and again, pulling with both hands clasped at her knee. It would not budge.

She thought of Brandon. His father was probably dead and his mother was probably dying. She pulled again, hard, groaning in pain as the twisted metal tore the skin of her ankle. It would not let go.

The water was now at her chin. Brandon's inflated SpongeBob doll nudged her, floating behind her head, caught between the frame and the seat. Suddenly she had a flash of inspiration. The seat! The seat might move. There were oblong controls on the passenger door---front, back, up, down---at the touch of a button. It could have been shorted out by now, but a few lights still glowed beneath the water. Maybe...

"Now, that's my Meg---think, think..."

Mama Neeley? It was her voice, clear as a bell. Now, I'm hallucinating, Meagan thought.

She felt her way along the door and bumped the control. She pushed. The seat moved forward, pinching her foot tighter. She winced as she pushed the control the other way. The seat moved back. Slowly. Oh, so slowly... She could taste the salty water as it bubbled at her lips.

The seat stopped. She pressed harder but it was no use. The last dim lights faded away as the power died off completely.

Meagan wanted to scream but the water was past her mouth. She strained up for a last gulp of air and plunged her head under, reaching for her ankle with both hands. She yanked with all the strength she had left.

Her foot popped free. She was released from the deathtrap! She arched upward, pressing her face against the roof of the car to sip a last breath from the sliver of remaining air and braced herself against the seat kicking hard, both feet slamming against the windshield. It didn't budge.

She quickly spun to the side window and kicked again. It didn't break, but it cracked along both edges. On the third try, the safety glass bent away from the frame in one fractured segment. Two more furious kicks and it gave way, bending far enough for Meg to wedge into the narrow opening.

For one awful moment she was trapped again, caught at her hips, the car dragging her down while the current buffeted her head and shoulders and her lungs screamed for air.

"Push hard, you can do it..."

She did. The glass scraped at her sides and released her. She tumbled with the force of the current, fighting her way to the surface.

She managed to get one precious breath before a whitecap slammed into her. She gagged on the water, coughed it up and gulped more air. Brandon's inflated doll bobbed to the surface next to her, a welcome companion. She pulled it to her and held tight, praying.

Alive, she thought, *I'm alive.*

She had only a second to enjoy the thought before the current grabbed her again and hurled her downriver.

◻

Curtis tried to make up distance, but the water was an obstacle course. He had to slow crawl. The only help was the searchlight mounted next to the cockpit. He flicked it on and a powerful burst of light shot straight ahead. He worked the hand lever to shift the beam right and left. He was just getting the hang of it when the light framed a crisscross of two thickly branched tree trunks toppled by the storm. There was something caught between, a blip of white in the muddy brown debris.

Cameron.

He hadn't gotten far when the skewed trees captured him like a giant pair of pliers. The current pushed him to the bank where it was entangled in the mangroves.

Curtis felt his heart sink as he steered closer. Cameron's head was down. He wasn't moving. Curtis was thinking the worst, when Cameron looked up, pulling one arm free.

"Curtis---get me out of here."

74

Cole worked his way to the line of trees near the river and down the winding path from the Big House. It was so dark in the trees that he could not see two feet in front of him. He used the flashlight to mark every step on the rain-slicked path, staying on his toes in the mud.

Once he broke through the trees, the water was only a few yards ahead. The rustic pier was jutting out of the dark, flooded, water swirling at the pylons. He shivered. It was here that he had taken on the waters last time and failed, thrown back, beaten and broken, only half alive. Now he was back to wrestle with the watery demons once more. He would either reclaim that part of him that he lost, or else die trying.

He stopped, fear clawing at his throat. He fought for a breath like a drowning man.

"It's all cool, my man. You can do this."

Andy?

"You hear me, Cole?"

It was Andy's voice, all right.

"You did it before, you can do it again. I'm telling you, you saved me. You were hauling ass through that river while I was sucking in water. I'm the one that hurt the team. You did everything right. You can do it again."

Real or imagined, the words energized Cole. He took a step to the water's edge and aimed the flashlight over the water, sweeping the turbulent surface. He didn't know what he was looking for but he kept at it, panning backwards and forwards. After a minute, he switched the light off in doubt and disgust. Maybe Eleanor was right---this is crazy. The wind shrieked. He took a step back and stopped. Wait. What was that?

He flicked the light back on, scanning the water again. Lightning lit up the night long enough for Cole to catch a glimpse of color in the distance. He pointed the flashlight and strained to see. Thunder cascaded overhead, then another blaze of lightning.

There! A speck of yellow, bobbing on the waves, a hundred yards upriver.

Cole took another step into the river, kept the flashlight on track as the lightning subsided and the world went dark again. He moved in waist-deep. Another burst and---there!

Oh my God. A woman caught up in the churning water.

Cole waded deeper, at a wide angle to the woman, hoping to intercept her down river. His feet pushed off the muddy bottom and he tried to swim, stroking hard, but it was like swimming through a waterfall. He only gained inches with every stroke no matter how hard he tried. The water resisted him at every step. He wouldn't make it before she was swept past.

Suddenly, the current stopped fighting him and propelled him forward. So now instead of speeding up, he had to slow down, stretch his body like a sail to slow the rush.

She was only a few yards away.

Meagan! It was Meagan, hanging on to something, struggling to keep afloat.

With a few hard strokes, he closed the gap between them, then he was pushed away again by the current. He tried again, five, six, seven thrusts to move ten feet. Finally, he stretched his arm and latched on to hers.

Meagan was stunned by the human touch in the midst of the wild water. She had not seen him working his way towards her. Who? She reached out for him, throwing her arm around his neck with her last bit of strength, pulling them both under.

Cole didn't panic. He freed her grasp, and kicked hard to hoist her back to the surface. They broke through together.

"It's all right," he gurgled. "I've got you."

She could not speak, barley lifting her head to look at him. The river still moving fast was taking them with it as Cole kicked and pawed the water with his free hand.

"Kick! Meagan---we can make it if you---"

Meagan tried, but the undertow tugged at her feet, pulling her down. Her head bobbed under. Cole's grasp began to slip.

Meagan felt the baby kick hard inside, fueled by the same adrenalin, fighting with her. She thrust both legs out in a mighty kick and broke to the surface where she was able to grasp a breath of air before she was torn from Cole's grip. He made a frantic grab for her and missed. Meagan was gone.

〇

Eleanor sat at the library window, watching the rain pound the sill. Gem sat silent and stoic. Chase clutched the phone, his vital link to Mac and the FBI. Almost all the news was bad. The car had gone in the water with Meagan, and Cameron had followed. The only good news was Brandon. He was safe and unharmed.

No one noticed as the television flashed the latest bulletins showing Chase edging past Dawson to take the lead for the first time.

The tension was unbearable for Eleanor. On top of the dreadful news about Meagan and Cameron, Cole had set off on a quixotic quest in the stormy night and not returned.

"How the hell could we let Cole go out there?"

"His fate called, and he answered," Gem said. "We could not keep him from it."

"God damn it," Elle sputtered. "I don't know if it's in those cards of yours, but---I should be with Cole. Maybe we can help. I can't just sit here anymore, Gem, I can't."

Gem's face lit up as she rose to join her.

"Let's go."

〇

Cole dove under. He hit the undertow and sur-rendered to it, letting it take him as it must have taken

Meagan. He had been under half a minute, lungs about to burst, hope all but gone, when it happened. His fingertips brushed her arm. He groped in her direction, bumped her arm again and grabbed for it. He pulled her close---he would not let go again---and he propelled them both toward the surface.

〇

With Curtis at the helm and Cameron on the bow guiding him through the treacherous waters, they had closed the distance in minutes, passed the bend where the channel widened at the approach to Port Royal and picked up speed as the quickened pace of the current helped clear the course. Curtis steered with one hand, working the searchlight with the other, probing the waters ahead as Cameron's unblinking eyes tracked with the light.

"There! Cam! Over there!" Curtis shouted and held the light steady. Cameron saw the two heads bobbing and leaned over the rope rail at the port side to get a better look.

Meagan!

She was gasping, struggling in the clutches of a man in the water with her.

Ross. It had to be Ross.

"Curtis, it's Meagan! Get over there, for Christ sake! Hurry! He's killing her!" Cameron raised his gun and tried to steady it with both hands as the boat jostled.

He could see the two heads clearly as the boat approached. He braced himself against the rail post, sighted the gun and waited for the boat to rock back and pause just long enough to---

"Cam, wait! Don't!" Curtis jerked the throttle, pitching Cameron off balance. "It's Cole! It's your brother!"

Cameron shielded his eyes from the rain. He could see Cole and Meagan framed in the spotlight, featured players on a watery stage.

"Christ Almighty." He lowered the gun. "Thank God for you, Curtis."

"That's what they all say." Curtis grinned. "I think I have a heroic nature."

▯

Cole saw the approaching boat but could not wait for assistance. Meagan was barely conscious, unable to keep her head up any longer. Cole hoisted her higher, using their combined weight to brace against the current.

With Meagan secure against his hip, he began to close the distance, one arm chopping through the waves. He stretched a leg to touch the muddy bottom and dug in, muscles throbbing. He took one wobbly step after another, ankle deep in the muck, as the current relented until he got to the shore where he laid Meagan gently on the bank and collapsed beside her. He could hardly move when he heard Eleanor call his name.

"Here," he answered in a hoarse whisper. "We're here."

Eleanor moved towards him. "Cole! Cole---"

And then she saw Meagan.

"Meagan! My God! Is she---Is she---"

"She's alive," Cole panted. "She's all right."

Eleanor fell to her knees as Gem stumbled in behind, drenched and splattered with mud.

"Cole, my shining star."

They heard the engine throttle down as the light approached and the boat glided in for a soft landing in the mud. Cameron couldn't get out quickly enough.

"Meagan!" He raced to her. "I thought I---"

"Oh, my God, Cam!" She embraced him. "Brandon! Is he---?"

"He's fine, darling. Brandon's fine."

Standing on the boat, arms folded, Curtis gazed down on the scene--- Cameron holding Meagan, both crying. Eleanor with her arms wrapped around Cole, both whispering. And Gem sitting placidly in the mud and rain like Buddha, perfectly content.

"Mrs. Chambers?"

She looked up with a weary smile.

"Did I ever tell you that you have a very interesting family?"

- 75 -

WILD NIGHT IN NAPLES
CANDIDATE PLAYS ROLE IN FBI MANHUNT
TWIN BROTHERS HAILED AS HEROES IN
ELECTION NIGHT DRAMA

The story captured headlines across the nation, going viral on the Internet, newspapers and networks topping each other with posts of the incredible details.

"The stunning victory of Chase Chambers over incumbent Lou Dawson in Florida's 9th District was overshadowed by a dramatic series of events that unfolded in Naples as the votes were being counted last night," read the lead story in the *New York Times*.

"Two FBI agents and two suspects were killed last night in a dramatic series of events in Naples. SA Harold Black and SA Benjamin Miller were slain at the home of financier Ross Hamilton, whom agents described as the focus of the investigation. Hamilton abducted his wife and son at gunpoint from their home and escaped in his vehicle. A high-speed chase ended at a roadblock near the Imperial Bridge where Hamilton's accomplice, an unidentified woman, was killed in a shootout with police and FBI agents. Hamilton apparently died after his car crashed through the bridge railing and plunged into the raging waters. His body has not been found. Mrs. Meagan Hamilton survived the crash. She was rescued from the river and rushed to the hospital where she was treated for her injuries. Her son was not injuried.

"MacNulty said that Ross Hamilton was involved in a "massive fraud and money laundering operation and the prime suspect in multiple related murders in Florida and elsewhere" and had been under FBI surveillance for months. More than $40 million in cash, negotiable bonds and securities had also been recovered.

"FBI spokesman John MacNulty released a statement thanking Chase Chambers and his brother, Cameron, for their assistance in the special investigation. The brothers are identical twins.

"Major Cameron Chambers, was reported as 'missing in action and presumed dead' by the Pentagon while on a Special Forces mission in Afghanistan last March. State Department officials now confirm that Chambers escaped capture and returned to the U. S. to join the FBI investigation of Ross Hamilton as an undercover agent.

"The FBI would not confirm or deny that Major Chambers had posed as his brother on several occasions during the recent campaign, but sources at Naples Police Department confirmed that Chambers adopted his brother's identity at times in the past three months for security reasons."

◻

The rain finally let up about dawn, but it was bedlam at the Big House through the night and the following day, with hordes of police, FBI and media swarming the estate.

The Coast Guard commander held an impromptu news conference on the front steps to report on the search for Ross Hamilton's body.

"We have eight craft in the channel, Naples Bay and the Gulf. We do not have a recovery yet. We may have had a sighting early this morning. One of the spotters saw something that may have been a body, but it was moving so fast and I can't give you confirmation on that.

"We'll keep looking, but with this rain---the river is moving too fast for a proper search---he could be ten miles out in the gulf by now."

He was peppered with questions and answered them all by holding up his hand. "That's really all I have for you right now. As soon as there's any news on our end, we'll let you know right away."

The commander stepped away from the battery of microphones quickly, glad to be out of the limelight.

It was late that evening before the last visitors departed and family members had their first moment of relative peace. Gem, Chase and Sandy, Cole and Eleanor gathered in the great room. Exhausted by the ordeal, no one said a word.

Brandon was asleep in a guest bedroom upstairs, converted to comfortable quarters for him and his mother when she returned from the hospital. The Hamilton house and property was a cordoned-off crime scene and would remain so for days. That morning, with Big Mac's intervention, Eleanor and Sandy had gone to Meagan's home and retrieved two armloads of clothes, toys and necessities for Meagan and Brandon, and brought them over to the estate.

Meagan's parents were out of the country in Ireland on a golf vacation with their country club group. They were sent the news and told not to return as Meagan would be kept in Mercy Hospital for only two days. She was lucky to be alive and to come away with only water in her lungs, a badly sprained ankle, gashes around her leg from where she wrestled with the car, and a wide assortment of cuts and bruises over other parts of her body. But all things considered, she was in surprisingly good shape. However, the doctors decided to keep her for observation a couple extra days. Cameron stayed with her the whole time. He hadn't left her side since they were reunited at the river. Brandon came to visit her each day brought by Eleanor, Gem and Sandy. Meagan felt blessed not only to be alive but to be loved by so many wonderful friends and family, her parents calling every few hours to see how she was doing.

The media circus was camped outside the hospital clamoring to get in, but police and hospital security kept them at bay. Meagan wasn't talking to the press, but all sorts of follow-up stories were dominating the cable channels and Internet.

MacNulty was on Larry King Live. Curtis LaFond was in top form for his appearance with Greta Van Sustern. Geraldo broadcasted live from a boat on the river, following the same course and explaining points of interest. CBS, NBC, FOX and CNN kept the story going.

Meagan did talk to the police and the team of FBI agents who came to her room the first evening, but they were there merely as a formality. She gave them a statement and answered all their questions, but there was little she could tell them that they didn't already know.

MacNulty was there, Curtis, and Curran, who had flown in from Washington. It took them less than half the following day to wrap up the details and pronounce the case closed. When they were finished, Big Mac escorted everyone out. He stopped at the door.

"Mrs. Hamilton, I want you to know how much we appreciate all that you did. I know it was hard on you. You're a brave lady. You'll be happy to know we're not going to bother you any more. You get your rest. I think Chambers here has a few more questions for you, and that'll be about it. You take care now."

MacNulty closed the hospital room door behind him, leaving Meagan and Cameron alone.

"A few more questions, Cam? What questions? There's nothing I haven't already answered."

"Oh, but there is. I just have one more question, Meg, and it's very important."

[]

A week later, the story was still in the news. When the Chambers camp confirmed that Cameron had indeed posed as his brother on several occasions as part of the undercover investigation involving Ross Hamilton, there was grumbling in some quarters about FBI interference in a federal election. Chase gallantly offered to concede his hard-won victory and step down, but his opponent would have none of it. Lou Dawson issued a statement saluting Chase for helping the FBI to bring a dangerous criminal to justice and declared he would not contest the results.

◻

Chase and Sandy were relaxing at the Big House, alone for the first time in weeks.

"Is it all right if we get married now?" Sandy teased. "Or is there some other earth-shaking event on your schedule?"

"Well, I'm glad you brought that up. I've been meaning to tell you. I think we're going to have to change our wedding plans."

"Oh, no." She playfully elbowed him in the side.

"I know you always wanted a big wedding. What's that word you always use---glorious, a glorious wedding---and you're going to get your wish. The wedding's going to be twice as big.

"Twice as----what are you up to, Chase Chambers?"

"Don't blame me. It's that brother of mine. You know he's always been the troublemaker. Which reminds me, we're also going to need a new best man."

"Chase, have you lost your mind? There's no way in the world that anyone but Cameron is going to be your best man."

"Unless he's getting married himself, on the same day."

Cameron and Meagan strolled in beaming, hand in hand.

"Welcome to the family!" Sandy ran to Meagan and embraced her.

"I hope that's the last big surprise from you for awhile, brother," Chase said. "I can't take much more of this."

Cameron mirrored his grin. "I can't either."

"I hope there's room for one more little surprise," Meagan ventured.

Cameron looked at her. "What do you mean?"

Before she could answer, MacNulty walked in, oddly out of character with a cluster of balloons tied to his finger. Curtis followed with a box of cigars tucked under his arm.

"What are you two doing here?" Cameron was baffled.

"Official business, Chambers," Big Mac boomed, winking at Meagan.

"A message from the Department," Curtis added solemnly.

"What message?" Cameron took the hook.

"Congratulations," Curtis announced.

Meagan braced herself.

"Guess the old saying is right---the father is always the last to know." Mac handed the balloons to Cameron.

"I'll be damned," Chase beamed.

Curtis offered the cigars around. "Please---these are the best. Contraband Cubans. We impound lots of them at the FBI."

Curtis winked.

Cameron turned inquiring eyes to Meagan.

"I've been meaning to tell you," she started. "And then everything got so crazy, and we never had time alone, then I started to tell you this morning. I did, but then I didn't---"

"Shut up." He pulled her close and kissed her.

God, he loved this woman.

- 76 -

The double wedding was scheduled for February 14th, a Valentine's Day ceremony. There was never a doubt that First Class would handle the event. Marsha and Eleanor, the new full partner in First Class, were on it from the time they got the wonderful news.

"OK, Ellie, listen up." Marsha was in a mood. "I'm going to do this wedding. Believe me, I want to do this wedding more than anything in my entire career, but you gotta tell me right now---I'm not going to lose another partner to the altar between now and then, am I? I mean, I really just couldn't take it."

Eleanor waited. She knew Marsha wasn't finished yet, just taking a breath.

"Never mind that it would leave me holding the bag on all the planning for the biggest event in Florida of the whole season with about a gazillion people

415

coming. That would be enough of a disaster. But you know what would really get to me?"

Eleanor didn't answer. She knew she didn't have to.

"I'll tell you what. If you and your precious Cole suddenly decide to up the ante on the twins and make it a triple wedding? Well, on top of everything else, that would make me the last spinster standing, and I don't think I could show my rapidly aging face in this town for about, I don't know, ten years at least."

Eleanor burst out laughing.

"Laugh if you want, but tell me now. Is that in the cards? Or, wait a second, maybe I'm supposed to ask Gem that question? Anyhow, am I making myself clear here or what?"

Eleanor gave her a hug. "Yes and no."

"Excuse me?"

"Yes, you are making yourself clear, and no..." Elle paused. "...There's no chance of a triple wedding. Cole---I love Cole, you know that, and he's come such a long way, but there's still a long way to go. For me, too. I don't want to rush him. We've got time now, all the time in the world."

Marsha clapped her hands like a cheerleader. "Yeah!"

"So what are we sitting around for---like lumps on a log? We've got work to do, don't we, boss lady?"

[]

Chase Chambers was sworn in as Congressman and star of the freshman class in Congress. Everyone wanted to have their picture taken with the famous Mr. Chambers. Even the President made time for a photo op in the Oval Office, welcoming Chase Chambers to Washington.

Sandy was going crazy, in a good way. Since the election night drama, she and Chase had become the hot couple of the year, celebrities on TV and in the tabloids, besieged for interviews on all sides. With all the hectic media, house hunting in Washington, rounds at the Capitol, and wedding arrangements---Sandy was run off her feet.

Cameron resigned his military commission, as he had promised Meagan. On his final day in uniform, he was awarded two more medals to add to his collection---one for distinguished combat service and another for his work with the FBI. Whilst mulling over offers for assignments with Homeland Security or the State Department, he was enjoying civilian life. He spent a lot of time with Brandon, easing into the role of surrogate father. The nights were for Meagan.

Cole and Eleanor were inseparable. He had genuine respect for her First Class work. His imagination and artistic sense helped with her planning and design. And in the meantime, she posed for another Cole painting, and this time it was a nude.

All was well in the Big House, except for Gem. She had seemed subdued for several days now, she withdrew to the cottage at night, walked the gardens and river bank by day, the lonely march of a troubled soul.

Cole noticed it first. He mentioned it to Cameron and they both discussed it with Chase when he returned from Washington. That evening, the three of them walked over to the cottage to see her.

A little family small talk, then Cameron took the initiative.

"What's the matter, Ma? You don't seem so happy lately. Don't you think you ought to tell us what's on your mind?"

"I hope it's not the weddings," Chase tried to keep it light. "Remember, you're not losing two sons, you're gaining two daughters."

"Oh, it's not that," Gem said. "I love those girls."

"Then what is it?" Cole implored.

"You see this?"

The Tarot cards were nowhere in sight but she produced one like a magician, holding it out for all her sons to see.

"Seven of swords. It rises up again and again now. Look."

"All right," Cam looked. "It's a man, a thief I guess, sneaking away with some swords."

"Look closer. Try to see everything."

Chase took the card from his mother's hand and scrutinized it carefully.

"There's a tent. A carnival or a camp. Lots of people. A party, maybe."

"They're busy celebrating, so he has time to strike," Cole got into it, too. "And make his getaway."

"So it is," Gem nodded. "It's that man, the man in the cards."

"Ross Hamilton?" Cameron was incredulous.

She recoiled. "An evil man, filled with hate for all of you. As long as he's alive…"

"But he's dead, Ma," Cameron said with certainty. "Trust me, the man's dead."

Chase agreed, "And officially so, as of today. We made a few phone calls to help speed the process so Meagan can get on with her life. The coroner issued a death certificate for the late Mr. Ross Hamilton today."

Gem was puzzled. "How could they do that without..."

"Without a body?" Chase shrugged. "All available evidence. They do it whenever there's a reasonable presumption of death."

"There you go," Cole said. "Even the government says he's dead, on the record, and that's coming from your favorite congressman. End of story."

She lowered her head. "That's not what the cards say."

Chase patted her shoulder. "They must be saying something else. It's over."

Gem was not persuaded. "It is not over yet. There is still a danger. Maybe not from him, but something... someone."

"Do you really think he's still alive?"

"I don't know. Impossible to tell. His soul is dead. That is certain. No light there."

"Well, if it's someone else, who could that be?"

"Who is William?" Gem asked, out of the blue.

"William?"

She groped for words. "William---determined, bitter---"

"Can you say what he looks like?"

"Tall, fair-haired. I cannot see him clearly. His face is distorted, twisted in pain, covered with something."

Cam shook his head. "Doesn't ring any bells."

"And the roses again," Gem added. "Yellow roses. Something wrong there."

Cam looked at his brother. "Well, they do have those thorns. They're a real hazard. Thorns, I mean."

"That's enough, Cam." Chase turned to his mother. "You know I'm a believer. I am. But I honestly believe, this time---you know how you always say it's in the eye of the beholder? The one who reads the cards can be mistaken, right?"

"Yes, it happens."

"So? Can it happen with you?"

"Of course," She said. "I can be wrong. I pray that I am. God help us if I'm not."

77

The rehearsal dinner was scheduled one week before the wedding and promised to be a preview of the grand event, a stylish soiree at the exclusive Cypress Country Club. Marsha and Eleanor had put it together, an intimate dinner for a hundred and twenty.

Meagan looked beautiful in an empire style dress that cleverly hid her condition under layers of colored silk. Sandy was gorgeous as always in a Stella McCartney gown. The wedding party was seated at an elevated table at one end of the immense dining room, with Gem in the center, flanked by her twin sons and their brides-to-be. Beyond them, Cole and Eleanor sat on one side, with Brandon and Meagan's mother and father on the other. Brandon looked older than his years in his precocious suit and tie. Katherine and Robert, Meagan's mother and father, had the proud look of parents of the bride, especially one who came so close to death so recently.

Meagan leaned over to Cameron with a self-conscious grin, whispering, "Nature's calling---again. Be right back." She dropped a kiss on Brandon's head on her way out.

She hurried down the long corridor toward the ladies' room, her hand flitting across her stomach, savoring the sweet life within. She was walking on a cloud.

As she set her silk purse on the marble counter, she gazed into the mirror. Yes, it's you. Little Meagan Neeley, soon to be Mrs. Meagan Chambers, married to the man of your dreams. She laughed at the thought of it all, and the amazing twists and turns her life had taken. It's unbelievable, she thought, but it's not a dream. It's real. It's all real.

"Did you miss your husband, darling?"

The words pulsed through Meagan like a shock. Stunned by the sound of his voice, she grabbed the edge of the vanity to steady herself and turned to where it was coming from, petrified at the thought of what she might see.

A powerful hand grabbed her by the back of the neck. She looked straight at the mirror. She could see him over her shoulder, snarling back at her.

Yes, it was Ross, or at least some bizarre version of Ross, barely recognizable with his scruffy mustache and ratty wig which didn't quite cover the zigzag reddish scar across his forehead, nor the ghastly pallor of his skin.

"Good to see you, too," he cracked.

This wasn't real. It couldn't be. She was dreaming! She stared at his image in the mirror, hoping she would wake from this nightmare, praying that when she turned, he would not be there. Her eyes welled with tears.

"Oh, is my Meagan going to cry?" His voice dripped with wicked sarcasm. "I thought you loved surprises. And I have another one for your precious Cameron, and all your new friends."

"Come along." He steered her forward roughly. "Time to enjoy the show."

As they moved, he took something out of his jacket pocket and held it in front of her. A small black box with a pulsing green light and a red button.

"Do you know what this is, darling?"

He didn't wait for an answer.

"Remote control. Simple, really," he said, as they continued the awkward march down the empty hall. "You can get one at Radio Shack for about ten bucks. Set the receptor to anything you want. Brandon has a few of them, I think, for that little truck, and the robot. This one's for a bomb."

Meagan tried to squirm from his grasp. He squeezed harder, holding fast.

"Oh no, Meagan, don't do that," he said calmly. "I'll push it right now. It will work."

"Oh God, Ross, please!" she implored. "You don't want, you can't---"

"Shut the fuck up!" he snapped. "Keep moving."

[]

The din of happy conversation filled the room as tuxedoed waiters slipped the plates teeming with Florida lobster in front of the guests. At the front table,

Cole picked up his fork, ready to start eating. He noticed that Eleanor was staring off into space.

"What's the matter?"

"Nothing. I---nothing."

"What? Come on…talk to me."

"It's the roses," she said, trying to shrug it off. "It's no big thing."

Cole turned. "Over there? What's wrong with them? They're beautiful."

"Marsha and I did all the arrangements for to-night."

"You did a wonderful job. Everything's perfect."

"Everything except the roses. We didn't order those----I don't know who did…or why?"

"Maybe Meagan wanted---"

"Hell, no! Not yellow roses. Never."

"The florist must have tossed them in, thought they would be a nice touch."

"Wilhelm? Please. He's so meticulous. He would never change a leaf from what we approved. And he'd be furious if anyone else did. He's an artist, he really is. But he's a regimented German, with an attitude, and he would never tolerate----"

Across the table, Cameron's Ranger ears perked up.

"What did you say, Elle?"

"I was just talking about the florist."

"And his name is---?"

"Wilhelm. Wilhelm Durman or Durfeld. Something like that. Why?"

Cameron looked at Meagan's empty chair, then beyond to see his twin returning his concerned look. Chase had been listening as well.

"William," Chase said quietly.

The hairs stood up on the back of Cameron's neck. He looked past Chase to the vase with the yellow roses on the high banquet table. He motioned toward it with his eyes.

Chase looked over his shoulder. His mother's words of warning rang in his ears as he stared at the lustrous bouquet. In his mind, the flowers morphed into something ugly and menacing.

"What do you think---are you a believer now?" Chase asked his twin.

"I believe we may have a problem." Cam stood. "Stay here for a sec."

He slipped out and walked briskly to the kitchen and made his way past the busy chefs and waiters to the service entrance and stepped outside. He saw the van parked a few yards away, "WILHELM FLORISTS" in appropriate flowered script on the side.

Cameron couldn't see through the tinted windows. He tried the doors. All locked. Never a patient man, he poked out the rear panel window with one neat thrust of his elbow, reached in and unlatched the door.

There, in the shadows toward the front of the compartment---the body of a man, wrists bound with tape, a clear plastic bag wrapped tight around his head.

Wilhelm. Dead.

Cameron rushed back to the dining room, hoping to see Meagan back in her chair. She wasn't anywhere in sight. And now his mother was absent as well.

He stepped cautiously toward the vase. Trying not to draw attention, he peered over the rim. It was filled to the brim with dirt instead of water. He thought that was odd for a floral arrangement, then saw the metal prongs poking through the dirt.

He showed no reaction, but inside, his stomach churned. He knew exactly what the prongs were. He had seen them a hundred times, in Afghanistan, Bosnia, Somalia---signatures of death, supersensitive antennae of land mines or explosives, ready to blow at the slightest touch ... or remote signal.

Cameron's eyes scanned the room. All their friends and family were laughing and talking, oblivious to the imminent threat of death and devastation.

He went to Chase. "Yeah. We've got a situation here. A bomb amongst those yellow roses. Could take out the whole room."

"Jesus."

"We've got to get these people out of here right now. But it's got to be quiet. No panic. You think of something. Use those persuasive powers of yours, congressman."

Chase nodded. "Where you going?"

"I've got to find Meagan."

Chase looked at the empty chair. When he looked back, Cameron was gone.

Chase rose, clinking his wine glass for attention. The chatter died down.

"Ladies and gentlemen, we have one more surprise this evening---This family is just full of surprises."

A few laughs and light applause from the comfortable crowd.

"And we need your help." He pointed. "I'm going to ask you all to join us on the terrace. Right now. It will only take a minute, so let's step out of the room now."

There was some good-natured grumbling as the guests shifted from the chairs and started to move towards the French doors leading to the terrace.

Sandy smiled at Chase. "What's this all about, darling?"

"Don't ask, honey," he said as he took her arm. "Just help me get everyone outside. And Sandy, for God's sake, hurry!"

The smile disappeared. Sandy shifted into serious mode, hustling stragglers toward the doors. Across the table, Cole and Eleanor picked up on the urgency. They followed Sandy's lead, helping to herd out the crowd.

78

In the main hall, Cameron pulled the slim 9mm Glock from his waistband. He always carried it. Force of habit. He crept down the hallway, flat against the wall, gun held head high, moving like a panther ready to pounce.

Who was this Wilhelm, William of Germany? He thought he knew. He didn't want to say the word, not even in his mind, but there it was. Ross. He couldn't believe it, wouldn't believe it, and still he knew it with a sickening certainty.

"God help her," he said aloud. If Ross was alive, then Meagan could be dead! At the corner, Cam hesitated, held the gun out front and pivoted to his right.

There they were, thirty feet away, moving toward him. A weird-looking man in a white jacket with a claw-like grip on Meagan's neck.

Ross Hamilton. He looked inhuman, a beast from some dark, demonic realm. And hard to kill. Cam had to give him that. He had been ripped up in a car wreck, drowned in a raging river, and here he was, a dead man walking, still a mortal threat to Meagan and everything Cameron held dear. Cameron's jaw clenched in determination. He had to put this creature down, once and for all.

Ross held something in his hand---Cameron couldn't see what---as he prodded Meagan along. Ross caught sight of Cameron and came to an abrupt halt.

"Cameron, look out!" Meagan shrieked.

Ross yanked her over in front of him, holding the remote aloft.

"Get back, Chambers! You don't want me to move a muscle."

He stood his ground, gun held steady. "Let her go, Hamilton."

"Let her go?" His maniacal laugh reverberated down the hall. "Do you know what this is?" He flashed the remote. "I'll let her go---I'll let her go to hell, along with you and everyone else in this building."

"And you, too? You don't want to do that," Cameron said coolly, focusing down the sightline of the gun. Ross was concealed behind Meagan, only one arm exposed. He took a half step to the side, looking for an angle.

"Oh, I don't?" Ross sneered. "Maybe you've forgotten what you've done to me. You and this---" He shook Meagan. "---Everything I had, everything I earned---I earned it---gone! You! You and this fucking woman!"

Cameron slid another half step.

"You think I care if I live or die?" Ross bellowed.

Cameron spoke calmly, "Aren't you forgetting one thing?"

"And what might that be?" he scoffed.

"You're already dead," the voice rang out from behind Ross.

Ross spun his head to see Gem only a few steps away. She had sensed the danger to Meagan and come to help, her powerful intuition leading her to them.

The distraction was all Cameron needed. Ross took his eye off him. He turned back a moment too late. Cameron pulled the trigger.

The bullet whizzed past Meagan's ear and caught Ross Hamilton in the right eye, tearing through his brain and out the back of his head. He wobbled for a moment, the remote still cradled in the palm of his hand, thumb twitching a hair's breadth from the button, and withered in a lifeless heap. The remote fell from his grasp, clattered across the marble floor and came to rest, green light blinking harmlessly.

Cameron rushed forward to catch Meagan as she fell in his arms.

Gem sighed, a weight removed, her spirits lifting.

79

"Is the President coming?"

The little boy in the striped shirt craned his neck to gawk at the helicopters overhead while he waited for an answer from the giant.

"I don't think so," Big Mac looked down. "But he might as well. We've got enough security to cover him and his whole cabinet right along with this wedding."

MacNulty was standing on the steps of St. John's Cathedral after completing his personal last-minute inspection. There were twenty-two agents assigned to the church and the surrounding area, two blocks in all directions, and every one was in position. The helicopters expanded to secure the perimeter to a full square mile. There was no real reason for concern, and even Big Mac admitted his precautions might be a bit excessive; but after the frightening close call at the rehearsal dinner, the FBI boss wasn't taking any chances.

"We're going to have a nice quiet wedding here today," is what he told his assembled team an hour before. "And for once, these Chambers folks are going to make it through an event without any calamities or crises of any kind. Nothing is going to happen. Nothing. By the end of the day, I expect to be bored stiff. I trust we are absolutely clear on that. Any questions?"

Not a peep from any of the assembled agents.

"All right, then." He waved them on. "Do your duty."

At noon, the caravan of limousines arrived. There were 1,200 guests packed inside and another throng of onlookers in front to witness the grand entrance of the celebrated couples, escorted by Gem, Meagan's parents, a bevy of bridesmaids, a phalanx of grooms-men, an adorable trio of flower girls and a beaming Brandon, proud ring-bearer.

It was the closest thing to a royal wedding they had ever seen in Southwest Florida. The front page of the Style section of the paper was filled with color photos, lists of VIP guests and all the glamorous details of the wedding gowns and bridal bouquets. Best of all, the press was happy to report that Cameron Chambers and Meagan Neeley, Chase Chambers and Sandra Simmons were married without incident on a cool Valentine's Day afternoon in Naples, Florida.

80

THE SUN .

Meagan screamed.

Her face was drenched in sweat, glistening in the too-bright light, hair plastered to her forehead; eyes squeezed shut against the agony. She didn't remember all the pain.

He stood over her, holding her arms down against the bed as her body buckled, then arched upward, wracked with another rush of pain.

"Come on, Meg," he said. "Just a little more. Push!"

She moaned as the last wave subsided, then opened her eyes to see Cameron above her. There were others in the room---one at her side and two more at the foot of the bed---but they were just a blur of pale green and white. She focused on Cam, only Cam.

Meagan took a great gulp of air and grimaced with determination. With a nod to Cam, she pushed, pushed, pushed.

"Doing fine, girl," came another voice from nowhere. "We're right there."

"I'll take it." Another voice, a woman, calm and assured. "Move the light a little, please."

"Doctor, do you want the---?"

"No, nothing. This is good. Let me get a shoulder and---"

Meagan felt one more stab of pain, then a rush of relief. She lifted her head, straining to see.

Prodded by sure hands, the slick bundle of new life tumbled from her. In one sure move, the doctor grasped the newborn, cradled him for the nurse to swipe the tiny nose and mouth, then held him aloft.

"Here's your new baby boy, Meagan."

The infant wailed a hearty greeting.

Meagan smiled. "He's so beautiful," she whispered.

Cameron beamed, and bent to kiss his wife. "You're beautiful."

The nurses scurried to their birthing chores. One stepped in to snip the umbilical cord, still pulsing with its ethereal blue-white life force. As it fell away, the doctor tied the knot at the baby's belly with a deft twist.

"Somebody give me a time."

"5:15 a.m."

"Baby Boy Chambers, 5:15 am. Mark it."

Another nurse stepped in, swathing the child with a cotton wrap and plopping a tiny blue knit cap on his head.

Meagan had only a few seconds to enjoy before she was jarred from her elation as pain shot up the base of her spine. She groaned as the anguish began again.

The doctor stepped to her side, taking her hand gently.

"This should go quick now, Meg," she said. "Hang in there."

She turned to the nurses. "All right, people, let's clear the decks. We've got some more work to do here."

◻

Baby Boy Two Chambers was born at 5:43 a.m., with the same blue eyes and wisps of flaxen hair as his barely older brother. Identical. A perfect pair.

Twins again.

Twins forever.

◻

"For me, it is the most wonderful of all the Tarot. Loving, nurturing and benevolent, abounding with fresh optimism, a bright new day. Some would disagree. It is not the orthodox view. The Sun card does not rank high in the Tarot hierarchy. But I believe it has no peer. It is always welcome, always a blessing."

Gem held the Sun Card up in the morning light. Vivid and bright, the sun filled the sky, the full-blossomed flowers, the noble white stallion and the exuberant child.

Exuberant child. She set her fountain pen on the desk and enjoyed the words.

Enough. No more today. No more profound thoughts or divinations.

[]

Gem stepped to the doublewide crib where her twin grandsons lay side by side, perfect faces glowing, hands touching, tiny fingers intertwined. Three months old and the magical twin bond was already strong.

Kyle Mitchell Chambers.

Quinn Michael Chambers.

Today, she would be Grandma Gem, passing the time with giggles and coos, Kyle on one knee, Quinn on the other. The future could wait until tomorrow. Today was for the joy of right now.

Comprends?